Madam President

Blayne Cooper and T Novan

P.D. Publishing, Inc.
Clayton, North Carolina

ISBN-13: 978-1-933720-13-5
ISBN-10: 1-933720-13-1

First Edition: 2001
Second Edition: 2001 (ISBN: 1-930928-69-6)
Third Edition: 2004 (ISBN: 0-9746210-2-1)

9 8 7 6 5 4

Published by:

P.D. Publishing, Inc.
P.O. Box 70
Clayton, NC 27528

http://www.pdpublishing.com

Acknowledgements:

Medora MacDougall, Maggie Sheridan, and Barbara Davies: Thank you for your technical assistance. TN, working with you is always a true pleasure.

~ Blayne Cooper (2004)

For my mom, I love you. As always, to RT, LL, and ROC, you inspire. To my writing partner, you're the best pal. To Tay, CN, Bridget and Judith...thank you all for being my friends. And to everyone I don't have room to mention here, thank you. I Love You All.

~ T. Novan (2004)

DEDICATION

To my parents, whose faith and support taught me to love myself. To my spouse, whose dedication and love fill my heart. To my children, whose smiles light up my life. I love you.

~ Blayne Cooper (2004)

To the victims, and heroes and their families of September 11, 2001. Because of your selfless sacrifices in the face of unmentionable terror and your dedication to service and duty, there is hope for a brighter and a safer future for generations to come. God Bless and thank you.

~ T. Novan (2004)

Prologue

Friday, November 6th

Her iron, slightly sweaty grip on the chair's armrests clamped down even harder, causing white knuckles to stand out in vivid relief against the dark blue vinyl. She would have chewed her lower lip in consternation if she could have. But she couldn't. Right now all she could do was pray. *I'm gonna be okay. I am. I can do this. Children do this, for Christ's sake!* Her head snapped to one side, wrinkling the white paper bib tied round her neck, and gray eyes went impossibly wide at the sound of footsteps. *Oh, no. Someone's coming. It'll be him!*

"Hello? Anybody home?" A cheerful voice chuckled for just a split second before a balding head, wreathed with white hair, peeked around the slightly open door. "Hi there!" The man smiled amiably at the frightened woman and marched happily into the room. "I'm Doctor Cardozo. So that means you must be…" He discreetly peeked at his patient's chart, having forgotten the name already, as he slipped into a pair of rubber gloves. Snapping the second glove loudly, he scanned for the pertinent information that his assistant had emphasized with hot pink highlighter.

> *Lauren Strayer*
> *Blood diseases: None reported*
> *Last checkup: 12/12/14*
> *Patient Assessment: Complains of chronic pain in…*

He glanced up from the chart and at Lauren. "Ms. Strayer, I think when you were here the last time you must have misunderstood one of my colleague's instructions. Checkup time comes around every six *month*s. Not every six *year*s." He shook his head sadly.

His voice was mildly chastising, and Lauren nodded but rolled her eyes. *Asshole*, she thought tartly. *I only come here because you're close to my apartment. One more snotty comment and I'm moving.*

Dr. Cardozo scanned the small diagram of the human mouth where an "X" was placed on the lower left wisdom tooth. He pursed his lips for a moment then set the chart down, pulling up a stool next to Lauren.

"Well now, let's see what we have." He grabbed a shiny silver pick from a tray full of instruments and pointed it at Lauren's mouth, which was already being held open by the jaw spreader that had been inserted by the dental assistant who had prepped her. One look, and the assistant had known that tooth was coming out – today.

Round, apprehensive eyes followed the instrument as it moved closer to its target. When it got within an inch or two of Lauren's mouth, she jerked her head away in pure reaction.

The dentist exhaled tiredly. "Come on now, Ms. Strayer. This is just a probe." He held out the pick for her to see. "I know you must be hurting. Your cheek is all pink and swollen." A cold finger poked the body part in question and Lauren winced, grunting her agreement.

She glared at him evilly, but, knowing he was right, dutifully turned her head and presented him with her wide-open mouth. *Not that I have a choice with this thing holding my mouth open like the catch of the day.* He immediately made a hissing noise that she correctly assumed meant something bad. Very bad.

"Needs to come out," he informed her bluntly. And, while he didn't do what he was about to do very often, he thought with this patient he'd make an exception. It was the reason he still kept the old machine around. "This will help." He reached over and turned a nozzle, then fiddled with a mask for a moment before placing it over Lauren's nose and mouth. "Just breathe normally."

She looked startled for a second, but then remembered getting laughing gas once as a child. *Nice bedside manner. You could have at least explained what you were doing first.* Lauren thought hard. *Would they need to use the* – she gulped – *laser to extract a tooth?* She couldn't imagine why. And with that self-serving conclusion, the woman felt her painfully rigid body begin to relax.

"You hold this." The dentist pried Lauren's fingers from one of the armrests and moved her hand to the mask. "I'll be back in a minute, and we'll fix you right up. Would you like to watch television while you wait?"

Lauren nodded gratefully. She would do anything to keep her mind off what was about to happen.

"TV on," he commanded. Three tiny, flat, gray boxes, each mounted strategically on a different wall, shot angled beams that, when combined, formed a stunning, three-dimensional picture whose edges simply fuzzed away into reality. Filling the space in the corner of the room there was now a handsome anchorman and his large paper-covered desk. "Election 2020" was written in red, white, and blue block letters and hovered over his left shoulder.

Lauren groaned loudly, but it was too late. Dr. Cardozo had already scuttled out of the room, presumably to attend to his next victim. Irritably, she pulled the mask away from her face and tried to give the voice command "change channel," but the current state of her mouth made it impossible. Her efforts served only to drip saliva down her chin. Then she tried to curse, but that didn't work either. Which only made her want to curse some more. Finally, she simply gave up and pressed the gas mask tightly against her face. Inhaling deeply, she prayed she'd be so stoned in a few seconds that she would miss the Ken doll-like anchorman droning on and on about President-elect Marlowe.

The election music cued up and, in the blink of an eye, Devlyn Marlowe, at her podium on the steps of the Governor's mansion in Columbus, Ohio, was standing at Lauren's feet. The late autumn breeze was tossing around the President-elect's dark hair, and her bright blue eyes were clear and intense as she gazed out into the cheering crowd.

"Oh, God!" *Not her again! Every day. Day after day after day after day...* The buzzing from the room's fluorescent lights began to grow louder and louder, and Lauren felt her body begin to magically sink into the chair as a lovely sense of dislocation overtook her. She stared at the charismatic woman dressed in a long, black trench coat who appeared oblivious to the light drizzle dampening her head and coat.

"How are you feeling, Ms. Strayer?" Dr. Cardozo reappeared at her side, and she blinked dazedly at him, not having heard him come in. He looked at her and grinned knowingly, quite certain she was feeling no pain at the moment. "I think we're finished with this now." The man gently pulled away Lauren's mask. "Don't you just love her?" He motioned over his shoulder with an instrument.

Lauren furrowed her brow. *Love her? Nooo. I'm sick of her and this entire election.* She allowed President-elect Marlowe's acceptance speech to roll right over her, the low tone of the dark haired woman's voice soothing her further. But even so, her gaze remained focused on Marlowe's image. *She's sure easy on the eyes. Nice hair, tall,* her mind rambled as the dentist began rooting around in her mouth.

After a few moments, the dentist began flushing Lauren's mouth with water and suctioning it back out, the noise preventing him from hearing the television. "Volume up two," he ordered absently.

Lauren jumped a little, shocked back to the moment when Marlowe's voice suddenly grew too loud to ignore.

Devlyn Marlowe leaned forward on the podium, her hands resting on its edges. Although she was physically exhausted from what had been a grueling campaign, one whose final numbers were the closest since the Gore/Bush fiasco twenty years prior, she fed off the crowd's energy, soaking up their excitement, the palpable charge in the air reinvigorating frazzled nerves. "We did it!" She raised a fist in victory, and the crowd roared.

The President-elect laughed warmly, then raised her palms to quiet them so she could continue speaking. Devlyn looked up and flashed a charismatic, heart-stopping smile at someone in the crowd. And Lauren sucked in a breath, her drug-induced stupor further adding to the feeling that Devlyn was smiling directly at her. *Wow.*

Marlowe's gaze dropped from Lauren's, and she stuck her wet hands in her coat pockets, stepping down several stairs so she could speak more directly to the crowd. A flurry of activity around her made it clear that that move wasn't expected by the Secret Service agents flanking the edge of the steps. Several of them moved smoothly into new positions before disappearing from view.

"As one of my favorite authors wrote, 'When faced with what seems like an insurmountable challenge, you have but one choice...to dig deeper within yourself than you ever believed possible...to question the dedication and worthiness of your very soul...and then to throw caution to the winds and take your fate in your own two hands.'"

Lauren began choking wildly, gasping for air, her flailing arms knocking into the instrument tray and sending several tools onto her lap. *Oh, my God!*

The crowd had gone respectfully silent, but exploded once again when Devlyn added, "We did that, folks...and we made history in the process!" Her voice was drowned out by the cheering masses, and the anchorman broke in to add his own commentary.

"Dammit!" Dr. Cardozo clumsily yanked his hand out of the convulsing woman's mouth, her tooth trapped between the bloody tips of his shaking forceps. *Thank God she didn't swallow it. My malpractice insurance is already hell.* "What's wrong? Are you hurt?"

"Cu-Cu-Cu–!"

"What? What?" he asked desperately, beginning to panic over Lauren's agitated state. Maybe she'd sue him anyway. He practically threw down the forceps onto the askew tray, sending Lauren's wisdom tooth bouncing across the carpet.

Without warning, the woman leaned over to a small porcelain basin and carelessly ripped the jaw spreader from her mouth, spitting and hacking several times in the process. Her lips were numb, and she could barely form the words. "Cu-Cu–" She swallowed and smacked her unresponsive cheeks and lips with her hands.

"Lord have mercy, girl. What is it?"

Lauren extended her finger toward the image of the anchorman who was still chatting away happily. A still head shot of Devlyn's was floating disembodied above him as election result percentages ran in a continuous stream just below her neck, disappearing into the area where Dr. Cardozo's coat rack stood.

"She cu-cu–"

Dr. Cardozo stared at her expectantly.

"She quoted me!" Lauren was finally able to blurt out. She frowned and wiped away a long string of saliva that was dangling freely from her chin.

The man rubbed his forehead, starting to suspect that Lauren's revelation didn't have anything to do with dentistry. "Huh?"

Lauren blinked in confusion, the laughing gas making her tongue feel thick and her senses dull. "I'm the...the author." She ran a hand through wavy, shoulder-length, blonde hair. "Sweet Jesus," she drawled, the words taking on a slur at the end. "I didn't even vote for the Yankee!"

A glimpse of color caught her eye, and Lauren suddenly peered down at her paper bib, which was speckled with red dots and several good-sized crimson smears. Her eyes widened, and the color drained from her face. "Is that blo-boo?"

"Blood," Dr. Cardozo finished, looking down at Lauren's limp form, which was lying peacefully in the dental chair. "Shit." Stepping around the unconscious woman's feet, he walked over to the doorway and motioned over the receptionist. "I need a phone number."

The receptionist peered inside the exam room. "Your lawyer?"

"My lawyer," he confirmed with a scowl.

Lauren pulled into her designated parking space outside her apartment complex, shutting down the engine with the voice command "engine off" followed by "4-2-1-3" which happened to be the last four digits of her Social Security number. In an effort to make her life simple, she used the same four numbers for every code she had, knowing full well that any thief with minimal brainstem activity could wipe her out financially in a heartbeat. Then again, she never got locked out of her apartment or accidentally routed her grocery bill to the phone company. *Simple was good,* she decided.

The fair-haired woman slipped off small, silver, wire-framed glasses and leaned over, resting her forehead against the steering wheel. After she had woken up at the dentist's office, it had taken nearly thirty minutes to convince the man that she wasn't going to sue him. She explained that passing out or throwing up was her typical reaction to the sight of her own blood. *Nothing like making a total and complete fool of myself to start the day off right.*

Lauren groaned slightly, her jaw feeling like she'd been hit in the face with a two-by-four. She plucked a small bottle of prescription pain pills she'd picked up on the way home out of her jacket pocket. Squinting, she studied the label, then shook her head and relented, sliding her glasses back into place. *Three more hours until I can take another one. Just great.* Her head felt like it was going to explode this very minute.

Stuffing the bottle back in her pocket, she exited her car and slowly made her way up the outdoor staircase to her second floor apartment. With one hand, she closed the lapels of her suede jacket to ward off the chill. November in Nashville was always unpredictable. Most of the time it rained; sometimes there were even flurries. Last week it had been a balmy sixty-five degrees and she'd pounded away on her computer out on her balcony in the warm afternoon sun. In contrast, today it was in the low forties, rain clouds loomed above, and the cold wind seemed to intensify the pain in her jaw.

She rounded a blind corner to her apartment, digging in her purse for the keys she'd already put away without thinking. When she glanced up, she stopped dead in her tracks. Three slightly shivering men, two dressed in suits and one in khakis and a sport coat, appeared to be waiting for her outside her apartment door.

The oldest of the trio, a heavy-set man in his late fifties with a slightly graying goatee, caught sight of Lauren and visibly relaxed. "Lauren! I'm glad we caught you. I tried to call you, but I kept getting your service."

Lauren scrunched up her face as she narrowed her eyes. "Wayne?" *My publishing agent? From New York City? Here?* While they had seen each other a hundred times via satellite video feeds, they'd never, in the seven years they'd been business associates and, finally, dear friends, met face-to-face. He was shorter than she'd imagined, but his virtual image had accurately portrayed his chubby, bland face, deeply-creased cheeks, and overall fatherly persona.

"Damn, I need to adjust the color on my machine. You're much more of a blonde than a redhead." His eyes twinkled happily. "Hiya, sweetheart. Ooo...how does the other guy look?" He grazed her slightly black and blue cheek with his fingertips.

Lauren didn't bother to answer his question. Instead, she grinned as much as her mouth, packed with cotton swabs, would allow. His rapid speech and nasal New York accent seemed much more pronounced in person.

He smiled back in response and felt himself pulled into a tight, heartfelt hug, wishing, as he had many times over the years, that he were young enough to turn this pretty woman's head.

Lauren caught a whiff of peppermint, and a light crunching sound near her ear confirmed that he was chewing a piece of hard candy. "What are you doing here?" she asked curiously, her hands grasping his biceps so she could push back and look him over again. "I sent you those contract revisions three days ago. There was no need to come all the way out here for that." She smacked his arm lightly.

Remembering that there were two strangers standing only a few feet away, Lauren allowed her gaze to travel to the other men who were both wearing navy blue, three-piece suits and gray overcoats. One of the men was large and intimidating, with shoulders so broad and bulky his head appeared to rest directly on them. He reminded the writer of a tree with legs. The other man was handsome, black, and slightly shorter than his companion. He had a neck, but was still imposing in his own way. She frowned and stopped talking, pressing her lips against Wayne's cold ear so she could whisper, "I told you I'm not doing a biography for Vinnie Lagulia! I don't care if he's sitting in a federal penitentiary with nothing but time on his hands. I don't do the mob!"

At the word "mob" the two other men's ears seemed to perk up like a curious German Shepherd's.

"Kidding," Wayne exclaimed, looking back at the men. "She's kidding, of course!" He gently grabbed Lauren's elbow and some-what nervously guided her the few remaining steps to the door. "If you let us all in, I'll make the introductions. I've got wonderful news!"

"No."

Wayne's jaw sagged. "No?" he repeated incredulously. *Dammit, what is wrong with her? It doesn't get any bigger than this!* "What do you mean 'no'?"

Arching a pale, slender eyebrow, Lauren crossed her arms over her chest. "It's a simple word, Wayne. Don't make me get out the dictionary." Before Wayne could argue his case further, she turned, picked up the other men's coats, and passed them over. Lauren extended her right hand once they had taken the hint and shrugged on the garments she was sure they wore to bed...along with their wing tips.

"Please let President-elect Marlowe know that I'm flattered beyond words that she wants me to do her biography, but that I'm afraid I'm going to have to decline. I'm sorry you had to come all the way to Nashville for nothing. I would have told you that over the phone."

Michael Oaks, one of Devlyn's most trusted aides, and soon-to-be Social Secretary for the new administration, reluctantly shook Lauren's hand, more than a little pissed off that he'd flown from Ohio to New York and then Tennessee, only to have the young woman shoot down his offer in five minutes flat. As far as he was concerned Devlyn could just find herself another writer – they had to be a dime a dozen. *And shouldn't they be falling all over them-selves to do this for Dev? For the country?*

But Michael knew his boss would expect him to give Strayer the full court press, no matter how he personally felt about the task. His dark eyes went serious. "Why, Ms. Strayer? Why won't you consider President-elect Marlowe's request? This is an unparalleled honor. Surely you don't have a better offer pending?" He looked over at Wayne, who wildly shook his head "no."

The writer smiled sweetly and did her best to hold her tongue. *Honor, my ass. This is one of those jobs where they tell you what to write, and then you slap your name on the book cover. No, thanks – she can find herself another propaganda puppet.* "I'm simply not interested." Her tone was polite but cooling quickly.

"The compensation offer is more than generous, but still negotiable. We consulted several major publishing companies who indicated what we are offering is well above what their highest paid historians and biographers command."

"I'm sure it is. But the answer is still 'no'," she insisted. *I don't respond well to overly aggressive, buddy. And you've already crossed that line.*

The young black man tried again. "But–"

Lauren lifted her hands in forestallment. "First of all, I don't specialize in politicians."

"If I'm not mistaken, your last biography was of Cardinal James O'Roarke. Are you going to stand here and tell me that the Catholic Church isn't a political institution?" His voice was rising in volume and had taken on a slightly sarcastic edge.

Lauren felt her temper beginning to rise. Who did he think he was? The man next to him, who might as well have had "Secret Service" tattooed on his forehead, stepped closer to her, invading her private space and looking at her with disapproving eyes, but she refused to back down. *Am I supposed to be intimidated by "no neck"? I think not. I can see how you operate, Devlyn Marlowe!* "I've only been home for a few months after spending nearly two years in Ireland and the Vatican, writing Cardinal O'Roarke's story. I'm simply not ready to commit myself to a job that will last for a minimum of four years."

"It's important to the nation that..." Oaks continued, not stopping when Lauren tried to get a word in edgewise several times.

Wayne noticed the woman's face turning pink, then, finally, a bright red. He crunched down a new mint nervously. *Oh, no. Here it comes. The IRS is going to audit Starlight Publishing – and me personally – every single year from now until the end of time!* "Lauren, please. I know you had your heart set on Maya Angelou." *She is in her nineties.* "But this is the President of the United States for God's sake!"

"No means no," Lauren ground out forcefully, her temper snapping. She marched over to the front door and flung it open with a loud bang. She automatically bent over and used one arm to keep her rambunctious pug, Gremlin, from escaping. "This conversation is over."

Saturday, November 7th

The sedan slowed. Actually, several sedans slowed. To the casual observer, they could've been mistaken for a procession carrying a family mourning the loss of someone it loved. And if it weren't for the identity of one of the people in the third car, that might have been true. Before her car had even come to a complete stop, men in dark suits who protected the life of the President-elect surrounded it. With a quick but thorough check, the area was deemed secure, and two long legs appeared from behind an automobile door as Devlyn Marlowe began to climb out of the car.

She leaned over, spoke to the other occupants, and retrieved a bouquet of roses before slowly walking to the stone that sat some thirty feet way. The men assigned to guard her were dutiful, but extremely respectful of her privacy at this moment, keeping as far away as safety permitted. She adjusted her scarf and tugged on the collar of her coat, raising it over the back of her neck. Dev gripped the roses and brought them to her nose, but most of their sweet, spicy fragrance was swept away by the cold autumn air.

She settled down in front of the gravestone, the damp, leaf-strewn grass soaking the knees of her slacks. Devlyn placed the flowers in a ceramic vase attached to the stone and brushed away a few twigs and leaves that had clustered around the base of the headstone. "Hiya, beautiful. I had to come today because things are going to get very nuts for me very shortly." Dev gave a slight chuckle as she intently studied a bright orange leaf with her gloved hands. "Look who I'm trying to kid. Things are already nuts for me."

Dev let go of the leaf and watched the wind carry it away. She leaned forward so her fingers could trace the outline of the letters carved in stone. "I miss you. Sometimes at night, I still wake up and reach for you." She smiled and her hand dropped away. "I've been thinking about you a lot lately. I wouldn't be where I am if it hadn't been for you. I wish we could be together now."

Her smile turned wistful. "You'd make a great First Lady." Dev settled back on her bottom, resting with her legs stretched before her. She crossed her ankles. "Wonder how they would have handled that? At least I think they would have called you 'First Lady'." She sighed, shaking her head. "Doesn't matter. You were, and always will be, *my* first lady, and that's what is important.

"I don't think I'll be coming back, Samantha. I'll bring the kids, of course. Anytime they want," she quickly added. "But I think...for me...I need to try to focus on the future for a while." She was silent for a long moment, listening to the faint howl of the wind and the sound of passing cars in the distance. "Yeah." She sighed and nodded a little. "I knew you'd understand."

Dev glanced back to the caravan and signaled. One of the agents opened the door to Dev's car, and three small children climbed out. Ashley, the dark-haired seven-year-old, patiently waited for her little brothers to make their way out of the back seat before carefully taking their hands.

The tall woman smiled affectionately as the children walked toward her. She turned back to face the stone. "You'd be so proud of all of them. They're very special. Aaron has a picture of you on his nightstand. He kisses you goodnight before bed." Her voice shook a little as she spoke. "I've made sure they know you. They know both their Moms." She chuckled suddenly. "Ashley, bless her, has learned to roll her eyes at me the same way you used to."

The children joined her, and Aaron, the youngest at four, settled himself into Dev's lap, snuggling round her neck, while the older two placed tiny bouquets of flowers on the grass in front of the grave.

"Hi, Mommy," Ashley greeted easily, taking a seat Indian style. "I got an 'A' in math today. Mom says I'm doing real good in math now."

On impulse, five-year-old Christopher gave the cold stone a little kiss, then joined his brother in Dev's lap. At five, the fair-haired little boy was by far the quietest of the three kids. Ashley and Aaron seemed to take their monthly visits in stride, but Christopher seemed to have as difficult a time as Dev herself. Even though he never complained, she wondered if she should stop bringing him.

But Devlyn knew it was important to make these wonderful children understand that they had, indeed, had two parents who loved them very much. Even if one had been cruelly ripped away from them by a drunk driver just a few weeks after Aaron was born. It hurt Devlyn's soul that none of them could really remember much about Samantha. Only Ashley had the smallest hint of a remembrance. And Dev wasn't sure if that was genuine or the product of their many family photos.

The Marlowes spent a few more minutes together, then the President-elect sent the children back to the car. She stood, leaning over to leave a soft kiss on the stone just as her son had done. "I love you, Samantha. You'll be in my prayers. Just like always." She took a deep breath and turned for the car. She didn't cry anymore as she walked away, and she knew that was a good thing.

Devlyn settled down in her padded seat at the head of the dining room table with the children and their nanny. Emma was a godsend. Samantha had hired her right after Devlyn had Ashley. And she had been right there to lend a hand when Samantha had Christopher and Aaron. Dev's career kept her so busy that she never had as much time to spend with the children as she wanted. Emma had helped take up even more slack after Samantha's death, and Dev wasn't sure whether she or the children would have made it without her.

Emma Drysdale was exactly what you'd want a nanny to be. Dedicated and loving. Her generous smile and heart were appreciated by all who knew her. She was a short but stout woman, with a fierce personality, ample hips, and a matronly bosom. She had a thick head of golden-gray hair and was as quick with a hug as she was to scold. Emma was more of a grandmother to the Marlowe children than a paid employee. And that suited Devlyn just fine. She was one of the family, and the older woman's wrath was nearly as legendary as her chocolate chip cookies.

"Don't you dare think you're gonna get up from this table until you've eaten every last bite on your plate."

Dev looked at each of the children, wondering which was in trouble. Then she glanced at her own plate, and she knew who was in Dutch. "I'm eating, Emma," she protested uselessly.

"You're too skinny as it is." Emma tsked her and pinched at a broad shoulder that was anything but skinny. "And you're not eating. You're pushing your food around to make it look like you're eating." Emma raised a gray brow, glancing down at the seated woman even as she moved over to Ashley and buttered another roll for the child. "You don't want to make a bad impression on your children now, do you?"

"You know," Dev stabbed a helpless stalk of asparagus, "I hate it when you do that."

"I know." The nanny nodded and refilled Aaron's milk. "That's why I do it."

"Sit down, Emma," she groaned. "The kids are fine. Eat something yourself." Dev shook her head and leaned back in her chair, knowing her protest would go ignored on this night just as it had on every other night. At least until Emma was ready to sit down.

She wasn't mistaken.

Ashley giggled and turned her large brown eyes on her mother. "Mom?"

"Yes, sweetheart?" Dev decided to make an effort to eat her dinner, even though she was so tired the only thought that really appealed to her was going straight to bed.

"Do I have to take *her* with me to the zoo tomorrow?"

"Huh?" Dev's forehead creased as she tried to figure out who *her* was. "Oh, you mean Agent Hamlin?"

Ashley scowled and Dev blinked, startled to see herself so clearly in her daughter's expression. "I'll take that as a yes. And I'm afraid you will, sweetheart."

With her fork, the little girl angrily smashed into the lava river she had created with her mashed potatoes and gravy. "None of the other kids have to."

"I know, honey. I'll tell you what, we'll tell her to wear jeans and a sweatshirt, okay?"

Ashley thought about that for a moment. *It couldn't hurt,* she figured. "Fine."

Christopher and Aaron stopped eating so they could listen intently to this conversation. They both had new bodyguards as well.

"You might as well get used to Agent Hamlin and try to make friends with her. She's probably going to be with you for the next four years."

"What about Amy?"

"Look, Moppet. Amy was a State Trooper. She took care of you before I was elected President. Now it's going to be a Secret Service agent and it's going to be Agent Hamlin." She patted the girl's hand and noticed that Christopher and Aaron didn't look any more pleased with the prospect than Ashley. Her eyes softened, and she smiled reassuringly. "You'll get to like her as much as you liked Amy. I'm sure of it."

"'Kay," the little girl muttered.

"Mom, can I go too?" Christopher piped up from his spot directly on Dev's right. "I want to go to the zoo."

"I'm sure you do, buddy, but this is a class trip that Moppet is taking." She grasped his small hand in hers. "But I'll tell you what, I'll try to arrange a trip for you and Aaron, okay?"

"Yes!" Aaron and Christopher cried simultaneously. The brothers gave each other the high five. Unfortunately, Aaron's aim was a little low, and he ended up smacking Christopher in the head. Christopher immediately struck back, and a mini slapping war ensued with the boys laughing and yelling.

"All right. Time to get ready for bed." Emma moved from her place at the end of the table and began herding the children toward the stairs.

Dev stood up as well, but sat back down like a chastised child when the older woman gave her a disapproving look. "I am the President-elect, you know!" the tall woman protested with a fake pout.

"Yeah, yeah, yeah. I'm very impressed, Madam President-elect." Emma pointed to the full plate. "Now eat your dinner."

"Am I ever going to do anything that impresses you?" Dev called to the retreating form.

"You already have. They're named Ashley, Christopher, and Aaron. Now eat."

It was nearly three more hours before Dev was finally finished for the day and wearily began climbing the stairs toward her bedroom. An aide caught her before her foot landed on the top step. "Governor?"

She let her head drop. "Yes?"

"The Secret Service just brought this file in for you. They said you wanted it immediately."

It's just a file. Thank you, God! I may get to bed yet tonight. "Thanks." She took it and gave the index a quick glance. "Strayer, Lauren Anna. Lauren not Loren, huh?" *I figured "L. Strayer" had to be a woman. The pictures she drew in my mind...*

"Governor?" The aide looked confused.

"Oh, nothing. Sorry. Good night."

"Good night, ma'am."

Devlyn made her way into Ashley's room first. It was a typical little girl's room. Filled with stuffed animals, dollhouses, and all the frills. The little canopy bed only served to remind Dev how precious her firstborn truly was.

"Hey, Moppet," she whispered into the darkness. "You asleep yet?"

"No, ma'am." The little girl rolled over, her soft, dark eyes glinting from the light coming from the hallway.

The tall woman took a seat on the bed, tucking the file under her arm. She studied her little girl, brushing aside messy bangs that needed trimming. "I know you don't understand everything that's going on right now, and it's kinda scary for you."

Ashley nodded.

"But I need you to trust me, okay? This is all a very good thing."

"My teacher says that you're gonna be the most powerful woman in the world. Is that true?"

Startled pale eyes blinked. "Well..."

"Even more powerful than Wonder Woman?" The girl popped up in her bed.

Dev looked into her daughter's round, brown eyes. "No. No way. Wonder Woman would kick my butt. Besides she's got that great invisible jet," Dev reminded, giving her daughter a friendly poke in the tummy.

Ashley nodded. "And the golden lasso."

"Right." She gently laid her little girl back down until Ashley's shoulders sank into the fluffy pillow. Then she leaned over and they rubbed noses. "But you trust me...right, Moppet?"

"Always and forever." Little arms tightened around Dev's neck.

They held each other for a long moment. "Did you tell Mommy good night?"

"Yes, ma'am. Right after my prayers."

"Good girl."

"You really miss her, don't you?"

Devlyn frowned. Today at the cemetery had been very hard for her, and her astute daughter had obviously picked up on that fact. She'd been trying to say goodbye to Samantha for over three years, and she was never very good at goodbye. Especially when it came to people she loved. "Sure, I do."

A pensive look crossed Ashley's face. "Maybe sometime you'll find a new mommy for us."

A lump formed in Dev's throat, and it took her several seconds to speak around it. "Maybe, Moppet," she conceded doubtfully. "But your mommy was very special. And I loved her very much."

"So did I...I...I think."

She tucked her daughter in, smoothing the covers underneath her chin. "I know you did. And Mommy knows you did, too. I'm sure of it."

Ashley yawned. "Do you think she's lonely, like you?"

The innocent words pierced Dev's heart, and she felt the beginnings of tears. "No, sweetie. She's happy up in heaven with grandma and grandpa. She's never lonely."

"'Kay." Sleepy eyes slipped shut.

Dev placed a kiss on her forehead. "Love you, Ash," she said softly, watching as the girl's breathing grew deep and even. "Sweet dreams." On her way out of the room she clicked on a tiny nightlight that cast the space in a muted blue glow.

Next, Dev quietly padded to the room the boys shared where they lay asleep, tucked down in matching racecar beds. She knelt between the beds and felt the tears come in earnest. These boys, with their blond hair and blue eyes, were the spitting image of the woman who had given birth to them. And neither would ever know the mother who loved them so much.

"Dammit, Samantha," she growled under her breath. Dev angrily sprang to her feet. "How could you just leave us?" She covered her face with trembling hands, immediately ashamed of her outburst. She wiped away the tears. "I'm sorry. I didn't mean it." The tired woman forced the tears to stop, cleaning the last of them away with the sleeve of her shirt. "I love you. I didn't mean it."

She bent over and gave each boy a soft kiss on the cheek. "Great adventures to you both tonight. I love you."

Closing the door gently behind her, she made her way to her own room. She tossed the file down on a desk near the stone fireplace. Where, true to Mrs. Drysdale's mothering nature, there was a sandwich and a glass of milk, waiting for the President-elect.

She snorted and threw herself into a large recliner. She hoisted the milk to her lips, then paused to take a moment and offer a toast. "To Emma Drysdale, I wouldn't get through the days or nights without you." She leaned over, flipping open the file as she sipped the creamy beverage.

"Well, well, Lauren Strayer. Aren't you just the cutest thing?" There were several pictures of the young woman, and she held up a five by seven inch candid shot of Lauren in the park with her dog. The blonde was wearing a baseball cap, and a short, wavy ponytail was poking out the back. She had on gray sweats and a bright orange and white University of Tennessee sweatshirt. She was laughing, her arm fully extended by the taut leash as the hideous little beast appeared to be walking her.

Dev examined the date on the back of the picture and confirmed it was taken recently. She flipped to the next photograph. In this one, Lauren was wearing a linen suit with a fitted skirt that stopped a few inches above her knees. The more sophisticated clothing made the writer look older, Dev noted. Lauren's suit jacket was draped over her shoulder and tanned arms peeked out from beneath a sleeveless, pale blue silk blouse. She was descending the steps of some office building and talking to a woman alongside her. Lauren's hand had been caught in mid-air as she gestured. A smile edged its way across Devlyn's lips as she took a good long moment to enjoy Lauren's youthful good looks, devastating gray eyes, and a smile that she was sure would melt butter.

The President-elect lifted the last picture, which was obviously Lauren's driver's license photo. Making a face, she shivered and pushed a button on the edge of her desk. The silent room was suddenly filled with a quiet hum. With one last grimace, she slid the enlarged photo into a paper-thin slot that ran along the corner of the desk, nodding happily as her shredder obliterated the unflattering shot.

She retrieved the picture of Lauren in the park and spoke to it. "The DMV will retake it if you ask them nicely, Lauren," she chuckled. Tossing down the photo, she picked up the neatly typed report and glanced at the bio cover sheet, but the words began to blur. She rubbed her eyes, knowing she still had several hours of pressing work ahead of her. *Hell, they told you she passed the security check, Dev. The rest can wait until later.*

"Well, Lauren Strayer, I don't need this file to tell me I want your help. I already knew that."

Dev finished her milk, ate her sandwich, and dug into a report on Chinese trade negotiations. She finally dropped into bed shortly after midnight.

Sunday, November 8th

Texas Governor Geoffrey Vincent was a man of middling height whose confident bearing always made him appear taller. He was undeniably attractive and his looks were often likened to the actor

Martin Sheen as he had appeared at the height of his popularity around the turn of the century.

As far as Devlyn Marlowe was concerned, he had been the perfect choice for her running mate and would serve the nation well as a Vice President. While they had their obvious political differences, with him leaning more towards conservatism than Dev herself, they shared enough common political goals and an unyielding dedication to public service to make them a formidable team. Simply put, Dev believed they made for a dynamic Presidential ticket.

The nation had agreed, and currently both families were in states of transition as they prepared for the big move to Washington. On this particular day, however, they were together in Ohio readying for a television interview where they would discuss their transition teams' progress and the upcoming Cabinet appointments.

It wasn't lost on anyone they were dear friends who were comfortable with each other and had a certain chemistry together that was compelling to watch. Under different circumstances, they would have looked like the perfect couple, a king and queen of a bygone era.

Devlyn, Geoff, and his wife, Brenda, were sitting quietly over lunch, waiting to be called into the Press Room for the briefing before the interview. "So, Dev," Geoff inquired as he stirred a spoon through his tea, cream clouding the dark liquid. "How are the kids adjusting to the idea of moving?"

Dev thought about that for a moment. "Well, luckily they're a little too young to put up too much of a fuss. Ash seems to be taking it the hardest though. She's sad about leaving her school, but her friends have apparently assured her that it's 'way cool'," Dev grinned, "that she's moving to the White House and that I'm going to be President. How about your kids?"

Brenda drew a deep breath and just shook her head. "Gary is just fine with it. But Erica is not a happy girl. We are seriously considering letting her stay with her grandparents to finish the school year, although that's just prolonging the inevitable. God help you, Dev, when yours hit teen and preteen."

"That's the whole point of me running for President, to pick up a few negotiating tips so I'll be ready when the time comes," she joked, giving them a wink.

"Don't bet on it," Geoff snorted. "There is nothing on this planet that prepares you for being the parent of a teenager."

"Truer words have never been spoken," Brenda agreed.

"Bren, have you had a chance to meet with Mrs. Clark yet?" Dev bit the inside of her cheek, trying to hold back the laugh that threatened to tumble forward. Brenda Vincent's dislike of the current Vice President's wife was well known. The traditional "wives meeting" was something the redheaded Texan was not looking forward to.

Brenda narrowed green eyes at Dev. "Not yet, Madam President-elect." That earned her a raised eyebrow. "But let's just say that our meeting will be as polite, but as brief as I can make it. That old crone and her self-righteous ways make me crazy. Dammit, Dev! I don't know how you've overlooked all those mean things she said about you during the election."

"I didn't overlook them, Bren." Dev smiled wickedly. "David, who is going to be the best Chief of Staff this country has ever seen, used them to get me and Geoff into the White House. I was thrilled every time that nasty old bat opened her mouth."

Geoff laughed. "I especially liked it when she said over and over again that you were on the fast track to hell and anyone who didn't believe that would be joining you there."

Dev's body shook with her own laughter. "Oh, yeah. I loved that too. Every time she said something, it was a point in our favor. You'd think Jack Clark would have been smart enough to hide her, or at the very least, hide the gin bottle, before public appearances. The woman needs treatment and did nothing but hurt her husband in the polls."

Geoff nodded, sipping his tea. "I thought Bren was going to launch herself off the couch when the Vice President's wife all but accused us of having an affair."

Brenda eyes turned to slits. "Hush, honey," she warned playfully.

He ignored her and continued. "You should have seen her, Dev. It was priceless." Geoff put his cup down and gestured wildly with his hands. "She jumped up, screaming at the TV, 'Dev Marlowe doesn't even play on our team, you old bi–'"

Brenda grabbed her husband's hand to quiet him, then she smiled at Dev. "For which I'm eternally grateful, Devlyn Marlowe."

Monday, November 9th

"No? What do you mean 'no'?" Dev scrawled her name at the bottom of a piece of paper and handed it to one aide while another was briefing her about her next three appointments.

Michael Oaks shook his head, wishing he could say to President-elect Marlowe what Lauren had told her publisher the day before. "She doesn't want the job, Dev." He shrugged. "It's as simple as that."

Dev shot him a look. "Nothing is ever 'as simple as that'. And you know it." She nodded absently to her secretary, who was going around the room and taking coffee orders from her staff. *"Why* doesn't she want it? No," she told her secretary, "that day is bad. Can we push it up to the twenty-first?"

Michael took a seat next to the tall woman. "Ms. Strayer gave me a few lame reasons, but I think it comes down to the fact that she just isn't interested in writing your biography."

"Then we need to get her interested."

"Dev, what does it matter? We can get someone else. Someone better. I know you love her work, but the woman didn't even vote for you, for God's sake!"

Now *that* got Dev's attention, and she looked up from her electronic organizer. Her customary smile slid from her face. "That information is private. And what do you mean she didn't vote for me? Why not?"

Michael nodded his thanks when a pot of coffee was set down in front of him and Dev, then moved his elbows to make room for a mammoth stack of papers. "Didn't you read the report on her?" He poured Dev a cup, then one for himself, drawing in a deep, appreciative sniff of the strong aroma.

"I looked at it," Dev said, her brow furrowing. *Okay, I looked at her picture. Shit.* "Jane?" Blue eyes scanned the crowded room.

"Here it is, Dev." Jane, Dev's personal secretary, thrust a manila folder into Dev's hand.

Twin eyebrows rose. "You frighten me sometimes, Jane. You do realize this, don't you?"

The plump woman smiled and winked. "After fifteen years, I know you better than you know yourself, Devlyn Marlowe." Her grin broadened. "And I can't wait to be President of the United States!"

The room exploded in laughter with Dev joining in. "And a wonderful President you'll make, too. Just give a me a little bump if I ever get in your way."

Dev took a sip of hot coffee and plucked a blueberry bagel from a loaded tray that was now circling the room. She opened the file. *Who are you, Lauren Strayer? And why did you turn me down?* The room faded away as she began to concentrate on the words before her. She speed-read the cover sheet bio before tackling the report in its totality.

Subject: Lauren Anna Strayer
D.O.B.: 7/4/1990
Ht.: 5'6"
Wt.: 124
Eyes: Gray
Hair: Blonde

Dev's eyes scanned beyond the address, non-remarkable medical history, lack of criminal history and employment information.

Marital Status: Divorced (dates of marriage 1/24/14–10/16/17)

Family: No children, no siblings, no significant other, parents still living

Devlyn's thoughts stopped there for a moment. *Sounds like a lonely existence.*

Education: BA in History, minor in English Literature, University of Tennessee, Magna Cum Laude, graduation date: 5/5/11

Devlyn laughed as she read about the eleven outstanding parking tickets the city of Nashville had against the woman. Her gaze drifted back to the photo that had caught her attention the night before, and she smiled again. *I wonder what the ugly little dog's name is?*

She flipped to the back of the file for the supplemental information she knew would be there, quickly examining a photograph of Lauren's ex-husband, Judd Radison, an architect living in Chicago who had remarried two months after his divorce from Lauren. He now had a two-and-a-half-year-old son. Dev did the math and stifled a curse. *Cheating rat bastard.* She decided to shred his picture later, too.

Devlyn frowned when there were no photographs of Lauren's parents, but the brief report indicated Howard Strayer was a retired plumber, and forty-five year member and former Union Steward for the American Plumbers' Union. *Blue collar background. I wouldn't have guessed that. Interesting.* Anna Strayer was a homemaker, who had been hospitalized for depression several times over the past twenty years.

When Dev looked up from her reading, ten minutes later, she was alone in the conference room. Empty cups were everywhere, paper plates were strewn around the room and for the first time she noticed the beeping of an alarm that had been set to remind her of her first appointment. Her coffee was cold, and she pushed the cup away with distaste. Devlyn shuffled back to the first page of the file and, taking a large bite of her bagel, she picked up her phone.

Lauren rooted around in her purse and finally found a small mirror. "Auto drive on. Preset destination number twelve. 4-2-1-3."

Lauren dropped her hand from the wheel and pushed her seat back as the car signaled and made a smooth lane change. She glanced at her watch. She was already late. "Increase speed by ten miles per hour. 4-2-1-3." She waited for the expected warning beep, then overrode the automatic speed control system with a voice command. "Speed override approved. 4-2-1-3."

Holding up a small hand mirror, she applied a light coat of pale lipstick. She jumped when her phone rang, causing her to smear her chin with a streak of pink. "Uck." She snagged a tissue from a holder between the seats, and let the phone continue to ring as she wiped her face. On the fifth ring she answered, "Hello."

"Hello," a strong but decidedly female voice burred. "Is this Ms. Lauren Strayer?"

Lauren held the phone away from her face and stared at it as though she'd never seen it before. *I know that voice.*

"Hello? Ms. Strayer?"

Lauren pressed the receiver back to her ear, impressed despite the fact that she truly didn't want to be. "This..." She cleared her throat gently. "This is Lauren Strayer."

Dev smiled, easily picking up on the younger woman's surprise and instantly loving the sweet, southern drawl. "I'm glad to be talking with you myself. Oh, I'm sorry. I'm–"

"The President of the United States," Lauren finished at a total loss. *My God! She's calling me about the biography? Herself?*

"President-elect, actually." Devlyn kicked her feet up on the table, wishing that her always-ravenous staff hadn't scarfed down all the bagels. She found herself wanting another. "You spoke with my aide, Michael Oaks, on Friday?"

Lauren nodded. "I did." Her shock began to give way to remembered anger. "And I don't appreciate being 'strong-armed'," she said, her tone suddenly cool.

Dev sat up straight, her feet sliding from the table and striking the ground with a loud thud. "What do you mean 'strong-armed'?" *What did you do, Michael?*

"Why else was Mr. Oaks accompanied by Mighty Joe Young?"

Mighty Joe Young? Dev closed her eyes. *Oh, God. Tell me he didn't bring Francis.* "Could you be referring to Francis Davies? The very intense and unfortunate Secret Service agent whose head happens to grow directly out of his shoulders?"

A laugh escaped Lauren, and she clamped down on it with the palm of her hand. *A politician with a genuine sense of humor? It's snowing in Hell.* "That name sounds familiar," she offered noncommittally, not bothering to wipe the smile off her face.

"Then please allow me to immediately apologize. I'm certain that Francis' presence wasn't intended to intimidate." *Please don't ask me why else he was there then.*

Lauren held the phone out again and looked at it, wishing could see Devlyn Marlowe's face. She sounded sincere enough. "Perhaps I misunderstood then," she heard herself say.

"Ms. Strayer, your work is both intelligent and insightful. I'm a huge fan."

Lauren was surprised again by Dev's enthusiastic praise and

felt her cheeks growing warm. "Th-Thank you." What she didn't know was that Dev was sporting a matching blush on the other end of the phone.

The President-elect mentally scolded herself for sounding like a star-struck teenager. "I need your help. I'm in a very unique position, Ms. Strayer. One that needs to be skillfully and, more importantly, accurately recorded." Dev's alarm went off, and she swatted at it with an irritated hand.

"I couldn't agree more."

Dark eyebrows lifted in surprise. "Then you'll do it?" People started filing into the conference room.

"I didn't say that."

Devlyn sighed in frustration. "Please, Ms. Strayer, help me out here. I've got a meeting in two minutes. Tell me what I need to do to get you to say yes."

Lauren's car came to a stop outside the public library and waited dutifully for her to give the command to kill the ignition. "I don't think there is anything you could say," she replied honestly.

"I'm flattered. Really, I am." *And curious as hell.* "But I don't want to have my copy ghost written by the Emancipation Party Chairman. That's not the type of work I do. I'd be happy to recommend someone—"

"What are you talking about?"

Lauren could hear the puzzlement in Devlyn's voice.

"That's not what I want." *What did Michael say to you?*

The writer blew out a breath, wanting to believe the other woman, but knowing better. "You say that now. But—"

"But nothing! I don't want a 'yes man' for the party. The party is paying you because I couldn't see asking the taxpayers to do it. And if I paid you myself it would call your professionalism into question, would it not?"

Lauren leaned forward, listening intently. "Yes, it would."

"I want someone with honesty and integrity and real talent. I want you, Ms. Strayer. You'd have free rein to write whatever you see fit." Dev waved in the woman who she hoped would be the next head of the Department of Health and Human Services. Cursing the time, she spoke rapidly. "I'm giving you full access to everything and complete editorial control of the content. Your only constraint will be working within the bounds of reasonable national security." Dev laughed. "And keeping up with me."

Lauren stared at the phone for the third time, not believing what she was hearing.

Dev held up a single finger indicating to the people in the room she'd be just one more minute as the last person sat down at the table and Jane closed the conference room door. The dark-haired woman turned her back to her guests and crossed her fingers. "Was that what you needed to hear, Ms. Strayer?"

Lauren nodded dumbly. *Full access? Editorial control? And a "subject" who is making history with every move she makes?* "Yeah." She swallowed hard. "That was what I needed to hear."

Thursday, January 21st

Dev took a deep breath and looked at David McMillian, her oldest and most trusted friend and the new White House Chief of Staff. She'd known him since her undergraduate days at Harvard. They'd studied and even roomed together for a semester before Dev met Samantha. Their time together cemented a friendship that had become a permanent fixture in both their lives.

While Devlyn's political aspirations put her squarely in the spotlight, David was more than content to play behind the scenes, where he often, and only half-jokingly, reminded Dev, the *real* power lay.

Dev reached out and grasped the cool metal knob, an astonished smile playing on her lips. "We did it."

"Yes, we did, Madam President."

"Cut that out." She scoffed at the title coming from him. They were beyond things like that, at least in private. And David knew it. But still, she was fun to tweak. "Or I'll make you call me Wonder Woman."

The tall, red-haired man scratched his jaw, and his tobacco brown eyes went slightly round. "Huh?"

"Never mind."

It was just after dawn and the offices were empty, an almost haunting quiet surrounding them. This was just the way Dev had wanted it to be the first time she and David entered the Oval Office as the President and the Chief of Staff. It had taken a horde of people to get her here. But without the support of her best friend she never would have made it. It was only appropriate that they should savor this moment alone together.

She pushed the door open but didn't step inside.

David smiled broadly and gestured. "After you, Wonder Woman."

"Smartass."

She stepped into the office and took a deep breath, stopping in the middle of the room to enjoy every crazy emotion, soaking in the pure thrill of it all. Devlyn had seen photographs of the room but never actually been inside before. It was just as impressive as she'd imagined. The oddly-shaped room had floor-to-ceiling windows dressed by heavy gold drapes that were pulled open to allow the sunlight to spill over the massive wooden desk.

The carpet was a steel blue and emblazoned in its center was an enormous Presidential seal done in shades of wheat, gold and beige.

The room contained little in the way of furniture: a desk, several chairs, a leather loveseat added by the last President. There were two bureaus topped with Presidential memorabilia including a bronze bucking bronco statue, inspired by Frederick Remington and added by Ronald Reagan in the 1980s that instantly made Dev think of Geoff – who would love it in his office. Several plants and rich oil paintings added splashes of color and flavor. And Old Glory stood right behind what was to be *her* desk.

An almost giddy laugh worked its way up from her chest.

She turned around to find David standing behind "the chair". He didn't feel it appropriate to mention that its back, for her protection, was lined with Kevlar, the same material used to make US Army helmets, and was found in the body panels of exotic automobiles. "The chair" could withstand a point-blank shotgun blast. He gave her a grin and patted the soft leather.

"Come on. Try it out."

"I'm almost afraid to," she admitted. "It's like, if I try to sit in that chair, I'll wake up from the dream, and it'll all be gone."

"Nah. It's real. You're here. And it's never gonna be the same again. You've already made history, Madam President. Now let's give 'em four years they'll never forget."

Devlyn took another slightly shaky breath and made her way to the chair, sinking into the soft leather with an inaudible sigh. She spread her hands over the desk in front of her, feeling the cool, smooth surface under her palms. "I am the President of the United States," she whispered, looking up to her Chief of Staff.

"Yes, you are." David sucked in a breath, biting the edge of his thick red mustache, fully aware of the power of the moment.

She blinked and stared across the room with unseeing eyes. "I've lost my mind."

"Yes, you have." David cleared his throat. "I'll leave you now, so that you can get your personal things out." He gestured as he moved back to the door. "They're in those two white boxes in the corner."

"Thanks, David." She looked up. "Hey, if we don't hate this too much, are we going for eight?"

"Ask me in two years. Have a good day, Madam President."

"David!" she called after him.

He poked his head back around the door. "Yes?"

"Thank you for getting me here."

"We did it together, Dev." Her friend gave her a smile and left the office.

Monday, January 25th

Dev had quickly adjusted to the flock of people that always seemed to be on her heels no matter where she was going. It was a lot like being Governor only to the nth degree. Luckily, she had long ago learned to listen to everyone at once. *Now, if someone could scare me up a good corned beef on rye without my having to fly back to Ohio, I'd be a happy woman.*

"You have a meeting with the Secretary of Energy at 3:30," Liza Dennis, her new assistant, told her, slipping another folder into Dev's hands. Liza was young and every bit as tall as Dev's seventy-one and a half inches. She was rail thin with tightly curled brown hair, and gums that showed just a little too much when she smiled. She was also saving Dev's life by getting her everywhere she needed to be with at least some semblance of punctuality.

Dev had learned early in her political career never to wear a watch. People read way too much into the gesture of glancing at the timepiece, which she tended to do often if she wore one. "What time is it now?" Devlyn eyed the door to the Oval Office, which was growing larger and larger with every step. She hoped to make it inside before someone declared war.

"One fifteen, Madam President."

"Remind me about the meeting at three fifteen."

"Yes, ma'am. You have an appointment now as well. With Lauren Strayer."

The President stopped dead in her tracks, turning to the young woman on her heels who nearly crashed into her. "Is that today?"

"Yes, ma'am. It was set for one o'clock."

Dev winced and then suddenly became very aware of her appearance. "Damn." She gave herself a quick once over, straightening her jacket and smoothing back long, ebony locks. "Do I look all right?"

The young woman's mind derailed at the sudden change of topic. "Umm...of course," she stammered. "I mean...yes, ma'am. You look fine."

"Good." She handed all the files back to Liza, then wiped her palms on her slacks, chiding herself for her nervousness. "How long is this scheduled to go?"

"Half an hour, ma'am."

Dev pursed her lips. That simply wouldn't do. "Push everything back and give me an hour here. I'm gonna need it."

"Yes, ma'am." Liza opened her notebook. This was only her second day, and she'd already figured out that the President was always going to need some wiggle room in her schedule. "That means you won't get back to the residence until sometime after seven-thirty."

"If I'm lucky," Dev grumbled as she stood in front of the door to her office and waited for an immaculately dressed man to let her in. She wondered if she'd ever become accustomed to people whose sole purpose appeared to be to open doors for her. *Okay. There's nothing to be nervous about. You respect her work. All right...you love her work. So what? You've met accomplished people before.* Dev drew in a deep breath. She was an expert at burying how she felt. "I'll be ready to move on in an hour." She reached over and tugged on Liza's sleeve. "Do me a favor and find me a corned beef sandwich, huh? The food they served at the luncheon wasn't even close to edible."

"Right away. What about...?" Liza gestured to the door.

"Oh, yeah." *Where are my manners?* "Hold on." Dev squared her shoulders and walked into the Oval Office, pushing aside the immediate thrill she felt just from entering the room. That's when the President got her first real life glimpse of Lauren Strayer. *Wow. Not just cute.* Dev mentally amended her assessment of Lauren's looks, based on her photograph. *Beautiful.* She cleared her throat gently, and the writer's head snapped around, slate gray eyes fastening on Dev's face. Dev's lips immediately curled into a smile, and she greeted Lauren warmly while remaining at the door. "Hi. I've been looking forward to meeting you. I'll be right with you, I promise. I'm just making sure I get enough sustenance to keep from passing out." She stopped and took a breath. *Okay, I usually don't talk that quickly.* "Would you like a sandwich?"

Lauren practically jumped to her feet. She hadn't even heard President Marlowe come in. It had taken her all of two seconds to commit her first breach of White House etiquette. "Hi." *God, television does not do her justice.*

Devlyn was wearing fashionably wide-legged, worsted wool trousers in the darkest of greens. Underneath a jacket that matched the slacks was a sleek-looking metallic silver turtleneck that complemented Dev's lightly tanned complexion and glossy black hair. She had the body of a track star, long and lean, with endless legs. Lauren's eyes widened as she realized she hadn't heard a word past "Hi". Her mind raced frantically. *Shit! I know her lips were moving!*

Devlyn wondered at the sudden look of confusion coloring the younger woman's face. "Sandwich?" she prompted hesitantly.

Right. That was it. "No, thank you, Madam President. I already had lunch." *The few bites that the bat-sized butterflies in my stomach would allow, that is.*

Sweet Southern accent. "Do you mind if I indulge? The NRA failed in its attempt to poison me over lunch. And I'm—"

"Of course, Madam President." Lauren smiled and tucked a strand of pale hair behind her ear. She slid off her glasses and began absently gnawing on the tip of one earpiece as Dev turned around.

Just like Christopher wears, the President mused. The boy was always fiddling with his glasses. Dev smiled again. He'd like knowing someone else who wore them. A lot. Glasses were unusual nowadays, and she knew Christopher hated wearing them, despite the fact that the lenses would actually correct his nearsightedness, so that he wouldn't have to wear them at all in a few years.

"Thanks," Dev said over her shoulder, breathing a slight sigh of relief. *Yes! She's not mad that I'm late.* "I swear I'll be right back." With that, Dev pulled the door closed and stepped back out into the outer office. "One sandwich and one hour," she told Liza, who was now explaining some White House protocol to Jane Shultz, Dev's longtime secretary. The President gave Jane a small wave and received a sympathetic smile in return.

"One sandwich, fifty-six minutes." Liza grinned tentatively and tapped her large-faced, gold watch.

Dev raised an eyebrow, glad – and a little surprised – that the young woman was already growing more at ease with her. Everyone had begun this new administration in a way that was almost painfully formal, and although it was to be expected, and wholly appropriate, it wasn't making her own adjustment any easier.

"Right. Thanks." Dev re-entered her office. Leaning her shoulders against the door to close it, her eyes slid shut, and she exhaled a long, slow breath. The breath turned into a happy whimper when the heavy door clicked shut, effectively locking away the rest of a very demanding world for another fifty-five minutes.

Lauren, who stood behind one of the rich leather chairs that sat in the center of the room, looked appropriately amused. Her hands restlessly rubbed at the back of the chair, and it looked as though she was trying very hard to stifle a laugh.

Dev stood up straight, intent on recovering at least a shred of her Presidential demeanor. With one look into understanding, even slightly indulgent eyes, she gave up instantly, grinning as she slumped back against the door. "Tell you what, let's make a deal right now. You let me be myself when we're alone, and we both might make it through the next few years without going insane." She smiled at Lauren's intently interested look. "Besides, if I have to be the President of the United States all of the time, the book's gonna be crap and we both know it."

"Deal." Lauren was grinning now, but her smile quickly faded. "Does 'you' being 'you' equal 'off the record'?" *Oh, boy. Here it comes.* The biographer instantly chastised herself for not listening to her first instincts and turning down this assignment.

Dev pushed away from the door. Padding over to the leather sofa across from Lauren, she gracelessly dropped into it, sighing with satisfaction. "Nope," she replied blithely, gesturing for Lauren to retake her seat. "The good, the bad, and the ugly of my life are an open book to you, Ms. Strayer." Unexpectedly, the President's voice grew serious, and she leveled a frank stare at the writer, one that caused Lauren to lean forward as she listened. "My children, however–"

"You don't have to be concerned about that, Madam President," Lauren interrupted urgently. "I would never invade their privacy. As far as your biography is concerned, they are only relevant in the ways that they directly affect you."

Dev looked at her curiously and barked out a tiny laugh. "Well, that would be in just about every way, wouldn't it?"

Lauren was about to disagree, but stopped herself. *Shut up, Lauren. It's not like you have kids. Well, at least ones that don't occasionally drink from the toilet. No assumptions, remember?*

The writer's first biography had been of Karina Jacobs, the star of the 2016 Olympics who had been born in Harlem addicted to crack cocaine. She was immediately touted as a twenty-first century Wilma Rudolph and ended up winning seven gold medals, despite several physical disabilities she'd been born with. Karina was single with no children.

Lauren's second biography had been of Peter Orlosky, the mega-nerd who had brought down the Microsoft empire with his single, non-proprietary operating system. It could handle everything from the desktop computer to the largest global networks – instantly resolving the problems of interoperability that had plagued computer and network operations people for years. Not only was he unmarried and childless, but Lauren was pretty damned sure he'd never even had sex. With another human being, that is. But ultimately that tidbit didn't make it into his biography because she reckoned everyone could figure that out just by looking at or listening to Peter. She certainly didn't need to tell them.

And, finally, her most recent biographical subject had been Cardinal O'Roarke. While she was certain that he and his long-time male secretary, Andre Ricardo, had a *very* up-close and personal relationship...as far as she could tell, he had never, literally, fathered any children. So how exactly could she know how President Marlowe's children affected her?

"Let me rephrase that." Lauren tried again, her tone every bit as serious as Devlyn's. Unconsciously, her gaze had softened. "You can trust me to know what's private in your children's lives...and what could hurt them. I promise," she swore intently.

Dev nodded. "If I weren't already certain of that, you wouldn't be here, Ms. Strayer. I don't take chances with the well being of my babies."

Lauren smiled engagingly, slightly taken aback by the President's choice of words. *"My babies"...so personal. Maternal. For some reason, I didn't think she'd be that way.* "But I'd be pleased if you felt like you could be relaxed and be yourself around me, despite my job." She raised a playful eyebrow at the woman who was comfortably reclining in front of her, with pleasure so complete it bordered on sensual. "I can see how hard that will be for you," Lauren teased gently.

Dev laughed, glad that her genuine nervousness didn't appear to be showing. "Good. Because this," she laid her hand on her abdomen and, as if on cue, it growled ferociously, "is me...tired, hungry," she glanced at one of the several clocks mounted on the wall, her eyes quickly finding the one showing the correct time zone, "and a little late."

She's a talker. Thank you, God!

"I really wanted to make a good first impression. But being late kinda blew that, didn't it?" Dev inquired sheepishly.

She wanted to impress me? Lauren cocked her head slightly to the side as she regarded the leader of the free world with ever-growing curiosity. "Some would say so." *But I wouldn't happen to be among them. You make a charming first impression, President Devlyn Marlowe. But I'll bet you already knew that.*

"Then I guess all I can do is say I'm sorry, and I hope you can find it in your heart to forgive me." A flash of white teeth brought Dev's face to life.

The writer's mind was already spinning, weaving a tapestry with words that would eventually form a picture of Devlyn herself. And there was one word that Lauren could already see was going to pop up again and again when it came to President Devlyn Marlowe. *Charisma...in spades.* It fairly oozed from the tall woman's pores, but it was in an understated kind of way that was both compelling and alluring. "I think, under the circumstances, I can forgive you, Madam President."

"Thanks." Dev scooted forward a little on the sofa and leaned forward, her arms resting on her thighs with her fingers interlaced. What she really wanted to do was ask the writer about some of her work – especially a few pieces that had been written under the pseudonym Lauren Gallager.

But now wasn't the time to be a goofy fan. There was still one major wrinkle to iron out that Dev had saved for a face-to-face discussion. Something she hoped would give this biography a sense of intimacy and candor that she found lacking in so many others.

Just ask her, Dev. The worst she can say is "no". Well, that's not quite true. She could laugh, accuse you of being insane and wanting to micromanage her work, and then say "no". "You just arrived in town this morning?" the President began casually.

Lauren shook her head. "Last night. The Emancipation Party is putting me up at the Hay-Adams Hotel."

"And your room is nice? You like it there, I mean?"

A wry smile wanted to twitch at Lauren's lips, but she felt a tiny kernel of worry germinate in her belly. *Where is she going with this?* "Well, it's Italian Renaissance. Not exactly the Motel 6, but *somehow* I'm making do," she said drolly.

"Good...good." Dev missed the joke. She was too wrapped up in what she was about to ask. "I, um...well, actually, I had something a little closer in mind. I mean, if you're going to follow me around on anything like a regular basis, you'll need to be close." *That was brilliant. Duh.*

Pale eyebrows lifted. "The Hay-Adams is less than three blocks away. Any closer and I'd be residing in your back pocket."

"Hmm...true." *Shut up, Dev. Don't scare her off now.*

"Okay, maybe not my back pocket, but how about in residence with me and my family?"

Lauren's jaw sagged. *"Inside* the White House?"

Dev grinned. "I've found inside the White House to be far more comfortable than outside the White House. The park benches around here suck." When Lauren didn't answer, Dev pressed on. "Look, if you really want to get to know me and understand what I do, you're going to have to tag along after me. And you can't very well do that from the Hay-Adams Hotel. I don't exactly keep regular hours, and there simply isn't enough time in the day for a lot of one-on-one research discussions." While that was true, Dev knew instantly that if Lauren Strayer asked, she'd make time for her anytime she wanted.

"I, umm...Madam President, I don't know what to say," Lauren admitted honestly. Sure it would make things interesting, but she knew she needed her privacy. Lauren wasn't at all sure that she could stand living in more of a fish bowl than she was already subjecting herself to.

"Living here is the only way to really know what I do," Dev continued reasonably. "It doesn't have to be for the entire term. Just until you feel like you've got a good handle on my day-to-day life." *C'mon, Lauren, say yes.* Lauren's head began to sway slightly, and Dev knew she was considering it. She went in for the kill. "I want a totally honest and accurate accounting of the first term of office for the first female American President. I don't take my legacy lightly, Ms. Strayer. The easiest way for me to give you full access is to have you nearby. I don't want to pull any punches."

"Do you really want that?" Lauren asked curiously. Giving her editorial control of the book was an enormous risk, and she knew it.

Sky blue eyes fastened on Lauren's with an almost painful honesty. "Yes. I really do."

Lauren found it nearly impossible to disbelieve the President's words. *Damn, I'll bet that comes in handy in her profession.* A tiny part of the writer still found this opportunity too good to be true. "And no one is going to be whispering in my ear, telling me what to write?"

The President smiled. *Don't even go there, Dev. Keep your*

mouth shut. "I promise you I won't censor you in any way. And once the book is done, as long as nothing concerning national security is revealed, I won't ask you to make any changes. There may be a few others that make requests of you...but you can take them on as you see fit."

"You'll back me up?"

"One hundred percent." It wasn't lost on Devlyn that Lauren hadn't agreed to move into the residence yet, but she was thinking about it. Something inside the President told her that this was a woman who didn't respond well to being pushed.

There was a gentle knock on the door, and Dev dragged her gaze away from her guest. "Come in."

A lunch table for two was rolled in and quickly set up. "Anything else, Madam President?" a young sandy-haired waiter asked, managing to sneak a peek at Lauren while he prepared the table.

"No. I think we're all set." Dev looked over at Liza, who was grinning. It was obvious the assistant had ordered lunch for two. The President gave her a smile and a wink. She nodded and the small group left the room, once again leaving the two women alone. "Are you sure you won't join me? I can see that my first executive order for one sandwich was completely ignored." Devlyn laughed, taking a seat at the table. "There's plenty. Everyone around here has been trying to feed me for days." She took a large bite and groaned with undisguised ecstasy.

Lauren swallowed hastily. "Well, if you insist." She smiled and took a seat across from the President.

Devlyn waved toward the other sandwich and took another bite, the smell of corned beef and horseradish wafting up to her nose. She drew in a deep, satisfied sniff. *Liza is getting a raise already. I'm in heaven.*

The writer took a bite and immediately mimicked Dev's reaction with a happy groan. "Oh, God," she mumbled, licking the corners of her lips. "This is so good."

Lauren's mind firmly told her living in the White House would give her fabulous access to the President, but would wreak havoc on her ability to keep a professional distance from her subject. She firmly told her mind to shut up and held up half a sandwich. "Will I get more of these if I say 'yes'?"

Dev suddenly stopped chewing and glanced up from her plate. "As many as you want," she promised seriously.

Lauren picked up her napkin and slid it over her knees. "Then set me up with a room, Madam President. It looks like you'll be having a guest for a while."

"Excellent!" Dev's honest pleasure was written all over her face. "And my name is Dev or Devlyn, not Madam President."

Unaccountably, the blonde woman felt a blush rising to her

cheeks. "Then please call me Lauren."

Dev extended her hand and when Lauren's found hers, she squeezed firmly, absorbing its warmth with idle pleasure. "It's a pleasure to meet you, Lauren."

"The pleasure is mine, Devlyn." Lauren exhaled and refocused on her sandwich as a knot that she didn't even know existed unraveled in her guts. "So...I know you must have nearly as many questions for me as I do for you."

Dev smirked and picked up a crunchy, cold pickle. "Yeah. How does someone rack up eleven parking tickets in two days?"

This time Lauren's blush was pronounced. "How...how did you know about that?" she mumbled in embarrassment.

Twin dark eyebrows lifted. Dev took a bite of pickle, enjoying its salty, tart flavor. "Do I really need to answer that?"

Lauren scratched just above her brow. "No, I guess you really don't. Let's just say it started with a really bad day."

"That ended two days later?"

Lauren chuckled. "Something like that." She picked up the bottle of spring water that was resting in a small bucket of ice and poured it into a crystal glass.

"I had a day like that once. It lasted for almost a week." Devlyn reached for a coffee carafe that was much closer to Lauren than her, and the smaller woman immediately intercepted Dev's hands with her own.

"Let me do that." She picked up the carafe and poured two cups, deciding she could probably use some as well. "How do you take it?"

"Black. And I'm praying it's strong. Thank you," Dev said as she took the cup from Lauren's outstretched hand. "How about you? How do you take your coffee? I want to know in case I need to get you a cup sometime."

"Cream and two sugars." Lauren poured in a little cream and began hunting for a teaspoon, which magically appeared right in front of her face. "Thanks." She smiled and plucked the spoon from Dev's fingers. "But somehow I can't see the President of the United States fetching my coffee."

"Hmm..." Dev begrudgingly nodded. "You're right, the President probably wouldn't. But Dev Marlowe will."

Tuesday, January 26th

The early morning meeting with her staff was just about ready to break up when Devlyn remembered something very important. "By the way," she straightened in her wingback, "I met with Lauren Strayer yesterday afternoon, and from now on she'll be attending these meetings. For those of you who don't know already—" Every set of eyes in the room turned downward, and Dev sighed loudly, mildly annoyed but not surprised. "Okay, you gossip hounds already know this, but I'm announcing it anyway. Ms. Strayer is going to be chronicling this term in office and will be moving into the residence today. Isn't that right, Michael?" Dev arched a challenging eyebrow in the direction of Michael Oaks, who nodded resignedly.

He'd tried to talk the President out of it, but the stubborn woman wasn't budging. There was something about Lauren Strayer he simply didn't like. Not only had she arrogantly refused his offer in Tennessee, but she'd said something to Dev that had made the President especially cross with him and had called his judgment into question. On top of that, whatever Lauren had told her had gotten Dev so angry that she'd had Secret Service agent Francis "No Neck" Davies transferred away from the White House. Permanently.

Dev took her last sip of coffee and carefully sat her cup back on its china saucer. "Ms. Strayer will be starting her assignment today. She has full privileges and complete access. Please be kind to her." This last part was delivered with a joking tone, but no one in the room doubted the sincerity of the request. The President looked around at the staff. "Anything else?"

The Chief of Staff glanced around the various faces in the room. Some were new to both him and Dev, but a few were loyal friends.

"We should do an announcement about Ms. Strayer being hired to write your memoirs," Press Secretary Sharon Allen stated firmly, opening her notebook and jotting down a few preliminary ideas. The fact that she didn't look thrilled about the prospect wasn't lost on Dev.

It wasn't that Lauren wasn't qualified. True, she was God-awful young. Her work, however, was well respected. But that didn't mean she had to live in the residence. Press Secretary Allen began to get slightly dizzy from the horrific scenarios that were playing out in her head. Someone older and fatter would have been a much safer choice.

"My memoirs? Ooo...I'm 38, not 88. And that makes me sound as old as the hills." Dev shifted in her chair, regretting the fact that she'd chosen a skirt instead of slacks today. "Biography has a less ancient ring to it, don't you think?" She gave Press Secretary Allen a pleading look.

The room filled with easy laughter, and Jane, who was standing against the back wall, shook her head. *Dev was such a pain in the butt sometimes. God love her.*

Taking the decision out of the Press Secretary's hands, Dev said, "Let's just call it a biography, Sharon. I'm not ready for a cane just yet."

Everyone stood up when the President did and filed out of the room, ready to start their incredibly busy days. The door closed, leaving behind Dev, Liza, and the Chief of Staff.

David looked at the young woman and silently asked for a moment alone with the boss. He smiled when she tapped her watch. Dev had a breakfast meeting with several members of the Democratic and Republican Parties, including the ultra-conservative Speaker of the House, this morning. He almost felt sorry for her. She had the unparalleled pleasure of facing two parties that resented and distrusted her. But that's the price she paid when she willingly joined a third party. David had always thought life would have been much easier if Dev had just stayed a Democrat.

Liza slipped out of the office quietly.

"Madam President?"

"Yes, David." Dev sighed, resting her head in her hand.

"I've got to tell you, I think Ms. Strayer being in residence is going to cause problems for you, Dev. Once the press gets wind of it, she's going to become more than an employee hired to write a book."

"You sound like Michael now. And I don't intend to tell the press she's in residence here. If it becomes an issue, we'll deal with it then."

David rolled his eyes. "It'll take them all of one or two days to figure it out. If that," he snorted. "And trust me, it will be an issue. A single, openly lesbian President moves in an attractive, single, female biographer..."

"You forgot very *straight*, single, well-respected biographer."

David put his hands on his hips. "And just how do you know she's straight? Did you ask her?"

"Uhh-buu-ahh–" Dev's mouth worked, but no words came out. "What!"

"Because I read that report, Dev. And I don't recall it mentioning any particular sexual orientation."

"But she was married to a man!" Dev blurted out a millisecond before covering her eyes with the palms of both hands. She shook her head furiously. "God, I can't believe I just said that."

David laughed. "Dev, whether Ms. Strayer is, in actuality, straight or gay isn't really the issue. Assumptions will be made. You're both single, and you've got three kids. You know what the conservatives will do when they–"

"Fuck the conservatives!" Dev hissed, suddenly angry. She had long ago grown tired of their painting her as the worst mother since Joan Crawford. "You know I don't give a shit about them."

"But you should," David insisted. He'd lost this argument a hundred times, but he never stopped trying. "They're out there, and they're not going away."

Dev leaned back against the edge of her desk. "Besides, I may be single, but I'm also still in mourning over my murdered spouse."

David's brown eyes softened. "I know, Dev. But we're talking about perceptions, not reality." He swallowed, wondering if he should go further. "Umm...you know Samantha wouldn't want you to mourn her forever."

Dev's shoulders slumped, and her voice dropped to an anguished whisper. "I know."

David moved over to the tall woman and sat alongside her. "Look, I don't want to argue. I know how important it is to you that this book be done right. But when this comes back to bite you in the ass, and it will," he smirked a little, "I'm going to be right here to say 'I told you so'."

"Like always?" Dev teased weakly.

"Exactly." He patted her thigh, a little surprised to feel warm skin through a pair of sheer hose. *Why is she wearing a skirt? She hates skirts.*

"Well, if moving Lauren into the residence, so she can work, is the worst thing to come back and bite me in the ass, I'll consider this a very successful month."

"It won't take a month."

Dev ignored David's pessimism and turned around, pulling over a couple of documents Liza had set in front of her earlier. She felt around in her blazer pockets, and David deftly handed her a shiny, metal pen. "We're talking legitimate press. *The Inquisitor* and the other scandal sheets don't count, David."

"The legit press will pick it up if it's hot enough. And we all know that if three of the scandal sheets pick up the story of Lauren living in the residence at the same time, it must be true. It's a law...like gravity or Murphy's."

Dev laughed to herself and stuffed David's pen into her pocket, rubbing her thumb along the warm metal. "It is true, Mr. Smarty Pants. Try to remember that."

Lauren sat down on her new bed, in her new room, in her new house...the White House. "Wow." She shook her head in amazement, allowing herself to absorb where she was and what she had gotten herself into.

Since November, she'd been on a continuous, whirlwind publicity tour for her last biography, making the big push to drive up holiday sales and keep her publisher very, very happy. That had left her with no time to even scratch the surface of who Devlyn Marlowe was. And it left her feeling unusually insecure, slightly disconcerted even, like the college student who had blown off studying for the big exam and was now getting ready to pay the piper.

Lauren chided herself for her worries. *It's not like you don't know anything about her. Hell, her face and those annoying, end-*

less sound bites have been plastered all over your TV for the past six months. Though the writer did admit to herself that the President was a lot more palatable when she wasn't being crammed down her throat. *Okay, more than palatable. Nice, really.*

She exhaled slowly. Lauren had finally been left alone for more than ten seconds at a stretch, her curious gaze unhampered by Secret Service agents and the milling, ever-present White House staff. It gave her a moment to order the mental snapshots she'd been taking since she met Devlyn. Although she itched to get her hands on her camera.

The thrill here, in this place, was the same she'd gotten when she was permitted inside some of the most private, holy areas of the Vatican while doing Cardinal O'Roarke's biography. Her stomach fluttered in a cross between nervousness and raw excitement, her palms moist and cool even as her keen intellect began cataloging information. But her tour of the Vatican had been a brief, escorted visit. She was actually going to *live* here. At least for a while. Lauren didn't think her penchant for privacy would allow her to stay here too long. But she was going to make the most of it while it lasted.

Her gaze glided across gleaming, Colonial style, cherry wood furnishings, and the rich oil paintings of previous Presidents in heavy wooden frames that adorned the walls. The room was nearly as big as her entire apartment back home. And while it didn't have a kitchen or laundry room, it did have what amounted to a full bedroom, a well-stocked bar, and a sitting area, complete with two small sofas that faced each other across a short, delicate-looking coffee table.

The bed was so tall that Lauren's feet barely touched the floor when she sat on the edge of the firm mattress. Predictably, it was a four-poster model made from the same cherry wood that dominated the room. Its deep, rich shine was so brilliant that Lauren could see her distorted reflection winking back at her when she looked at it. She immediately lifted her hand and ran her finger across it, smudging it with the same weird delight a kid gets when she rolls around in a pristine bank of even, white snow, happily making her mark by destroying its almost unnatural perfection.

A slender, matching dresser, nightstand with brass handles, and massive armoire flanked the bed. On the nightstand, in a cut crystal vase, sat two dozen long-stemmed yellow roses, their gentle fragrance filling the room and mingling with the scent of wood polish. Long, cream colored curtains that matched the impossibly soft comforter had been pulled open a few feet and tied with a gold sash, allowing the early evening's moonlight to spill in through the frosty glass.

Her few boxes had been unpacked by White House staffers, after, of course, everything had been properly inspected, X-rayed, sniffed and scanned...and that included her pug, Gremlin, who was scampering around her feet, trying furiously to jump up onto the too tall bed. Lauren was actually surprised the little dog didn't glow by now.

"I must be dreaming, Gremlin." *But, God, talk about pressure.* "I hope I'm this good." Lauren blew pale golden hair off her forehead with a puff of warm air. An incredulous laugh bubbled up from inside her. "This is totally surreal." The fingertips of one hand idly grazed the satiny soft top of the bed's comforter, while she leaned over and scratched Gremlin behind the ears as the dog growled in pleasure. Slate gray eyes flecked with blue and green widened when the woman peered down at her watch and realized that it was already time to meet Devlyn and be introduced to the President's children. She wondered if they'd all be lined up like the von Trapp family, awaiting inspection from their Commander-in-Chief. *Ewww...I hope not.* Lauren cringed. *Plus, I can't sing for crap.*

She was a little nervous. Life as an only child hadn't prepared her for dealing with kids. And always having your nose in a book when you were a child yourself didn't help make you Miss Popularity. Then again, she was pretty sure she wouldn't do something embarrassing like lift up her shirt and show her boobies in exchange for two Hershey bars and the window seat on the school bus. *Again.* A grin tugged at her lips...of course that might depend on who was asking, and how good the candy was. She decided not to rule anything out for the time being.

The writer stood up and straightened the belt to her russet colored slacks, sparing a wistful thought for the blue jeans she didn't think she'd be seeing a lot of in the next four years. Then, out of the corner of her eye, she saw it. *Should I?* She thought for a moment then nodded. "I think we've got a minute, Grem. Let's call him, huh?" Lauren chuckled. "Let's just hope this doesn't give Wayne that heart attack he's been worrying over for the past five years. Because he is going to die when I tell him where I ended up staying."

The second shelf of the dark nightstand slid out, forming a small table, and made the phone easily accessible from the bed, but still kept it mostly hidden from view, so as not to spoil the decor of the room.

The blonde woman opened her mouth to give the voice command to "call", but stopped when she got a good look at the smooth machine. It didn't have a voice box on the top. "Huh." *Must be a genuine old phone.* Next she picked up the phone and stared at the cord, pulling at it a few times and looking slightly annoyed. "Pain in the...okay, I can do it the hard way." She lifted the receiver and flipped it over to press the button pad, but there wasn't one. In fact, there was no visible way to call anyone.

Suddenly, a genuine smile lit up Lauren's face. "Hot damn, Gremlin!" The dog finally took a running jump and was able to make it onto the bed. His tail wiggled furiously in victory, and his beady, black eyes fixed on the object in his mistress' hand. "It's the Bat Phone!"

A light knocking sound drew Lauren and Gremlin's attention to the door. "Time to go meet the miniature humans. Wish me luck, boy." She waggled her finger at the mutt. "No, you can't come." She almost ordered him off the beautiful comforter but shrugged instead. If she was going to live here, this would be Grem's home too. And he'd be up there for bed tonight anyway. "Just be careful," she pleaded, straightening the pillow Gremlin had mashed in his excitement. "Martha Washington or somebody probably made that. And I don't want to have to take out a loan to replace it."

Unlike most pugs, who were solid black, or tended towards a dingy-looking crème color, Gremlin was a pristine white with only a few black markings on his face and ears. The dog jumped to the edge of the bed to follow her, but hesitated when he looked down at the floor. He whined softly.

"Uh huh. Now you're stuck, aren't you?" Lauren laughed as she made her way to the door. "Serves you right."

She opened the door to find Michael Oaks standing there. Lauren was vaguely disappointed. *Why was I expecting Devlyn?* She looked over the slender black man's shoulder. "What? No reinforcements this time?"

Michael stiffened at her reference to his visit to Nashville. "The Secret Service agent assigned to this hall is properly positioned at his post, Ms. Strayer, I assure you. I saw no reason to bring him to the door." He tucked his purple necktie deeper behind his suit coat. "You're ready, I assume?"

"Yes...err...no...just one minute." Lauren dashed back to the desk perched against the wall opposite the bed. Digging into a bag, she pulled out a camera and quickly slid in a fresh roll of film. She waited to click the cover closed before she spoke.

"Now I'm ready."

"You can't..." He pointed toward the camera. "That's not..." he began to sputter.

Lauren arched an eyebrow. "*Full* access, Mr. Oaks. These will be for my own research purposes, not for publication. And I already have David McMillian's full permission. Do you outrank him?" she asked innocently, chuckling inwardly.

"Well, umm...of course not." Michael's frustration began to mount. "But..."

"Get over it." She looked at her watch. "We're going to be late. Shall we continue to stand here and discuss it?" Lauren was fully aware of how much she was annoying the aide, and she was loving every minute of it.

He gave her a thin lipped smile. *Bitch.* "So we are." He extended his arm, and Lauren brushed past him, closing the door behind her. She hadn't taken two steps when a surprisingly loud, prolonged howl rang out from inside her room.

Gray eyes slid closed. *Not now, Grem!* Lauren bit her lip and turned back around to face Michael, who looked appalled. "I'm sorry," she apologized sincerely. "He's not used to his surroundings yet. Let me go calm him down. Or I could bring him? We're only going a few doors down to see the kids, right?"

"I'll have a cage and muzzle delivered immediately."

Lauren stopped dead in her tracks and turned icy eyes on the well-dressed man. "You can order those things if you'd like. But they certainly won't be for Gremlin," she ground out harshly.

"He can't continue to howl like that."

Lauren's hands moved to her hips. "Actually, he can."

"That's unacceptable."

"I agree. I should go get him."

"No," Michael said flatly.

Lauren sighed. God, she was already tired of this person, and she'd only been living here for three hours! "The apartment I had all picked out before my plans changed permitted pets. Gremlin is doing the best he can here."

"This isn't an apartment complex."

"No, it's not. And I don't have a problem with calling the apartment manager and seeing if the place is still available," she shot back. "Look, Mr. Oaks, it isn't as though there are a lot of options here. Either I leave him alone and he howls. Or I bring him with me and he's quiet. Or I stay in the room with him for a little while and get him settled down and he's quiet." Lauren crossed her arms over her chest defiantly. "Your call."

"Do you expect that...that *thing* is going to have the run of the White House?" Michael was almost yelling now, his anger getting the best of him.

"No," Lauren answered evenly. "He'll calm down soon. He's used to traveling, but he's only been here a few hours. Gremlin's also been poked, scanned, prodded, and don't even get me started on that glowing, bright green liquid they made him drink. Then they X-rayed him *several* times as though I had hidden a nuclear bomb in his Dog Chow! He's only an animal. He can't be expected to endure endless disruption and not react."

With that, she marched back into the room and sat down next to Gremlin, who quieted immediately and happily laid his slobbery face on her thigh.

"I thought we had an appointment?" Dev poked her head into the room, acting as though she hadn't heard the voices raised in anger. She had been waiting impatiently for Lauren and finally came to seek her out. Michael scampered out of Devlyn's way.

Lauren jumped to her feet. "We did...I...I'm sorry."

"No problem," the tall woman said casually, feeling a little guilty for her childish impatience. But all throughout the day her mind kept drifting to tonight. *Well, tonight is here, dammit!* She tilted her head toward the inside of the room. "Can we come in?"

Lauren nodded dumbly as Ashley, Christopher, and Aaron raced in past their mother without giving the writer a second glance. They headed straight to Gremlin, who managed to jump to the floor with no problem whatsoever and basked in their attention. "Faker," the blonde woman mumbled.

"I told you I heard a dog, Ash!" Aaron exclaimed excitedly, his hands fighting with the other children's as Gremlin lay on his back, enjoying his belly scratching with orgasmic delight. He even groaned.

"I hope he didn't disturb you." Lauren approached Dev, relieved beyond measure that the President didn't seem to be angry. "He's only been here a couple of hours and wasn't too happy about me leaving him so soon."

Dev smiled at her kids and spoke to Lauren without turning her head. "Why didn't you just bring him along then?" *God, I know they're going to want their own dog now. Maybe I am the meanest mother since "Mommy Dearest".*

Lauren almost laughed out loud. She looked past Dev to Michael, who was still hovering in the doorway like an annoying horsefly that didn't know when to scat. "Gee, what a great idea."

Michael turned on his heel and left in a huff, but by that time no one was paying any attention to him anyway.

"You look like you're settling in," Dev commented. Actually, the room looked exactly as it had before Lauren moved in, except for the slightly rumpled bed and a few boxes sitting on the desk.

Lauren glanced around the room and gave a slight nod. "I am." She extended her hand towards the sofas. "Won't you sit down?"

"Absolutely." Dev flashed Lauren a smile. "You know how much I love to relax. But I believe introductions are in order first." Both women looked down to find the children on the floor with the dog, giggling as he licked their fingers. Without thinking, Lauren lifted her camera and crouched down, effortlessly snapping off several quick shots.

"I'm sorry." Dev sighed. "They were supposed to wait by me and be introduced."

"Please." Lauren waved a dismissive hand and chuckled, setting the camera on the coffee table. "If I were them, I'd be far more interested in Gremlin, too."

Oh, I don't know about that. You seem pretty interesting to me.

"Kids?" Dev raised her voice just a hair and three sets of little eyes immediately snapped up.

"Uh oh," Ashley mumbled, pushing up to her feet. Christopher and Aaron quickly followed, although the youngest boy's attention remained firmly divided between his mother and the dog.

"We forgot to wait at the door, Mom," Ashley admitted honestly, her toe twisting its way into the carpet.

"I know you did. We'll work on that later," Dev promised, but the words were tempered by an indulgent smile. "Kids, this is Lauren Strayer. Ms. Strayer is going to be writing a book about my time as President. We talked about how she's going to be staying with us for a while."

"Nice to meet you, Ms. Strayer," Ashley said politely, hoping she could make up for her earlier mistake. Her brothers just nodded.

Lauren smiled. "Call me Lauren."

The little girl's eyes darted to Dev and the President nodded, letting Ashley know she was, indeed, allowed to call Lauren by her first name.

"It's nice to meet you, too," Lauren continued, unaware of the silent exchange between mother and daughter. *Ashley's a carbon copy of her mama, except for the brown eyes.* She gestured toward the floor. "And you've already met Gremlin."

Christopher was smiling so broadly that Dev feared he would fracture his cheeks. He unconsciously pulled at the stems of his glasses, his gaze riveted to Lauren's glasses.

Lauren caught his obnoxiously pleased look and laughed gently, moving over to the children. Gray eyes twinkled. "Yours are just like mine," she needlessly informed Christopher.

Christopher nodded, mesmerized.

Lauren chuckled again and ruffled hair the same color as her own.

The little boy's face turned brick red and he suddenly ran for Devlyn, burying his head in her legs.

Lauren blinked. "What did I–?"

"He's just a little shy." Dev patted the boy's back. "No worries," she assured, amused by the startled look that flickered across Lauren's face. *She hasn't been around children. Oh, boy. This is going to be interesting.*

Aaron walked over to Lauren and tugged on her pant leg, causing Lauren to drop to one knee so she was level with his bright blue eyes. "I have a very important question to ask you."

Lauren swallowed, suddenly apprehensive. "You do?"

He nodded solemnly. "Can we pet the dog again?"

Lauren burst out laughing. "Umm..." She had barely dipped her head into a nod when the kids, including Christopher, threw themselves down to the floor to pet Gremlin. Bemused, Lauren watched her pet. She stuck out a tongue at the lounging dog.

"Spoiled."

"I'd pay good money to any PR firm that could get me a greeting like that," Dev commented wryly.

"Oh, yeah."

Dev knelt down alongside Lauren. She held her hand out to the dog. "Why, hello...Jesus Christ!" She snatched her hand away when Gremlin growled unexpectedly, showing two rows of tiny, uneven teeth.

"No. That name was already taken," Lauren deadpanned.

Then, as though Gremlin didn't have a care in the world, he yawned widely. His mouth clicked shut and he innocently resumed playing with the children.

Lauren's voice turned scolding as she glared at her four-legged friend. "Gremlin!" *You are in so much trouble, you little shit.* "I'm so sorry, Madam President."

"Devlyn, remember?"

Lauren ducked her head. "Right. And I am sorry. That's so strange." Pale brows furrowed. "Grem loves everybody." Seeing Dev's scowl, she realized how that must have sounded and added, "He has had a really stressful day. But he's totally, one hundred percent safe, I swear. He's usually afraid of his own shadow."

Dev suddenly growled back at the dog and he jumped, scooting under the bed with a loud yelp just as fast as his tiny legs would take him. "Okay, I'll buy that," Dev agreed amiably, quite pleased with herself. *Mental note: consult David about finding the best dog bribes for dogs more chicken than canine who obviously hate me.*

Dev pushed herself to her feet, groaning. It had been a long day. And she'd been looking forward to relaxing. Reluctantly, she roused the kids. "I think we should give Ms. Strayer her privacy now."

"Don't go," Lauren heard herself say, a little bewildered by the urgency in her own voice. She could feel her cheeks tingling with heat.

"Okay," Dev replied immediately, a grin forming. "Wanna chat while the kids play?"

Gremlin took that as his cue to that it was safe to come out from under the bed.

Lauren nodded, and the women moved to the sofas. The younger woman sat down first, and Dev fought the urge to plop down next to her, moving to the opposite couch instead.

Lauren's gaze swept down Dev's legs "That's a pretty skirt." *She should wear them more often. Fantastic legs.* The thought might have been startling, but for the fact that it was so undeniably true.

Dev's voice called Lauren back to the moment, and now it was the President's turn to blush as she picked nervously at the material. "Thanks." Devlyn rooted around in her blazer pocket until her hand emerged holding a foil wrapper. A sweet aroma drifted towards the writer.

"Wanna share my Hershey Bar?" Dev passed over a piece of chocolate.

"Sure!" Lauren reached out happily. *A Hershey Bar? Oh, boy. Thank God we're not on a bus.*

February 2021

Monday, February 15th

Lauren paused in her writing and pushed away from her desk. She tilted her head to the side in deep thought, her fingers absently twirling a pen as she read over her latest journal entry. This wasn't a private journal, although her personal thoughts were woven around her professional observations. She would extract them later. Or not. Depending on exactly what they were and how they related to what she was trying to convey. This was her collection of hand-written notes about her "subject". And they already filled a single, heavy duty, three ring binder.

The writer had to admit that her few weeks as Devlyn's biographer had been little more than a blur. A whirlwind of motion and activity. Pledges and compromises. Deals and sacrifices.

It had taken every single one of the last twenty days for her to begin to become accustomed to rising at five in the morning so she could start the day with Dev. Lauren had actually groaned out loud when she found out that on Mondays, Wednesdays, and Fridays the President and a flock of Secret Service agents went jogging. She smirked to herself as she scratched out a few more thoughts. That wasn't quite true. They didn't *jog*. They *raced* the entire three miles around the South Lawn jogging path, which had been installed in the 1990s by a pudgy Bill Clinton, as though their feet were on fire. Their blistering pace kept Press Corps participation, which was permitted if not openly encouraged, to a bare minimum. Lauren already knew Devlyn well enough to know that was no accident.

The President approached her workouts with the same single-minded intensity with which she approached everything. Dev wanted to sweat. She didn't mind if some good conversation took place while she was doing it though, which was the only reason Lauren could make herself attend. But President Marlowe wasn't going to slow down to let it happen. *She* set the pace. And that made Lauren more determined than ever not to fall out. After the first week she stopped wishing Dev were dead and started wishing *she* was. But then, begrudgingly, grouchily, as the days ticked by, her body began to accept this new demand.

On Tuesdays, Thursdays, and Saturdays Dev worked out in the White House's private gym for at least an hour and a half, which was something Lauren found infinitely more palatable than the running. In this arena she had even shown the President a thing or two. Sunday was "family day". And Dev, "the no-good, lazy whelp", Lauren underlined the words, drawing a wickedly smiling devil's face, complete with horns and flames shooting from her nose – didn't "officially" exercise. Though the woman got twice as much of a workout as normal because she always gave Emma the day off and took to chasing after Ashley, Christopher, and Aaron herself.

Dev even slept in until 7:30 or 8:00 on Sundays, unless something crucial required her attention. Which, so far, had happened the last four Sundays in a row. But to Devlyn's credit, she usually wrapped up her business before the children even woke up and didn't pick back up with it until they were tucked safely in bed.

The blonde woman quickly discovered that Devlyn was always working, even when she wasn't. And while Lauren could sneak back to the privacy of her room and collapse on her bed, Dev was always in a series of meetings or just one more phone call away from a little time to herself. Many nights Lauren would lie awake in bed, listening for Devlyn's quiet footsteps as she slowly padded her way from her office to her bedroom – well after midnight. Lauren privately wondered if anyone could keep up the maddening pace established in this first month. And more importantly, why would they want to?

Despite what she'd come to call the "grind", there were still a heaping handful of pleasant memories that stood out in her mind and made her smile just to recall them. She had discovered that Dev was at her most Presidential *away* from the White House.

Lauren got a surprising thrill when she traveled with Devlyn in the Presidential motorcade. It wasn't the motorcade itself. *Well, okay,* she admitted privately, *it is a great ego trip to feel like the world is spinning just for you.* But even better, it gave her the opportunity to sneak a few moments alone with Devlyn. And although she wasn't positive, she suspected that Devlyn felt the same way. The older woman's sly grin as she would shuffle them toward the waiting cars gave her away.

It was at times like these, alone in the back of Dev's limousine, that they enjoyed some of their best conversations. In the past, Lauren had always prepared questions on note cards for her subjects, stuffing them into her pockets to be used at a moment's notice. So far, with Devlyn, she hadn't even bothered. Dev was always willing to talk. She was honest and funny, and Lauren wasn't sure how it happened, but one day she heard herself laughing and telling Devlyn about her own college days, her research long forgotten in the wake of genuine smiles and a growing camaraderie.

They were becoming friends. Lauren could feel it. And while professionally she was certain this was a bad idea, personally she couldn't dredge up a single drop of will power to fight against it. She liked Devlyn Marlowe. And the more she got to know her, the more she wanted to know.

During the times she wasn't trailing after the President like a wayward puppy, Lauren was researching Devlyn's family tree, consulting several well-known genealogists and even a cultural geographer. While Devlyn's lineage wasn't going to be the focus of the biography any more than the campaign was, most readers seemed to appreciate it if you started at the beginning. On occasion, Lauren would skip around chronologically and focus on the present day, trying to fit pieces of information with other bits and scraps of knowledge that would ultimately paint a portrait of an American President and a truly unique woman.

Lauren had already turned up at least one interesting tidbit that had required considerable digging. All evidence pointed to the fact that Devlyn's great-great-great-grandfather was a Native American. Chippewa to be precise. And the biographer suspected that Devlyn could trace her dark hair, lightly tanned complexion, and angular bone structure back to this side of her family. It was likely that this information had never come to light before because, by the early 1800s, the Marlowe family had evolved from French fur trappers into society bluebloods. And in 19th century America, having an Indian lover was something no daughter of privilege would have ever admitted to.

Lauren turned the page in her notebook. She dropped her pen when the newest pile of photographs she'd taken caught her eye. One in particular captured her attention and she pulled it from the stack.

It was of Dev and the kids, stretched out on the floor of the residence living room. Dev was sprawled on her back, holding a book slightly above her face, and the children were all lying on her, their heads each resting on a different body part. *It was a fairy tale,* Lauren recalled. She had been invited to spend the evening with the family and remembered enjoying the story nearly as much as the children. Dev looked younger, her face relaxed and happy. Dark hair spilled onto the light colored carpet and her blue eyes stood out vividly against the shadows created by the book and the fireplace.

The writer sighed audibly as she traced the photograph carefully, lingering over Devlyn's face. *She has such interesting eyes and lips. So expressive.*

It was a beautiful picture. A portrait of domestic bliss that, to Lauren, looked as alien as it did comforting. For the most part, her own childhood had been unremarkable. While not overly loving, it wasn't abusive either and was characterized more by simple indifference than anything else.

Her parents were stuck in their roles as "provider" and "keeper of the house", and she always considered them in a never-ending rut. Each living out his and her lot in life with a stoic acceptance of their place in the world and an almost intentional blind eye to their own happiness or the happiness of those around them.

Lauren's own dreams of travel and education were neither

encouraged nor discouraged. And she learned very early on that she was expected to make her own way in life, unburdened by the sentimentality and support of family. Still, she loved them and felt that love timidly returned in the form of actions, if not words.

There were sporadic moments of harshness amidst the general blandness of her youth, but she didn't dwell on them. She had grown up and gotten out, saving most of her contact with her parents for her monthly telephone calls home and short visits at the holidays. Lauren glanced at the photograph again and a bittersweet smile flickered across her lips before disappearing completely. No. She shook her head a little. Her childhood hadn't been anything like that.

She compared the photo in her hand to several others where Dev was in full Chief Executive mode, exuding power, intellect, and an unsurpassed determination. Lauren grinned in amazement. Each picture perfectly suited a different aspect of the President's personality. She was never "in" or "out" of character like so many people. These were *all* Devlyn. Every last one.

At first, four years studying Devlyn and her life sounded like more of a prison sentence than an opportunity.

Now Lauren wondered whether four would be nearly enough.

Friday, February 19th

"Well," David stood directly in front of the boss' desk, a thick stack of newspapers in his arms. "Twenty-four days isn't quite a month."

Dev didn't even bother to look up; she just sighed and extended her hand. "What?" she asked in a voice that wavered somewhere between amused and annoyed.

"I." He dropped a copy of the *Washington Post* on the desk under her nose. "Told." Next came the *New York Times*. "You." Followed by the *Los Angeles Times*. "So." Then he just tossed the rest of the stack, which consisted of a majority of the papers with the largest circulation in the United States, on the pile.

Dev picked through them until she found *The Columbus Dispatch*. "Oh, look. They're trying to figure out what caused the explosion at the gunpowder factory." She drew a deep breath, pursing her lips and covering them with a finger as her face scrunched up in contemplation. "Could it be...oh, I dunno...*gunpowder?*"

"Top half of the front page, Madam Smartass." David flipped the paper over and pinned it to the desk with a long, ruddy finger. He gestured with his chin.

Devlyn made a show of squinting at the page. "You mean that tiny, little one column, barely two inches long announcement that my biographer has been hired?" She snorted. "Big deal."

"That one is nice to you because it's your home state, and you know it. The *New York Post* is comparing you to John Kennedy and Bill Clinton and wants to know if you and Lauren are "playing house" inside the White House."

She grinned rakishly. "No, but you can call the AMA and let them know I wouldn't mind playing doctor." Dev instantly bit down on her tongue and chanced another glance up into David's wide, practically bulging, brown eyes. "You didn't hear that." She shook her finger at David. "I didn't say that!"

"Oh, yes, I did! And, oh, yes, you did!" He nervously tugged at his tie. This was not good. No. Actually, this was outright bad. "Deeev," he drew out her name menacingly.

"What happened to Madam President? Hell, I even liked Wonder Woman better than Deeev." She imitated his worried tone perfectly.

"What aren't you telling me here?"

His voice was low and stern, and Dev felt like a child caught with her hand firmly entrenched in the cookie jar. "Nothing, I swear." She crossed her heart. "Nothing is going on; nothing will be going on." Dev frowned, unable to keep how she felt about that prospect from showing on her face. "She's writing a book, and I'm the subject of that book. End of story."

"Me thinks thou doth protest too much." David pushed aside Dev's steaming mug of coffee and leaned forward. "Something is going on between you and Lauren Strayer, isn't it?"

"No." She looked him straight in the eye.

He searched her face. She was telling the truth. *So far.* "Do you *want* something to be going on between you and Lauren Strayer?" David carefully enunciated the words, not giving her a way out.

Devlyn's eyes went slightly round. She wasn't expecting that. *Damn you, David.* "No." Then she shook her head, knowing that was a bald faced lie. "I mean 'yes'." But that wasn't quite the truth either. "Shit! I mean, 'maybe'." *Jesus Christ, I sound like a hardcore Democrat.* "I don't know, David."

David's eyes softened at the look of distress and confusion on his friend's face. He backed off a little, sitting on the edge of the desk and dropping his hands to his lap as he waited for Devlyn to continue.

"I know that when I'm in the room with her, I feel like a giddy teenager. I find myself thinking about her all the time. Wondering what she's doing. What she's thinking." *Why she always smells so nice and what she's wearing,* she added privately. Dev stood, turning around to stare out the window and into the dingy, gray, winter sky. "I think I've been alone so long that I'd forgotten what it's like to spend time with someone new, where it felt easy...comfortable.

"Lauren doesn't want anything from me except for me to talk

and be myself. I mean...I know she's just doing her job." She shrugged one shoulder. "But it feels like more. Like she really cares about what I think and feel. Not like I'm under her microscope."

David blew out a frustrated breath. He didn't want to see his friend hurt. And Lauren could devastate both Dev's career and her heart. But it was time that Devlyn started living again. Samantha had been the love of her life, but that life was over. And Dev had embarked on a new one the moment her wife had died. David was more than anxious to acknowledge that it was okay to feel again...even if the timing and circumstances royally sucked. "Feels good, doesn't it?"

She nodded without turning around, but he caught her weak smile in the window's reflection. "Yeah," she admittedly softly. A pause. "It really does."

David allowed the conversation to dwindle down, which was never very hard to do when Dev was working through something in her mind. The tall woman was prone to lapse into long moments of silence as she thought, even if it was in the middle of a conversation. He chewed at his mustache for a moment, and just as he was about to speak again, there was a knock on the door, and Liza announced herself as she hurried into the office.

"I'm sorry for the interruption, Madam President." Liza gave her watch a perfunctory glance – the eighth one in the past five minutes. "It's time for your press conference."

"Don't make that girl use a cattle prod," Jane called from somewhere behind Liza.

Liza smothered a smile. Jane would say anything to her boss, and, to Liza, President Marlowe's secretary from Ohio walked on water...a goddess of the highest order.

Dev rolled her eyes, properly chastised by Jane. "Right. Of course." She turned and retrieved her jacket from the coat rack, handing it to David. As per their ritual, he held it for her, and she shrugged into it, buttoning all the buttons as he smoothed the shoulders. It was simple and intimate in a way that spoke of their affection and true friendship. Dev had done the same thing for him on many occasions.

The President picked an imaginary piece of lint off the black, wool blazer. "Send copies of those to Lauren." She motioned toward the stack of newspapers. "I don't want her blindsided. And could you...umm...tell her I'm sorry about all this?"

David nodded. "I've already done it. And I asked her to skip the press conference today, too. I told her you'd call her right after."

"Good man. I knew there was a reason I kept you."

"Yeah, my charming personality and good looks."

Dev burst out laughing. She punched David in the gut, making him instantly regret stopping at the McDonald's drive-thru for breakfast. "No, it's because you're the best damn handler in the business, and we both know it." Dev reached out and took the note cards from Liza and placed them in her left pocket.

"Are you saying I'm not good looking?" He squared his shoulders indignantly and wrinkled his slightly pug nose.

Devlyn grinned. "I'd never say that. Your wife would kick my butt."

"Madam President, we really need to go," Liza reminded, already walking to the door.

"Cattle prod time!" was heard from somewhere in the distance.

Lauren opened the folded paper, her mouth still hanging open from the last article she had read. Impossibly, her face turned a darker shade of red as she scanned the words. "Playing house? The President's little blonde toy? Hanky Panky Washington Style?"

She crumpled the paper and tossed it onto the pile of balled up newspapers on the floor by her bed. "Arrgghh! You *slimy* sons of bitches!" Then she read the byline and snorted angrily, tearing the article with her name and horrific college yearbook photo right out of the paper. "You were an asshole in college, Marjorie. And you're still one!"

Gremlin whined and buried himself under Lauren's pillow.

A toneless but soothing female voice rang out in Lauren's room. "Estimated time to press conference, one minute. Activate image feed."

"Activation authorized...umm...um...crap...186...um...1868... ugh! Pause activation."

She tried valiantly to remember the number, her hands flailing the entire time. Michael Oaks had informed her that the last four digits of her Social Security number were an unacceptable password and had insisted she come up with another one. Lauren agreed just so he would shut up and leave her room. She'd been sorry ever since.

Grabbing Gremlin by his back legs, she pulled the pooch out from under her pillow. "Get," she snatched a squirming leg and gave another tug as he tried to scramble back under her pillow, "get out of there, you coward! I'm not mad at you!"

Once she freed him, she flipped him over and peered down at his dog collar, the shiny tags reflecting off her glasses. She raised her voice and read aloud his license number. "Activation authorized. 18686GH89ZDC." *Let someone figure out that code!* she thought defiantly.

The video image popped into being, and a life-size Devlyn was now standing next to Press Secretary Allen, a few feet from her podium in the Press Room, and in front of Lauren's desk. The writer's first thought was that the image that had once seemed so vivid and intense paled in comparison to the real woman. *Of course, I was stoned at the time.*

Gremlin began to growl at the dark-haired women. Though even in the best of circumstances, he couldn't quite muster "ferocious".

"Hush!" Lauren wrapped her palm around Gremlin's slightly damp mouth and pulled him into her lap. "And for the last time, you can't bite that...it's just an image."

He gave a hopeful whine, wiggling his bottom as he got comfortable.

Lauren rolled her eyes. "You can't bite the real thing either. It's about to start...quiet." She absently kissed the top of his head and folded her legs up underneath her Indian style, staring intently. "Devlyn will take care of this." Lauren nodded. "They won't know what hit 'em."

Dev shifted back and forth, waiting for the Press Secretary to introduce her. She couldn't help but wonder how Lauren was taking this news. *Lauren is a reasonable, mature woman. She'll understand that this was inevitable and really couldn't be helped.*

"Tear 'em to shreds, Dev!" Lauren crowed eagerly.

"Ladies and gentlemen, President Marlowe will now take a few questions on the topics we've covered this morning." Press Secretary Allen adjusted the microphone on the podium so that it was more suitable for the President's height.

Dev stepped out, and the cameras followed her every move. When she took her place, her gaze immediately drifted to where Lauren usually stood. Holding in the sigh and hoping the disappointment didn't show on her face, Devlyn greeted the press. "Good morning."

Murmurs of "Madam President" and "Mornin" answered her.

Devlyn shuffled her notes on the podium. "Let's start with the DNA Registration Act, shall we?" She pointed to a man in the front row and smiled. "Let's have it, Bill. I know you're dying to get into this."

The balding reporter from the *Chicago Tribune* stood and adjusted the mini-recorder he held in one hand and the notepad he held in the other, jumbling them for just a second as he settled himself. "Actually, Madam President, what can you tell us about Lauren Strayer?"

Lauren all but snarled. "Set him straight, Dev."

Dev's expression hardened just a bit, but she answered smoothly, "She's a very talented biographer and I'm delighted she's agreed to write mine."

"What?" Lauren exclaimed to Dev's image. She released Gremlin, who stuck his non-existent nose under the edge of the comforter and scooted underneath it to hide again. "That's it?" The writer's tone was incredulous. "That's all you're going to say?"

Dev gestured to a woman in the middle of the room. "C'mon, Kathleen. I'm sure you can do better than that."

The correspondent from CNN rose to her feet, pushing a lock of hair from her eyes. "I don't know about that, Madam President. Maybe you could fill us in on the details, like when did Ms. Strayer move into the White House and why wasn't she put in VIP quarters? Why the residence? There was no press release to that effect. What are you hiding?"

"Nothing, you moron! We're hiding nothing!" Lauren tore her glasses from her face and tossed them onto the bed.

Dev raised a sharp eyebrow at the CNN reporter. "Just because I don't disclose every detail of my private life to the press does not mean I'm hiding anything," Dev growled.

"Oh, my God," Lauren muttered, covering her face with her hands.

Press Secretary Allen, who was waiting in the wings, closed her eyes briefly as she let out a long string of expletives under her breath. She turned to David. "Tell me she didn't use the word 'private'."

David threw his hands in the air. "I don't think she meant it like it sounded." He shook his head. "Out of the frying pan into the fire, my friend."

Dev immediately knew she had misspoken, and it wasn't just because the room exploded with questions.

"Where did you meet Ms. Strayer?

"How long have you known her?"

"What's it like trying to go out on a date as the President of the United States?"

"Is she a real blonde?"

Two pale eyebrows disappeared into Lauren's hairline. "You'll never have the pleasure of knowing, buddy," she answered tartly.

Dev silently endured the barrage of questions. She did consider what happened in her private residence to be private, despite the fact that Lauren was there on a professional basis. *But why do I think the press isn't going to take it that way? Shit!*

"How do your children like her and how do they feel about her living with you?"

With that question, the color rose to Dev's cheeks, and she drew in a deep, calming breath before speaking. "Ladies and gentleman, I know Press Secretary Allen came out here and gave you a full briefing about three very important pieces of legislation I'm working on. I came here to answer questions about those and other important issues facing our nation."

Lauren's eyes were drawn to Dev's white-knuckled grip on the podium.

"I did *not* come here to answer questions about something that is of no significance at all."

"No significance?" Lauren sprang to her feet, knocking her glasses onto the carpet. "I've just been crucified in every major newspaper in the country, and it's not *significant?*" she shouted at Dev's hologram. "Thanks so much!"

A chorus of voices protested and Dev raised her hands to silence them. "I'm sure, overall, that the American public is far more interested in how I intend to make sure every child has adequate health care and whether or not there will be a Social Security program at the end of my time in office."

Press Secretary Allen and David looked at each other, rolling knowing eyes simultaneously.

"And when you're ready to talk about those things, you let Press Secretary Allen know and I'll be back. Your current line of questioning is a waste of my time, and, therefore, the public's money. Good day, ladies and gentlemen."

And with that, she left the room. *I need to see Lauren.*

Lauren sat on her bed with her head in her hands. Her career was dying on the vine. What good was an historian and biographer who couldn't be trusted to be objective and honest? None. *Jesus, I'm going to end up doing Ricky Martin's life story for* Reader's Digest. *I just know it.*

The blonde woman heard a light rapping on her door. "Go away."

Devlyn pressed her forehead against Lauren's door, not caring who saw her. "Lauren, please give me a moment."

"You had your moment. And, if I recall, you decided to go with 'no comment'." But, despite herself, she was drawn to the door. She took several steps towards it, but decided she wasn't ready to see Devlyn yet. Instead, she gracelessly plopped down on the coffee table, only to have it collapse under her weight.

Devlyn pounded on the door several more times, but waved away a Secret Service agent who had jumped to her assistance. When he was back at his post she called softly, "Are you all right?" *God, she's stubborn.* "C'mon, please let me in. At least let me apologize to you face to face."

Lauren pushed up from the rubble. *Great. There go my next ten paychecks. I hope Gremlin can learn to appreciate generic dog food.* Her gaze traveled to the door. Dev sounded sincere enough. Brushing off her pants, she reluctantly crossed the room and pulled the door open just a crack. "Yes?"

Now that they were face to face Dev found herself a little tongue tied, but one look into flashing gray eyes and she got over it quickly. "I'm sorry."

Lauren felt a pang in her chest at the look of regret etched across Dev's face and fought the urge to accept Devlyn's apology on the spot. But the words from the press conference were still too fresh in the writer's mind. She turned her back on the President and moved deeper into her room with Dev trailing behind her, the door left open just a crack. "Why are you sorry about such an *insignificant* little thing as the career I've worked my ass off for, President Marlowe?"

Devlyn flinched at Lauren's icy tone and the use of her title. Not to mention the fact that she didn't particularly enjoy having her own words thrown back at her. *Patience.* "Yeah." She sighed. "I know that came out wrong. Lauren, I didn't mean to say, or even imply, that you or your career were insignificant. I just meant that this was something the public didn't need to concern itself with. I am sorry."

Lauren shook her head. Apologies were all well and good, but Devlyn didn't seem to grasp what this meant for both of them. "I record. I observe. I can't be the subject of speculation!" *How blind am I that I didn't even see this coming?* "You had one chance to nip this in the bud, and you didn't do it. You promised you'd go to bat for me, and you didn't. If I'm not credible, I'm worthless as your biographer." *And anyone else's.*

The President straightened as Lauren's accusations hit home. "You are not worthless and you never will be! Lauren, if I take the time to address this issue, it won't just go away. The best thing to do is let it run its course and let it die a slow, quiet death. Trust me. Tomorrow," she paused. "Okay, maybe not tomorrow, but next week or next month, this will just be a memory and the world will move on to other pieces of gossip."

Devlyn ignored the slumped set of Lauren's shoulders and pressed on when all she really wanted to do was give the woman a hug. "Haven't you been paying attention these last few weeks? Haven't you watched me jump from one issue to the next so quickly that sometimes I feel like a trick pony? If you haven't, then maybe you aren't the person for the job after all."

The dark-haired woman's jaw worked for a few seconds, and she let out an explosive breath. She didn't want to say the next part, but she knew she had to. She stared at the wall beyond Lauren with unseeing eyes. "We're not involved and...well...you're not a prisoner. You're free to leave anytime you like with the highest recommendation I can offer."

Lauren's shoulders dropped further, and Devlyn felt her guts twist into a solid knot with the knowledge that she was the cause. This was all her idea. "Just know that I'm sorry for what happened.

I would never intentionally cause you pain, Lauren." *Please believe me.*

The shorter woman closed her eyes at Devlyn's words. She never blamed Dev for this happening, only for not handling it differently. *Or am I just upset that she didn't handle it* my *way?* "Leave?" she whispered weakly. Did she want to leave? *No.* She wanted the day to start itself over again and to not have a stack of newspapers, and a room full of reporters, questioning her morals and professionalism, and Devlyn's good sense.

Her anger began to drain away, and when she turned around and peered up into concerned blue eyes, her own filled with tears. "But we didn't do anything wrong. It's not fair!" She knew how naïve that sounded, but at that moment, she didn't care. It was the truth.

Devlyn's lips curved into a sad smile. "I know what's true and so do you. That's all that matters today, because tomorrow we're old news," she cocked her head to the side, "remember?" Then her forehead creased and she bit her lip, unable to stop the question that was on the tip of her tongue. "Would it be so horrible? People thinking that there was something between us. If it weren't for the job, I mean." *That was smooth, Marlowe. Even I'm confused about what I just asked.*

Lauren shook her head as a few unshed tears spilled over. She wiped them away angrily, hating that when she was upset her first reaction was to yell, her temper boiling over. Her second was to cry. And, to her embarrassment, Devlyn had just been treated to both. "I...um..." Her brows knitted together. Was Devlyn asking if it bothered her because they were both women? She wasn't quite sure so she guessed. "It's not that."

Devlyn's voice was softer now, and she crossed the final steps to Lauren, not stopping until she was close enough to see the crystal scattering of tears that remained in the pale lashes. "It's hard to have everything you are put under a microscope. Trust me, I know. I just need you to believe that I'm sorry."

Dev swallowed hard, morbidly picking at what she immediately recognized as a sore spot. "If you want to resign, I'll understand. And I'll make sure that Sharon puts out a proper press release as to why. You just...umm...just let me know. In the meantime, if there is anything I can do, you let me know that too."

Their eyes locked, and Lauren found herself unable to break Dev's intense gaze. "Is that...?" She paused and licked her lips. "I mean...do you want me to resign?" Lauren had never stood quite this close to Dev before and she felt a slight, inexplicable yearning to move even closer.

Dev shook her head gravely. "No. That's the last thing I want. What I want is for you to be happy and comfortable here."

Lauren nodded. She didn't know if that was still possible, but she was bound and determined to try. The writer lifted her chin. "I'm no quitter, Devlyn." She blinked away her remaining tears, splashing a salty drop on her cheek.

Dev reached out tentatively, her hand moving so slowly that Lauren could detect its faint trembling. "I know you're not." Devlyn chuckled softly. "Why do you think I wanted you in the first place?"

Lauren smiled when soft fingertips grazed her cheek, gently brushing away her tear. She laughed nervously, unconsciously leaning into Dev's touch.

"Are we done arguing?"

A quick bob of the head.

"Good. Because I just discovered that I really hate arguing with you." Dev smiled, the relief coursing through her nearly enough to make her dizzy.

They stood there awkwardly for a moment and Dev dropped her hand from Lauren's cheek. "Sometimes, after fussing with a friend, a hug can feel really nice," she offered gingerly, still not sure she was on solid footing with the biographer.

Lauren needed no further invitation. She leaned forward and wrapped her arms around Dev's solid, lanky form, sighing with relief when Dev mirrored her actions and squeezed her gently but firmly. Her face was pressed against Dev's shirt and she realized her heart was thumping double time. She could feel Devlyn's pounding pulse in return. Lauren pulled in a deep, comforting breath, catching the faintest whiff of the President's perfume.

Oh, God. Devlyn pressed her face into Lauren's soft, wavy hair, praying – hoping – that the smaller woman couldn't feel her heart, which was about ready to pound out of her chest. She squeezed a little tighter, then realized that her friendly two or three seconds were up, and she'd have to release Lauren. Dev was about to speak when Lauren's door opened and she looked up to find Christopher and Aaron staring back at her.

Lauren's gaze flicked to the door and she affected a deer in the headlights look as the boys watched on, oblivious to the room's mounting tension.

"The dog," Dev whispered in Lauren's ear, her warm breath causing a slight tremor in the writer. "They're here for him."

Lauren suddenly whistled and Gremlin poked his head out from under the bed where he was hiding. He saw Devlyn and immediately growled, baring tiny, crooked teeth.

"Gremlin!" the boys shouted happily.

The dog bounded across the room, but not before stopping in front of Devlyn and offering another short growl. Then he ran over to Christopher and Aaron, who immediately began playing with him, forgetting all about the fact that their mother and Lauren were still wrapped in a loose embrace.

Lauren stared for a moment. "That's amazing. Gremlin hypnotizes them."

"It's true. My children are slaves to the cult of Gremlin."

They both burst out laughing and reluctantly disentangled themselves from each other.

Dev spied the broken coffee table. "Next time you get mad at me, you might want to hit me. I doubt I'm worth as much as that table."

"Sweet Jesus," Lauren drawled, her southern accent popping out in full force. She examined the shards of wood scattered on the carpet and gulped. "How much was it worth?" *Not that I really want to know. But I'm sure Michael Oaks is running me a tab, so I might as well hear it now.*

Devlyn crossed her arms. "Dunno. It was made for Andrew Jackson. It's a one of a kind historical piece. Completely irreplaceable." *I will not laugh. I will not.*

Lauren's eyes grew wide as her voice grew weak. "It was," she uttered glumly. *I so should have stayed in bed this morning. Well, except for that hug. I'd get out of bed for one of those any day of the week.*

"Yeah. It was," Dev commiserated. "I heard they had appraisals done on it last year, from both Christie's and Lloyds of London. It was too expensive to insure."

Lauren could hear the smile in Dev's voice and she glanced up from the coffee table to see twinkling eyes. "Lloyds of London, huh?" Her tone was skeptical.

Dev laughed. "Okay, would it make you feel any better to know that I bought it at a yard sale in college, paid four bucks for it, and refinished it myself? It came with me from Ohio."

"You rat!" She made a mock angry face, but still said a small prayer of thanks. "Does this mean I don't have to sell a kidney?"

"No kidney." Dev arched a droll brow. "But you owe me four bucks."

"C'mon in." Lauren opened the door to her quarters, a soft, yellow light from the lamp she'd left on spilling into the hallway. "You're going to love this picture. I just developed it over lunch. She was giving a speech to Congress."

Dev's eyebrows crawled up her forehead. "Ashley?" *Please tell me she wasn't a Republican.*

The women stopped in front of Lauren's desk. The shorter woman grinned and handed Devlyn the picture. "Uh huh."

Dev chuckled and held the photo at eye level. "So that's why she's wearing my blazer." The navy jacket hung nearly to the floor on the seven-year-old, its broad shoulders making her head appear tiny. "She's so cute."

"She looks just like you."

Devlyn felt a flush working its way up her neck. "I suppose so," she admitted sheepishly, although Lauren could still hear the pride in her voice. "Samantha always told me the same thing." Dev suddenly paused as though she'd said something wrong. She felt a twinge of guilt and her throat began to close. With a start, she realized that she hadn't thought of Samantha in days...hadn't said her name in weeks. Tears filled her eyes, coming so fast she couldn't stop them.

Lauren laid a gentle hand on Devlyn's arm. "You miss her a lot, I'm sure." She smiled sympathetically, at a total loss as to what else she could say.

By the time Lauren had divorced her ex-husband, there were no tears of grief for her; not that there had been many to begin with. She had been more upset by her own failure to make the marriage work than by losing him. By the bitter end, she was more than ready for it to all be over and to let go. Looking at the older woman, Lauren felt a little ashamed that she hadn't ever mirrored the stinging loss that was so evident in Dev's face.

Dev nodded weakly. "She was a very special person, but the world does keep spinning." *Even if it took me a long time to really believe it.* Her eyes fastened on Lauren's. "I don't think I was meant to walk through life alone." A wistful smile touched her face. "It's much more fun with somebody else."

"Depends on the somebody," Lauren said seriously.

Dev's voice was just as serious. "I guess it does."

A smooth, female voice interrupted the suddenly silent room and Lauren tore her gaze away from the riveting blue. "Incoming call from (865) 555-9537. Call forwarded from cell phone. Status: emergency."

Lauren sucked in a breath. Calls designated as emergencies didn't ring on the phone. An automated voice system kicked in instead. She'd had her cell phone off all day. While she called home once a month, she had never, *ever* received a long distance phone call from her parents. Not caring that Devlyn was still in the room, she took the call.

"Lauri?" a deep, male voice boomed in an accent that was far more pronounced than Lauren's.

"What's wrong, Daddy? Is it Mama?"

Dev wrapped her arm around Lauren's waist, bracing them both for bad news. *Don't let someone be dead,* she thought hastily.

There was a long pause and then a sigh. "Your mama's been in bed all week. You know her."

Lauren looked concerned and Devlyn wanted to ask about her

mother, but Lauren's father spoke before she could.

"Holy hell, girl! I've been trying to get a hold of you since this morning. Do you know what time it is?"

"I know it's late. I just got back to my bedroom."

"Doesn't that lady President let you sleep?"

This, coming from a man who got up every morning at 4:30a.m. for work. "Never mind about that. Daddy, what's wrong?"

"I'll tell you what's wrong." He quoted *The Revealer* at length and both women cringed. That was the tabloid rag that had used the phrase "brainy sex kitten". "Everybody is talking about it! Our phone has been ringing off the hook. I had to unplug the damned thing. And now there are a bunch of newspeople parked on our front lawn and they won't leave!"

"Oh, Daddy, I'm so sorry. We never meant for that to happen. And for the millionth time, tell Mama to stop reading that trash." *Not that the "respectable" papers were much better,* she thought sourly.

"We?" The word was said with as much rancor as the man could muster. This couldn't possibly be true, could it? "Who exactly is 'we'?"

"Ummm..." Lauren fumbled for something to say, suddenly feeling very guilty despite the fact that she and Dev hadn't done anything wrong.

"Girl, are you really living there? In the White House?"

"Surprise," she teased listlessly. "I was going to tell you next weekend when I called."

"You didn't tell them?" Dev whispered harshly in Lauren's ear.

Lauren shrugged a little defensively as she pulled away from Dev. She had been abroad for nearly two years when she did Cardinal O'Roarke's biography. And her parents never inquired once about her exact whereabouts. Never asked her for her address. They were content to have her phone number, which they never used. It hadn't occurred to her to let them know anything other than the fact that she'd be in Washington, D.C.

There was a pause while Howard Strayer covered the receiver with his palm. "I told you to get away from those bushes, God dammit!"

Lauren looked at Devlyn in panic when she heard the unmistakable sounds of her father's shotgun being loaded.

"Mr. Strayer, this is Devlyn Marlowe," Dev jumped in. "Please don't shoot the press. I'll make sure your local police keep them from trespassing on your lawn."

Lauren turned and looked at Dev, her jaw sagging. *What are you doing, Devlyn?*

"Yeah, right!" the man snorted. "You're the President and I'm the King of France."

Lauren covered her mouth, stifling a sudden laugh.

"I, um...but I am Devlyn Marlowe!" Dev persisted indignantly.

"Girl, this is no laughing matter. And stop making your voice all deep and gravely like a man's. I should think you're too old for such nonsense."

Two sable eyebrows curved upwards. Dev put her hands on her hips and mouthed "Like a man?" to Lauren, who was now doubled over with laughter.

"Daddy, this really is President Marlowe," Lauren finally choked out when she caught her breath. She motioned to Dev. "Say something while I'm talking, so he'll believe me."

"Mr. Strayer, it really is me." Devlyn spoke over Lauren's renewed laughter.

"No shit?"

"No shit." Dev replied smoothly, now smiling herself.

"Well then, Madam President, I only have one question for you."

Dev tilted her head toward the intercom. "Yes?"

"What in the Sam Hill are you doing in my daughter's room at 11:30 *p.m.?*"

Dev's eyes widened at the scolding, parental tone. *Could someone else's father ground you?* "Uhh..." *Oh, boy.*

Sunday, February 21st

The writer liked Sundays. This Sunday, her fourth in the White House, was quiet and nearly what an ordinary person would call normal.

Why would anyone want to be President? There was never really any time to rest. Even today Dev was called into a meeting over a brewing crisis in the Middle East. This was the time she had set aside for the kids and they all wanted to go outside and play in the fresh two inches of snow that had fallen overnight.

Lauren's plan was to stay in and write. Though she knew she needed to take Gremlin for a walk soon. She was craving some time outside herself. Gray eyes slid over to her little companion, who was curled in a tight ball at her feet.

A noise drew her attention outside the window next to her bed, where she could see Christopher, Aaron, and their Secret Service agents romping in the snow and having a good time squealing as they pelted each other with soggy snowballs. The two young agents who were assigned to them were honestly playing and looked to be having nearly as good a time as the children. She noticed several other agents standing in the background, drinking steaming beverages, and keeping a watchful eye over the snowball fight.

The blonde woman stood up to get a better view of the winter mayhem and wondered where Ashley was in the melee. Her eyes searched the lawn, pale brows drawing together when she realized the little girl wasn't there. "Come on, Gremlin, let's go for a walk."

Gremlin jumped up as though he hadn't been snoring only seconds before. He was ready to go in an instant, bouncing wildly at Lauren's feet, circling her madly as she gathered up her jacket and his leash. She shook her head and laughed at the dog's antics. "Crazy." Bringing along Grem's leash was more a habit than anything else. At the White House he wasn't required to be on his lead.

There were faster ways for Lauren to get to the lawn, but she strolled along the route that took her by the kids' bedrooms and the President's living room. Sitting in the hall outside the living room was Agent Hamlin. As she and the dog approached, Gremlin darted into the living room ahead of her. Lauren laughed to herself. *I'm going to have to leave you here when I'm finished with this assignment, aren't I, Grem?*

At the doorway the writer paused, leaning on the frame and watching the dark-haired little girl who had a few coloring books laid out in front of her. Her jacket and cap were balled up on the table next to her crayons.

Gremlin gave a little bark and Ashley immediately perked up, wiggled herself out of her chair, and flopped onto the carpet to give him a loving scratching. Gremlin purred as though he were a fat cat. He was clearly in canine heaven and Lauren wondered what she could do in this life to insure coming back as a spoiled pooch in her next.

The woman took off her glasses and stuffed them into her jacket pocket, knowing they'd just get so steamy outside they'd be of no use anyway. Besides, they were bifocals and she really only needed them for reading and writing, but it was just easier to leave them on all day and not worry about it. She pushed off from the doorframe. "Hey, we're just about to go out for a walk. Would you like to go with us?"

Ashley looked up and gave her a little shake of her head, her chin length hair swaying with the motion.

The profoundly sad look in the little girl's eyes said more than most of the words the writer had ever put on paper. Lauren knelt down next to Gremlin. "You sure?" she asked gently. "Your brothers are having a ball. Why aren't you out with them?"

Ashley glanced to the door but didn't say anything. Lauren sighed. "C'mon," she coaxed. "I think Gremlin wants to play. And I'm sort of tired this morning. You'd be doing me a big favor if you'd play with him for a while and wear him out."

"Really?" Ashley asked interestedly, allowing the dog to lick her hand.

"Sure."

"But isn't it cold out?"

Lauren pursed her lips. *Since when did a kid care about the temperature when it came to playing outside?* "Well, I suppose. But you'll be bundled up, right? And we can always come back inside if it gets too chilly."

"'Kay." The girl immediately brightened.

"Good." Lauren nodded. "You put on your coat and gloves and..." she looked at the big pile of clothes on the table, gesturing vaguely with her hands, "And whatever else is in that pile and I'll let Agent Hamlin know."

Ashley didn't bothering answering; she was already tugging on her boots.

Lauren marched purposefully to the door. Leaning out, she spoke very quietly. "Get your ass up out of that chair and get ready to go out. Ashley and I are taking Gremlin for a walk. It is *not* too cold to have a little fun outside. What do you think her brothers are doing at this very moment?" *God, no wonder Ashley wasn't hitting it off with the agent. The woman acted like she was an old lady! Wasn't Emma enough for any household?*

"But..." The agent looked into a pair of very unamused, slate-gray eyes, and her protest died on her lips.

The blonde turned back to see Ashley and Gremlin happily bounding towards her. As they stepped into the hall, Lauren heard Agent Hamlin speaking behind them. "Princess and Mighty Mouse are on the move. We're headed out to walk the dog."

Mighty Mouse? Mighty Mouse! Oooo, Devlyn Marlowe, they had better not have gotten that moniker from you. Then she laughed at what David had covertly suggested the Secret Service call Devlyn. As Lauren followed behind Ashley and Gremlin she hoped her name didn't fit as well as the President's. A wry smile pulled at her lips. *Hope your meetings are going okay, Wonder Woman.*

Friday, February 26th

They were sitting in Devlyn's living room, the warm toned blue walls looking gray in the wan light. Upon her arrival at the White House, the President had only requested that the décor of one room be significantly altered. And this was it.

Formerly known as the Yellow Oval Room, the family living room had undergone a transformation in Dev's first month in office. No longer a predominantly drab banana color, with floor coverings that, while tasteful, were still dreary, the space had been warmed by a dozen shades of blue and accented with strong greens, rich browns, and natural finished wood furnishings.

While Dev would still undoubtedly entertain there, she meant for the space to appear more homey and less Presidential. It was a place she could put her feet up without worry and the children could play without fear of breaking some priceless piece of Americana. Gone were the oil paintings of people long dead and landscapes in heavy gilded frames. In their place hung family photos and art that meant something to Dev or her kids because they knew the artist or especially admired their work. The many furnishings from the Marlowe home in Ohio lent the room a private, comfortable quality it had never known before.

Lauren and Dev were both exhausted. The writer looked at her watch. It was almost midnight and they had been up since 5:00 in the morning. Almost nineteen hours straight. She glanced into the face of the woman next to her, watching as Devlyn sipped a tall glass of milk.

Dev shoved a plate of cookies at Lauren. Sighing, she kicked off her shoes and propped her feet on the coffee table. The fireplace was softly glowing, but Dev didn't think the flames were responsible for the dark shadows under Lauren's eyes. It had been a bear of a day, and she herself was drained to the bone. "Tired?" she asked needlessly.

Lauren looked at her like she was crazy, but answered the rhetorical question anyway. "Hell, yes. I'm dead." She stared into her glass of milk with mild distaste. Lauren hadn't drunk milk since she was a little girl. *What was Emma's obsession with the white liquid?* When they'd walked into the living room the older woman, with her hair up in rollers that had to be antiques, simply pressed the cold glasses into their hands and then marched off to bed without another word. *Weird.*

"I don't know how you do it day in and day out. I don't know how *I* follow you day in and day out." The shorter woman yawned. "And I'm not sure how we're going to survive four years." She picked up several double stuffed Oreos and sat them in her lap, not giving a rat's ass about the black crumbs on her crème colored skirt. *That's why God invented dry cleaning.* She passed the plate back to Dev.

"Today actually got a little out of hand, and you know it." Blue eyes rolled. "That little fit the Secretary of Defense threw was quite unexpected, and it totally FUBARed my schedule."

"That man," Lauren plucked up a hapless Oreo and twisted it apart, digging out the impossibly sweet, creamy filling with her teeth, "is an ass."

Dev shrugged, dunking her own cookie in her milk until it was properly soaked. "He hates me."

"Then he's a bigger ass than I thought. Why does he hate you?" Lauren moaned a little as she sipped her milk. It was actually good. *Who knew?*

"Because," Devlyn quickly popped the soggy cookie in her

mouth, sucking out the milk before swallowing, "and these are his words, not mine," Dev affected a heavy Bostonian accent, "'She's queer as a three dollar bill.'"

"All that fuss today was because you're gay?"

The tall woman snorted. "Lots of people hate me because I'm gay." She sipped her milk as an evil grin crossed her lips, nearly causing the milk to drip out of the corner of mouth. Dev leaned forward just a bit and whispered in a conspiratorial tone, "I want the Federal Treasury to print three dollar bills just to piss him off."

Lauren burst out laughing and was only able to keep from spraying Devlyn with cookie crumbs by slapping her palm over her mouth. An impish smile twitched at her lips. "You might not want to start out with something so drastic. Maybe you could start small? Like with a Devlyn Marlowe rainbow postage stamp?" *I know I'd buy a book.* Then Lauren's face grew serious. "Why have a Cabinet member who hates you?" She glanced down enviously at Dev's feet.

Dev made a show of wiggling her happy, socked toes. "Please do. And, by the way, you have to be dead before they put you on a stamp. I don't want to give him *that* much satisfaction."

Somewhat hesitantly, Lauren pushed off her medium heeled pumps. She sighed with relief at the feeling of the soft, cool carpet against her nylon covered toes.

"C'mon," Dev encouraged, wiggling her feet again. "It's always better on the coffee table."

"You're sure?"

"Oh, please. This one didn't belong to Andrew Jackson either." She reached down and wrapped her fingers around Lauren's ankles.

The younger woman yelped at the unexpectedly cold hands.

"Sorry." Dev gestured at the glass of icy milk she'd been holding. "My fingers aren't normally cold."

Lauren remembered their hug from the week before. "I know."

"Now, back to your question." Dev smiled, looking at their feet sitting side-by-side on the coffee table. *She has cute toes.*

"Yes?" Lauren prompted, wondering why Dev was staring at her feet.

Dev's head popped up. "Right. Why have Cabinet members who hate me? Well, it took a lot, and I mean *a lot,* of dealing to get me here. I agreed to put people in important positions in return for support within the Emancipation Party itself. It got me the Presidential nomination and then four years of putting up with assholes like Secretary of Defense Brendwell. It's a political game. And that's how it's played." She drowned another cookie.

"I see," Lauren answered thoughtfully. But she didn't really. At least not until that very moment. "So, you're not only fighting the Democrats and the Republicans...you have to worry about your own people, too?"

"Well, sort of. My party supports me now. It would be stupid for them not to. A lot of sacrifices were made along the way. I've got a lot more enemies around here than friends. The friends I do have are the key. Geoff, for example, who was not only a strong running mate in the eyes of the public and Emancipation Party, but is someone I can really count on. Or David, who is a Democrat." Dev shifted on the couch. "So he's my deal man. He can cross party lines and not look like a total phony. I also trust him with my life."

Lauren mumbled her agreement. If the public knew how much influence David, and even Jane, really had, America would have a collective heart attack. But Washington was a shark tank and Devlyn needed a few friendly sharks swimming in her waters to make sure she didn't get eaten alive. Lauren turned her head slightly, watching as the President shoveled in what had to be her twentieth cookie.

Dev stopped mid-bite. "What?"

"You don't ever have to watch your weight, do you?" she asked enviously. "I think I hate you."

Given the opportunity, Dev gave Lauren's toned body a thorough once-over. "I don't think you have anything to be complaining about, Ms. Strayer," she teased, but had to drag her eyes back up to meet Lauren's. "Trust me, with the way we move around, very soon you will learn to eat anything and everything that is put before you. And you won't gain an ounce. In fact, you've lost a little already, haven't you?"

Lauren blinked. "Only five pounds." She arched an eyebrow. "Are you spying on my scale?"

"No," Dev laughed. *I'm just noticing everything about you.* "But that's the cool part about being here. Suddenly, all food is good for you. You'll need all the extra energy you can find to get through marathon days like this one." She popped another cookie into her mouth followed by another deep swallow of milk. "Besides, I don't have to bother keeping track of my weight. All of America is watching it for me. Three hundred and twenty million people are all interested in how wide my ass will get in the next four years."

Lauren made a face. "Well, all America may be watching your ass, but no one is watching mine."

Dev grinned. "I wouldn't say that." In a heartbeat, her faced flushed a deep red, and she covered her eyes with her hands. "I'm...ah...I..." Dev scrubbed her cheeks, trying to erase the blush. "I cer-certainly didn't mean to say something as out of line as that." She shook her head. "Sometimes I wonder how I made it this far. David's right; open mouth, insert foot." Worriedly, she peeked between her fingers and saw Lauren's indulgent smile. "I'm sorry." Dev really wanted to kick her own ass right now. *God, I can't remember ever being this embarrassed!*

Lauren just laughed, enjoying the rosy tint of Dev's cheeks. *Is she actually flirting?* "It's all right, Dev. Just a little slip of the tongue, right?"

Dev's eyes widened slightly and her blush deepened. "Yeah," she croaked, bringing her glass to her lips.

How am I even going to maintain the pretense of any professional distance from you, Devlyn? Jesus, just look at us now! They were sitting so close together their thighs were nearly touching. And Lauren's brain nearly seized up on the spot when she found herself leaning a little closer, willingly losing herself in sky blue eyes. *I am in so much trouble.*

Dev offered her the last Oreo by way of a peace offering and Lauren chuckled. "A bribe?"

"Well, we are in Washington. Would you expect any less?" She wiggled the cookie, wondering what brand of perfume her biographer wore and whether it smelled that intoxicating on anybody else. *Oh, man, I'm never going to make it through four years.*

Wednesday, March 3rd

Washington, D.C. was a mud pit. Snow had given way to a deep, icy slush, which, in turn, mutated into a soupy, dirty sludge. Thankfully, the spring warm front had parked itself over the nation's capital and had finally vanquished even the last signs of what had been a brutal winter. Lauren cocked her head toward the window, hearing the faintest chirping of a robin. *Oh, yeah, she sighed. I am so ready for spring.*

The writer smiled at the vase of fresh cut, yellow roses that brightened her desk. Every evening when she made her way to her room, a new bouquet was there to greet her. At first she assumed that they were delivered to every room in the residence as a matter of course. Then she realized she hadn't seen them anywhere but her room, unless the President was entertaining or the room was open to the public. She had asked David McMillian about it and the man just snorted, never really answering her question.

This sunny morning the President was in a meeting with her National Security Advisor, and Lauren took the time to start researching a topic that had been niggling at her for weeks. She had thought Devlyn might discuss it with her herself, but the few times that it naturally came up in the conversation, Devlyn looked tense, even angry perhaps. Unable to bear the shadows of pain behind Dev's eyes, Lauren steered the conversation into different waters, despite the fact that Dev appeared willing to press forward.

Thankfully, this part of the President's past had already been very well publicized.

With a series of quick commands, Lauren fired up her computer and logged on.

"Good morning, Ms. Strayer," the soft computer voice greeted her.

"Good morning." She laughed at her response. She always answered the greeting, even though it was a machine. It somehow just seemed rude not to. "Search files. Marlowe, Devlyn."

"Searching. ... Files located. Directory?"

Lauren leaned back in her chair, removed her glasses, and rubbed the end of the bridge of her nose. The end of an earpiece soon found its way into her mouth. "Sub-directory: Marlowe, Samantha. Source: All available."

"Searching. ... Files located. Directory?"

"Open all files. Most recent first. Current directory."

"File name: Sentencing Hearing. Harris, Theodore, 5/17/2017."

A three-dimensional video image cued up and Lauren replaced her glasses, sliding her chair back a foot or two to maximize the resolution of the image. Dev was in a wood paneled courtroom and the mere sight of her caused Lauren to suck in an unexpected breath. The dark-haired woman was standing alongside a podium, her face drawn and tired looking, dark circles ringing normally bright eyes. *She looks like she's been to Hell and back.*

"If it pleases the Court," Dev paused and took a sip of water. "I stand here before you today, not as the Governor of the state of Ohio, but as a victim. I stand before you, a spouse in mourning over the loss of my...my wife..."

Dev's eyes flashed and Lauren could see a barely suppressed rage mingled with a profound sadness, both begging to be released.

"I spent nearly fifteen years with Samantha and intended to spend many more." Her penetrating gaze flickered sideways and her face hardened. "Except that that man," she pointed to a bearded, frazzled-looking man who appeared to be in his early thirties, "decided to get behind the wheel of a car after drinking all night. As has already been proven, he was speeding along in a drunken stupor when he broadsided the car that Samantha was driving. Mind you, his car was fully equipped with auto-drive and that would have prevented the accident – if he had bothered to turn it on!"

Lauren leaned forward, watching intently as Devlyn paused again, fighting to keep her emotions in check. Her chest felt tight, Dev's tension making it hard for her to breathe.

"The defendant left that crash scene with barely a scratch to show for it. And while Samantha Marlowe lay...ble-bleed-bleed-ing and dying, trapped in her car, he continued on his merry way to the liquor store to buy more alcohol!"

The image quickly shifted to the defendant, whose head was now in his hands, before panning back to Devlyn.

Lauren recognized Jane in the gallery.

"It took the fire department nearly an hour to tear apart the car and get her out. And...and by that time she was already," Dev's voice dropped to a whisper, "she was dead."

The sound of weeping could be heard in the background, and Lauren wondered whether it was a friend or family member of Samantha's or the defendant himself.

Dev's jaw worked for a moment and she stepped back around behind the podium. Her eyes dropped down to look at the notes she had spread out on the slanted wooden surface. They were crinkled and tattered and Dev suddenly pushed them away as though deciding not to use them after all.

Lauren looked from the papers to Dev. *It was too personal to be read in open court, wasn't it?*

"She left behind three beautiful children," a tiny smile edged

her lips, and Lauren smiled back sadly. No matter what the circumstances, Dev always smiled when she mentioned her kids. "Our
three-year-old daughter, Ashley, whom Samantha adopted as soon
as I had her. Our son, Christopher, who is one. He...um...he took his
first steps the day after Samantha was killed." Sniffles joined the
sound of muted weeping in the background. "And our youngest
baby, Aaron, who was barely four weeks old when she was killed."
Dev's composure began to crack and hot tears slowly crept down her
cheeks, plunking lightly onto the papers in front of her.

Lauren closed her eyes briefly, her stomach churning. She
didn't want to see any more, but knew she had to.

"These three bright and wonderful children will never know the
love of this woman who took care of them, and in the case of Christopher and Aaron carried them in her body and gave them the very
lives they live today. Because of his carelessness...his reckless-
ness...his indifference and disregard for human life..." Devlyn spat.
"Because of his refusal to seek treatment after his *previous two*
DUIs, I have lost my partner and my best friend. He destroyed my
family," Dev stopped, completely unable to continue.

She won't even say his name, Lauren thought.

Devlyn took a deep breath and stilled her shaking hands, making firm eye contact with the judge. "I request that this Court do the
right thing and sentence this man to the maximum time allowed by
Ohio state law for the crimes of which he has been convicted. I'll
never get Samantha back." Her voice shook. "Our children have lost
an irreplaceable part of their lives. The community has lost an outstanding, contributing member. He," she jerked her head toward
the defendant, "should lose as much as we have." Dev squared her
shoulders. "But that's not possible. So his freedom is the least that
he can give."

David suddenly entered the picture, wrapping a strong arm
around Devlyn's waist as she appeared to falter for just a second.

"Halt image." Lauren reached under the lens of her glasses,
catching a salty tear just as it began to fall. She'd had enough.
"Computer, tell me the sentencing of one," she glanced down at the
handwritten notes in her lap, "Teddy or Theodore E. Harris. Convicted of aggravated vehicular manslaughter in Ohio, 5/14/2017."

"Searching. ... File located. No visual."

The writer stared at the frozen image on the screen, looking
directly at Dev's shell-shocked face. "Open," she said quietly.

"Harris, Theodore, a k a, Harris, Teddy, case number
12843CR17, sentenced on 5/18/2017 to two years in Lebanon State
Prison..."

Lauren's jaw dropped. "Two years?" She shook her head in disbelief. "Two lousy years!"

The computer continued, unfazed by the woman's outburst.

"Paroled on 5/19/2018, after serving twelve months."

"My God," Lauren whispered. She took off her glasses and dis-gustedly tossed them onto the desk, rubbing her watery eyes.

The ringing phone startled her from her thoughts. "Computer off." She wiped her eyes once more and reached over, tapping the video feature on the phone. She was immediately greeted by Dev's smiling face. "Hi there."

The President leaned back in her chair, and Lauren could tell by the background that Dev was in the Oval Office. "How was your meeting?"

"Top secret." Dev grinned and wrinkled her nose in a way Lau-ren found impossibly endearing.

It would be nice to watch laugh lines form around those baby blues. I'll bet Samantha was looking forward to that. "Of course. I'm sorry."

"No problem. Listen, it just so happens that I'm sort of free for lunch. If you don't mind eating in my office, that is. I can sign my name, talk to you and eat my lunch at the same time." The smile slipped from Devlyn's face and she eyed Lauren worriedly, idly not-ing the absence of her glasses. "Is...um...are you okay, Lauren? You look a little upset."

Lauren smiled softly and made a conscious effort to brighten her somber mood. "I'm fine. And you can do all those things at the same time?" Her voice was playful. "My, my, you are multitalented."

Hush, Dev. But she couldn't keep a charming, slightly mischie-vous grin from stretching across her face. "Years of experience. How about it?"

"Dunno," the blonde teased. "Lemme check my calendar and see if the Prime Minister of Great Britain has–"

"Hardy har har."

Lauren chuckled. "I'll be right down."

"I don't give a good goddamn!" Dev slammed her fist against her desk.

Lauren heard the jarring thud and winced at its intensity as she quietly closed the door. The entire White House didn't need to hear this. When she turned, Dev was on her feet, the receiver pressed tightly against her ear. "What do you mean they changed their minds? They're only allowed to do that when they disagree with...well...me! Get those votes back. I won't lose this because some lame ass Democrats can't decide which side of the fence to stand on!"

The biographer couldn't resist. She brought her camera up and began clicking off several frames. *Damn, Dev, you do have a tem-per, don't you?* Lauren smiled inwardly. *That pulsing vein on your forehead would make an impressive book cover shot.*

"Find them! And don't call me back until you do." She slammed the phone down and then hit the intercom switch. She took a deep breath, purposely calming herself before speaking. "Jane—"

"The Chief of Staff is already on his way, Madam President. He was at a meeting on the Hill, but he's coming now. I put the call in as soon as the Deputy Chief of Staff phoned you."

"God bless you, Jane." Dev leaned against her desk with her palms against the flat surface. "Thank you." She sighed. "Are you having fun being President yet?"

Jane laughed. "Uh huh...and you're welcome."

The President switched off the intercom and sheepishly glanced up at Lauren.

"Hold it!" Lauren commanded, crouching down and changing the angle of the picture as she focused the lens.

Dev shook her head and burst out laughing. She moved around the desk and leaned on its edge, crossing her long, silk covered arms across her chest. "Suddenly I feel like a fashion model." She struck a pose, causing Lauren to giggle.

"You could have done that, you know...been a model. The camera loves you." Lauren lowered her camera. "Do I want to know what's got you so upset?"

Dev pursed her lips unhappily. "Ah, my DNA Registration legislation is meeting with some last minute and very unexpected resistance."

"I knew that was gonna happen," Lauren said absentmindedly as she fussed with her camera lens.

Twin eyebrows jumped.

Lauren shrugged. "During that meeting last week, well, they just didn't seem like they'd made up their minds. I didn't believe them when they said they'd support you. It was those Yankees from New Jersey that turned on you, wasn't it?" She made a face. "I think they were just here for the free lunch."

"Well, next time feel free to warn me, okay?" Dev chuckled. "Speaking of lunch, looks like I'm skipping it today. There is a little bipartisan butt that needs kicking." For once the Emancipation Party seemed to unite behind an issue. *It's really not a good idea for you boys to stab me in the back like that. Time a few people found that out.*

"No problem." Lauren waved a dismissive hand, bringing the camera to her ear to listen to the film rewind. There were easier ways to take pictures, but she loved this old camera, enjoying that she had to think to use it. "Want a spectator? It's been, oooh," she put her fingertip to her chin, pretending to think, "at least a week since I've seen a bipartisan butt kicking. I need my fix." The writer grinned.

"I'd be honored, madam." The President jumped down and bowed slightly at the waist before retaking her perch. "I'll even be your escort." Dev stopped speaking for a moment and stared intently at Lauren. "Would you vote 'yes' for my bill? You've heard more than enough about it to make a well-informed decision."

Lauren sighed resignedly. *Why did Devlyn always do this?* She winced then drew in a deep breath. "Well...um..."

"Lauren." Dev's impatient voice dropped an octave.

"No."

"No?" Dev exploded off the desk and marched over to other woman.

Lauren shook her head firmly, adopting a more stubborn pose as Devlyn approached. "No."

"No?"

"Nope."

"You're joking."

The younger woman just waited.

Devlyn threw her hands in the air. "But why? I rejected the Republican proposal requiring every person to submit a DNA sample at birth."

Lauren lifted a sassy eyebrow, letting Dev know exactly how she felt about the little suggestion made by the Speaker of the House. Despite his bent towards conservatism, even Vice President Vincent couldn't get behind that idea.

"My proposal only registers people when they're arrested. Isn't there a *single* Democrat who will see reason?"

"Apparently not. And innocent people get arrested every day," Lauren said reasonably, opening the door to Dev's office. "The DNA thing is invasive and creepy. Like Big Brother or something."

Dev motioned with her hands as they walked. She was in full "persuasion" mode. "We already fingerprint people when they're arrested. And this will ultimately save lives and help solve future crimes."

The younger woman stopped walking. "Fingerprints are not..." Lauren shivered and said her next word with so much distaste that Dev nearly laughed, *"blood.* You can't clone people from their fingerprints. And what if someone decided to do something hinky with all those samples, huh?" Okay, she was half teasing about that last part, but she knew Devlyn would bite.

"Arrgghh! I don't want to clone anyone! God," Dev rolled her eyes as they turned the corner and made their way down the hallway that lead to the Green Room, passing several Secret Service agents and cleaning staff on their way. "They're *still* showing those damned *X-Files* reruns on television, aren't they?"

Round, gray eyes were the picture of innocence as the women continued their trek.

Thursday, March 4th

"So," from the door of Lauren's room, Dev grinned over her mug of coffee, "you want to take a trip with me?"

"Business or personal?" The blonde smiled back as she looked up from her journal at the President.

Devlyn privately cheered that Lauren would even consider her request might be personal. "Does it really matter?"

"I'll need to know what to pack."

Dev rolled her shoulders and with her free hand unbuttoned her blazer, leaving it on. "It's business. Our protocol specialist, Mrs. Baldridge, will help you with what to take." She took another sip, then set her ruby red mug on a coaster on the corner of Lauren's second coffee table. Silently she gestured at the couch.

Lauren nodded her approval and snagged a stack of mail from her desk as she joined the President.

Dev settled down across from Lauren, bouncing a little on the springy cushion. She looked around covertly for Gremlin, the Demon Dog. "Your room smells nice," she commented idly.

"It's the flowers."

"Umm, nice." Dev figured Gremlin was hiding someplace and would jump out and growl at her later. But for now, she'd focus on Grem's mistress. "Lauren, I'd love for you to come, of course. But I'll understand if you need a break." Though she didn't like the idea of not seeing the writer every day, Dev did appreciate that the daily grind could be oppressive at times. "We've been at this for nearly two solid months. Surely you're getting tired of me."

"Nah." Lauren stretched. "Compared to Supergeek, who spoke computer gibberish most of the time and Cardinal O'Roarke, who napped from noon to 4:00 p.m. every single day, you're a dream," she teased.

Dev bit the inside of her cheek. "Gee, thanks."

Lauren laughed softly as she sorted through her mail. Most of it was junk, which she left unopened, but she did notice a thick manila envelope that was from Starlight Publishing. She was certain it was an advance copy of her latest book, but she was slightly embarrassed by the notion of Dev's seeing this particular piece of work. Lauren dragged her eyes up from the envelope.

"You're very dedicated. I appreciate that," Dev commented sincerely.

Lauren flushed with pleasure. Coming from a true workaholic, that was a big compliment. "So, where are we going, Madam President?"

"We're going to the U.S. Embassy in the United Arab Alliance. I need to oversee some trade negotiations. And there are certain – shall we call them 'diplomatic' – issues that are more easily resolved if I host the talks at our Embassy."

Lauren gave Dev a confused look, still fingering the envelope in her hand. "Diplomatic issues?"

Dev grunted her agreement. "The whole 'she's a woman and an evil lesbian' diplomatic issue." She smiled wryly. "In the Embassy we're technically on American soil. What is punishable by death in their country, is, well, it will be begrudgingly accepted at the U.S. Embassy. It would also be a great insult for them to turn down my invitation. These people are very respectful of their traditions, and they won't want to insult me."

"Sneaky." Lauren was continually impressed by the way that Dev worked around the limitations placed on her by her gender and sexual orientation.

Dev chuckled. "Thank David. That's why he gets the big bucks and bigger headaches." She gestured at Lauren's hands. "You gonna open that, or would you rather I leave first?" Dev didn't want to leave at all, but she couldn't take another second of Lauren picking at that envelope. She was nearly ready to reach over and rip it open herself. *But,* she conceded inwardly, *that would be just a tad difficult to explain.*

"No!" *Okay, that was way too quick.* Lauren cleared her throat awkwardly. "I um...you don't have to leave. I mean, you don't have a meeting or anything, right?" she asked hopefully.

"Not a single one, and it's only 5:30." Dev crossed herself. "It's a miracle."

Lauren moved to get up, clutching the envelope. "Let me just put this away. I'm sure it's nothing."

"Aw, c'mon, Lauren." Dev smiled charmingly and poked at the slightly dingy, golden paper. "I'm dying to see what happens next to the intrepid female explorer, Adrienne Nash. Or do I have to call you Ms. Gallager when I talk about your series?"

Lauren looked at Dev blankly, thinking she must have heard her wrong. *She couldn't mean...*"You...you read these?" The younger woman waved the envelope.

"Oh, yeah! Devour is more like it. I've read all of them. Been waiting like an idiot for the new one."

Lauren fell back onto the sofa limply. "You knew and you *still* hired me?" *Duh! Of course she knew. She's the President of the United Friggin' States of America! She probably knows more about me than I do.*

Dev scoffed at the question. "Your biographies are the best I've ever read. And your credentials as a biographer and historian are impeccable." Dev picked up her mug again and took a healthy swallow. "But I never have understood the notion that writers couldn't do both fiction and non-fiction and still be respected in each field. Plus...well...um..."

"Plus, I use a pen name for my fiction so I can still 'pass' as respectable because nobody knows?" Lauren's voice was resigned, but tinged with sarcasm.

Dev stiffened. "I control a lot of things, Lauren. But I don't set the standards of acceptability for the publishing industry."

Lauren's gaze dropped to her shoes. *Quit being such a bitch about it. It's not her fault you can't own up to most of the writing you do.* "Of course you don't. I'm sorry." A thought suddenly occurred to her and she smiled tentatively, hoping to make up for her misdirected anger. She handed the envelope to Dev. "Here, enjoy it. A gift from me to you; the proof copy of Lauren Gallager's newest tale."

Devlyn snatched the book like a little kid who had just been handed her first present on Christmas morning. She practically squealed with delight. "Ooo, neat!"

Lauren burst out laughing as Dev tore open the envelope with abandon. The tall woman looked up as she slipped the book out. "What?" she complained somewhat bashfully. "You gave it to me. Don't laugh at me now."

Lauren watched in surprise as Devlyn flipped the book over in her hands, examining it from every angle and running her fingers over its shiny cover. Then she looked up at Lauren with eyes so filled with innocent pleasure that they immediately brought to mind Ashley's, despite the difference in color.

A slow blush worked its way across Dev's cheeks. "Don't suppose you'd autograph it for me?"

Mutely, Lauren bobbed her head. *Wow. I can't believe this.* "I'd be happy to. Let me get a pen."

Before she could move, Dev was seated next to her, eagerly handing her the book and a pen. Lauren was a little startled, but recovered quickly. "Umm...wow, that was fast. Okay, any particular way you want this signed?"

"No." Dev shook her head as she tapped her knees excitedly. "Just think of me as your biggest, geekiest fan."

Lauren chuckled as she took the book back, opening it carefully. She'd lay money on the fact that Devlyn Marlowe didn't break the bindings on books. The tip of her tongue appeared for just a second as she thought of what to write. Then she quickly inscribed the book and handed it back. "You're all set."

Dev gingerly opened the novel, peeking at the inside cover.

To Wonder Woman: Please enjoy it, my geeky friend.
– Lauren Gallager

Dev shook her head. "Cute," she snorted. "Veeery cute." The President was loving this and it showed in the sparkle of her eyes and the bright smile that creased her cheeks. "Well, now I have something to read on the plane."

"Holy shit!"

Dev jumped, fumbling with the book as it threatened to fly out of her hands. "What? What is it?" She searched Lauren's face.

"We'll be taking the Bat Plane, won't we?"

Dev blew out a relieved breath, her eyebrow twitching in amused annoyance. "I'm thirty-eight years old. One more unexpected exclamation like that and I won't see thirty-nine." She clutched her chest for effect, and Lauren rolled her eyes. "And, yes, we'll be aboard Air Force One, if that's what you mean. And Lauren?"

A pale head tilted.

A reckless grin made Dev feel like a kid again. "It's so much better than the Bat Plane."

Friday, March 5th

"Come on now, give me a hug." Dev was on her knees with the children.

The looks of disappointment on their faces tore at Lauren in a way she never thought possible. *Sweet Jesus, is it always like this? I'd never be able to go anywhere!*

"You gonna be gone long?" Christopher asked, his face buried in Dev's long, glossy hair.

"I'll only be gone as long as I have to, pal. You know that. I'll be back as soon as I can."

"Miss you." Aaron gave her a kiss on the cheek as Dev wrapped her other arm around him.

"I'll miss all you guys. And I promise, when I come home, we'll do pizza and Disney movies all day on my first Sunday back, okay?"

"Can Lauren and Grem watch movies and eat pizza, too?" Christopher asked, pushing his glasses up his nose, looking at Lauren with a bashful grin.

Dev glanced up at the writer, giving her a tiny smile. *So, you've bewitched my children too, huh?* "If she wants to." Her eyes flicked to Lauren's and held the same look of adoration that Christopher was currently sporting. "But you'll have to ask her yourself."

Before Christopher could open his mouth, Lauren answered. She held Dev's penetrating gaze as she spoke. "I wouldn't miss it for the world. I enjoy spending time with you guys," she heard herself say. *Huh. I really do. Judd would keel over from a heart attack if he heard me say that.* She glanced over to Christopher and wagged her finger in warning. "But no pizza for Grem. It makes him burp."

Aaron and Christopher began giggling and whispering to each other conspiratorially, causing Lauren to realize she'd just guaranteed Gremlin his very own slice of pepperoni pizza.

Dev winced at the mention of the dog's name. "Speaking of Gremlin." *The hateful little fleabag.* "Lauren's gonna need someone to look after him while we're gone and we agreed you guys can do it if you want. What do you think?"

The boys cheered, but Ashley, who was standing next to Emma, only shrugged noncommittally. Dev rose and moved past the tow-headed boys to her daughter. "Now c'mon, Moppet." Her dark head tilted in entreaty. "You're the oldest, you have to agree too."

"'Kay." Ashley tried to smile, but it was weak and watery at best.

Dev leaned in and touched noses with her daughter. "I have a surprise for you."

Despite herself, Ashley's eyes suddenly glittered with youthful excitement. "Yeah?"

"Yeah." Dev gave a whistle and the door opened. Gremlin came charging into the room, followed by a certain *former* Ohio State Trooper who had finally been coaxed into joining the Secret Service. Devlyn had pulled out all the stops, breaking with longtime tradition and training regulations in order to secure this White House assignment right way.

Ashley's eyes grew wide as saucers when she saw her friend. "Amy!" She bolted past Dev, her brothers, and Lauren to grab the woman around the waist, squeezing as tightly as she could.

Dev said a prayer of thanks that she was finally able to do something to make Ashley smile. She knew it had been a difficult winter for the girl.

Devlyn asked Emma, "You're sure you're okay with dog sitting?"

"Tch. Why not? I've been taking care of you for years. The dog might actually listen to me." The older woman gave a playful poke to presidential ribs.

"I really appreciate it too, Emma," Lauren offered, delighted by the motherly interplay between Emma and Devlyn. "I think he'd be miserable in a kennel after all the attention he's used to getting from the kids. They love him."

The nanny smiled knowingly. "It's springtime." She waved her hand out in front of her. "It's in the air."

Dev regarded the ugly white dog that looked like his face had been smashed flat by a cast iron skillet. She just knew he was a Republican. "Hey, you little beastie."

Grem's ears perked up, and his tail began wagging furiously. Then he saw who called him and he grumbled, baring crooked teeth and mottled gums.

Dev reached into her pocket and pulled out a small zip locked baggie. "I've got something for you," she taunted wickedly. Dropping to the ground, she sat back on her heels and pulled a treat from the clear plastic, pretending to eat. She moaned and hummed "boy, eating this is one hell of an orgasmic experience" sounds the entire time.

Lauren unconsciously licked her lips.

Gremlin took a nervous step forward, his beady eyes trained on Dev's hand.

Devlyn waved the dog snack in front of his face, watching as his little nostrils flared with wary interest.

"Now you're bribing my dog?" Lauren's hands moved to her hips. "Good grief, have you no shame?"

"Nope. None." Dev shrugged lightly. "I figured if you could be bought for a double stuffed Oreo, Gremlin would be ripe for the taking with a few Snausages." *You'd better not make me look stupid in front of your mommy by biting me, Gremlin! I hear NASA is looking for a few test animals for their next mission to Mars.* Devlyn was careful to hold the treat at the very tips of her fingers as the dog sniffed it cautiously. "Oh, yeah. You know you want it." Dev's eyes narrowed with a predatory glint. "C'mon...take it."

Lauren watched in fascination as the President of the United States and her pug faced off in a battle of wills. She was taking even odds. *I can't believe I'm seeing this.*

But Grem broke first, snatching the fragrant treat from extended fingers before he retreated behind Emma's legs. Dev felt a big, satisfied smile edge its way onto her face. "Ahhh, progress. I wish Congress were that easy." The tall woman put her palms on her knees and pushed to her feet so she could hand the bag to Emma. "Keep those handy in case he turns on you."

Emma nodded. "Be careful, Devlyn Marlowe. These babies need you." She gave the President a long hug.

"I will, Emma. And we'll be home soon." Dev disentangled herself and opened her arms to her children once more. "Last chance. You know just one is never enough for me." She sighed. "I have to go before Liza has a conniption and gets the cattle prod after me."

All the kids ran over and hugged their mother in turn. Ash tugged her down to her level. "Thank you, Mommy. Amy is the best present ever."

"I'm glad, Moppet. Take good care of her. She just finished a very accelerated version of Secret Service training, where she had to work really hard. I think she could use a little TLC."

The girl giggled. "I will. I promise." Then, without thought, she darted over to Lauren and threw her arms around her.

Lauren started in surprise but managed to gently, albeit a little awkwardly, lower her hands and softly rub Ashley's back. She wasn't sure what to say and felt a flood of relief course through her when Ashley spoke first.

"I promise we'll take good care of Grem, too."

Lauren relaxed and returned the girl's hug with more vigor. "I know you will, Ash. Have fun while we're gone."

Lauren tried not to let the excitement show in her face as the limousine pulled up to the plane. *It's just a plane. It's just a plane. You've been on a plane before.* Her eyes were riveted on the enormous steel monster. *Oh, man, for two Hershey bars and a window seat on that bad boy, I'd have Dev's baby.* Her face turned bright red as the direction of her thoughts registered.

"I've arranged for you to have your own office onboard," Dev commented casually, oblivious to the sometimes profound, but always unique, mental machinations of her biographer. She leaned closer to Lauren, wondering exactly when it was that they'd gone from sitting across from each other to sitting side by side. Not that she was complaining. "It's the office normally reserved for the First Lady. I um...I hope you like it. And the plane, too. It's really nice and um...fast," she babbled. *Great, now I sound like a sixteen-year-old trying to impress a pretty girl with a ride in my Daddy's Corvette.*

"Oh, well, I'll just have to make do. I don't know how I'll manage," Lauren drawled, fanning herself in mock distress and doing her best Southern belle imitation.

Dev laughed. "Well, it's only fitting that you have the First Lady's office on Air Force One since you've been sleeping in her room in the White House." Dev pulled Lauren's new novel from the bag at her feet and eagerly set it on her lap. "I don't intend to work any more than I have to on this flight. I'm going to read."

Lauren's ego practically purred under Dev's gentle stroking. She never got to enjoy a real live fan's reaction to her novels. "Any suggestions for the next Adrienne Nash book? Since you've read them all?"

Dev nodded emphatically. "Oh, absolutely. She needs a girlfriend."

Lauren crossed her arms, drawing back from Dev. "Oh, she does, does she?" *Could be interesting. A tall, beautiful one with piercing blue eyes perhaps? That would sure throw a few readers for a loop.*

"Yup!" Dev grinned. "She'd be much more at peace with herself. More content. And completely satisfied."

Pale brows lifted. "That's one hell of a girlfriend."

"Uh huh."

Lauren glanced sideways at the President. "And what makes you think Adrienne Nash is interested in women?"

Before Dev could answer, the car stopped and her door was opened from the outside. She smiled and climbed out, turning to give the waiting Press a quick wave before extending her hand to Lauren. With a slight tug, she helped the writer out of the car. "What makes you think she's not?" Dev asked, pressing her hand lightly against the small of Lauren's back and giving her a gentle nudge in the right direction.

"Good point."

The women were pelted with a flurry of questions from the waiting Press, their shouts barely heard above the general hum of car and plane engines and other airport activity. Dev completely ignored the reporters, but noticed that Lauren's back went ramrod straight and that her stride slowed after a particularly personal and inappropriate question was thrown her way. The President leaned down a little and told Lauren, "Just keep walking. Ignore it."

The blonde woman lifted her jaw and Dev felt a flash of worry. She could tell that Lauren was considering doing or saying something, and Dev shivered when she imagined what it could be. "Ahh...Lauren, I'm sure whatever you're thinking about doing would be extremely satisfying."

Lauren nodded tersely, kicking a pebble across the concrete as she picked up the pace. "So very satisfying."

"But please don't. It will only add fuel to the fire."

Dev paused, allowing Lauren to start the climb up the stairs ahead of her. She was very well aware of the cameras going off all around them as they boarded. At the top Lauren paused to wait for Dev, but quickly stepped inside when Dev motioned her back. "Go inside so they'll leave you alone." The President winked, then turned at the top of the steps to give a final wave before stepping onboard herself.

David met them at the door, as did Liza, who slipped a file into Dev's hand. "We have a call waiting for you, Madam President."

Dev's head dropped forward and she groaned. "Of course you do. I'll take it in my office. David, will you show Lauren to her office and make sure that her computer and other things were deliv—"

David nodded and gave Dev a push towards her office. "Everything is ready, and I'll be happy to show her where she can set up."

Dev gave Lauren an aggrieved look, then peeled off, following Liza down the hall. Before she disappeared into her office, she turned around and tapped Lauren's novel, yelling, "I am telling you—"

"I'm thinking about it," Lauren shot back with a grin.

"Thinking about what?" David gingerly took the writer by the elbow and pointed to the opposite end of the hallway.

"Lots of things," the blonde admitted cryptically.

David opened the door to the office and gestured for Lauren to enter. "Wow." She took a moment to take it all in. "This is incredible. I can't believe I'm on an airplane."

"Well, it's not called 'The Flying Oval Office' for nothing. It really is amazing. Did you know that two hundred and thirty-eight miles of wire wind through the plane? That is more than twice the wiring found in the old 747 models. The wire protects the plane from electro-magnetic pulses generated by a thermonuclear blast. Even in a nuclear war, we'll still be able to receive electronic signals," he enthused.

The blood drained from Lauren's face.

"Oh! Sorry. Not that I expect a nuclear war," David explained quickly.

"Thanks for clearing that up."

He unbuttoned his jacket and ran a hand through his close cropped red hair. Taking a deep breath he asked, "Can I come in for a moment? I'd like to talk to you."

Lauren eyed him seriously, chewing her lip as she wondered if she'd done something wrong. She and David had been getting along just fine these past few months. Lauren moved behind her desk and dropped into a soft leather swivel chair. It forced David to talk to her across the desk and put her in an immediate position of power. It was a trick she'd subconsciously picked up from Dev. "Sure. Is something wrong?"

"Truth is," David closed the door and took a seat on the couch, skipping over the chair in front of the desk, "I'm not sure."

"What do you mean? Is there a problem with the book?" Lauren had agreed to let David read the rough notes that would form the beginning of the prologue to Dev's biography. It was mostly background and family information and wouldn't change, no matter what happened in the next four years. She'd never shared any part of her preliminary work before, but, as Dev's best friend and the President's Chief of Staff, she valued David's unique insight.

"No! Everything looks great so far. Dev is going to love it. She'll get a big chuckle out of the fact that one of her ancestors was a convicted horse thief. Must be where her natural talent for politics comes from."

"Then what?"

"It's Dev." He looked her directly in the eye. "She's, umm, really opened up to you, you know?"

Lauren nodded reluctantly, suddenly feeling very uncomfortable with where this was heading. "That's true. For a biography to be good, a subject has to open up to the writer."

"I'm not talking about the book, Lauren. I'm talking about on a personal level. She's really taking a chance here. In fact, I haven't seen her warm up to another person so quickly since..." his words trailed off and Lauren caught the significance.

"Samantha?" Her voice conveyed her astonishment.

David nodded. "I can see you understand." He stood and buttoned his jacket. "I trust you not to hurt her. You're the first person in a long time who has seemed to make her happy." He paused. "Just don't lead her on. Please." The man turned and quietly left the office.

Dumbfounded, Lauren blinked several times in rapid succession. *Lead her on?* Coming to her senses, she jumped up from her desk. "David, wait!"

The Chief of Staff stopped and turned around in the hall. "Yeah?"

"You believe the rumors, don't you?" Lauren lowered her voice, looking around a little nervously. "The ones about Devlyn and me."

"I'm not sure what to believe at this point." He placed his hand on the plane wall as he felt the big machine begin to taxi down the runway. "I'm just asking you to be careful."

"Then, just like Devlyn, you're going to have to trust me." She could see the hesitancy in his eyes. "I'll admit it probably wasn't the smartest professional move I've ever made. But somewhere in the last two months, we became real friends, David. Please know that I wouldn't do anything I thought would hurt her. I'm not leading anyone on."

Her voice was pleading, and he had no choice but to believe her. David hated being surrounded by honest people. *This is Washington politics for God's sake.* "I do trust you." He smiled softly. "And I'm glad she has you for a friend. Now, if you'll excuse me, I have a call to make myself."

Lauren's notebook was in her lap as she sat hunched over on the long sofa in her office aboard the "Flying Oval Office", scrawling away. She glanced up at the steward, who placed the milk on the table in front of her. After so many weeks with Dev, the writer had grown rather fond of the beverage as well, but she discovered it had to be ice cold for her to truly enjoy it. *Do I need to wonder where this came from?* "Thank you."

"My pleasure, Ms. Strayer. Is there anything else I can do for you?"

"No, I'm fine, thanks." She pushed her glasses up on her nose, rolling her neck to work out its tightness before taking the glass. She was amazed that it was, indeed, ice cold. *Are they all mind readers?*

Lauren glanced at her watch. They'd been in the air almost two hours and she hadn't seen hide nor hair of Devlyn since they parted in the hallway. *Quit your whining. You're a big girl and you know she's busy.* With a soundless sigh, she went back to her notebook and her milk.

Dev finally showed up outside her door almost an hour later.

The President gave a light rap and heard Lauren's answering "Come in."

Blue eyes rolled at Lauren as Dev marched into the office, arms outstretched in front of her like Frankenstein's monster. She walked stiff legged across the room to the couch, where she collapsed face down. "I'm such a bad mother," she mumbled into the cushion.

"What?" Lauren snorted. "No way."

Dev rolled over, clutching a small throw pillow to her chest. "I just realized that I'm not going to be home for Christopher's birthday next week." She folded her arms around the pillow and tucked it under her chin, looking down the couch at Lauren. "Maybe I can airmail him a camel."

The writer turned her body, lifting one arm to rest it on the back of the couch. "Nah, that's overkill. Besides, you get him a camel, and next he'll want an elephant, and before you know it: poof! You've got rhinos eating the bushes in the Rose Garden and the South Lawn is a petting zoo." *C'mon, Dev, smile.*

Dev's laughter rang out through the plane so loudly that Lauren wondered if the press rats, who were housed near the rear of the plane and went along on every Air Force One flight, could hear her. Then she got hit in the head with the pillow Dev had been using.

"Hey, be nice!" Lauren scolded as she confiscated Dev's pillow and pressed her face into the soft cloth.

"I'm always nice." Dev grinned, but the happy expression faded quickly. "I'll figure out some way to make it up to Christopher." She stopped speaking for a moment, and a contemplative look crossed her face. Dev's eyes went serious. "This is the kind of thing he's never going to forget though, isn't it?"

Lauren felt a pang deep in her chest. *It was only a birthday, right?* He would eventually understand that Dev had pressing commitments that were of global importance...things that couldn't wait for a little boy's party. She smiled sadly at the President. "No, it's not something he'll ever forget."

Dev nodded slowly and pushed up off the couch, moving towards the door. She exhaled tiredly. "That's pretty much what I figured."

Tuesday, March 9th

They had been at the Embassy for three days and this was the first time that Lauren had had more than a moment to enjoy her room's balcony. She stared out at a city that pulsed with life. It was congested and colorful. Foreigners stood out like sore thumbs, their business suits or touristy shorts and T-shirts clashing with the natives' traditional white robes. Car horns mixed with the angry shouts of pedestrians and the occasionally whinny from a donkey or horse. It was a curious mix of old and new world technology, culture, and attitudes that Lauren found more interesting than appealing.

The writer snapped off a few photographs and then headed back inside her room, stepping out of the heavy perfume of highly seasoned, roasting meats, local pastries, and car exhaust.

She was amazed when Dev ordered everyone to take their third day "in country" to rest and relax. "Everyone", Lauren found out, was a relative term. David was still working like a madman, as were several aides and advisors on foreign policy. However most of the other staff, including Dev herself, used the day to relax.

The President slept away the entire day and Lauren suspected that the dark-haired woman was still fighting a nasty case of jet lag. While she slumbered, David had easily taken charge, giving orders that Dev not be disturbed for anything. He made it perfectly clear that she needed to be well rested for the upcoming meetings.

Lauren had managed to take a nap herself, but felt restless and was up long before Dev. She took the time to do some exploring and shot two rolls of film, but was hesitant to venture too far from the executive quarters. There were just too many strange faces milling about, constantly staring at her, and whispering as she, or anyone connected to Devlyn, passed. No. Lauren preferred to stick close to her friends, especially the beautiful one who ran the most powerful nation on earth.

The first meeting was set for tomorrow morning at 9:00 a.m. Tonight, however, Dev was hosting a reception for the dignitaries who would be attending the meetings. The Embassy was simply crawling with workers, ranging from kitchen and cleaning staff to security personnel and military.

Lauren was now back out on her balcony, soaking up the dry heat, and watching the ordered chaos on the street below, before a knock at the door drew her back inside. She settled her camera on a table and opened the door to be greeted by Dev's thousand watt smile.

Devlyn was holding a garment bag and looking incredibly pleased with herself. "You know," Lauren started, her hands coming to rest on her hips, "I've known you long enough now to know that that smile is trouble." Yet even as she teased, her eyes worriedly searched Dev's face, relieved to find that the lines of fatigue and tension that she'd seen yesterday appeared to be gone.

"Oh, so that's how it is, huh? I bring you a present, and you accuse me of causing trouble." Dev shrugged nonchalantly and threw her nose in the air. "Fine. I'll just take this incredibly gorgeous evening gown and find some other short, cute blonde to give it to." She sniffed in mock indignation and turned around, barely clearing Lauren's line of sight before an enormous grin sprang to her lips.

Lauren's arm shot out, grabbing the back of Dev's shirt. "Wait just a minute, Madam Commander-in-Chief!" She tugged the woman into her room and eagerly closed the door. "Number one, I'm not short—"

"You're shorter than I am."

"Everyone without male plumbing is shorter than you are, Stretch."

Dev laughed. "True."

"And number two—" Lauren held up two fingers.

Dev draped the garment bag over her arm. Her eyes twinkled. "You're not gonna try and deny that you're cute, are you?"

"Do I look stupid?" Dev opened her mouth, and Lauren clamped her hand over it. "There's really no need to answer that, Devlyn."

The President's eyes screamed, "Who, me?" But she prudently remained silent.

Lauren smirked and pulled away her hand. She eyed the bag. "So are you gonna show me? Or do I have to beg?"

Dev didn't say a word. Her evil laugh alone was more than enough to make Lauren blush to the roots of her hair. *I love it when she does that,* Dev thought affectionately. "All right, Mighty Mouse – ouch!" The President grasped her arm and scowled. "I bruise easily, you know!"

"Then you shouldn't call people names," came the reasonable response.

"You know, I'm pretty sure it's a Federal crime to hit me."

Lauren lifted both brows as she liberated the garment bag from Dev's arms. It was deceptively heavy for a garment bag. "Call a cop." Her gaze flitted around the room, looking for a place to hang it, but before she could move, Dev took it back and held it up for Lauren's easy inspection.

The blonde carefully unzipped the leather bag. She gasped when the dress came into view. Dev hadn't lied. *Wow.* "Oh, my." She fingered the black, sequined material reverently. "It's..." She swallowed emotionally. Nobody had ever given her anything so lovely. "It's beautiful. I can't um...I can't believe it's for me." Suddenly bashful eyes tilted upward, and she gazed at Dev from beneath pale lashes. "Thanks," she said softly.

Dev sighed happily. *God, Marlowe, she's got you hook, line, and sinker. I'm totally and irreversibly twitter-pated.* "It's-it-it's for the reception tonight," she explained needlessly, her tongue failing to comply quickly enough with her brain's command to start talking and stop looking like a moron.

Lauren nodded and mercifully dropped her gaze from Dev so she could refocus on the dress.

Once out of the beam of those intense gray eyes, Dev found she could think much more clearly. "I personally thought the most beautiful woman in the room should have the most beautiful dress."

Lauren lifted a skeptical brow.

"But since I'm wearing a pantsuit..."

"God, I so knew that was coming."

They both laughed, but Dev's face soon took on a serious expression and she cleared her throat. "As I was saying, the most beautiful woman should have nothing less than the most beautiful dress. Though I'm quite certain it won't nearly do you justice."

Lauren blushed again, unsure how she should take these compliments. Dev was as solicitous as a lover, but surely she didn't feel that way about her. Other than a little harmless flirting, Dev had never given Lauren any indication that she felt something other than friendship for her. Still, she was flattered by the attention, and the way Dev was looking at her caused her belly to flutter nervously and her palms to go moist.

The biographer dismissed the most obvious explanation of what she was feeling, chalking up the sweet talking to Dev's being well rested, in a really good mood, and charming as hell. "You know, you're gonna spoil me if you keep this up. I mean, gee, great big white house, a private plane, permanent dog sitters." She grinned, scrunching up her nose and wrinkling the corners of her eyes. "I think I'm ruined for anyone else."

Dev nearly bit her lip through. *From your lips to God's ears, Lauren.*

"If I didn't know better, I'd think you were someone awfully important."

"Nah, I'm just a geek stalking her favorite author, remember?" She laughed. "Okay, I've got a meeting and Liza is gonna be here to drag me downstairs by my ear any moment. She has learned way too much from Jane, I tell you. But I'll be back to get you at about six and we'll go down for the reception. I'd invite you to join me for the meeting, but it wouldn't go over well."

"I thought the first meeting was tomorrow?"

"The first official meeting is tomorrow. This afternoon's is with the Crown Prince. It's nothing important. Photo op and sound bites for the press, that sort of thing." Dev grimaced inwardly, wondering how much longer she had to hold up her arm before she could discreetly lower the garment bag without looking like a wuss in front of Lauren. "It'll be boring as hell. And you've already been there and done that a million times, so please continue to enjoy your day off. If I didn't have to go, I wouldn't. Just relax and enjoy. You can watch the dog and pony show on closed circuit if you like."

"I'll do that." She closed her eyes for a moment, scratching just above her eyebrow. "Umm, please don't tell me I need my password to activate anything here. It's several thousand miles away at the moment. Probably eating Snausages."

Dev shot her a slightly confused look. "No, everything here is simple voice activation."

Lauren threw her hands in the air. "Finally, something simple!" She studied Dev's face, her eyes widening with realization. "Jesus, put that down." Without a warning, Lauren plucked the bag from Dev's hand. She grunted at its weight and peered interestedly inside, pulling open one of the black leather flaps. There were several pairs of shoes, a handbag that matched the dress and any pair of the shoes she might select, and several jewelry boxes resting on the bottom. "My goodness, Devlyn! No wonder this weighs a ton!"

"Nah. I barely noticed it," Dev lied. "I just wanted to make sure you had a decent selection of accessories to go with your surprise." She suppressed a smug grin. "There are a few baubles in there I hope you'll like." Her fingers idly played with the bag's zipper. "But I borrowed them. So no losing them, okay?"

Lauren nodded, gulping a little. "This wasn't necessary, Devlyn. I could have—"

"Don't be silly," Dev admonished gently. "I wanted to." She gestured toward the bag, excitedly picturing how lovely Lauren was going to look. "I'll be back in a couple of hours to escort you. Unless you've got someone else in mind," she commented with forced casualness. Half the Press Corps and a good portion of her own staff were in love with the beauty.

Lauren shook her head. "I'm all yours, Madam President."

Now that's more like it. Dev's heart began to swell. She knew that those simple words shouldn't mean so much, that they didn't mean what she wanted them to. But still, they made her happy, and she found herself lacking the willpower or inclination to fight the feeling. "See you soon then."

When Dev left, Lauren unzipped the bag fully and pulled out several pairs of shoes. She held them up to the dress and, with a little nod, selected a medium black heel with a thin strap around the ankle. Then she set them aside, along with a small evening bag, and pulled out several velvet jewelry boxes that had Cartier imprinted on them in gold letters.

Gray eyes widened when she realized that when Dev said she had "borrowed" them that meant the jewelry was on loan from one of the finest jewelers in the world. Lauren shook her head in simple disbelief. "Good God, Devlyn. Don't ever let it be said that you don't know how to make a woman feel special." She tugged over the dress and let out a nervous breath. "I only hope I can do all this justice."

Lauren flopped down on the bed and ordered the TV on,

requesting a translation in English so that she could watch the photo op. Dev stood proud and tall, looking absolutely incredible. The power of her presence alone drew every eye to her and captured the viewer's attention completely.

Almost resentfully, she dragged her gaze from Dev to inspect the shorter man standing alongside her, who was undoubtedly Crown Prince Karim Sami Hassan. He was nice enough looking, she considered thoughtfully, estimating his age somewhere between twenty-five and thirty. He had a generous mouth and a well-trimmed, dark beard that disappeared into a thick mass of wavy, black hair. The Prince's olive coloring made him appear more Mediterranean than Middle Eastern, and his dusky skin was set off nicely by his loose, white robes, which were streaked with red. He wore the traditional headgear of his people.

The United Arab Alliance had chosen him to attend these meetings because most of his formal education had taken place at Cambridge. Once, he had even visited Devlyn's own alma mater, Harvard. They believed his youth and open mind would serve him well in dealing with such an infidel. He wouldn't be as quickly offended as the older and more experienced members of the Alliance.

They spoke quietly with one another and then shook hands, dragging out the normally quick ritual for the flashing cameras. After a few moments, the Prince leaned over and whispered something to Dev. When she pulled back, she was still smiling, but something had changed.

Lauren sat up on the bed and pulled a pillow into her lap, missing Grem at that very moment. She studied the image, looking into eyes that were normally rich and vibrant, but now appeared as cold and stony as a grave. "Oh, boy, I do believe that Madam President is pissed."

The meeting ended, and the Press Corps shuffled out of the room. David began making his way over to Dev, but she waved him off, needing a few moments with the Prince. She did her best to maintain her calm demeanor, but she could already feel the sneer forming on her lips.

"Your Highness." She stopped and cleared her throat. "I appreciate the fact that you saw Ms. Strayer today on television. And I also appreciate the fact that you find her an attractive, desirable woman." Dev's nostrils flared. "But let me make something perfectly clear to you. She is *not* approachable. And she is most certainly *not* interested in remaining behind in your lovely country upon my departure." Dev's heart clenched at the very thought.

The man's eyes narrowed and he ran the back of his hand over his dark, closely cropped beard. "I was under the impression that there was no romantic involvement between you and Ms. Strayer," he said in perfect, though slightly accented, English. "My people were assured by your people that your newspapers were simply looking for a sensational story and that Ms. Strayer was free to be, shall we say, pursued."

When I find out who said that, he's walking back to the United States! So what if it's true! Dev's teeth actually ground together when he looked at her with eyes daring her to say differently, which she immediately did. "You were misinformed," Dev answered flatly. "I'm sure that you understand I must deny our involvement to the press for appearances' sake. But I assure you, Ms. Strayer is very much taken. She will be accompanying me to the reception tonight."

The Prince looked Dev directly in the eye. "She is your lover then?"

"Absolutely," Devlyn practically snarled, startled by the proprietary ring to her voice.

"But she is not your wife," he clarified smugly. The young man tilted his head to the side, waiting for Dev's response. With a quick jerk of his chin, he kept his own approaching entourage at bay.

Dev's jaw clenched. *Asswipe isn't getting the picture.* "That changes nothing." *Except for the fact that if she were my wife and you were saying these things, I'd wring your scrawny neck on the spot.* "The fact remains that Ms. Strayer is unavailable to you, Your Highness." She straightened to her full height and looked down at the Prince with barely contained rage. *How dare he?* "I trust, Your Highness, that this is a closed issue?"

"This discussion is over," he agreed amiably, flashing Dev a smile that was anything but reassuring. "Madam President."

Dev could see that the Prince was used to getting his way in every matter. *Too bad that's not going to happen with this, junior.* Dev stiffened, her body unconsciously responding to the challenge that was flashing in his eyes. To him, Lauren was still a prize to be won, and she'd just made things worse by tossing the gauntlet at his feet. *God, Lauren, I hope you trust me this much. Because he's gonna be watching us like a hawk tonight.*

Dev knocked on Lauren's door. She nervously ran her hands over her long, white jacket, tugging on its hem and smoothing it against her wide-legged silk trousers. It wasn't what she normally would have worn for such an occasion, but it was still formal attire and she wasn't about to put on a stitch of clothing that would detract from Lauren tonight.

Despite Dev's loosely worn hair, elegant jewelry, and modest makeup, her outfit would help Prince Hassan see her as Lauren's escort and his peer, not just a woman. In this male-dominated region of the world, Dev's trousers were more than a fashion statement. *Besides, I'm the President of the United States, I'll wear whatever I damn well please.*

Devlyn's mind was awhirl with tomorrow's likely headlines. She sighed. There was no choice now. If the Prince found out that she'd outright lied to him about her relationship with Lauren, the entire trip could be in jeopardy. She had put Lauren's feelings ahead of a summit that had actually been in the works for more than ten years. But she wouldn't see Lauren harassed as though she were an object to be owned.

The door suddenly swung open, and Dev's breath was simply stolen from her body. "Stunning," she whispered reverently as wide blue eyes eagerly absorbed every detail of Lauren's appearance.

Her pale hair had been swept up into a low knot that rested snuggly on her neck. Several fair tendrils had already worked their way free and served to frame Lauren's youthful face in a quietly graceful way. The black sequin dress was strapless, showing off a slender, succulent neck and slightly muscular shoulders that were covered with creamy, white skin and dotted with faint freckles. The snug cloth clung to every curve of the writer's body, outlining firm breasts, a trim waist and the womanly flair of her hips. Dev found herself wishing it were shorter, say mid thigh, but this was an evening event, so the floor length gown was already pushing the limits of propriety by showing so much of those incredible shoulders.

Dev sucked in a breath, very conscious of the low burn that had ignited deep in her belly.

"Can I take your staring at me as though I had sprouted a tail as a good sign?" Lauren asked a little insecurely. She felt her heat rise to her cheeks. Dev's eyes raked over her body in a way that was making her pulse flutter happily. Unfortunately, it was also making her even more nervous than she already was – which was pretty damned nervous.

"Wow," Dev mumbled. "You look..." She shook her head, unable to form the words. *Fabulous,* her mind screamed. *She looks fabulous! Uh oh. Too fabulous. Prince What's-his-name is gonna drop dead at first sight.*

Lauren tucked a wisp of hair behind her ear, her earrings glittering gently in the waning evening light. Her hand dropped to her throat. "Thank you. And for these especially. I feel like some sort of princess." Her fingers shifted and grazed the sparkling diamonds wreathing her neck, then moved down to the matching bracelet that hung loosely around her wrist. She smiled warmly. "I'm a little concerned about turning into a pumpkin at midnight." Lauren spoke without paying much attention to her words. Her gaze was firmly fixed on Devlyn. The mere sight of the President, whose elegant suit contrasted with her dark hair and luminous blue eyes, threatened to seize up Lauren's brain entirely.

"You, um..." Lauren laughed helplessly, finding herself tongue tied and with the inexplicable urge to run her hands up and down Dev's body. *And kiss the hollow of her throat? Okay, that's new.*

"Clean up pretty good?" *No, I cannot lean in and nuzzle that sweet smelling hair.*

"Mmm..." Lauren agreed. "That's an understatement, Devlyn."

"Shall we?" Dev offered the smaller woman her elbow.

"Oh, yeah."

"Wait a second." Dev frowned a little and pointed back toward the room. "Don't you need your glasses?"

"Will I have to read or write?"

"Well, we were all going to sit around and retake our SATs for fun." Dev slapped her forehead. "But so much for that. Now what will we do after drinks?" *I have a few suggestions. One of them includes whipped cream and...STOP IT!*

Lauren laughed. "We'd better get going, President Marlowe." She spied Dev's Secret Service men lurking down the hall. "I'm sure Liza is stroking out someplace, waiting for you." Lauren tucked her arm around Dev's as they made their way down the hall.

"Umm...Lauren?" *Time to face the music, Marlowe.*

"Yes?"

"Do you trust me?"

"You did *what!*" Lauren stopped dead in her tracks just as the couple entered the reception hall. She stared at Dev in disbelief.

The room went dead silent and every set of eyes turned to the two women.

"Don't make me say it again," Dev pleaded under her breath as she grinned at the crowd and gave a quick wave. "I know by the way your jaw just hit the carpet that you heard me the first time."

"Devlyn!" Lauren huffed through her plastered on smile. She was temporarily blinded by a dozen quick flashes from the waiting cameras. "The gossip just started to die down back home." The writer spoke without moving her lips. "If we put on some show tonight so we can convince Prince Hassan, it's just going to start all over again."

David rushed to Dev's side, pushing down his irritation. Dev knew the drill. Why was she being difficult? She'd been in an unusually foul mood ever since the photo op that afternoon. "Good evening, Madam President" was what he said.

Devlyn, however, heard exactly what David meant, which was, "Why didn't you wait for your introduction, bozo?" "Sorry, David. I was distracted. Besides, I was already introduced to everyone this afternoon. This is just a little reception. Relax." She glanced sideways at her Chief of Staff and elbowed him in the ribs affectionately. "Nice tux. Your tie is crooked, by the way."

"Thanks." He fussed with the tie until it was straight. "And you know we have to follow protocol, Madam President."

Prince Hassan made a beeline for the women and Dev immediately wrapped her arm around Lauren's waist, tugging her closer and surprising the hell out of both David and Lauren. A flurry of camera flashes lit up the room, and the press hounds began to murmur among themselves. "Let's just skip it and say we didn't, David. I've got something else I need to take care of right now anyway. If you'll excuse us?"

David turned round eyes on Lauren who could only shrug helplessly. "Fine," he mumbled. "I'll be back in a few moments. I'll handle it."

Dev nodded absently, her eyes tracking the Prince and the advisors that flanked him like bookends.

Prince Hassan stopped right in front of Devlyn and Lauren. He motioned his men back a few feet. "Madam President, it's a pleasure to see you again." Yet somehow Dev just couldn't believe him. It might have been the fact that he was looking at Lauren the entire time he spoke. "I don't believe I've been introduced to your lovely biographer."

Dev remained stubbornly silent until Lauren nudged her. "Your Highness, Prince Hassan, may I present Ms. Lauren Strayer?"

"It's a true pleasure." Prince Hassan bowed deeply at the waist and grasped Lauren's hands. He kissed her knuckles, lingering for several seconds too long.

"Hello," Lauren replied cordially, wanting her hands back.

Dev fought not to roll her eyes. *If I strangled him, I wonder if it would start a war?* Dev knew she wasn't acting very presidential – she couldn't seem to help herself.

"What a lovely necklace, Ms. Strayer." The Prince gestured to the glittering stones then let go of one of Lauren's hands to reach out and touch them. Using the grip on the hand he still held, he tugged Lauren closer.

"Thank you." Lauren pulled her hand away and discreetly moved out of his reach, trying not to appear as repulsed as she felt. *Okay, now I know why Dev didn't want him to feel like I was fair game. Yuck.* "It was a gift from...Mad...Devlyn." *Her lover would say her name,* she admonished herself. Lauren smiled up at Dev, who glanced back down at her with apologetic eyes.

Prince Hassan retracted his hand casually, although he felt stung by Lauren's actions. "I trust that you are enjoying all that my lovely nation has to offer."

"Unfortunately, this is a business trip, Your Highness," Dev interrupted. "We've had no free time for sight seeing. Perhaps another time." *Like ten minutes after never.*

He frowned. "Perhaps." Then his frown shifted into a smile that the women were sure only *he* found charming. "I believe then that I need to make the most out of our short time together." The man handed a full glass of champagne to Dev, who took the glass without thinking. Then he turned to Lauren and smiled broadly. "It seems that I need some more champagne. Would you care to join me, Ms. Strayer?"

Dev stepped in between Lauren and the Prince, her temper flaring. "No, she would not, you son—"

"Why, yes." Lauren laid a calming hand against Dev's back and then moved around her. "Thank you, Your Highness. I would be delighted."

The man's chest immediately puffed out, and he tossed Devlyn a conceited grin. No unmarried woman would refuse him. And that a woman could be chosen over him? That was unthinkable.

"One moment please, Your Highness. I need to speak with Devlyn." Lauren immediately grasped Dev's hand and walked them several feet away. She lowered her voice to a whisper. "Let me handle this, Devlyn."

"I will not!" Dev whispered back angrily. "He's making a play for you right in front of me! Of all the arrogant pieces of—"

"I know." Lauren made a face. "He's a pig. But I've got the sneaking suspicion that you punching him in the nose wouldn't do anything for our two countries' relations." A pale brow lifted. "Right?"

Dev's expression turned sulky. "I wasn't going to punch him." *Yes, I was. Shit. I'm going insane.*

"Uh huh." Lauren smiled gently. "I know you were only trying to get him to leave me alone by telling him we were lovers. And for most men, I think that would do it. But Prince Hassan is apparently the overeager type who needs a little extra convincing." She patted Dev's arm reassuringly. "Trust me."

Devlyn exhaled unhappily. "Do I have a choice?"

Lauren pretended to think for a moment before she smiled sassily. "Ummm...not really."

Blue eyes took on a dangerous glint as Dev peeked over her shoulder at the Prince. "I'm going to be watching him. And if he gets even the tiniest bit out of hand—"

"I know. I know. Now go greet your other guests before you get a reputation for being a horrible hostess." Lauren squared her shoulders, realizing that she'd never even had the chance to be nervous in her surroundings. Things had just happened too quickly. "I'll be fine."

Dev flashed her a gleaming smile full of admiration and affection. But there was a serious edge to her voice that garnered the younger woman's complete attention. Piercing eyes bore straight into Lauren, and they stopped speaking for a long moment as the rest of the world faded away. "Just don't forget who your escort is tonight," Dev finally whispered softly, her heart thundering in her ears. *This should be for real. Not some stupid ruse.*

Lauren swallowed. "I won't." Several more seconds passed before their surroundings seeped back into their consciousness. Lauren closed her eyes for a moment to clear her head. *Time to get this fixed.* She purposefully strode over to Prince Hassan, who had been waiting, stealing furtive glances at the women and wondering if his bed might be warmed by more than just Lauren tonight. Lauren wrapped her arm around his and headed them in the general direction of the bar. "We need to have a little talk."

"I was hoping you would see me alone."

"I...um...I wanted to make something clear to you, Your Highness. I thought it best if we spoke privately. That's all."

"But a woman as beautiful as you should not be required to think."

Lord, help me. Maybe I'll be the one to punch him. Prudently, Lauren decided to plow ahead, ignoring his last remark. "I'm flattered by your attentions, Your Highness." *Gag.* "But I'm perfectly happy with Devlyn."

"Obviously, President Marlowe values you, or you would not be attending a function such as this. But you are merely a lover and not her wife, correct? I have four wives and several lovers. And it is you that I am interested in tonight."

Lucky them. "Be that as it may, I only have one lover, and I'm not interested in any others." Lauren was running out of patience quickly. *What is it going to take to put off Romeo?* Her imaginary status as Devlyn's lover was apparently far enough below that of a spouse that Prince Hormones felt free to try his luck. A server finally passed them, and she snatched a flute of champagne from the tray, tossing it back in one deep swallow.

"Your Highness, I'm trying to be discreet here. But you've left me no choice but to be rather explicit."

He leaned closer, obviously extremely interested.

"I am *completely* satisfied." Lauren wriggled pale brows, and her voice dropped to a sexual purr that did an excellent job of conveying in *exactly* what ways Dev satisfied her. "I wouldn't trade Devlyn for ten men." She licked her lips slowly and tried not to burst out laughing at the look of surprise, then arousal, that swept across his face. "No offense."

The Prince cleared his throat, suddenly embarrassed. His respect for the tall American jumped several notches. "None taken,

Ms. Strayer. I'm glad that you are so," he paused and smiled with open appreciation, "satisfied." Lauren was a beauty. But he wasn't foolish enough to chase after a lost cause.

"Thank you. I am a very lucky woman." Relief flooded her. *Finally.* Just then David joined them. *Perfect timing.* "It was a pleasure to meet you, Your Highness. I hope your meetings tomorrow go very smoothly."

"I'm sure they will. It seems that President Marlowe is a master at getting and keeping what she desires most."

Lauren ducked her head and smiled. "I agree. Good night." She turned to David. "I believe there was someone you wanted to introduce me to?"

David stared at her blankly.

"Across the room," she prompted, tilting her head in a direction she's chosen randomly, hoping it would put her as far away from Prince Dipshit as she could get.

David's eyes widened slightly with recognition. "Oh, yes, of course." He quickly scanned the crowd and threw out a name. "If you'll excuse us, Your Highness?"

The Prince nodded and insisted on taking Lauren's hand and giving it another little kiss.

"You're a lifesaver, David," Lauren said softly as soon as they were out of the Prince's earshot.

He stopped walking and looked at her curiously. "How'd you know my Secret Service name?"

The Prince smiled at Dev. He had managed to avoid her for the past two hours, but he was about ready to retire and decided a quick goodbye was in order. "It seems that your Ms. Strayer is very much taken," he conceded.

Dev spun around at the sound of the Prince's voice and another glass of champagne was thrust into her hand.

She had downed hers in one swallow when Lauren and the Prince left in search of a server or the bar. And even as she tried to mingle, she found her attention drifting across to Lauren. It was only after Lauren had finally broken away with David that she felt comfortable enough to begin mixing with her guests. "I told you that this afternoon," Dev stated flatly. "What finally convinced you?"

The young man burst out laughing. "Ms. Strayer's declaration of her 'satisfaction' in your 'arrangement'."

Dev blinked. *What? Ooo...Well, thank you, Lauren!* She grinned rakishly at the Prince, who looked as though he would high-five her if he were familiar with the gesture. Instead, he slapped her between the shoulders with gusto. Apparently, Dev had been accepted as "one of the boys".

"I have no hard feelings, Madam President." His brow furrowed a little, not quite understanding why this whole thing seemed to bother the American President so. Lauren was merely her lover. President Marlowe was a beautiful and powerful woman and her nation obviously accepted her sinful ways. Surely she had dozens of lovers. "She's just a woman," he finally said, still puzzled but willing to let it go. He waved a hand dismissively. "Nothing that we should allow to interfere in our negotiations tomorrow."

"Until tomorrow then," Dev ground out, needing to make a hasty retreat before she did something stupid. *It'll only make Lauren mad if I go ahead and punch him in the nose.*

"Anxious to get back to your beautiful blonde?" he laughed. "Ahh...I cannot blame you a bit. Lucky for me, she can easily be replaced with another beautiful blonde."

Dev's eyes darkened with unspent anger, and she moved to shake Prince Hassan's hand. She grasped it firmly and leaned forward, placing her lips near his ear. "That, Your Highness, is where you are dead wrong."

Sunday, April 4th

"Why so glum, chum?" David leaned over the chessboard, wondering why he always fell for that same gambit.

"Oh, I don't know." Dev sighed, then sipped her brandy. She leaned back in her chair and watched pensively as David tried to get out of trouble...again. Would he never learn?

They were in the spare office in the private residence of the White House. It was a cozy room that Dev had turned into a family game room of sorts. The kids loved it. On this chilly spring night, however, her babies were fast asleep, as was, Dev suspected, nearly everyone else in Washington, D.C. without insomnia. David's wife was out of town visiting relatives and her old buddy was lingering in Dev's quarters, not wanting to go back to his empty house.

"The only time you drink is when you're having women troubles," David said casually, his eyes never leaving the board.

Dev looked into her snifter and frowned. "It's brandy, for God's sake. And I certainly don't have women troubles. No women, no troubles."

"Well, I'm really glad to hear that." *Here goes nothing.* "Because guess who's in town this week?"

"The Emperor of Japan?"

"Nooo." David moved his knight.

Dev leaned forward and made a move that would allow the game to continue as long as David didn't do something stupid. She wasn't ready to be alone either. "King of England?"

"Nooo." His brows knitted together. *Why didn't she go for the quick kill?* "Think a little less political. More, umm, your type."

"My type?" Dev kicked her long legs out in front of her. "David, I don't have a type."

He leaned back in his chair after making his move and leveled his best brotherly stare at his friend. "Yeah, I know. And it's about time we changed that."

Dev glared at the ruddy-skinned man. "David, please don't tell me that you went and did something incredibly stupid like—"

"I set you up on a date."

A dark head dropped. "Oh, God!" Dev set her snifter on the table next to her, its heavy crystal bottom making a loud thump. Then she changed her mind and irritably jerked it back up again. "Isn't my life already complicated enough without you fixing me up? Half the U.S. and one horny Arab prince already think I'm sleeping with Lauren."

"And since you're not," David said sensibly, "there's no reason you shouldn't go out with Candy Delaney."

Devlyn began choking on her drink, wincing as the strong liquor stung her sinuses. She covered her mouth with her fist and tried to breathe through her nose.

"Surprise."

When Dev could finally speak she managed to gasp, "You mean you fixed me up with 'C'mere and get a piece of Candy' Delaney? Jesus, David, why didn't you just hire me a hooker and call the press in to take pictures!"

David chewed the inside of his cheek unhappily. He was starting to get the idea that the only person who was going to satisfy Dev was one Lauren Strayer. "I'll have you know that Candy Delaney is now Candice Delaney, *M.D.*, and she's in town attending the Surgeon General's conference on STDs."

"Well, she had enough of them in college. She should be an expert by now."

"Deeeev..." But he couldn't stifle a laugh.

"You know how I hate being set up!"

"I set you up with Samantha, Dev."

"Oh, yeah." She frowned, slumping back into her seat. "But you'll never get that lucky again. And I still don't want to be set up now."

"C'mon! You're being ridiculous!"

"I am not going out with Candy 'Check out my crème filling' Delaney!" Dev extended her arm and lazily moved her bishop. "Checkmate."

"You're right. You're not going out. You're the President of the United States, for God's sake."

Dev snorted. "'Bout time you remembered that."

"She's coming here. Friday night, seven o'clock. I thought a nice dinner in residence. Maybe a movie after. Or a tour of–"

"How very Andy Hardy of you."

"*She's* not even going to be here on Friday. *She's* got a date," David said quietly. He knew the words would sting, but there was no use in Dev's continuing to brood about it.

Devlyn didn't have to ask who "she" was. Liza had practically been beaming because of it all week. The President's personal assistant had happily blabbed to everyone who would listen that Lauren had agreed to go out with her favorite cousin, Casey Dennis. "Thanks for reminding me, pal." Dev glowered. "I had almost forgotten," she mumbled sarcastically. *And where is that damn FBI report I ordered on Liza's cousin? I asked for it hours ago!*

David made a face at the chessboard and lifted his palms in a gesture of defeat.

Dev thought of Lauren being wined and dined, having an intimate evening out with someone else. They might hold hands or...*God, what if he kisses her? Or she kisses him? And what if that leads to... No. No. No! I will not think about that. I won't!* Her face screwed up with anger and she knocked David's king across the room with her bishop.

Both sets of eyes followed the king, as the white wooden chess piece sailed through the air and landed in the lit fireplace. It burst instantly into flames and David gulped audibly.

"Oh, yeah, buddy, you're just lucky you won't fit."

Friday, April 9th

Dev sighed as she entered the hallway. She looked at her Secret Service agent who pushed up out of his chair and stood the moment she left her room. "Don't suppose you'd just shoot me now?"

The man paled a little. "Madam President?"

"Did you ever do something that you didn't really want to do just to keep your busybody friends happy?"

He relaxed and gave her a knowing grin. "Blind date, Madam President?"

"Almost. I haven't seen her since college." Dev sighed. "Well, at least I made it clear to my Chief of Staff that he and his wife were coming too." Her head jerked up when Lauren's door opened several paces in front of her. *Oh, shit. She looks great. Why does she have to look so damned good? If I didn't know better, I'd almost say she was trying to drive me insane.*

They approached each other very slowly. Lauren slid her purse over her shoulder as she moved alongside Dev. "So, you ready for the big evening?" She'd heard about Dev's blind date from Emma and the thought did *not* make her happy. Dev had been looking tired these past few days. *She only gets ten free minutes a week as it is. She should be relaxing or watching TV or reading my book, or something,* Lauren thought petulantly. *Not making her life more complicated. So what if this chick is a big time doctor from Harvard? Big deal. I know I'm not impressed. University of Tennessee is a great school!*

Dev nodded and tried to sound positive. "Yeah, it'll be nice to see Candy...eh...Candice...um, Dr. Delaney again." A tiny frown line appeared on Lauren's forehead and Devlyn barely stopped herself from reaching out and smoothing it away.

"Well, I should be going. Liza asked me to come along with her and her boyfriend. Umm...her cousin is going to be there. And...well..."

"Really? I hadn't heard," Dev said casually, hoping no divine being actually kept track of little white lies, especially where Lauren was concerned. If he did, she was in deep shit.

Lauren tugged on her glasses uncomfortably. She felt an inexplicable urge to explain herself to Dev. "I've been going kind of stir crazy lately. It's been months since I've really gone out. And she asked...um...Liza, I mean, and really wanted a fourth person so her cousin wouldn't feel uncomfortable." *Why do I feel like I'm cheating on her? We're not a couple!*

"Oh, I understand completely." *I am going straight to Hell.* "You never know when you might meet Mr. Right."

Lauren smiled weakly and shrugged. Somehow she didn't think she'd be meeting Mr. Right tonight. "Or Ms. Right."

Dev's ears pricked up. "Huh?" she practically shouted.

"Candice Delaney?" Lauren clarified, puzzled by Dev's outburst. "Your date tonight?" Her cheeks turned pink with embarrassment. "Um...Emma mentioned it a couple of days ago." *And I haven't been able to think of anything else since.*

"Oh. Right." Dev tried not to look too crestfallen. She tilted her head in the opposite direction from the one Lauren was heading in. "I'm on my way there now, as a matter of fact."

Lauren eyed Dev's casual suit appreciatively, perversely pleased that Dr. Delaney didn't rate a skirt or heels. "I can see that. That's a pretty outfit."

"Thanks." A tiny smile edged onto Dev's face. "Same back." Awkwardly, she stuffed her hands in her pockets and rocked on her heels. "Well, I'll see you around." Yet she made no effort to move.

Lauren sighed wistfully, already sorry she had agreed to Liza's double date offer. She firmly commanded her feet to move, when what she really wanted to do was stay here and visit with Devlyn. *Ugh. Except that Dev is going to spend the evening with Ms. Harvard. She sees me all the time. I'm sure I'm the last person she wants to spend more time with.* "Yeah. See ya around."

By the time Lauren's taxi dropped her off in front of the Been Gi Palace, a cloud of depression had settled over her. She glanced up at the restaurant sign and wrinkled her nose. *Why did I agree to Korean food? I hate not being sure about what I'm ordering. I'm from Tennessee, dammit! I'm very happy knowing that the "C" in KFC stands for "chicken" and not "cat".* The irksome thought made her shiver.

"This is what I get for wanting a life," she mumbled to herself as she squared her shoulders and pushed open the restaurant's heavy wooden door, allowing the strong aroma of the Korean food to waft out onto the sidewalk.

A smiling hostess immediately rushed to greet her. Lauren slid off her trench coat and draped it over her arm.

"Hewo, hewo," the young woman greeted, bowing her head several times. She looked exceedingly pleased to see Lauren.

"Hi." Lauren began bowing her head too, until she caught herself and realized what she was doing. She stopped and smiled at the petite woman. "I'm here to meet the Dennis party."

"Party of one?" the hostess chirped. Her accent was so thick Lauren found herself leaning forward as though the words might somehow make sense if their volume were increased.

"No."

The hostess looked confused. "You no want food?"

"No...I mean yes. I'm meeting some friends here. The Dennis party," Lauren tried again.

"If you no want food, you just go! This not funny joke." The young woman began shooing Lauren back toward the door.

"No...I do. I mean yes, I want food." *Just not this food.* The odor was making her a little sick. Lauren exhaled impatiently and peered around the small woman.

The restaurant was dark, illuminated only by the candles dotting the tables and by several yellow toned lights hanging over the bar. She squinted as her eyes continued to adjust to the dim light. Liza was no place to be seen, so she started looking for Casey, which was no easy task considering she had no idea what the guy looked like. A handsome, clean-shaven, dark-haired man in a sports coat and tie was sitting at the end of the bar nursing a drink. The seats on either side of him were empty.

Lauren decided to take a chance. She stepped forward, past the hostess, and waved in his direction. Despite the darkness, the man spotted Lauren and his head popped up. He smiled broadly, gesturing her over. Lauren sighed in relief. Liza and her date must just be late.

She turned to the confused hostess, who had moved back in front of her, apparently prepared to block her path if necessary. "I found my party. See?" Lauren pointed to the man who raised his drink in acknowledgement.

The hostess nodded furiously, finally understanding that Lauren was meeting the man at the bar. "You go then," she said happily. "I get you table and waiter leave menus."

Lauren just stared, not having understood a blessed word.

"Go!" the hostess finally huffed. "Tourists so stupid," she grumbled as she stepped back to the door, her head bobbing again as she greeted an elderly couple who had just stepped inside.

Lauren took the bull by the horns and approached the man. He stood up and offered her the seat next to him. She extended her hand, and he shook it briskly. "I'm sorry I'm a little late." She slid onto the stool next to him. "I'm Laur–"

"That's okay, honey," he interrupted. His eyes tried their best to focus, but this was his fifth drink and things were a little fuzzy around the edges. Still, he could see enough to know this was the luckiest damned day of his life. "You were worth the wait." He smiled triumphantly. And his friends tried to tell him that munching down the worm at the end of a bottle of Cuervo wasn't really good luck. Ha!

Lauren's eyes narrowed, and she caught a good look at the man for the first time, noticing his slightly disheveled shirt and askew necktie. "What's your name?"

The man suddenly grasped the importance of this question and thought wildly. "John?"

Lauren rolled her eyes. "More like 'asshole'." She pushed off the bar.

"Bill?" he valiantly tried again. "David? Sam? Rick? Steve? Bob? David?"

"You already said that one."

"It's the right one then?"

"Nope."

"C'mon! Give me a hint at least."

"Sorry, pal. None of those are close to Casey." *Thank God.* The woman two seats down, who had been listening to the exchange with mild amusement, suddenly jumped to her feet. "Lauren?"

Lauren's eyes jerked toward the sandy-haired woman. "Yes?"

"I'm so glad to finally meet you. I'm Liza's cousin, Casey Dennis." She extended her hand and Lauren lifted hers in utter shock. "Your date," Casey added when Lauren continued to stare at her blankly. The writer's hand was as limp as a spaghetti noodle.

"You're a woman," Lauren said needlessly, her jaw sagging slightly. *Do I look totally gay or what?*

Two eyebrows jumped. "Yeeeah," Casey drew out the word. "Last time I checked, anyway. Surely you knew that. I mean, Liza said–" She stopped, noticing that Lauren looked a little spooked. "Hey, are you okay?"

Lauren scratched her jaw. "Boy, that's a good question." *The idea's not totally new to you, Lauri, and you know it. You've thought about it before. Especially lately. So don't even think about acting all shocked.*

She'd been mildly interested in a few women over the years. Lauren had wondered, if given the chance, whether things might have developed beyond friendship, but time marched on and opportunity never knocked. Her marriage to Judd had been one long study in unfulfillment for them both. So maybe it was time to broaden her horizons? She'd been skirting the edge of it for years. Lauren had to admit that it wasn't a lack of interest in women that had held her back. More like a lack of attraction. Or at least a feeling of attraction that was more than fleeting.

Attraction should be... her mind immediately hit upon the answer, and she sighed quietly... *like what I feel for Dev.* To pretend to be anything other than attracted to Devlyn was simply a lie, and she knew it. She was drawn to the older woman like a moth to a flame. Her heart hadn't as much as spared a second thought toward Dev's gender. Lauren tried not to think that Dev was probably kissing Dr. Delaney at this very moment.

The writer firmly clamped down on her wandering thoughts and glanced up at Casey, who was, admittedly, a pretty woman. She concentrated on her for a second, holding her breath and purposely looking long and deep into Casey's warm brown eyes. *Nothing. No glimmer of interest. No spark of desire. No attraction. No pull.* It was nothing like what she felt with Dev, even from the very first. Lauren exhaled. *But she's not Dev. So stop doing that!*

"I'm sorry. And I'm fine," Lauren finally answered, realizing that she was staring. "What I meant to say earlier is that you're a woman...who looks really familiar. Have we met?" *Okay, that was pathetic.* But Casey seemed to buy her answer without question.

"No, I'm sure I'd remember you." Casey led the way to the empty table that awaited her return.

"Where's Liza?" Lauren hoped the question came off casually, despite the fact that she was starting to get a little worried.

"Oh, she called a few minutes ago. Something came up at the White House and so she and Art won't be meeting us tonight." Casey smiled as she slid into her seat, tossing her menu onto the empty place setting next to her. "It's just you and me for the whole night!"

Lauren's eyebrows crawled behind her bangs. "Umm...wow. The whole evening?" *What time is it?* She fought the urge to glance at her watch. *Give the woman a chance. If Dev were interested in you, she wouldn't be dating someone else, right?* "That's great," Lauren said with as much enthusiasm as she could muster. *The whole night.*

In the dining room of the residence, David and Beth chatted with Candy, while Dev tried not to look totally miserable. She smiled at all the right times and feigned interest in what was being said as she pushed her pasta around on her plate.

Dev had lost her appetite long before dinner even made it to the table. It had been totally vanquished between the soup and salad. She had nearly dislocated her knee by smacking it into the table when she felt Candy's hand land on her thigh.

Once she had managed to get Candy's insistent hand off her leg, she looked up to find the woman openly leering at her. It had been a long time since anyone had looked at her like she was the main course, but coming from Candy it was downright unappealing. It actually made her a little sick to her stomach. *Candice Delaney, respected M.D. by day, Superslut by night. Some things just never change.* Dev just shook her head.

She imagined Lauren looking at her like that, with lust filled, slate gray eyes, and her cheeks immediately flamed a bright scarlet. *Oh, God.* An involuntary moan escaped from deep in her throat.

The conversation around her suddenly stopped and everyone stared.

Okay, that wasn't a good idea. "Hot pasta," Dev explained lamely, fanning the tepid entree.

With dessert, things went from bad to worse. While David and his wife were lost in their own conversation, Candy whispered an obscene suggestion to Dev, explaining just how she'd like to use the cherry sauce once they were alone. Dev cringed at the mere thought. *Not even with someone else's tongue!* Her shoulders slumped and she tossed her napkin onto the table. *How am I gonna survive this? Wonder how Lauren's doing? Couldn't be any worse than this.*

Lauren's head bobbed dutifully as she poked her fork around her plate, barely listening to Casey's endless droning, but fascinated by the stinky conglomeration of *something* that had been placed in front of her. *Are those tiny legs?* She gulped. *Or tentacles? I didn't order anything with legs!* A mental pause. *I think.*

"And that's how I became a medical technician at the morgue."

Lauren nearly dropped her fork. Her eyes shot upward. "You're what?"

"A morgue clerk," Casey enthused, heartened to see that Lauren was as excited about it as she was. Maybe the writer wasn't as big a dud as she seemed. "It's such a totally interesting job! Why one time, after a mob hit downtown–"

The biographer felt the blood drain from her face. *She's not going to tell me about it, is she? Oh, God!* "So, what's your favorite book?" Lauren changed the subject as quickly as she could. The legs mixed in with what she thought were noodles on her plate were nearly enough to make her barf. Hearing about corpses would surely push her over the edge.

"You know, people are always asking each other that," Casey commented sagely. "I don't really have one. I've always preferred the movies." She rattled off a half dozen titles, none of which Lauren had even heard of. "Aren't those great? They're my favorites."

"Um...sorry, I haven't seen any of those."

"Oh." Casey looked mortally wounded, and Lauren wasn't sure whether to feel bad or relieved. Maybe she could cut the evening short.

Both women were silent for several awkward moments. "What

about travel?" Lauren prompted. "Have you been anywhere interesting? Or is there someplace you'd like to visit?"

"No. Not really."

More painful silence.

"Oh."

Casey took a long drink of Korean beer. "Astrology is a hobby of mine. I'm a Virgo. What's your sign?"

"Cancer."

Casey suddenly found the contents of her glass very interesting. "Oh."

Lauren cocked her head to the side. "Oh, what? Is that bad or something?"

"No. Not really. Well, they just aren't very compatible with Virgoans." She shrugged lightly. "That's all."

No shit, Sherlock. Lauren covertly studied her watch. *Who knew two hours could feel like this?*

"You gonna eat that?" Without waiting for Lauren to answer, Casey reached over and stuck her fingers in Lauren's dinner, fishing out something green and slimy that she immediately popped into her mouth.

Lauren's eyes turned to slits and she considered stabbing Casey with her fork. If that had been a French fry, Casey would be sporting fork marks on her hand right now. As it was, she really wouldn't miss one more piece of slimy thing.

"Umm." Casey chewed happily. "Thanks, those are great. And I can't believe you didn't eat them right off. I can never wait. Ooo...have I told you how much I love the symphony? Have you heard our local symphony? They're fabulous."

Lauren shook her head. "I've heard they're wonderful, but I'm not really a big fan of the symphony. So I haven't seen them myself. But I like opera," she tried hopefully.

Casey's face twisted in disgust and she stated flatly, "I hate opera."

Lauren looked down at her plate hopelessly. She scooped up a big bite, legs and all, and shoveled it into her mouth. She reasoned that she'd probably have to be rushed to the emergency room soon and then she could escape the date from hell. Or she'd be dead. Either way worked.

Casey's face suddenly brightened. "But this body we had down at the morgue last week sort of looked like one of those fat opera guys."

Lauren didn't even look up. She just took another enormous bite.

"He was pale and bloated. I think they fished his carcass out of the river near National Airport. But that's not the worst thing I've seen. Not by a long shot! The worst was this..."

Dev seriously considered hurting David when he and Beth excused themselves after an insufferably long dinner, but suggested that the President give Candy a tour. She grabbed his arm as he was leaving. "I will make you pay for this!" she growled under her breath, knowing that only David was close enough to hear her.

"Well, you know what the old song says," he whispered back. "If you can't be with the one you love, love the one you're with."

"Not in this lifetime, David."

"Good night, Madam President." He leaned over and spoke very quietly into Dev's ear. "I didn't remember her coming off this strong, Dev. This was a slight miscalculation on my part. I'm sorry."

Slight? "Good night, former Chief of Staff."

David and Beth made a hasty exit, and Dev turned to face the music. *Why do I keep hearing "Little Red Corvette" playing in my mind? Dear God, I promise you I'll do something* really *good for the environment if you'll just get me out of this.*

"Well," the President gestured nervously down the hall, "let's go see what we can find to look at around here."

"Come on, Dev." The woman moved closer and Dev took a step back. "I don't bite." She grinned. "Unless you ask real nice. How about a tour of the Executive Bedroom?"

"They say Lincoln's bedroom is haunted. Mine too." Dev stepped around Candy, only to have her ass pinched in the process.

"Thanks for the ride, Casey." *Which you* insisted *on giving me.*

"No problem. I was coming back here to meet Liza anyway." The women made their way around to one of the staff entrances just as Casey's phone rang. It was Liza. "Well, what are you doing there?" Casey practically crowed into her cell phone. "We just came from there!" She placed her hand over the receiver and turned to Lauren, who was quietly digging for the ID that was required before she could sign in and gain entrance to the White House, even though the guard at the door knew exactly who she was and that she lived there.

God, I'm totally screwed if I ever lose this thing. Lauren finally pulled it out and signed the clipboard before turning a bored, slightly frustrated expression on her companion. "Let me guess," Lauren sighed. "She's at Been Gi's?" *Please don't tell me this means I have to spend anymore time with you.*

"Yup. And she wants to know if you wouldn't mind giving me the nickel tour." Casey gave her a hopeful expression. "She doesn't want to drive all the way back. She lives in the opposite direction."

Lauren held out an impatient hand. "Let me talk to Liza."

"Okay." Casey put the phone to her mouth again to say goodbye, but didn't pass it to Lauren. "Liza says it's not necessary to thank her, that you can do that on Monday. She, umm...she hung up."

Lauren's shoulders slumped and she exhaled wearily. *Won't this date ever end?* "C'mon, Casey, the nickel tour is really quick."

Dev wondered if she could still be President after her brain finally exploded in her skull. She figured if Ford could do it, she might be able to get away with it too. There were bigger stumbling blocks than brain death when it came to the Oval Office. Devlyn decided that if she had to remove Candy's hand from some part of her anatomy just one more time, she was going to have to throw "polite" out the window and simply kick Candy out on her ass.

"The...umm...China Room is this way." Dev gestured again.

As the pair entered from one side, Dev was more than relieved to see Lauren enter from the other doorway. Then the fact that she was with a woman registered just a millisecond behind that. *What in the hell? A woman! Casey is a woman?* "Lauren, you're home." It slipped out before Dev could get her lips and brain in sync with each other. The one thing that her mouth and brain could readily agree on, however, was to smile at Lauren. Which she did, quite readily, despite the fact that she felt hurt. It was clear that Lauren liked women. Just not her. *Whoever didn't get me that FBI report is going to be looking for a new job come Monday.*

"Hi, Devlyn." Lauren smiled warmly at the President, but threw a look of solid ice at the attractive woman standing next to her. "I don't believe I've met your friend."

"Oh, yeah." *And what does this Casey woman have that I don't, Lauren Strayer?* "Uh, Lauren, may I present Dr. Candice Delaney? Dr. Delaney, this is Ms. Lauren Strayer, the very talented young woman who is writing my biography."

Candy slipped a possessive arm through Dev's, only to have the tall woman shift away. She gave the President an annoyed look and then offered her hand and a catty smile to Lauren, instantly sniffing the blonde out as her competition. "Nice to meet you, Ms. Strayer. I have some great Dev Marlowe stories from college," her voice was condescending, "if you need them."

Candy's Bostonian accent grated on Lauren's nerves like fingernails running down a blackboard. "Nice to meet you, too. And I see Devlyn everyday. I don't need any *old* stories. She's perfectly willing to tell me anything I want to know." The smile she gave Dr. Delaney was every bit as catty as the one she'd received. "I'm sure that Dev was pleased with how well you've held up over the years."

Dev snorted, but tried to cover it by pretending to cough. Then she got a good look at the woman with Lauren, who hadn't so much as given her the time of day, and whose eyes were feasting on Candy like she was...well, a piece of candy. "Uh, Lauren, you haven't introduced us to your friend." Dev shifted her gaze back and forth between the two women, hoping to hell Lauren would pick up on it.

Lauren was too busy mentally cataloging every reason that Candy Delaney wasn't nearly good enough for Devlyn to notice. It wasn't until Dev repeated her question that Lauren said, "Madam President, may I introduce Casey Dennis, Liza's cousin?"

Casey completely ignored Dev and continued to stare lustily at Candy. "Please tell me you're not *the* Dr. Candice Delaney," she said in awe. "I read your article on crabs last year, and I haven't been able to pee in a public restroom since." Casey's brown eyes grew moist, and her voice trembled. "You are...I mean, *it* was magnificent."

An enormous smile split Candy's face, and she openly appraised Lauren's date. "Why, thank you very much, Ms. Dennis. Tell me, are you in the field?" Candy stepped past Dev and offered her limp hand to Casey.

"Oh, *yeah!*" Lauren said, almost too loudly. "Casey has a fascinating job, and she just loves to talk and talk about it."

Casey nodded enthusiastically. "It would be a honor to discuss my passion with someone as accomplished as you."

Lauren turned her best Southern charm on Casey for the first and last time this evening. "Casey, darlin', maybe you could give Dr. Delaney a ride back to her hotel?"

"I'd be delighted." Casey grinned dumbly.

"Well," Dev clapped her hands together in sheer joy. "I'm glad that's settled. Jack!"

A young Secret Service agent popped into the room. "Yes, Madam President?"

"Would you please show Ms. Dennis and Dr. Delaney out?"

"But—"

"Don't worry, Jack. I'll be going back to the residence, and I doubt that Ms. Strayer is out to hurt me."

"Yes, ma'am. Right this way, ladies." The young man gestured toward the door.

Casey and Candy were so wrapped up in talking with each other that they barely mumbled a hasty goodnight to their original dates.

Lauren and Dev both held their breath until the women were gone. After a few seconds, they sighed in unison.

"Thank God," Dev mumbled.

"Amen to that," Lauren agreed.

"What does Casey do for a living?"

"Morgue attendant."

Dev suddenly took a big step away from Lauren. "Well, eeww," she teased.

Dev and Lauren started back to the residence. Dev stared at her shoes as she walked. She hated that seeing Lauren with another woman hurt. But it did. A lot, actually. She was feeling anger as well. Anger that she didn't have a right to. Lauren hadn't done anything wrong. So she was obviously only interested in Dev as a friend. *That's my problem not hers.* Dev shoved back the disappointment that stung her heart and threatened to give her away by leaking from her eyes. She cleared her throat, determined to try to salvage a little of her evening and spend it with...her friend.

"Lauren?"

"Hmm?" Lauren stopped walking and faced Dev. She looked up into eyes brimming with sadness and...something else. And she felt a twinge deep in her chest. "Are you okay?"

"Yeah." Dev smiled softly. "I, umm, well I didn't really get much to eat tonight. Don't suppose you'd like to come back to the residence with me. We could order up a couple of corned beef sandwiches and maybe watch a movie or...or...something." *And then I can torture myself all night with something I'll never have.*

Lauren felt a genuine, heartfelt smile stretch her lips for the first time that night. "I'd love to." That earned her a broad grin from Devlyn and both women started for the residence once again. "Dev, I cannot believe I was ditched by Casey!"

"I'm sorry. Did you really like her?" *Twist the knife, Dev.*

"Right," Lauren snorted indignantly. "Give me more credit than that please."

Dev sighed inwardly. Even if Lauren didn't care for her the way she cared for Lauren, she didn't want to see her friend hurt. "Yeah, well, can you imagine how I feel?" she teased. "The biggest slut I've ever met just dumped me–"

"The President of the United States," Lauren chimed in for effect, grateful that Devlyn was taking this all in stride.

A dark eyebrow rose, but Dev continued, "–for a morgue clerk. Not a great evening for my ego."

Lauren chuckled. "No. I suppose not." Dev's hand brushed hers as they walked and she wondered for a brief moment what would happen if she reached out and took it. "Can I ask you something?" she said in a soft voice.

Dev smiled, placing her hand gently on the small of Lauren's back as they climbed a short flight of stairs. "Why would you stop now? You know you can ask me anything."

"You didn't seem very surprised that Casey was a woman. Were you?" She smiled wryly. *Like I was.*

For a moment Devlyn didn't know what to say. Somehow, she didn't think it was a good idea to tell Lauren she had nearly swallowed her damned tongue. "Well, I mean, I was surprised." The words tumbled out nervously. "But what was I supposed to say? 'Gee, Lauren, didn't realize you'd gone all lesbian on me'."

Lauren slid off her glasses and tucked them into the front pocket of her blouse. "I didn't realize that I had either." She held her breath, waiting for Dev's reaction.

"See, there you go. It would have been rude for me to point it out in front of your date." *What do you mean, you didn't realize!*

Lauren laughed weakly. "Yeah, I guess it would have."

"So, um, this was your first date with a woman?" *Please don't let me be totally misunderstanding this conversation.* Lauren nodded as Dev opened the door to the living room and ushered her inside. Blue eyes widened a little. "Wow."

"Yeah, wow. I guess I've always known there was some interest there," Lauren clarified, wanting to be honest. "But this was just my first actual date...that, um...didn't include a man." She could sense Dev was upset about something and she wasn't sure if that "something" was her.

Dev grunted with satisfaction at the softly lit room and the fireplace, which was already burning. She chewed on the inside of her lip as she reached for the house phone. She was dying to hear more from Lauren, but it seemed so personal. Dev kicked off her shoes, then removed her jacket. "Yes, send up two corned beef sandwiches with all the trimmings." She paused and looked at Lauren. "What do you want to drink?"

"Beer. And since I'm being brave and asking you outright, does it bother you that I like women?" *Something is bothering you. You always chew your lip like that when you're upset.*

Dev took a deep breath. "Send up an ice bucket full of beer, too." *I'm gonna need it.* She put the phone down and put her fists on her hips. "Why would it bother me? I like women too, in case you hadn't noticed."

Lauren shrugged, her insecurity showing. "I dunno, Devlyn. We're friends, right?" She looked up at the older women with an expression so open it was nearly painful in its intensity.

Dev sighed and took a seat next to Lauren on the sofa. "I'd really like to think we are. I'm...well, I'm very fond of you." She really wanted to pull the young woman into her arms and just hold her until they both felt better. "I always have such a good time when we're together. And, God, I was so miserable tonight. Then, when I saw you, I wanted to..." *Kiss you senseless,* she finished silently. *Of course, I'd probably have a heart attack before I got the nerve up to try it. But it's still a nice thought.* "Well, let's just say I'm really glad we're here now."

Lauren let out a shuddering breath and felt every ounce of tension leave her body. "That's how I feel too, Devlyn. I just wanted to make sure that that wouldn't change after you saw me with Casey."

She pushed off her shoes and tucked her legs underneath her until she was sitting Indian style. "So, do you want me to tell you about my horrendous evening? Or would you like to start?" She leaned back, her eyes twinkling gently. *You are so stupid, Lauri. This is where you should have been all along.*

Saturday, April 10th

When her alarm went off, Lauren's hand crept out from under the comforter and she slapped it silent. Then her hand retreated back under the warm thick blankets with the rest of her body. *Wonder what it would take to keep her in bed for just one morning?* She groaned and tossed back the covers, rolling over to look at the clock. *Five a.m. on a Saturday morning. It just doesn't get any more disgusting than this.* It took a moment for her to figure out what exercise was on tap for the torture of the day it was. "Ughhh, the gym today. Thank God we're not jogging."

She briefly contemplated covering back up and playing hooky when Grem crawled up from the foot of the bed and placed his head on her stomach. "Yeah, yeah, I know, Grem. If you can't take the heat, you shouldn't be in the kitchen.

"But at least this is your favorite day of the week. In a few hours those kids will be here just begging for you to come out and play, so they can spoil you rotten." Gremlin growled contentedly as his mistress rubbed his belly. "And I've got two phone interviews set up for some of Devlyn's old high school teachers. That should be interesting, huh?" She pictured an adolescent Devlyn, all gangly arms and legs, tall, and sparkling baby blue eyes. A smile came to her lips unbidden.

Lauren gave her pal a long scratch behind the ears, trying to find the energy to get up and pull her sweats on so she could go watch Dev sweat. Not that she minded that part. She laughed softly.

Her attention was drawn away from her pooch by a loud commotion in the hallway. Not once since she had been here in residence had she heard anything like it. It sounded like the world was coming to an end. Lauren jumped out of bed and pulled a robe on over her pajamas. Haphazardly, she ran her hands through her hair and grabbed her glasses from the nightstand on the way to the door.

The hallway was teeming with dark-suited Secret Service agents. She stuck her head out and a hand reached out to stop her, until the agent recognized her and allowed her to step out into the hall.

Mixed in with the Secret Service were medical personnel. They were dragging or carrying armloads of equipment into Dev's bedroom. For a brief moment, Lauren could have sworn her heart stopped.

"Wha–" She cleared her throat and tried again. "What's going on?" She pulled her robe closed at her throat and ordered her stomach to stop roiling in protest at what her eyes were seeing.

"The President won't be going out today, Ms. Strayer. You may go back to bed if you'd like."

"I didn't ask if she was going out. I asked what was going on."

"I'm not at liberty to say, Ms. Strayer." Michael Oaks gave her a frosty smile. They had stopped pretending they liked each other a long time ago. "And even if I were, it's none of your concern."

A Secret Service agent tapped Michael on the shoulder, and his attention shifted away from the biographer.

Lauren tried to peer around the milling men, but she wasn't tall enough to see into the outer room that led to Dev's bedroom. She grabbed another agent as he shuffled past. "What is going on? Is she okay?"

He only shrugged and then continued on his way.

Gray eyes flitted from face to face, and she heard more raised, panicky voices from inside Devlyn's room. Then she did the only thing she could think of – Lauren started screaming at the top of her lungs. "Emma!" She knew that if something was wrong with Dev, the nanny would be close by.

The men around her jumped back as though she were insane. And, from the look on Lauren's face, more than a few of them were sure that that was, indeed, the case. They knew better than to touch her, however. For something like that, President Marlowe would likely have them transferred to the North Pole to guard Santa's ass.

Emma rushed out into the hallway to see what had happened now. "What in the world is the matter?" she asked, trying to grasp why Lauren was yelling at the top of her lungs.

Lauren immediately stopped and composed herself. She was a little lightheaded from her exertion. "What's wrong with Devlyn? No one will tell me a damned thing!"

"Didn't you tell her?" Emma looked to Michael Oaks. Her tone was scolding.

"Somebody tell me!"

"C'mon inside." Emma shook her head sadly. "You need to see this for yourself."

Lauren braced herself for the worst. She swallowed hard and followed Emma into the confusion.

Dev opened her eyes. *Is that Lauren's voice?* Then she saw a fair head in the crowd outside her room. A very raspy voice gave the low order. "Make way for the lady."

The flurry of motion around the bed ceased for just a moment as the doctors and nurses parted and allowed Lauren to take a seat on the bed. Without thinking twice, she took Dev's clammy hand in her own and squeezed gently. She heard the doctors talking to Dev, but only got about every other word. Her eyes and her mind were firmly focused on the sick woman.

Lauren was about to ask Dev what was wrong when a doctor said, "Madam President, we're going to start an IV." He set down two large test tubes full of crimson blood that he'd drawn from Dev only seconds before. "You're going to feel another prick."

Lauren's stomach twisted. The thought of Devlyn being impaled by a sharp object was every bit as distressing as if they'd informed her that she herself was next. Shivering, she tore her eyes away from the test tubes.

The doctor stepped forward, but was stopped dead in his tracks by Dev's grumpy bark. "Get that damned needle away from me." *Can't you see you're freaking out Lauren?* Dev's bleary eyes focused on Lauren's robe and the pajamas that were peeking out. *God, are those pink elephants on her pajamas? Could she be more adorable? I wonder what she'd think if I invited her to a slumber party.* "This is food poisoning, not the plague. I don't need any IVs." She motioned weakly toward the tank next to the bed. "Or oxygen."

Lauren cringed at the words "food poisoning", fully knowing how miserable that was, but totally bewildered by the staff around Devlyn who were acting as if she were on her deathbed. She expected the flag outside the White House to be flying at half-mast. Lauren put her face in her hand. "Food poisoning?" she breathed somewhat shakily, reassuring herself that it wasn't any more serious. She willed her heart to resume beating.

"Mornin', Mighty Mouse. You sure do know how to get attention when you want it."

Lauren smiled weakly and stroked Devlyn's palm with her fingertips. "Well, I got tired of you hogging the spotlight all the time. And I'll let the Mighty Mouse comment slide only because you're sick. All this," she motioned around the room to the doctors and Secret Service agents, "scared the crap out of me, you know."

Dev rolled her eyes. *God, people overreacted around you when you were President.* "Sorry about that. I'm not really sick. It's just a ruse to get the day off." But her pale face told a different story.

A tiny, unexpected laugh escaped Lauren's throat. "How are you feeling?" she asked gently. Before Dev could answer, Lauren hurriedly broke in, "And I want an honest answer, Devlyn."

"Been up the entire night worshipping the porcelain goddess. How do I look?"

"Like crap."

"Funny, I don't feel that good."

Lauren's brow creased with worry. Dev did look terrible. She glanced up at one of the doctors. "It's just food poisoning, right?" She knew she was being nosey, but Lauren couldn't help but worry.

The doctor, a short, middle-aged man with a bald head and

slightly protruding belly, looked annoyed that Lauren had interrupted the notes he was making on Dev's chart. He pulled two labels
from a small packet and placed them on the President's blood samples, deliberately ignoring the interruption.

Dev's brows creased, and she turned her head. "Doctor?"

"Yes, Madam President?" he answered immediately, giving Dev
his undivided attention.

"Ms. Strayer just asked you a question. It would be in your best
interest to answer her. Right now!" Dev growled, pale eyes flashing
with sudden anger.

The writer and doctor jumped, and the man fumbled with the
tubes in his hands before settling them on the tray. "The President
appears to have a serious case of Salmonellosis, which is commonly
referred to as 'food poisoning'. We believe the culprit was the
shrimp from her dinner last night. The blood work is just a precaution."

Lauren nodded slowly, trying not to lose her temper at the doctor's rudeness. *They don't owe you an explanation. Get that
through your head.* "Thank you." She turned back to Dev and
smiled sympathetically. "If you'd seen what I ate on my date last
night, you'd never believe that you'd be the one who was sick in
bed."

A nurse approached Dev with a long needle and a tourniquet
once again. "I'm sorry, Madam President, I'm afraid we need one
more sample. One of your doctors just requested another series of
tests be run." She shifted uneasily, not missing Lauren's wide-eyed
stare. "This will need to go to a different lab. That's why we need
another sample."

"Oh, all right." Dev held out her arm.

The color drained from Lauren's cheeks. "You're going
to...right now...?" Darkness invaded her peripheral vision, and her
eyes rolled back in her head as she bonelessly lurched forward onto
Devlyn.

Dev looked down at the woman who had passed out right in her
lap. She grinned tiredly at the doctor. "I swear to you, doc, this is
not the normal reaction to being in bed with me."

The doctor rolled his eyes and ordered the nurses to pull the
limp blonde off the President. Dev chuckled and told them just to
get Lauren settled next to her. The bed was queen sized and Dev
wasn't quite ready to give up her hand. It made her feel better to
know Lauren was close.

After the blood had been drawn, on Dev's orders, one by one,
the medical personnel and staff reluctantly filed out of the room.
Emma raised a sharp eyebrow at Dev and, with a nod from the President, left the door open a crack after leaving.

Then, and only then, did Devlyn bring the young woman around with a little help from an ammonia capsule. She waved the powerful chemical capsule under Lauren's nose and, after a few seconds, the shorter woman's head began to thrash. Confused eyes popped open, and she immediately sat up and looked around the room. She stared at Devlyn and then back at herself. "We're in bed together?"

Dev coughed and laughed. "Yes. But I assure you, your integrity is firmly intact, Ms. Strayer. You passed out in my lap."

"Oh, my God. I did, didn't I?" Her hands immediately went to her face, to straighten her slightly askew glasses. Devlyn's hand covered her own, and before she knew it, the glasses were slid off and placed on the nightstand. "Thank you." Lauren swallowed hard, feeling her stomach flutter, although this time it wasn't only because of worry.

Dev smiled gently. "Would you do me a favor?"

"Anything I can," Lauren answered sincerely.

Dev completely bit back the request she wanted to make and trudged on with her second choice. "Well, you see, when I'm sick, I'm like the biggest baby in the world." She smiled sheepishly. "I hate to be alone. Emma is far too busy with the children to sit here and hold my hand. Would you stay with me? We could work on the book if you like."

Lauren nodded mutely. Of course she wanted to stay. If Devlyn hadn't asked, she would have offered. "But...um..." She gestured to their half reclined, pajama-clad bodies. "Is this okay?"

Dev took a deep breath. "Well, I have to be here like this, but...well..." *I can't believe I'm saying this. She looks so damn good with her hair all mussed and in her wrinkled pajamas. But I don't want her to be uncomfortable.* "If you want to go get a shower and change, I think I can manage for a few minutes."

Lauren was vaguely disappointed, but Devlyn's words caused her to suddenly feel self-conscious. "You're right. I don't know what I was thinking coming out of my room like this. I was just worried...and−"

Dev placed her fingers against Lauren's lips. "I'm glad you did. Thank you for being worried about me." Reluctantly, she pulled her hand back, struck by the softness of those coral lips.

"But it's just food poisoning, right?" Lauren asked warily, her eyes flitting to the various pieces of medical equipment that were sitting around the room. "You'd tell me if it were more serious?"

"This is just a precaution." She yawned. "If I weren't the President, I'd be left to my own devices just like any other normal human being. They're not worried about me. They're worried about their boss."

Lauren frowned. "That's not true." *I'm worried about you.*

Dev's eyes started to grow heavy, and she wondered if the doctor had slipped a little something extra in her last dose of medication. "Sure it...is. But...you...care..." She couldn't help the fact that she was falling asleep right in the middle of the conversation. She had been up all night.

Lauren smiled softly and whispered, "Don't fight it."

Devlyn's eyes immediately slid closed and the dark-haired woman let out a slow, deep breath.

Lauren lifted their intertwined fingers, looking at them as though she had forgotten she was holding Devlyn's hand. She pulled up the covers and smoothed them around the taller woman's body, then glanced at the nearly closed door. *Do it. You know you've wanted to since you walked into the room.* "Longer than that," her mind whispered stubbornly.

Refocusing on Devlyn, she tenderly brushed the President's cheek with her knuckles before dropping a soft kiss on the warm skin. "Pleasant dreams, Devlyn. I'll be here when you wake up." Lauren snuggled back into her own side and allowed her eyes to flutter closed. A gentle peace stole over her as she dropped off to sleep.

Lauren woke well before Dev. She lifted her head and looked at the woman. Instinctively, she raised her hand and checked Dev's forehead for fever. She was relieved to find it cool, not only because she didn't like the thought of Dev being sick, but she wasn't really sure if she could tell whether she had a fever or not.

Lauren moved away slowly, not wanting to wake the President, and retrieved her glasses from the nightstand. Carefully, she climbed out of the bed and started for her own room. She paused briefly to speak the Secret Service agent and the nurse seated outside the room. "I'll be back in a few minutes. Please let her know if she wakes up in the meantime."

The nurse nodded. "Yes, Ms. Strayer."

As Lauren walked away she heard a comment pass between the people she had left behind. "Not sleeping together, my ass."

Lauren turned on her heel and marched up to the Secret Service agent and the nurse. She opened her mouth to deny the rumor, but stopped herself before saying a word. Her mouth clicked closed and her lips curved into a delighted, borderline shit-eating grin. She winked. "You don't know the half of it." Then her tone cooled. "And you never will. So instead of spending your time gossiping, why not do your jobs before you end up as a security guard at Sears and an orderly at the morgue?" *It's not like I don't know someone there now,* she thought wryly.

Squaring her shoulders, she marched back to her room, not quite believing what she'd just done. She took the fastest shower known to man, threw on her sweats, grabbed Grem up for the quickest walk of his little life and returned to her room.

Lauren gathered her notebook and her laptop together and, with a quick nod, started back for Dev's room. Just as her hand touched the knob, Gremlin began to whine. Her shoulders drooped and she pressed her forehead against the door. "Come on, Grem. Not now. Not today. Please?" she mumbled, turning around. "I'll buy you the biggest, fluffiest dog bed you've ever seen if you just behave today."

The dog was not impressed. He bounded over to his mistress and flipped over on his back, presenting his belly for a good scratching.

Lauren blew out a frustrated breath and glanced at her watch. It was still too early for the kids to be up. "Okay, you can come with me, but you have to promise to behave. Devlyn doesn't feel well. No growling at her."

The dog rolled over happily, his tail wagging furiously.

"You spoiled little, snaggle-toothed extortionist," Lauren grumbled. "C'mon. And I mean it. One growl and you're history." She pulled open the door.

A nurse was just exiting Dev's room to rejoin the agent outside the door. Lauren gave them a raised brow before she and Grem disappeared inside. After setting down her things, she moved to the bed to check on the President. Dev whimpered slightly, her head tossed from side to side. She seemed to be having trouble breathing, or she was gagging in her sleep, Lauren couldn't tell which.

"Devlyn?" Lauren peered down at the President's ashen face.

Pale eyes blinked open.

"Hey." Lauren smiled. "What's wrong?" She quickly ran her thumb over dry lips. "Is your throat sore or are you thirsty?"

The tall woman shook her head wildly and groaned piteously. "Laur..." A swallow. "You...you'd better..."

Lauren leaned in closer to hear Dev better. "What is it?"

Dev's entire body convulsed and she leaned forward and heaved, throwing up all over Lauren's chest.

Lauren's eyes went impossibly wide as warm, chunky liquid slowly slid down the front of her shirt, pooling in a great blob in her bra. She moaned, her own stomach furiously roiling at the rancid smell. "Oh, God! Ewww!" She pawed at her shirt as Dev leaned forward again, and Gremlin ran out of the room. "No, you don't!" Lauren grabbed a basin from the nightstand next to Dev's bed and thrust it in front of her just in time to catch round two.

After a moment that felt like ten lifetimes, Dev stopped retching and turned red, watery eyes on her friend. "I'm so," she paused, gagging momentarily on the taste of bile, "so sorry."

Lauren moved the basin back under Dev's chin and left it there until she was sure the President was finished.

"I can't believe I did that."

The blonde's skin itched everywhere, and she couldn't believe she'd lasted this long without puking herself. "Are you all right?" she managed, trying to hold her breath.

Devlyn nodded, too mortified and weak to do much else. "Sorry."

"It's okay." Lauren stood up, consciously not looking down at her shirt. "Nurse!" she called to the woman, hoping she'd hear her. She expelled a huge breath when the matronly woman quickly burst through the door. "Please see to the President. I need...I need to...I'll be back after I shower. You'll be okay?" She pushed Dev's bangs back from her eyes. *Please say yes. Please say yes.*

Even behind Lauren's revulsion, Dev could see her genuine concern. *You are something else, Lauren. I could fall in love with somebody like you.* "Yeah, I'm feeling much better now." She gave a weak grin. "Save time, use my shower. There are fresh clothes and robes in the closet. Take what you like. I owe you." Dev gestured behind Lauren. "Through that door."

Lauren could tell that Dev was in good hands as two more nurses entered the room and immediately got to work. They could handle getting Dev cleaned up. Which really wouldn't be that hard, considering she'd thrown up all over Lauren and not herself. Lauren needed to get to the bathroom...fast.

She stood in the multi-jet shower in Dev's bathroom. If it weren't for the completely disgusting circumstances that had brought her here, she'd be impressed by this bathroom.

It was as large as a normal bedroom, well lit, with limestone floors, polished, Italian marble countertops, and a sunken tub that could easily hold two adults. The fixtures were gold and accented the room's pale green décor. The enormous shower had benches all along its sides and sprayed powerful jets of water from four different directions.

Lauren scrubbed herself furiously. She just wanted to get clean fast. Very clean.

Twenty minutes later she emerged, dressed in a set of Dev's sweats, which had to be cuffed several times – towel drying her hair. The clothes were big, but they were comfortable and after the recent turn of events she decided comfortable was good.

Lauren reentered Devlyn's room without being stopped by the Secret Service. She stood back and watched as the medical staff tucked Dev back into bed. They took away her toothbrush and a small basin and propped her up against the headboard, putting several pillows at her back and head. Dev's bedding and pajamas had been changed and she was looking much better. Even a hint of her normal color had returned to formerly pale cheeks.

Thank goodness. Lauren approached slowly.

A nurse fluffed the President's pillow one last time. "We've given her a shot for the nausea."

"Better late than never," Lauren mumbled playfully, knowing Dev could hear her. "And thanks for doing it while I was gone." She was serious about that last part.

Soon Dev and Lauren were alone again. "So, have you used the puking thing to get women out of their clothes before?" Lauren teased. Then she took a seat on the bed next to Dev. "Next time, just ask."

Dev blushed fiercely, but quickly recovered. "Don't tease me. I'm not a well woman."

"Oh, trust me, I know. At least we can find comfort in the fact that Candy is probably barfing all over Casey at this very moment."

Both women smiled broadly at the thought.

"I know something that will make me feel even better than that." Dev's grin turned wicked. "Phone activate."

A soothing, female voice said, "Voice recognition system on. Activation code?"

"I am Devlyn Marlowe. Code: 18758OHIO6236ACA." Dev waited for the phone to verify her access code and recognize her voice.

Pale eyebrows lifted at Dev's far more sophisticated phone set up. *She's leaving it on speakerphone?*

"Call David McMillian."

Why do I think David is in trouble?

After six rings David picked up his phone.

"David?" Dev smirked when the only sound she heard was a deep groan. "How you feelin' this morning, pal?"

"I'm dying, Dev," he whined, hoarsely.

"Yeah, me too, you pain in the ass. We got food poisoning from the shrimp last night, the shrimp you insisted the cook get specially for Candy 'The Slut' Delaney."

"Ohhh, God."

Dev could almost imagine David hiding under the covers of his bed. "The doctor says it'll pass in a few days, David, but you know what?"

He shook his head unhappily and then remembered there was no video link on this call. "What?"

"You'll be in your office bright and early Monday morning."

"Yes, Madam President, you bitch."

Lauren burst out laughing and grabbed a spare pillow, pressing it against her face to muffle the sound. *Oh, God. Only David could get away with that.*

Dev chuckled. "And what will I be doing on Monday, you ask?" Dev continued cruelly. "I'll be taking the day off and spending it in bed. Just me and my body pillow." *And I might be lucky enough to continue enjoying the company of the beautiful, blonde biographer who is in my room right now. I wonder if I can make up enough stories about myself to fill up two days.* Then Dev's brain kicked into gear. *What am I thinking? I'm a politician for God's sake. No sweat.*

David let off a few more choice words that nearly had Lauren in tears.

"See you Monday. Oh, and did I mention that you can take the Secret Service on their run? They get all twitchy without it."

Another loud groan.

Dev laughed wickedly. "Phone call end. Code: 18758OHIO6236ACA." She turned to Lauren, who was shaking her head and smiling at Dev's antics. She shrugged, only somewhat guilty. "Sometimes it's great to be President."

Monday, May 3rd

Dev was whistling as she tucked a newspaper under her arm and gathered up two steaming coffee mugs. She strode out of her office with Liza trailing behind her. "I just need ten minutes alone, Liza."

"Can you live with five?"

"I'll settle for seven."

"Deal."

David met her in the hall. "Madam President?"

"Not now, David. I have a very important meeting."

Rust colored brows furrowed. "With whom?" David's mind raced. Had he missed an appointment?

Dev flashed him a grin.

The tall man rolled his eyes. "Never mind. That silly smile says it all. How long will you be, Madam President? You have a meeting with the Secretary of Health and–"

"Yeah, I know. Liza has granted me a seven minute parole from my duties as President. Go talk to Jane. She's got the job until I get back."

David shook his head. "Have a good time."

"I intend to." She smirked. *Boy, I hope Lauren's in a good mood. She sure sounded like it when I asked her to meet me.*

Dev walked quickly to her destination, waving off the small tribe that was following her. She pushed the door to her destination open with her hip and drew in an appreciative breath. The earliest of the spring roses were blooming in the Rose Garden and their sweet aroma wafted over Dev.

Lauren was sitting on a bench with her arms across the back and her face turned towards the warm spring sunlight. Though Dev could see only her profile, she could tell that Lauren's eyes were closed, but she was awake. She looked content. A grin tugged at Dev's lips at the sight.

"Morning, Mighty Mouse." Dev couldn't resist teasing the writer with her Secret Service name. She got a different reaction every time she used it.

Lauren's body remained perfectly still as she continued to soak in the morning sun and Dev's good natured taunt. "It's amazing. I hear the words, but I know no one is talking to me," she drawled calmly. "Because there is no one here by that ridiculous name."

Dev chuckled and took a seat next to Lauren, nudging her over on the bench. "Do you luuvv me, Lauren?" she asked in a playful voice. When a single, questioning, gray eyeball slowly opened and rolled in her direction, the President offered the blonde woman a cup of steaming coffee, which just happened to be in Lauren's very own red mug. It was prepared with two sugars and cream, just the way she liked it.

Lauren smiled coyly as she took the warm mug. "Thanks. And I love anyone who brings me coffee the way I like it."

Dev grabbed the neatly folded paper from under her arm and made a show of looking at it. "Huh." She set her mug on the bench and scratched her chin. "Looks like they're right then. You are cheap and easy." She handed the paper to the writer. "And cheating on me." Dev pulled a nonexistent knife from her chest. "Why am I always the last to know?" she moaned piteously.

Lauren reached for the paper. Using her hand to block the sun, she scanned the spot where Dev was pointing, which was the social column. "White House live in, Lauren Strayer, was caught rendez-vousing with her new love at Been Gi's last month." Her eyes scanned the rest of the short article, stopping on the small, unflattering photograph of her getting into Casey's car. Lauren wrinkled her nose. "God, I have no taste whatsoever. I'm cheating on you with a morgue attendant named 'Lacey'."

"It would appear so. Yes." Dev braced herself for the pending explosion, but it never came.

"Oh, well," Lauren casually tossed the paper aside and took a sip of coffee, hiding her smile behind the rim of the cup, "if you'd keep your woman satisfied, I wouldn't be forced to look elsewhere for romance."

"Ouch!" Dev clutched her heart. "And just so cold about it, too. Gee, I have all the popularity of the plague. I can't catch a damned break. My live in lover *and* my date threw me over for this Casey/Lacey woman. Who knew the morgue had such appeal?" Dev shook her head, sending her dark hair spilling over one shoulder. "Maybe I should try the other team. I'm batting zero with my own."

Lauren burst out laughing. She bumped shoulders with the older woman. "Don't tell me something in the papers finally got to you? They've been writing about us for months. And the 'other team' has its faults, too. Trust me."

"I just didn't want you to see this and explode," Dev explained sincerely. "It's just another attempt to get a reaction out of us." She leaned back and tried to act nonchalant about putting her arm over the back of the bench and dropping it down to rest lightly on Lauren's shoulders. *I am sooo pathetic.*

Lauren jerked away at the feeling of Dev's arm on her shoulder. "What is it? A bug?" She began slapping where Dev's arm had been, her eyes searching her pale green blouse.

Dev threw her head back and laughed. "Might as well have

been, the way my luck is running lately." She sighed and this time, decisively wrapped her arm around Lauren's shoulders, pulling the younger woman closer to her. "No, it wasn't a bug." She grinned devilishly and added a belated, "Mighty Mouse." *I should just gather up my courage and ask her out. What's the worst she can say – no? That wouldn't be a big surprise either. I've got nothing to lose.* "Uh...Lauren?"

Lauren blushed when she realized what Dev had tried to do and what her response had been. *Sorry, Devlyn. And I'm glad it wasn't a bug.* She happily snuggled closer. *Is she going to? Oh, my God.* Lauren crossed her fingers and toes. "Yes, Devlyn?" *Ask me before I die!*

"I was wondering...I mean...umm..." *I am six feet of pure, unadulterated chickenshit. Good thing I don't run the government the way I run my love life. If I had a love life, that is.*

Dev cleared her throat and lifted her chin. It was now or never. "Okay. What I wanted to know was–"

Liza opened the door to the Rose Garden looking slightly harried. She winced, clearly seeing she was interrupting something. "I'm sorry, Madam President."

Lauren nearly groaned with disappointment, letting off a string of curse words in her mind.

Dev's mouth clicked shut and her head dropped forward. *That was not seven minutes!*

"There is an emergency phone call for Ms. Strayer."

Friday, May 7th
The loudspeaker crackled and the school auditorium was alight with excitement, when the school principal nervously announced, "Ladies and gentlemen, students, staff and faculty of Jefferson High School, the President of the United States!"

The high school band fired up "Hail to the Chief", and Dev grinned at Liza as she stuck her notes in her jacket pocket. She tilted her head towards the drums. "Hey, they're not bad."

"No, Madam President. And they were very honored that you picked them to play for you."

Dev buttoned her jacket. "Well, for some of these kids it's a big deal." She shrugged. "Guess I'd better get out there, huh?"

This was another of Dev's many community visits. Her goal was to do at least one a month. They were already wildly popular and requests from communities across the nation had come pouring in. Thus far, however, none of the visits had taken her too far from Washington, but she had plans to change that once she'd made a complete transition into office and things settled down.

These visits were held in high schools or community centers

and were open to the public, but, at Dev's request, not televised. She wanted the most intimate setting and feeling possible and she believed this was her chance to give something back and stay connected to the people.

"Bzzz..." Liza sounded off like a cattle prod in action, just as Jane had taught her.

Dev laughed. "I'm ready. I'm ready. There's nothing after this, is there, Liza? I want to try to get home early tonight."

"No, Madam President." Pushing a few buttons, the tall assistant checked her electronic organizer and nodded. "This is it."

Dev leaned over to her assistant. "Don't suppose you've heard from Ms. Strayer."

"I'm sorry, Madam President. I haven't. I could call and have someone...?"

Dev's eyes strayed to her Secret Service agent, who was about to give her the cue to walk onto the stage. "No. That's okay. She'll call if she needs something." *Like me, for instance.* Dev inwardly cursed the Cabinet meeting that morning that had kept her from flying out to Tennessee to check on Lauren herself.

Receiving a short nod from the dark-suited agent, the President strolled onto the stage of the high school auditorium. She smiled and waved to the crowd as a thousand cameras clicked furiously, their flickering flashes illuminating the room. Dev had learned to give everyone a moment or two before she tried to speak. This time she walked back and forth across the stage, waving and making eye contact with as many people as she could.

The last time she had done one of these community visits, she'd gone down into the audience, causing the Secret Service and David to go nuts. After her Chief of Staff had lectured her incessantly, she did promise to be good.

Once the audience settled down, she took a seat in a tall stool. She smiled at the crowd and said, "Hi."

The auditorium exploded into applause.

Lauren shifted in her chair as she watched her mother sleep. Dark circles ringed the older woman's eyes and her fair hair looked thin and lifeless. They were in Nashville's St. Andrews Hospital, in the same wing where Lauren had visited her mother on several other occasions. The very hallways stirred up dark memories she'd rather forget, and, at this moment, the writer was wishing herself anyplace but here.

Earlier in the week, Howard Strayer had called and calmly explained that Anna's depression had taken a turn for the worse. Her mother had steadily been going downhill since Christmas, really, and that she had tried to take her own life.

Lauren's mother had gone grocery shopping and fed the cat before stripping naked and climbing into the cold, empty bathtub. Howard wasn't sure why, but for whatever reason, she didn't bother to fill it with any water. Using his razor sharp, fish scaling knife, she had slit both her wrists to the bone and closed her eyes, patiently waiting to die.

Anna had burst into uncontrollable, gut wrenching sobs when Howard had come home in search of an aspirin and found her still alive, bleeding profusely.

Lauren stared bleakly at her mother's ghostly white figure. The sight of her, combined with the antiseptic smell of the hospital and the stomach churning tension of the last day, made her shiver. Lauren couldn't honestly say she was surprised by the suicide attempt. The older woman had fought nearly debilitating bouts of depression all of her adult life. This was the third suicide attempt that Lauren could remember, the other two haunting her otherwise unremarkable childhood like annoying, out of place specters.

When Lauren was eight she'd walked in on her mother trying to cut her wrists. The woman was weeping and fumbling helplessly with a safety razor, whose blades she'd somehow popped free of their plastic casing. Lauren had tried to calm her, but in the end was forced to wait until her mother actually passed out from blood loss before she could get near enough to her to help.

On her second attempt Anna Strayer tried sleeping pills, but ended up vomiting before they could do much damage. The result was a killer headache and six months of institutionalization, at the end of which, she was functional. She was sent home with an armload of antidepressant drugs and, ironically, a prescription for sleeping pills...in the event that her insomnia should make a reappearance.

Those days seemed far away, even as the pain from this most recent attempt came in fresh waves. Howard had gone to the cafeteria for a much needed cup of coffee, leaving Lauren alone in the room with her mother.

Golden rays of spring sunshine poured in through the sparkling clean windows, warming the room that was painted in soothing tones of green. The writer's eyelids felt heavy, but she knew she was too wired to sleep. Instead, she sat quietly, watching over the person who was supposed to watch over her.

Lauren felt chiefly sad. But there was also anger and a crushing guilt, because a big part of her wondered if her mother wouldn't be better off finding the peace in oblivion she so obviously craved. Was it selfish to force her to continue when she so clearly didn't want to? This was no cry for help. Howard was supposed to be gone for the morning, and, unlike Anna's other attempts, this couldn't be painted as half-hearted. She had wanted to die. It was as simple and as complicated as that. Who were the doctors, or Howard Strayer, or Lauren herself, to tell her that she couldn't?

Anna stirred, slowly turning her head towards Lauren and opening her eyes for the first time since the day before. "Hi, honey," she said softly, when her gaze landed on her daughter. Anna's expression was the very picture of despair, and Lauren watched in agony as her mother's face contorted with pain as she took in her surroundings, realizing what had happened, and what the likely outcome would be.

"Hi, Mama," Lauren croaked weakly. Her chin quivered slightly, but she took a calming breath and slowly made her way to her mother's bedside. What could she say? *I'm glad you're alive, even though I know that you're not? Daddy and the doctors saved you, only so you can spend God knows how long back in the institution or spaced out on drugs?*

Anna tried to lift her arms. She looked with wide, dazed eyes at the strong bindings that strapped her to the bed. "I can't do anything right, can I?" she whispered brokenly, then turned away from Lauren, wallowing in just one more failure.

A soft knock on the door caused Lauren's bowed head to swing around.

Anna Strayer tried to sit up, confusion written all over her face. A low keening sound suddenly erupted from her throat. Why wouldn't everyone leave her alone!

"Shh...rest now, Mama," Lauren said quietly, doing her best to block out the almost inhuman noise that was hurting her ears and shredding her heart. She tenderly straightened her mother's covers, intentionally keeping her eyes away from the wide leather straps that tightly held her arms and legs to the bed, and the stark white bandages that wrapped her wrists. "I'll go see who it is."

Lauren bent and placed an awkward kiss on her mother's cheek, then headed for the door, which was already being pushed open by a heavy set black nurse. "Yes?" Lauren asked, wondering why she'd bothered to knock. They never had before.

"Ms. Strayer?" The woman's voice was deep, her thick accent drawing out each word and adding syllables where there were none.

"Yes."

"You have a phone call, ma'am. It's from the White House," the nurse said, awe reflected in her warm chocolate eyes. "The doctor said you could take it in the conference room, even though it's for staff only. You need to come now. It's urgent, ma'am."

Lauren nodded slowly, another kernel of worry blossoming in her belly. *What now?* "One second." She turned back to her mother. "I need to take this call for work, Mama. I'll be right back."

For a moment she thought her mother hadn't heard her, then Lauren noticed that the gray eyes, whose color so closely matched her own, were vacant and unseeing, staring off into space. She was awake but somewhere else. Lauren had tried to understand...tried to figure out where her mother went when she just disappeared inside herself. Tried to reach her and begged her to come home...

It wasn't until she was a teenager that Lauren fully grasped that that far away place would forever be Anna Strayer's alone. Despite her best efforts, in her heart she fully believed that there was no bringing her mother back, no helping her find her way home. Ever.

With a soundless sigh, Lauren stepped out into the hall with the nurse. "Let's go."

At the end of the corridor was a small room with a round table and six chairs, a coffee maker, and a phone with video link. That was all. *Sad conference room.*

"You can take the call in here, ma'am. When I get back to the nurse's station, I'll tell the operator to transfer it."

"Do you–?"

"I'm sorry," the nurse said sincerely. "I don't know anything more." She shut the door quietly, and Lauren wrung her hands for the thirty seconds it took for the video link to fire into life.

An image of Jane, from the shoulders up, appeared above the phone and across the small table from Lauren. The older woman's eyes were teary and lines of worry cut deeply into her forehead. "Lauren?"

Lauren paled at the expression on Jane's face. She licked her lips. "Yes?"

"I'm sorry to have to be," Jane paused for a moment to collect herself, and Lauren felt her anxiety ratchet higher. Whatever it was, it was bad. Very bad. "It's Dev...there's been an accident. No, that's not right," Jane corrected herself quickly. "She's been shot, Lauren."

Lauren blinked, staring stupidly at Jane's image, the secretary's words not quite penetrating her brain. "Wh-what?"

"Devlyn's been shot, Lauren." This time Jane's voice was firm. "About twenty minutes ago. David asked me to call you."

Lauren swallowed around an enormous lump in her throat. *Devlyn's been shot? Someone shot her? Jesus.* She felt sick. "Is she...is she–?" The blonde woman choked out the words.

Jane shook her head. "Not at last report, dear. But we don't know how bad it is yet."

Lauren's eyes fluttered closed. "Oh, thank God," she muttered softly, her stomach still roiling. "Thank God." She let out a shuddering breath and scrubbed her face with slightly shaking hands. "What happened?"

"She had a speech at a local high school today. When she was leaving the stage someone opened fire. We're still putting all the information together." Tears leaked from Jane's eyes and trickled down her round cheeks. "David wanted me to call you. He didn't want you to think...well, he wanted to make sure you didn't just hear it on the news."

"So...so, the kids were at home. They didn't see. They're okay, right?" Lauren asked in a rush, her mind desperately trying to process what she was being told. *I need to get back there. I need...*

"The children are safe with Emma and Amy. They haven't been told yet. We didn't want to tell them until we had some real news." Jane hesitated, knowing she was putting Lauren in a terrible spot just by mentioning it. But she needed to. "Should I tell David you'll be coming back? Or–?"

"No! I'll be there just as soon as I can." There wasn't a second's hesitation. She could tell her father on the way out of the hospital. "Where is she?"

"David will send someone to meet you at the airport. They'll take you to her then. Her location is classified. They'll be doing a press announcement in about five minutes."

"Classified? Shit! Fine. I guess I'll come into National. I'm not sure when." Lauren rubbed her temples. "And I'm not sure what airline. Maybe I can book a private plane or–" She was starting to panic.

"Lauren, calm down, dear. I'll make all the calls. Just go to the airport. We'll get you to her no matter what. I'll call you on your cell phone and let you know where to go."

Lauren nodded furiously. "Okay, okay. I'm leaving right now." She jumped to her feet, swaying a little as her knees threatened to give way. Lauren was on her way out of the room before she realized she hadn't said goodbye . She turned back to Jane. "You tell Devlyn...well...just...you tell her not to do something stupid like die, okay? I'll be there as soon as I can, Jane." Without waiting for a reply, she ran out of the room, leaving Jane to hear the fading sound of her pounding footsteps as they echoed down the hospital hall.

David stood at the front of the limousine, pushing his hands in and out of his pants pockets over and over again as the private jet he'd arranged to pick up Lauren taxied to a stop. He'd just gotten off one of the worst and most emotionally draining phone calls of his life to Janet and Frank Marlowe, who weren't home when he tried to contact them immediately after the shooting. David wondered if he had any ass left at all. And now it was time to face Lauren.

She'd made it from the hospital in Nashville back to Washington, D.C. in just a little more than three hours. The jet door burst open and Lauren jumped out, toting a small carry-on bag. She broke into a dead run for the thirty or so yards it took to reach the Chief of

Staff.

She was panting by the time she reached David and skidded to a stop. *Please don't let me be too late. No, David wouldn't be here if she were...* "David! Is–?"

He waved her off, indicating that the press hounds were waiting nearby, their cameras snapping away and recorders waiting to pick up any part of the conversation. The world had simply imploded since the announcement had been made. The press was everywhere, dogging every move every White House staffer made, and looking for hidden meanings behind every activity or decision. Geoff Vincent was on the television at this very moment, calming down the nation and doing his best to appear utterly Presidential.

David pulled open the limo door and hustled Lauren inside the car. The door had barely slammed shut when the car jerked forward, a police escort clearing their path. He took a seat across from her. The first words out of his mouth once they were alone were, "She's alive."

Lauren let out a shuddering breath and said another prayer. A wave of anger assailed her, overwhelming her and guiding her actions before she could even savor a moment of relief. She leaned forward and poked David in the chest with a furious finger. "Where was all her security, David?" The volume of her voice increased with every word. "They were supposed to protect her!"

Guilt clouded his eyes. "Lauren, she was shot leaving the stage. They reacted quickly, exactly the way they're trained to. They got her out of there and to the hospital. They caught the assassin." His jaw clenched. "You know as well as I do, if someone is determined enough, nothing will stop him!"

Lauren lowered her hand, but her posture remained challenging. "Those sound like nothing but excuses to me. If they were doing their job, they would have gotten the assassin *before* she was shot!" She slumped back in her seat with her arms crossed. Lauren knew she was being unreasonable. That she was lashing out at someone who didn't deserve it. David loved Devlyn and would do anything in his power to keep her safe. Lauren was furious, and she felt like she was losing the tenuous control she had over her emotions. It was too much at the same time. Her mother. Dev.

David took a chance and moved next to Lauren who remained deathly still. He could see she was trembling slightly and he wrapped his arms around her, pulling her against his shoulder. "Have you cried yet?"

Lauren violently tried to shove him away, unable to stand the closeness, not wanting to let go of the fraying emotional thread she was clinging to.

But David didn't move. He was as solid as a rock.

Lauren's pushing soon gave way to weak pawing, punctuated by ragged, pained breaths as the writer fought more with herself than David. "I...don't need...to..." She tried to grind out the words between clenched teeth, but her speech was interrupted by her quivering chin and by broken sniffles she foggily realized were her own. She felt long arms tighten around her and she sank into their warmth and comfort. Another sniffle and the dam simply broke. Lauren buried her face in David's chest and began to cry in earnest. For everything.

"That's it. Get it all out. It's okay," he soothed softly, knowing damn well that he'd be doing the same thing in his wife's arms tonight. "Get it out before we get to the hospital."

They traveled several miles before the hot tears began to slow and Lauren began to hiccup.

David blew out a deep breath. "I'm gonna tell you something she'll kill me for later, but you need to know. In the ambulance, it was you she was calling for."

"Real-really?" Lauren sniffed, wiping her eyes with the clean, white handkerchief David pressed into her hand.

He nodded, backing off a little to give Lauren some breathing room so that she could compose herself. "Really. She wanted you. She only relaxed after we all assured her you were on your way back."

Lauren wiped her face one more time and expelled a shaky sigh. *God, I needed that.* "Thank you, David." Her eyes conveyed her true regret and she reached out and squeezed his forearm gently. "I'm so sorry. I shouldn't have said those things, especially to you."

He laughed quietly, though there was no humor behind it. "What do you think the first thing I said was? Only I wasn't very nice about it." He rolled his neck and shoulders, popping the joints. "It's been a long day. Okay, do you want me to fill you in before we get there, or do you need more time to just let it all soak in?"

Lauren shook her head. "No. Tell me now so I don't fall apart at the hospital." She turned a watery smile on David. "Instead, I'll just fall apart – again – here with you if I need to."

He gave her a reassuring grin. "That's what I'm here for. I've got broad shoulders." David placed his hand over the one Lauren had resting on his arm. "There were four shots and Dev was hit three times. Once in the hip, once in the shoulder, and one grazed her head." He stopped when he saw the color drain from Lauren's face. *Poor kid. It's been a helluva couple of days for her.*

Lauren's eyes widened and she swallowed against a wave of nausea. "Three times? My God," she breathed. Lauren shivered and wrapped her arms around herself in mute comfort. She pinned David with shiny, determined eyes. "Is she going to be okay?"

David nodded. "With rest and lots of help from her friends, yeah, she's gonna be fine. She got out of a couple of relatively minor surgeries to repair the damage about an hour ago. They went very well. Dev is a strong woman."

He wrapped his arms around Lauren and she didn't resist his reassuring touch. "When you see the video, it'll seem worse than it really is; scalp wounds like to bleed a lot. The shoulder wound was clean and the bullet traveled clear through. The bullet had to be removed from her hip. She's going to need a lot of TLC and therapy to get back on her feet. And if her bout with food poisoning was anything to go by, boy, is she gonna be grumpy. She's not accustomed to being inactive and I would imagine we are going to have our hands full."

Lauren wiped her eyes with the back of her hands. "As long as she's okay. She can be as grumpy as she wants."

David's real laughter rang out for the first time all day. "You and I are talking about the same Devlyn Marlowe, aren't we? You know how she gets. You think you're ready for that?"

Lauren chuckled along with the Chief of Staff. "Umm...well." She scratched her forehead. "It sounded good at the time. But you're right, this is Devlyn we're talking about. So *nobody* is ready for that."

David lowered his head to give her a very serious look. "She cares for you, Lauren." There was more to it and he knew it. So a second later he added, "A lot. She's going to need you now. Need your friendship." He searched to gauge her reaction.

Gray eyes brimmed with tears again. She straightened David's wrinkled suit coat and smiled warmly at the man she had coming to regard as a friend. "Don't you worry, David. She's got that." *And a lot more.*

Dev's nose began to twitch as a familiar fragrance washed over her senses. It was so faint that it was barely detectable, but it was an aroma easily recognizable even in her drug-induced stupor. *Lauren's perfume.* Dev forced open impossibly heavy eyelids, blinking with exaggerated slowness. "Is...she–?" Her voice was scratchy, and her tongue felt thick and unresponsive. She licked dry lips to moisten them. "Is Lauren home yet?" She tried to look around the quiet room, but her mind was in a murky haze brought on by painkillers and the lingering effects of anesthesia.

Dev felt the bed move slightly and the heat of another human being press up against her. Her cool, limp hand was lifted and cradled by two, smaller, warmer ones. "Hiya, Wonder Woman," a soft, Southern voice burred. "I can't leave you alone for a minute, can I?"

Devlyn tried to wrestle the silly grin off her face as she blearily focused on Lauren. "Hey, Mighty Mouse. Know what?"

Lauren ran her fingertips down Dev's cheek. *She's okay. She's here.* "What, Devlyn?"

"Morphine is my friend. And I luvvv your accent. Did you know that it slips out more when you're not thinking? It's so sweet." She giggled, for some reason finding that incredibly humorous. "There's just so much about you..." Her rambling paused when her eyes began slipping closed.

Tears filled Lauren's eyes again, even as she blushed. "Thanks," she chuckled weakly. Her fingertips gently moved up to trace the bandage circling Devlyn's head. *How that must have felt.* The dilated eyes that tried so valiantly to maintain contact with hers were confused, but hopeful. They held none of the soul weary despair of her mother's and Lauren was able to draw a sharp contrast between the two hospital room scenes, having been in this same position only hours before.

The President's eyes opened and rolled up slightly to track Lauren's hand. "Don't worry, sweetheart, it's too tough to do any real damage." She licked her lips again and tried to knock on her own head to demonstrate its hardness, but her hand fell limply to the bed after valiantly lifting a few inches. Which was okay, Dev decided, because she had already forgotten why she was raising it. She let out another small laugh and then began to mumble just loud enough for everyone to hear. "Have I mentioned lately how beautiful I think you are?" A dreamy expression crossed her face.

Lauren's gaze flickered around the room, lighting on indulgent, smiling faces. Her blush deepened. "Oh, God," she muttered, raising her hands to her cheeks to feel their flaming heat. "Devlyn, um...you know we're not alone right now, right?" she asked in a low voice. But even in the midst of her embarrassment, a smile formed unbidden on Lauren's lips. *Sweetheart? She thinks* I'm *beautiful?* She nearly swooned.

Dev still couldn't focus her eyes clearly, but she could hear the smile in Lauren's voice. "Yeah, so? I'm never alone. That's part of my problem." She took a deep breath. "Do you have any idea how nervous you make me? I babble like an idiot when I'm around you."

"No, you don't," Lauren lied. Her tone was mildly scolding, but there was a playful edge there as well. "You're perfectly charming and you know it."

David, Jane, and several Secret Service agents politely turned away from the women's conversation, feeling very much like they were intruding on a private moment.

"How are you feeling, Devlyn?" Pale brows drew together at the sight of Dev's multiple IVs and the machines monitoring her heart rate, blood gases, breathing, and a host of other things Lauren didn't pretend to understand. She had mentally prepared herself the best that she could, but it was still so hard, seeing someone she cared about hurt.

When the President didn't answer she continued, "You scared the crap out of me again, ya know?" Lauren cocked her head to the side and smiled at her friend's vain attempts to keep her eyes pried open. This was second time she'd seen Dev flanked by hospital equipment. "That's becoming a habit I don't much care for. We need to work on that."

"Didn't mean to..." Dev wanted to apologize for scaring Lauren. She didn't want to do anything that would upset the young woman, but words began to go fuzzy in her mind. She grumbled like a petulant child trying to fight the irresistible call of sleep. Her mind drifted helplessly, but she felt better with the warm body perched on her bed.

Lauren patted Dev's chest comfortingly, carefully avoiding her heavily bandaged shoulder. She leaned close to Dev's ear and placed a gentle kiss on her cheek before crooning softly, "Sweet dreams, darlin'. I'll be here when you wake up."

Monday, May 10th

The agent outside Dev's hospital room door gave Lauren a small, slightly irritated smile as he went in search of some caffeine. His replacement was already standing in place alongside the President's door in Bethesda's Naval Hospital. When Lauren entered Dev's room, she was greeted by the sound of frustrated voices.

"I don't want to wait!" Dev rasped.

Lauren could hear the taller woman fighting to catch her breath, even before she could see her. "I want to see it now, David!"

"Madam President—"

"Cut the Madam President bullshit, David. Order in the video link before I have to call someone else in here to do it!"

"But—" David tried again.

Lauren stepped around the Chief of Staff to see Dev struggling with her IV tubing and a host of wires as she futilely tried to get more upright. "Jesus, Devlyn." Lauren rushed to her side. "Are you crazy? You're going to tear your stitches!"

Dev seemed to calm almost as soon as soon as she saw Lauren. "Help me, then."

Lauren immediately reached out to take Dev's hand. "I don't understand. What's the matter?" She set to untangling Dev's IV tubing, cursing mildly at the mess the President had made. *Why didn't she call a nurse if she wanted to sit up? Or ask David?* Lauren fished around for the bed controls, which ended up being on a detachable panel on the side of Dev's railing. *Just how old is this bed?*

"I want to see the video of the shooting." Devlyn was breathing hard and shooting daggers at David. "But some people don't think

I'm ready."

Lauren pressed a button and slowly raised the back of the bed until Dev nodded. "'Some people' are probably right, Devlyn. The recording isn't going anywhere. It's been less than three days."

Dev turned her stare on Lauren, whose cheeks were tinged pink from the cool, spring air and whose hair smelled like flowers. "Oh, don't you go rebel on me too! I am still in charge around here!"

Lauren flashed a look at Dev that was part irritation and part trepidation. "You're going to insist on doing this, aren't you?"

"I shouldn't have to insist, I should only have to ask." She glared at David again, who threw his hands into the air disgustedly.

"Then I'm staying too," Lauren insisted, her tone making it clear that she wouldn't be dissuaded. Every single cell in her body told her that she did not want to see the recording of Dev being shot. But if Dev ever needed a friend to stand by her...this was the moment. Lauren swore to herself that she wouldn't fail her. *But please don't let it be too horrible.* She took a deep breath. *How could it not be horrible? Somebody shot her three times!*

"Fine! I give up." David picked up the phone and made the call.

Dev glanced at Lauren and gave her hand a little tug to bring her down to sit on the edge of the bed. "I don't want you to see this." *I don't ever want to see you sad.*

A tiny crease appeared on Dev's forehead, and the writer had the strongest urge to smooth it away. Lauren's determined gaze softened as she looked into Dev's eyes. "And I feel exactly the same way about your seeing it."

"Yeah, but I need to see it. If for nothing else, so I'll know what not to do next time." Devlyn chuckled humorlessly, wincing as a burning bolt of pain shot through her shoulder and hip from the movement. "I guess not getting hit would be a step in the right direction."

David's gaze dropped to his shoes. Though intellectually he knew he had done everything he could to keep this from happening, he still felt like he'd let down Dev and her kids. He sighed...and Lauren and the entire damned nation.

Lauren squeezed Dev's hand. "You know I'll have to see it eventually. Let's get it over with together." *She needs you to be strong. Don't get sick or start crying like some pathetic baby again.*

In only a few moments everything was ready and Dev had ordered the room cleared of everyone but Lauren. She leaned a little closer to the writer. "You ready?" The younger woman's nod seemed hesitant and Dev briefly considered simply calling the whole thing off and waiting to view the video disc after Lauren had gone home for the day, but Lauren was right. She would have to see it eventually for the book anyway. At least now they'd be together. "Um...Lauren, this is a combination of several recordings that were running at the same time and have been put together for the best angles. These weren't made for television. The Secret Service films all my public appearances for security reasons. But what happened, the shooting part, is unedited. You know that, right?"

Lauren kept her voice even and her eyes focused straight ahead, though her words were slightly strained. "I know."

Dev gave a short nod. "Start disc."

Lauren found herself taking in a deep breath and holding it when the image came to life in front of them. She smiled at Dev, standing on stage in her dark slacks, tan shirt and camel hair jacket, which was a few shades darker than the shirt. The applause in the auditorium died down and Dev perched on a stool to address the students.

"Who called you and told you what had happened?" the dark-haired woman asked quietly, her mouth near Lauren's ear, but her eyes on the unfolding scene.

Lauren licked her lips, remembering Jane's pale face and shaky voice. "Umm...Jane," she replied softly. "Jane called me."

The President nodded. "She was a good choice for the job. Jane always holds together, no matter what." Dev briefly remembered getting word about Samantha's accident. It was Jane who had broken the news.

Lauren nodded, her attention split between Dev's real life voice, burring quietly in her ear and the image of Devlyn at the foot of the bed. "She was great."

Dev's grip on Lauren's hand tightened as the video continued to play. With a start she realized she could be hurting the smaller woman, though Lauren hadn't mentioned it. She loosened her grip and patted the slender hand before regretfully resting her palm on her own thigh. Dev immediately felt the loss and balled her hand into a fist.

Lauren had been so busy over the past couple of days she hadn't spent a lot of time thinking about the exact circumstances of the shooting. She'd spent countless hours at the hospital and, at Dev's request, made sure the children knew what had happened and weren't scared out of their wits. Though she wasn't convinced she had been completely successful on that front. The kids had already lost one mother. The looks on their little faces when Lauren told them Devlyn was in the hospital nearly broke her heart. Thank God for Emma, who immediately stepped in to help when Lauren began to flounder.

Lauren watched the video with intent eyes, scanning the shots of the crowd for the crazy boy who had tried to kill Dev. But no one looked out of place. Everyone seemed happy and excited that the President had made time for them in her busy schedule.

"Where is he?" Lauren whispered to herself, frustrated that she couldn't spot him right away. *A killer should be immediately recognizable, shouldn't he? He should...well...look guilty, sinister, something.* Lauren knew it was a ridiculously naïve thought, but she couldn't help thinking it. It would make things so much easier. "I always foreshadow in my books," she mumbled.

Dev turned away from the playback. "What? Pause disc," she ordered in a louder voice. "What did you say?"

Lauren frowned. "I don't see him anywhere. The camera is panning the audience, but I can't spot him."

"Well, if he'd been that easy to spot I'm sure the Secret Service would have picked him up before he got off four shots. I don't know for sure which one he was either. But the shots came from the center of the audience just as the crowd began to applaud when I was about to get off stage." Dev waved a hand in the direction of her frozen image. "Let's skip all the boring stuff about how my DNA Registration legislation could help capture criminals on the loose." She chuckled. "Funny that in this case it wouldn't have mattered either way. The shooter had never even had as much as a speeding ticket."

Lauren smiled weakly, not quite able to enjoy the irony that Dev seemed to. She could feel her stomach turning into a solid knot of tension and her palms growing sweaty. Her heart rate picked up in anticipation of what was to come and she unconsciously leaned closer to Devlyn, reassuring herself that she was here. That she was alive.

"Disc playback advance." Dev's eyes scanned the events as they flew by at five times their normal speed. She moved her hand slowly, letting it come to rest on Lauren's arm, stroking gently. "Halt. Regular play."

They watched together as Dev made a few parting comments and cracked a joke that had the students laughing and clapping. Then she gave a short wave and turned to leave. The band hadn't even cued up again before a well-dressed teenager, who had only seconds before been smiling and applauding like everyone else in the audience, stood and yanked a gun from the back waistband of his pants. He held it straight out and screamed, "Die, bitch!" as he pulled the trigger four times, with a brief pause between the third and fourth shots.

Dev flinched when the shots rang out. She watched with an odd sense of detachment as her body recoiled and blood began pouring from her shoulder, hip, and face. The last shot, the one that hit her head, dropped her instantly.

Lauren's entire body jerked with the loud crack of the pistol. Her stomach lurched and her heart jumped to her throat, the raw pain of the moment shocking her for several dazed seconds. She had known it was coming. Yet that still hadn't prepared her for witnessing Dev's body recoiling violently, then crumpling to the ground from the vicious impact of the shots. "God, Devlyn," Lauren whispered. She squeezed her eyes tightly shut just as a warm arm wrapped around her shoulder and pulled her close.

Suddenly, the camera angle changed, and the image of Dev on the stage was magnified to a close up. The sound quality was slightly worse because the background noise had risen to a dull roar, but it was still focused, allowing the viewer to hear every raspy, ragged breath Dev took.

"God..." Dev groaned, reaching up and smearing away the blood that was dripping into her eyes.

Three agents immediately descended upon her, using their bodies to shield her as several more Secret Service members tackled the boy in the audience and disarmed him.

The camera angle shifted again, this time to an overhead shot. Michael Oaks was the first member of the President's staff to reach her side.

"They got the shooter. The Chief of Staff and Vice President Vincent are being notified, Madam President," Michael explained worriedly as an agent pressed his suit coat jacket into Dev's shoulder to stop the bleeding. Dev gasped.

Lauren sucked in a quick breath in response to seeing Dev's pain.

"The kids...?" Dev winced as two men rolled her onto a backboard.

Michael looked out into the audience, which was being herded out of the auditorium like spooked cattle. "They're fine, Madam President. No one else in the auditorium was hit."

"My children?" Dev's eyes closed as she struggled to move her left arm, but found it impossible.

"They're fine too. The Nest has been notified and all security precautions are being taken."

Devlyn opened her eyes and focused on one of the agents who was pressing a thick pile of bandages against her hip. "Bad?"

"No, Madam President." The agent leaned over and whispered to her, "This is nothing for Wonder Woman."

Dev blinked and they were moving. Her confusion was evident and she looked as though she was going into shock. "Mighty Mouse..."

Lauren burst into tears at the sound of her Secret Service name.

"It's okay," Dev whispered. "It all turned out all right." The President's men had done everything right. They had covered her and gotten her out of there more quickly than she remembered. Although, to be honest, she couldn't remember much, beyond a searing pain in her hip and shoulder and the smell of her own blood.

Then the video simply stopped after Dev's gurney was wheeled away, freezing on a shot of the bloodstained stage. Dev's gaze dropped to her lap and she concentrated on that day. "That boy. I remember him. He...he kept smiling at me."

"You remember him?" Lauren turned in her friend's loose embrace so that she could see Dev's face. The President had watched with little more than a flinch, though Lauren didn't miss that her face was slightly paler than when the disc began. "Out of that entire crowd?"

"Yeah. He was right there. Smiling at me. Listening to me. Watching me." Dev shook her head. "Hell, I thought he was interested in what I had to say."

Lauren's anger mounted as she imagined the teenager biding his time, waiting to murder Dev, smiling as she tried to connect with him, just knowing that he was going to kill her. *Little bastard!* She turned away from Dev and was struck again by the image of the bloodstained stage. "Jesus." She pointed at the image. "Can you...?"

"I'm sorry. Image off." Dev looked to Lauren, who looked like she was going to throw up. "Are you all right?"

Tears filled the blonde's eyes again. "I-I..."

"Hey," Dev said softly as she reached out and cupped Lauren's cheek in her palm. "I'm okay. I might leak when I drink now, but I'm okay," she joked.

This time Lauren did laugh through her tears. "Okay," she sniffed. "You're right. I'm sorry for being a baby."

"Don't be sorry." *God, Dev. You haven't even asked about her mother. What kind of a lousy friend are you?* "How's your mom?" She felt Lauren stiffen. "Do you need to go back to Tennessee to be with her?" Her heart went out to the younger woman.

Lauren pulled away a little, suddenly uncomfortable. "What, um...what exactly do you know about my mom?" She eyed Dev warily.

"I know what happened, Lauren. And I understand if you don't want to talk with me about it. I mean, I'm not family." *She's been here for me these last few days when her heart is probably back in Tennessee.* "If you want to talk, I'm here, okay?"

Lauren nodded, but continued to pull away. She wasn't ready for this discussion. Especially not now. Not after everything that had just happened with Dev. Lauren felt like she was on an emotional roller coaster, and, while a big part of her wanted to talk about it with someone, she just wasn't ready.

The blonde woman's father hadn't understood her leaving Anna to come back to Washington, D.C. She'd tried to explain that Devlyn wasn't just part of her job, that she was a good friend, but that hadn't worked either. They'd had a horrible argument in the hospital, and, despite the fact that she wasn't close to either of her parents, her father's parting words had hurt her more than she'd thought possible.

The writer grabbed a tissue from the stand next to Dev's hospital bed. "I don't need to go back." She wiped her eyes. "There's nothing I can do back...there." Dev remained silent, but Lauren could tell she wanted to know more, and her chest constricted at the prospect. The room began to close in on her. Air. That's what she needed. Clean air, without the scent of disinfectant. She needed to be *out* of the hospital.

Lauren nearly jumped from the bed, startling Dev in the process. "I...um...I'm going to tell David we're finished here." And without looking back she bolted across the room and flew out the door.

"Lauren! Wait!" Dev cursed inwardly when the shorter woman disappeared out the door. She wanted to follow her and try to apologize for upsetting her. She wanted to hold her and tell her everything would be all right.

Dev groaned as she pushed herself forward and a jolt of pain shot through her hip. She dislodged her heart monitor in the process and the room was suddenly pierced with a shrill beeping noise as an alarm sounded.

Several doctors burst through the door with David right alongside them. His eyes shut in pure relief when he saw that Dev was all right. "Oh, no you don't!"

"David," Dev grunted as she swung one leg off the bed. Another blast of pain made her feel lightheaded.

Jane joined David at Dev's bedside and after several moments she and David were finally able to wave off the panicky medical staff. "You can't get up, Dev!"

"Lauren—"

"Lauren is a big girl." David eased the President onto her back and carefully repositioned the leg she still had hanging off the bed. "She'll be back, Dev."

Devlyn had asked David to keep tabs on Lauren's mother. And what David had learned did not make him happy.

Apparently, everyone in the hospital had been talking about the very public argument between Lauren and her father. The old man had yelled at Lauren as she'd left the hospital. Screaming for everyone to hear that if some woman she'd barely known for a few months was more important than her own damned mother, that she didn't need to bother coming back home – ever.

David let out an unhappy breath. "Dev, she's been through more than you know. Give her some space."

Dev settled back into her bed with an angry sigh. "She's going to be okay, because I'm going to make sure of it." She looked up at her Chief of Staff, determination glinting harshly in pale blue eyes. "Sit down, David. I think you've got something to tell me."

June 2021

Tuesday, June 1st

Dev sat with her head bowed. She was panting slightly as her physical therapist stood back and made notes on the President's chart. The therapist was young and fit and a rising star in his field, having earned glowing recommendations from Devlyn's leading physicians. The man took a breath and girded his mental loins before turning back to face the tall woman straddling the weight bench. They were about two-thirds of the way through their rehabilitation routine for Dev's shoulder and hip and he could clearly read the lines of exhaustion and pain on his patient's face. Things were about to get ugly.

"Madam President?"

"What?" she growled, not bothering to lift her head. Sweat was dripping from her forehead and chin onto the vinyl covered bench between her legs.

"We need to do another set to work your arm." The therapist looked up to see Lauren slipping quietly into the room.

Lauren closed the door behind her and motioned for the man not to alert Devlyn of her presence.

"Don't want to." The President shook her head, grimacing at the bolt of pain even that small movement caused her stressed muscles. "We're done for the day."

"Ma'am, you have a routine that we need–" He ducked just in time for a small water bottle to sail past his head.

"Fuck the routine! I said we're done for the day!" Dev's shoulders slumped even further. "Now leave me alone," she whispered, ignoring the twinge of guilt she already felt over her outburst.

Lauren cleared her throat, causing two sets of frustrated eyes to swing her way. "Hi. It's Julio, right?" The blonde extended her hand to the therapist. "I'm Lauren Strayer."

The young man smiled and moved several steps towards Lauren to take her hand. "Nice to meet you, Ms. Strayer. I was just on my way out. I'll be outside if you need me."

Lauren watched as the therapist made a hasty exit. She decided to ignore Dev's mini-meltdown. Lauren had been meaning to come to one of Dev's sessions earlier, but something always seemed to come up. *Be honest, Lauri. You don't want to see her in pain. And you don't know what to say to her after tearing out of the hospital like an idiot a couple of weeks ago. You're embarrassed to face her in private.*

The writer slowly padded to a bench near Dev and sat down.

She studied the President carefully. Other than a quick initial glance, the older woman hadn't even acknowledged her presence. Dev's face was flushed and drawn and it was clear that she was hurting. Lauren's thoughts turned to Dev's would-be assassin, Louis Henry, and how his actions had affected so many lives. *The little bastard.*

When it was clear that the President wasn't going to say anything, Lauren blew out an unhappy breath. "Hello, Devlyn," she drawled softly. "Are you finished for the day?" She cocked her head to the side. "Liza said you'd be going for at least another half an hour or so."

"Liza was wrong." Dev self-consciously wiped her eyes with the back of her hand. "That's the beauty of being the President. I can tell people to fuck off and they actually have to do it."

Lauren sat up a little straighter at Devlyn's choice of words. "I see," she answered seriously. "And does that include me as well?"

Dev shot Lauren a contrite look and shook her head. "No."

Lauren watched as the President tried to make a fist with the arm that had been injured. She couldn't do it. "I'm just so tired." Her voice was resigned. "And it hurts a lot."

Lauren had to sit on her hands to keep from literally reaching out for Dev. She wasn't sure it would be welcomed and she was already treading on dangerous ground. "I know it does. But there's something else I'll bet you didn't know."

"What?" Dev reached for her sling and looped it over her head.

"You're the strongest person I've ever met." Unable to stop herself, Lauren stood up and moved behind Dev, carefully tugging long hair out from under the sling's strap. "And you're not a quitter." *Okay, this is where she blasts you for not understanding what she's going through.* Lauren closed her eyes and waited.

"I'm not as strong as you think, Lauren. I've been through an awful lot and I'm just damned tired. I only want to go to my room and go to bed."

Okay, that didn't work. "And you can go back to your room and take a nap." She waited until she saw Dev's head bob before adding firmly, "Right after you finish your physical therapy."

Dev looked up. "Excuse me? What happened to the 'Fuck you' factor?"

Lauren raised an eyebrow and gave Dev's sling a little tug. "It was just trumped by the 'Lauren factor'. Go figure. Don't make me get tough with you, Devlyn. Southern women are relentless and you'll lose eventually." Gray eyes twinkled.

Dev stared at her for a moment. Lauren was serious, but the words still held a teasing edge. It was something she'd missed sorely in the past few weeks. "I knew somewhere along the line I'd find someone who had the trump card. I always figured it'd be Jane or

Emma though." Dev visibly squared her shoulders and lifted her chin. "I guess I should apologize to Julio for being a royal bitch, huh?" She eased her arm into the sling.

"It couldn't hurt, Madam President." *Way to go, Devlyn.* "I'll go tell him you're ready to continue."

"'Kay. I'm not going anywhere. Umm...thanks." Dev sat stock still as Lauren walked away. She wanted Lauren to stay, but a bigger part of her didn't want Lauren to see her like this. Weak. Miserable. A disgusted look crossed Dev's face. Most of all, she just wanted this day to be over.

Lauren paused at the doorway, waiting for any reason, any word from Dev that she wanted her to stay. After a few seconds she swallowed hard and opened the door. "The President is ready to continue her therapy, Julio." She smiled at him sympathetically. "Thank you for being so patient."

The man blushed and stared at his sneakers. "No problem, Ms. Strayer. That's my job." He glanced back up. "She's really hurting."

Lauren's brow creased with worry. "I know."

He inclined his head toward the gym. "You coming back?"

"Nah." Lauren pursed her lips before pushing her glasses up higher on her nose. "She doesn't need me." *But I wish she did.*

David entered the debriefing room just as the video of the assassination attempt ended on a freeze frame shot of the bloody stage floor. He shook his head. *Why do they always stop it at that very second?* His temper flared and angry brown eyes flickered around the room, landing on each man and woman before moving on and glaring at their next target.

"How in the hell did that happen!" He pointed at the video image. "Would somebody like to tell me why the President of the United States is currently undergoing physical therapy to heal her three bullet wounds?" David bolted across the floor and slammed his fists hard on the long table where the agents sat. "Well?"

The silence was deafening and not a single agent could meet David's glare. He angrily tugged at his tie and unbuttoned the top button of his shirt. "Get comfortable, ladies and gentlemen, because no one's leaving this room until I have the answers I want," he boomed.

Several agents flinched.

David took his jacket off and tossed it onto a chair. With quick, angry tugs he rolled up his sleeves. "I want to know how a fifteen-year-old kid got a gun in the first place. How he got it into that high school." David's already red skin tone turned an angry shade of scarlet. "And how he managed to get it and himself in perfect position to kill the President of the United States! Goddammit, I want to know *why* he did it!"

An older man at the end of the table drew in a deep breath and rose to his feet before speaking.

David's jaw worked. "Yes, Agent Rothsberg?"

"It was a hate crime, sir," he stated tentatively.

"Speak up!"

"A hate crime, sir." His voice was a little more solid this time. "The suspect tried to shoot the President because she is a woman and a lesbian." The agent pushed a file towards David, sending it sliding down the glossy tabletop.

"He didn't try," David barked, "he *did* shoot the President. Several times!"

The agent nodded quickly. "Yes, sir. All the information we have is in there." He pointed to the file David was now holding. "That's the latest intelligence."

David picked up the file and thumbed through it. "He very nearly succeeded in killing her." The Chief of Staff continued to chastise as he read. "Which one of you in here wants to have to confess that it was on their watch that the President of the United States got killed? Because if we continue to be this sloppy, that's exactly what's going to happen!"

David yanked an empty chair out from under the table and gracelessly plopped down in it, his nose still buried in the file. "Hell, it's been almost sixty years since Kennedy died. I guess most of those guys are dead now too. Trying to fill their shoes? You all had better hope that the investigation proves that kid got lucky." He closed the file. "Because if I find out any of you were lacking in your sworn duty to protect the President, or that you in some way made the attempt possible..." The rest of the threat remained unspoken, but was crystal clear.

Deep brown eyes traveled to every face in the room. All David saw was sadness, embarrassment, and regret, which actually made him feel a little bit better. For now he could believe that the kid had gotten lucky. This couldn't happen again. Somehow, someway, they would find where they had made their mistake. There might not be a second chance.

"Disc rewind," David commanded. "Okay, kiddies, here we go again. We're gonna watch it over and over again until I know where everyone was and what they were doing when our President was struck down. Disc start."

Friday, June 4th

Dev groaned as she eased herself back down into the bed and propped her cane against the wall. Her hip still hurt like hell and she missed not being able to run or work out. She wondered if anyone would be surprised when she pulled her sling off and choked several people with it. *Probably not,* she mused silently, knowing full well she could be a bitch on wheels when she didn't feel well. Since she'd lost her cool with her physical therapist, she'd tried her best to rein in her frustration. Maybe she'd only choke one person.

She sighed as the warm sun spilled into the room through the tall windows that stretched from floor to ceiling. Devlyn was recovering in the Solarium, which also happened to be another one of her favorite rooms in the residence. Ironically enough, it was in this very same room that President Reagan had recuperated after being shot some forty years before.

The room was on the third floor of the residence, its location making it quiet and affording it a privacy that was generally lacking throughout the rest of the White House. Its décor was contemporary, shades of white, creams, and ivory. An entire wall was a window with four enormous paned panels that allowed generous amounts of sunlight to filter in unimpeded. The Marlowes used the Solarium for a reading room or a place where Dev could do some light paper work while the children used the large, airy space to play.

Devlyn's gaze lazily strayed out the window. *Well, I'm the first American President of this century that someone hated enough to try to murder. Too bad it was some woman/lesbian hating punk that did it. He doesn't even care about my politics!* Her ego squawked indignantly.

Liza strode in through the open door and past two Secret Service agents so she could drop a pile of folders onto a table next to Dev. "If you feel up to it, Madam President, you really need to look through these and sign off on them."

Dev snatched up the first folder, happy to be able to wallow in something besides self pity. "I'd be happy to do that. I'll have them for you by dinnertime."

Liza smiled. Jane had insisted she give Devlyn something to do so she'd stop terrorizing the entire White House staff. As usual, the President's long time secretary knew best.

"Lauren's gone to get the kids. We're going to spend a few minutes with them in here." *Or at least I am. I dunno if Lauren will stay. Seems like since I got shot she's almost afraid to be around me. Not that I can blame her. Who wants to walk next to a target? I might as well have a big red bull's eye tattooed on my ass. And then I had to go and pry into her family's private affairs. If she wanted to talk to me about her mother she would have. Good going, moron. Fuck. So much for ditching the self-pity.*

"That's wonderful news." Liza looked at her watch. Ever since she set up Lauren with Casey, she'd been avoiding the writer like the plague. She'd heard from Emma that Lauren was after her "no good Yankee ass". Liza wasn't quite sure what that meant, but she was pretty sure it was bad. Very bad. At least Casey was happy. She and Candice Delaney were getting married in the fall.

Liza handed Dev a pen and looked nervously towards the doorway. "Should I have the call from the British Prime Minister transferred up here?" She began edging her way out. "It's a social call, but he may want to discuss the State Dinner coming up in September for His Majesty."

Dev nodded absently. "Sure. I'll probably spend the rest of the afternoon in here. So transfer everything up here that's not classified."

"Yes, ma'am." Liza turned to leave as the children came barreling in and skidded to halt just before they crashed into their mom's bed. She scooted around Ashley, purposely avoiding Lauren's evil gray gaze as they passed each other just outside the room. Liza winced when she heard a growl. *Gremlin or Lauren? Does it matter?*

The children were careful to mind their mother's injuries but still gave her enthusiastic hugs and kisses before settling down with coloring books and crayons. Ashley's Secret Service agent, Amy, joined them on the carpet, leaving Dev and Lauren to talk quietly.

Dev tilted her head towards her children. "I wanted to thank you for taking extra time with them these past few weeks," she said in hushed voice, noticing that Lauren had taken a seat in the center of the couch instead of closer to the end and nearer to the bed.

Lauren twisted uncomfortably on the cushion. Devlyn had already thanked her for this very thing. Several times. They'd never discussed her bolting from Dev's hospital room several weeks before, and ever since then things between them had been – she sighed inwardly – strained. Dev was on pins and needles around her; she wasn't doing much better. Their brief conversation during Dev's therapy session three days ago had been the most they'd spoken all week.

Silences that were once comfortable now felt uneasy. And at this very moment, it was painfully obvious that Devlyn was making small talk to avoid one of those silences. It was equally obvious that it was a strain for the older woman.

Lauren chewed her lip. This was her fault. She glanced apologetically at Dev. "I haven't minded spending the extra time, Devlyn." It was the truth. "The book will be better because of it. And I lo...I mean...your kids are great."

Dev couldn't stop the grin that transformed her face. "Thanks. They're all crazy about you. Except for Christopher, that is."

Lauren leaned forward and frowned. "Really?" Her gaze darted to the tow-headed boy sprawled out on the carpet. She looked back at Dev helplessly as her mind raced for what could have possibly happened that she didn't know about. They always got along great! "But...but..."

"He's not *just* crazy about you," Dev clarified, "he's madly in *love* with you and asked me the other day if you were married."

Lauren laughed. "Wow. You had me worried there. Did you tell him I'd be available when he gets legal?"

Like hell you will. Dev smiled. This was going better than she'd hoped. The banter that had been missing over the past few weeks was edging its way back. She hoped. "I most certainly did not. I want grandchildren and by then you'll be—"

"Not that many years older than you are now!" Lauren crossed her arms over her chest and narrowed her eyes.

"Yeah. An old lady!" Dev winked and they both laughed softly.

Devlyn was determined to keep the conversation going. "From what I can squeeze out of David, he seems to think the book is going great so far. But he keeps threatening to reveal a few really embarrassing stories if I don't behave and do all my therapy." Her face colored when she remembered the last time they were together. "He always was a blackmailer at heart, and if he'd seen how I behaved the other day in the gym he'd have kicked my sorry ass."

Lauren made a face but didn't disagree.

"I'm sorry."

"You don't have—"

Dev stopped her with a stern look.

Lauren grinned and ducked her head graciously. "Apology accepted, Devlyn." Her gaze dropped to her lap for a moment before she changed the subject. She looked a little nervous. She wasn't sure how Dev would feel about the personal interviews she wanted. "Speaking of my progress on the book, I...um...I think I've done all the background research I can do from the White House."

Dev's suddenly felt her heart stop and her throat close up tight. So much so, as a matter of fact, that she was having trouble breathing and had to clear her throat and take a drink of her coffee before she could speak again. She wondered briefly if her panic was showing on her face. *God, she's gonna leave! She wants to move out. Think of something quick!* "Ahhh..." Dev's mind went absolutely blank for all of a horrifying second. "How about a chance to meet my parents?" she blurted out, a little faster and a lot louder than she meant to, but she didn't think her heart could take losing Lauren right now. *Maybe in a few weeks when I feel better, but not now. Please, God, not now. I can't lose her, too.*

Lauren's brow wrinkled and she stood up and crossed over to the bed. She hesitated for only a moment before sitting on its edge. She wanted to pat Dev's leg or hold her hand, but she didn't. Instead, she trapped her hand under her own leg to keep it from roaming. "What's wrong, Devlyn?" Her concerned voice was soft and warm and made the President want to burst into tears.

"I-I...umm...was just thinking that, after everything that has happened, maybe a vacation was in order. My folks own a beautiful little cabin back in Ohio and we could have a few days off. The kids could see their grandparents and we...I mean, I...uh...well, we could get some rest and peace and quiet if you wanted to go with us. And my folks could be interviewed for the biography." Dev took a chance and let the back of her fingers graze Lauren's leg very lightly. If Lauren was going to leave, she wanted to have every possible memory she could get.

At the word "Ohio", Ashley excitedly jumped up and ran to Dev's bedside. "Grandma and Grandpa! Can we? Please, Mom? That would be great! Can we take Gremlin with us?"

Dev patted her little girl's back. "Yes, sweetheart," she chuckled. "We'll go see them. But we can only take Grem if Lauren goes with us." The President smiled unrepentantly, knowing she was putting Lauren on the spot, but willing to use any advantage she could.

Lauren's lips quirked. "Very sneaky, President Marlowe. You know your kids get their way with me nearly as much as Gremlin." She tried not to laugh as Christopher, who was now standing at the foot of Dev's bed with Aaron, nervously tugged at his glasses, waiting for her answer. Then she blinked. *Did he pick that up from me?*

Before Lauren could answer Dev, Aaron trotted over and climbed up into her lap, turning blue eyes that rivaled his mother's on the writer. The little boy, like his best buddy Gremlin, had no shame whatsoever when it came to manipulating Lauren. "Please," he asked pathetically.

Lauren's head dropped forward and her shoulders started to shake with silent laughter. She was outnumbered and couldn't care less. "Yes!" she crowed, happily. "Yes, Gremlin and I will come."

The children cheered and Aaron jumped off Lauren's lap to go play with his brother. His work here was done.

Lauren turned back to Dev, who was grinning like a Cheshire cat. She leaned into the fingers that were still lightly pressed against her thigh. "I'd love to talk to your parents. I've been meaning to ask David about the possibility of a phone interview. But seeing you with them and talking to them in person will be so much better." *She needs this. We all do.*

Dev still had dark circles under her eyes and she'd lost weight over the last few weeks. She was still the most beautiful woman Lauren had ever seen, but the shooting and stress had taken an obvious physical toll. "I think we could both use a vacation." She grinned. "I'd love to get out of the city for a while." *With you.*

Dev's answering smile caused her to laugh out loud. Suddenly, her eyes took on added depth and she lowered her voice so that only the President could hear her. Lauren hesitated and glanced around the room, gauging their level of privacy. "We need to have a talk soon though, okay?" She inclined her head, waiting for Dev's reply.

"Okay." Dev nodded, suddenly apprehensive. "Anything you want. Whenever you want it." She licked her lips. "Lauren, if I've done something to upset you, you'd tell me now, right?"

"No, I wouldn't," the blonde replied seriously. "I'd rather do this alone."

The knot in Dev's stomach tightened. "Son of a–" she stopped when she realized that the kids were only a few feet away. The phone rang and she let out a frustrated grunt, before giving the appropriate codes. "Activate phone."

The image of the British Prime Minister took shape. "Madam President." He looked around and smiled. "I hope I'm not interrupting some family time. I was just concerned for you. How are you today?"

Devlyn went into full Presidential mode. "Well, to be honest, Prime Minister Hawkins, I've had better days. But I'm hoping things will turn around soon. And how are you and your family?"

Friday, June 11th

Dev, with the help of her cane, walked slowly down the hall. This was her first day back in the Oval Office after being shot. Geoff had taken up an enormous amount of slack, further solidifying in Dev's mind that he was the right running mate and Vice President. But even from her hospital room she'd been performing most of her duties as Chief Executive.

David and Sharon had done a wonderful job of keeping the press updated, and she was currently enjoying an approval rating near sixty-five percent. *Damn, if he'd hit me with that fourth bullet I'd either be dead or at eighty percent!*

"Good morning, Madam President." Jane was already on her feet when Dev entered the outer office, having heard the rhythmic thumping of her cane as Dev progressed down the hall. Jane smiled and handed Dev what would be her first of six or seven cups of coffee.

A few feet behind Dev came Liza, her nose stuck firmly in her electronic organizer.

"Good morning, Jane." Dev did her best to smile despite the throbbing pain in her shoulder and hip. "Would you come into my office for a moment, please?"

"Of course."

The three women entered but Liza broke away from the other two, taking the mug out of Dev's hand and setting it on the President's desk. She immediately went to work on her half-day schedule, pounding away on her organizer with one hand while writing in

Dev's leather bound appointment book with the other.

Dev turned to Jane when the door clicked shut. She stepped forward and gave the woman a hug. "Thank you. Thank you for being a rock for my family once again, Jane. I don't know what I'd do without you."

Jane, who was never big on emotional scenes, gave Dev a quick hug and then pulled back. "You'd leave your own head lying about if David, Emma, and I didn't keep it fastened there."

The President rolled her eyes but quickly acquiesced. "You're absolutely right."

"And now Liza has earned her place on the roster as well, Devlyn. That girl doesn't earn nearly enough money for chasing around after you like she does."

Dev's eyebrows jumped. "You're right *again*. I should send her some flowers, don't you think?" she asked in a whisper.

"What a grand idea, Madam President," Jane whispered back with a grin. "I'll get right on that."

"Thank you." Dev turned toward her desk, then paused. "Oh, and, Jane?"

"Yes?"

"Why don't you get yourself one of those ugly cactuses you like, too."

Jane huffed, "I may get two. And expensive ones at that!"

Dev grinned and shook her head as she listened to the older woman leave the Oval Office. The President gingerly settled down at her desk, taking time to look over her schedule and sip her coffee. "Liza, where did Lauren rush off to this morning? Do you know?" She propped her cane up alongside her desk, out of sight.

"Yes, ma'am." Liza winced inwardly at the mention of the writer's name. "Ms. Strayer had several meetings on the Hill today. Doing interviews for the book with the Congressmen and Senators from Ohio, I believe."

"God, I hope everybody is in a good mood up there this morning," Dev mumbled as she signed her name to several documents. She paused, staring long and hard at the paper in front of her. "What the hell is this? A grocery list?"

Liza peered over Dev's shoulder. "It's the suggested menu for the State Dinner, Madam President."

"Ah, well give this back to the Social Secretary to go over. If Michael Oaks has any questions, have him direct them to Jane or even Beth McMillian. They make much better stand-ins for the First Lady than I do. Besides, as long as they don't serve sauerkraut, I don't care what we eat."

Liza's eyes widened. "I'll meet with Jane immediately."

Dev chuckled. "You do that, Liza."

The young woman took the file from Dev's hand and handed her a half a dozen more.

Dev glared at her, but there was no real heat behind the look. She lifted a single dark eyebrow. "You get a perverse pleasure out of doing that, don't you?"

Liza smiled. "I refuse to answer that question on the grounds that it might incriminate me."

"Oh yeah? Well, you haven't looked at your watch in at least ten seconds."

"I don't need to look at my watch to know that you have precisely four minutes until the Chief of Staff and the Special Prosecutor arrive."

The smile slid from Dev's face. She sighed and dropped her head forward onto her desk. "Do I have to?"

"Yes, ma'am, but look at it this way. Today is the last day for a week. This time tomorrow, you, the children, Ms. Strayer, and the McMillians will be on your way home to Ohio for a much deserved vacation."

"This is true. Tomorrow night, Lauren will no doubt be treated to my mother's pot roast."

Liza bit back a smile. *How many times has the President already mentioned Lauren this morning?* "Is it good?"

Devlyn read over another paper before answering. "I never said that." She signed her named, never looking up.

Laughing, Liza excused herself just as David and a tall, dark-haired man entered the Oval Office. David moved over to Dev's desk and leaned forward, bracing his hands on the desk's edge. "Liza looked pretty happy. Glad to see you haven't lost your ability to make people laugh."

"That was pity, my friend. She knows we're having dinner with my folks tomorrow night."

David's eyes grew wide and he crossed himself. Twice. "Is your mom cooking?" He gulped. "If she is, I need to tell Beth to pack the antacid."

"Well, that's the threat currently hanging over our heads, old buddy. Her world famous pot roast. And don't even think of backing out now. You know it would hurt her feelings." She closed the last folder and looked up at the man quietly waiting behind David. She started to stand, but David motioned her back down.

Dev grunted her thanks and interlaced her fingers. "So, gentlemen, I take it you're here to discuss the prosecution of a fifteen-year-old boy."

"Madam President," David began, "this is special prosecutor William Miller."

"Mr. Miller." Dev extended her hand, they shook formally, and then the President gestured. "Please have a seat."

The slim, clean-shaven man unbuttoned his suit coat and carefully dropped into one of the wingback chairs that sat in front of Dev's massive desk. David was already in the other one. "Thank you, Madam President."

Dev pressed an intercom button. "Jane could you have someone—"

"Send up a tray of coffee? It's on its way, Madam President."

"Of course it is. I'm sorry I doubted you, Jane."

David winced at Dev's *faux pas*. Jane *never* forgot coffee and cookies.

"It's the painkillers. I forgive you," Jane chuckled from the other end of the intercom.

"Thanks so much." Devlyn looked at David who gave her a disapproving look. "Can I help it if I'm addicted to coffee? That's got to be why Emma makes me drink a glass of milk every night. She's trying to coat the hole in my stomach." She leaned back in her chair, took a deep breath, and studied both men seriously. "So tell me what's going on with this young man."

"We intend to prosecute him to the fullest extent of the law, Madam President," Miller stated authoritatively as he removed a file from his briefcase.

"What about the people who put the gun in his hand and taught him how to use it?" David took one of the files offered to him, flipping through it. "A boy doesn't materialize a handgun out of nowhere. He stole it, bought it, or it was given to him. He had help."

Miller nodded. "We are looking for accomplices, sir. But so far we haven't come up with anything on that particular front yet."

"Good. Because I want everyone who had a hand in this brought to justice."

Dev crossed her arms. "David?"

"Yes, Madam President?"

"Suppose he did it on his own. No law against being a bigot."

"But there is one against attempted murder," David shot back. "And where'd he get the gun? That person is responsible too, Madam President."

Special Prosecutor Miller broke in. "The gun was purchased on the street. It's been traced back to a small police department in Wyoming where it was stolen from an officer who was shot and killed in the line of duty. The gun is a complete deadend."

"Jesus." Dev let her head drop. "The gun has quite the history doesn't it?"

"Yes, ma'am, it does."

"You know," Dev said. "That gives me an idea." She reached over and scribbled a note on a pad.

"Your ideas can be dangerous, Dev," David mumbled. "Don't forget we're going on vacation tomorrow."

"I'm not." Dev looked back up. "Mr. Miller, if the boy is prosecuted what kind of sentence can he expect to get?"

"Life."

She blew out a disgusted breath and closed her eyes. "Such a waste." *He's not that much older than Ash. And his whole life is probably over.*

"Dev, what that boy tried to do to you...well, it isn't that different from what Ted Harris did to Sam." David shifted uncomfortably in his chair. He knew he was hitting below the belt by mentioning Samantha, but he could tell Dev was on the verge of doing something stupid, like publicly coming across as soft on what Louis Henry had done. It was one thing for her to appear sympathetic to the boy's parents, to his brothers and sisters, and the community that helped raise him. It was quite another for her to openly act as though what he did could be forgiven. If she did, she'd be opening the door for every nut in the world that wanted to take a potshot at the President.

Saturday, June 12th

Lauren nervously wiped her hands on her jeans, shifting from one foot to the other as she stood outside the President's office on Air Force One. They'd been in the air for forty-five minutes and she'd finally mustered her courage, knowing that she couldn't put off this discussion with Devlyn for much longer. This had already been a month in coming and that was way too long.

Despite the fact that things seemed to have improved over the last few days, their friendship was still suffering and she wasn't sleeping well because of it. Lauren hadn't realized how much she counted on the little intimacies between them until this awkwardness sprang up, robbing her of something she'd come to want...maybe even need in her life. She felt foolish and guilty. Their relationship was slipping between her fingers like fine grains of sand and she was letting it happen. *No more. I need to put this right.*

Taking a deep breath, she lifted her hand and gave the door three light raps. There was no answer. She tried a second time. Still nothing. *That's odd. I know she's in there.* Taking a chance, she quietly turned the handle and peered around the door. "Devlyn?"

Dev was lying asleep on the sofa with Lauren's very first Adrienne Nash novel fanned open on her chest as her gentle snores filled the room. The blonde's eyes softened and her heart swelled with affection as she took in the sight of the President sleeping curled up on the sofa, her chest rising and falling in a slow, even pattern.

Lauren started to retreat when Dev cried out quietly and her eyes began to working beneath closed lids. "Don't," she whispered.

"Please."

The writer hesitated for only a second, before clicking the office door closed behind her and crossing the room. She knelt on the floor next to Dev. "Devlyn," Lauren soothed. "It's okay."

Dev's arms began to thrash and she knocked the book that was lying on her chest onto the floor. "Please don't," she whimpered again as her breathing increased and she began to struggle weakly.

The urge to touch Devlyn was too strong to ignore. Lauren reached out and laid warm hands on Dev's arms, using her thumbs to stroke soft skin. "Everything is just fine, darlin'. You're not alone. It's only a dream." The thrashing stopped at once, and the older woman's short breaths began to lengthen and even out again.

Lauren gnawed her lower lip, wondering what Dev's nightmare was about. *Samantha? The shooting? Or something else perhaps.* She smoothed a dark lock of hair off Dev's forehead, careful of the still healing pink scar that ran along the left side of her temple. *So close.*

In this quiet, semi-private setting, with Devlyn asleep, Lauren felt comfortable indulging herself. She studied Dev's relaxed face carefully, her eyes lovingly tracing every line and contour. *God, you are so beautiful.* Her gaze dropped to full, red lips and she felt herself drawn closer. A shock of pale hair tumbled forward and Lauren tucked it behind her ear as she leaned in and allowed the light scent of Devlyn's shampoo and skin to wash over her senses. *I need to kiss her.* The familiar thought came unbidden. Only this time a sense of urgency was attached. *If I don't kiss her, I'm going to die.*

An unexpected patch of turbulence caused the plane to lurch slightly and Dev's face twitched and her eyes fluttered open. She blinked, mildly alarmed until the face so close to hers came into focus.

Lauren immediately pulled away, her heart hammering in her chest. *Oh yeah. I was going to do it. I was going to kiss her!*

"Hi." Dev's voice was rough with sleep. She leaned forward a little, rubbing her eyes with one hand and bracing herself with her good arm. "What are you doing in here?"

Lauren immediately stumbled to her feet. "I'm sorry," she said in a rush. "I knocked and there was no answer and—"

"Lauren," Dev stopped the younger woman's stream of words. Before Lauren could escape, Dev reached up and grabbed the writer's hand, holding it tightly. She sat up all the way, her eyes searching around for her book. "I'm glad you're here."

Lauren reached down and fished it off the floor, wordlessly handing it to Dev.

Dev shrugged. "I was just reading."

Lauren chuckled at the deep creases the sofa had made on one of Dev's cheeks. She decided not to mention the nightmare since

Dev didn't seem affected by it. "I can see that." Lauren waggled her finger at Dev's sleep-marked face. "I hope that isn't a reflection of the story."

"Oh, no!" Dev corrected her quickly, flushing slightly. "The first one is still one of my favorites." With a slight groan, she threw her feet over the edge of the sofa, making room for Lauren. She patted the cushion next to her in invitation.

Butterflies began to flutter wildly in the younger woman's belly. *Apologize now, you coward, before another minute goes by. And then just kiss her.*

"So," Dev prompted, knowing that Lauren was here for the private talk she'd alluded to in the Solarium. She purposely didn't let go of Lauren's hand and her body tensed in reaction to Lauren, who did not look happy.

"Yeah." Lauren exhaled slowly. "So."

Dev lifted her jaw. "What have I done to upset you, Lauren? Please tell me. Things haven't been the same between us since that day in the hospital." *And it's killing me.*

Lauren's shoulders slumped and she restlessly picked at the couch's navy colored fabric. "You didn't do anything. I just..." She swallowed. "I just—"

"Are mad at me?" Dev ventured, bracing herself for Lauren's anger.

"No!" Lauren's brow furrowed and she shook her head. "It's me, not you."

Dev's lips formed a thin line. "Me, not you," she muttered. *That's sounds like the kiss off. She can't break up with me! We're not even together...like that.* "What does that mean...exactly?"

Lauren licked her lips, letting out a slow breath. "It means you didn't do anything wrong. I need...um...I need to apologize for running out on you in the hospital." Lauren felt a pang deep in her chest when she thought about what she'd done. "You needed a friend and I just ran away," she admitted softly. "I'm so, so sorry."

"Hey." Dev scooted closer to her companion, though there was already almost no space between them. She forced herself not to flinch as she lifted her arm and wrapped it around Lauren's shoulder. It had only been out of her sling for a few days and she still had weeks of physical therapy to go before it would be back to close to normal. "You don't have to apologize. I've been worried about you."

Lauren voice was full of self-loathing and she pulled away from the comforting embrace. "But I just left you after you sat through that horrible video!"

"That doesn't matter." Dev pulled her back.

"It does matter, Devlyn!"

"No, it doesn't. And if I'd known that's what was bothering you, I would have made that clear weeks ago."

Lauren's watery gaze lifted to meet Dev's and she found only genuine curiosity and concern shining in those pale blue eyes. There wasn't an ounce of anger. Or worse yet, the pity she feared she'd find. "I see you every day and I still miss you."

At the sweet words, Dev found herself gulping back tears. "I miss you, too."

"That day I was embarrassed and ashamed." Lauren paused and then added, "And tired and angry."

"Angry?"

A blonde head nodded. "When you told me that you knew about Mama, it suddenly felt like you were spying on me. It was like all my family's dirty laundry was being paraded in front of you whether I wanted it to be or not."

Dev winced at the truth of the words. She'd known Lauren was having trouble adjusting to life in a fishbowl. And her actions, though started with only the sincerest of intentions, hadn't helped much. "I-I...didn't mean for you to feel that way. I was worried about you. I only had David check into things so I could help." Dev's gaze dropped to her lap. "I didn't mean to pry. I just wanted to be able to help if you needed me, but..." *I couldn't go with you when I wanted to. I couldn't be there when you really needed a friend.*

"I know." *God, how can I explain this?* "But it's so hard. Mama...my mother...I mean..." She paused to let out a frustrated breath. "If I'd been thinking straight I would have assumed that you'd find out what happened." Lauren winced, seeing flashes of her younger self and slashed wrists and a pool of dark crimson blood spreading across the floor in her mind's eye. "It's so personal and ugly what she tried to do."

"It's hard." Dev swallowed back the pain of her next admission. She'd never lied to Lauren and she wasn't about to start now. But this went beyond that. Her political mind wanted to say "off the record", but she believed deep down that Lauren wouldn't betray her trust and that that kind of lack of faith on her part would seal a future for herself *without* Lauren. Dev's face was deadly serious, but her voice was still even and soft. "Some people just can't fight the urge. They want to escape. Lauren, I'm going to tell you something I've never told another living soul." She could feel the weight of Lauren's expectant stare and slender fingers threaded themselves tightly between her own. Devlyn looked the smaller woman square in the eye. "When Sam was killed, I thought about it." Dark brows creased in thought. "I didn't know how to deal with the loss. I wouldn't...I couldn't find a place for the anger and pain and it started to overwhelm me. I couldn't breathe without it hurting. Every heartbeat was painful." The tears welling in Lauren's eyes nearly made her stop, but she didn't. "Somehow, after a long while, I found a way back. Through my children. But some people just can't fight."

Lauren squeezed her eyes shut. She had trouble picturing the strong woman beside her giving up on anything. Then she remembered the video image of Dev testifying at Theodore Harris' sentencing hearing. Only one word came to mind. Broken. She was broken. But somehow, someone had fixed her. Or she'd fixed herself. "But I can't help Mama," Lauren whispered in anguish. "I've tried! My whole life I've tried and nothing works. I'm not enough." *Nothing is ever enough.*

Oh, Lauren. Don't do that to yourself. "Sweetheart, you've helped her even if you don't know it. By growing up into such an intelligent, generous woman, by being there for her when she needed you, and by trying your best. Sometimes people just can't help what they do or how they feel. If you want, we'll hire new doctors to see her. They can try to help her. Maybe there is a new technique or medicine or–"

"She's got the best doctors I could find. My royalty checks are enough to see to that." *Sweetheart?* She let the word soak deep down inside her, soothing spots made raw by worry and fear. *She hasn't said something like that to me since she was in the hospital.* "I appreciate your offer, but I don't think there's anything you can help us with." She squeezed Dev's hand. "Other than continuing to be my best friend."

Lauren sniffed, then smiled when she heard Dev doing the same thing. They were quite a pair. "After I ran out of the hospital, I felt like I wasn't enough to help you either. All you were doing was being kind to me. But all I could think about was running away." Lauren reached up and wiped away a shimmering tear that was hanging suspended in the corner of Dev's eye. "I'm so sorry about that," she whispered. "And especially sorry about being too embarrassed to apologize sooner." *Say the rest!* "Things between us have been awkward and I don't like it. I, um..." A breath. "I want to hold your hand...a lot...and I can't do it if we won't sit by each other." She held her breath and waited, praying that Devlyn felt the same way.

A brilliant smile edged its way onto Dev's lips and she instantly saw its echo on Lauren's. "So," the President shrugged a little, hoping to lighten the mood and barely able to keep herself from jumping up and down like a little kid. "Sit next to me. I don't bite." Her expression turned playful. "I'll even give you a hug if you need one. And my hands are *always* free to be held."

Lauren nodded shyly. She lifted their linked hands. "We're halfway there. But how about that hug?"

"Okay." Dev used the arm lying loosely across Lauren's shoulder to pull her closer. "This is not a bug," she teased. "This is me hugging you. I don't want any confusion." She eased her arm around

Lauren's shoulders and pulled her close. When Lauren was pressed tightly against her, both women let out long, shuddering breaths. Dev rested her cheek atop strands of fair, wavy hair. "I know we're not done talking about the privacy issue. But maybe we can take things a little bit at a time, you know?"

Lauren murmured her agreement against Dev's collarbone. "I won't let things get so out of hand again. I promise." She sank into the warm embrace, not thinking about what it meant or where they were going, just accepting the affection and comfort Devlyn was offering and doing her best to return it in kind.

"But you know what else?"

"Mmm?"

"Nash still needs a girlfriend."

Lauren began to shake with silent laughter.

Then Devlyn felt the softest of touches graze the hollow of her throat. She went completely still and her eyes fluttered closed. *Oh God, she's kissing me!*

Lauren pressed her lips against the soft skin again, marveling at the tiny tingles that chased their way up and down her spine and the flood of warmth that flowed through her veins like a strong wine, heating her from within. The feather light kisses were painfully intimate and it felt so good to finally be showing Dev how she felt, how deeply she cared for her, that Lauren had no intention of stopping yet. She leaned forward and barely brushed Dev's throat with her mouth and felt the dark-haired woman's pulse pound wildly in response.

The plane lurched again, sending Lauren a little sideways and interrupting the perfect moment. Dev drew in a breath to speak and the writer pulled back a little, tilting her head up and regarding Dev seriously. "No." Her voice was gentle but insistent. Lauren brought up both hands and gently cupped Dev's cheeks, enjoying the warm, smooth skin against her palms. She stared deeply into panicky eyes tinged with desire and affection. "Nothing is going to interrupt us again. Okay?" A tiny bit of insecurity popped through but was quickly quashed by Dev's response.

The taller woman let out a shaky breath and nodded once, tilting her head and pressing her cheek more firmly against Lauren's steady but delicate touch. She fell willingly into warm gray eyes that were so full of honest friendship and devotion that Dev's chest constricted at the sight. "Okay," she croaked softly, honestly surprised she could speak, considering her heart felt like it was going to burst the confines of her chest at any moment. She already felt lightheaded and they hadn't even really kissed yet. *Please don't let me pass out now.*

Lauren smiled shyly and licked her lips to moisten them. With a tiny tug of her hands, she drew Dev's face to hers. "I've been wanting to kiss you for forever." Dev's warm exhale caressed her lips and she forgot the rest of what she was going to say.

The President's eyes slid closed when as light as a feather, impossibly soft lips brushed against her own, and then settled more firmly there. A moan escaped from deep in her throat and she threaded one hand in Lauren's hair, holding her gently in place as she returned the kiss. Lauren's mouth was soft; inquisitive lips were setting her on fire. The younger woman let Dev set the pace of their heartfelt exploration and Devlyn felt like her entire body had been placed on a slow burn.

It lasted a long, sweet moment, not stopping until tentative tongues had reached out and tasted what both had been wanting for so long. Finally, Lauren began to pull back, slightly breathless, but Dev surged forward and nipped at her bottom lip, tugging it into her mouth in a move that earned a gasp and then a low, sensual groan. But the high intensity of the moment quickly shifted when Dev began nipping and teasing with her teeth until both women were laughing.

This time it was Dev who loosened the fingers she had threaded in Lauren's hair, but before she could pull completely away, Lauren exacted her revenge by surging forward and passionately kissing Devlyn into insensibility. Her initial fears had melted away and now she acted on pure instinct, letting the rightness of the moment sweep them both away and easily deepening the kiss. She swirled her tongue around Devlyn's until the taller woman began to whimper. *God, yes!* Lauren's mind cried. This is what she wanted. It was the desire and hunger that lurked behind every touch, every innocent glance, and tender gesture. And now she was tasting it.

Lauren felt her body responding, as much to the sounds she was evoking from Dev as to the wonderful touch she was receiving. Her belly was beginning to clench as a combination of rampant hormones and adrenaline sang through her blood. When they finally parted, she drew in a deep breath, slightly dumb-founded and more than a little giddy. Lauren happily smiled and Dev's face immediately flushed a bright red. The younger woman laughed.

"That was...um..." Dev searched for the right words with slightly wide eyes.

"That was wonderful, Devlyn, and I wish we would have done it ages ago."

The President was nodding before Lauren could finish her sentence. She sighed with relief, still a little tongue tied from the effects of the mind-blowing kiss.

Lauren smiled again, finding Devlyn's bashfulness, mixed with pleasure and a good dose of nerves, utterly charming. "I think, considering that I'm the one who's never done that before...with a woman, that is, that I'm the one who is supposed to be scared witless." She reached up and with the very tip of her finger traced the delicious mouth that was already beckoning her back with its softness.

Dev grinned then nipped at Lauren's finger. "You would think that, wouldn't you?"

The pilot's voice came over the loudspeaker, informing the plane's passengers that they were making their final descent into Port Columbus International airport and that they were advised to buckle their seat belts.

Devlyn stood up and pulled Lauren up with her. Together they moved to two side-by-side seats that they could buckle into.

"I think we've got some things to talk about on this trip, Lauren," Dev said seriously, but her twinkling eyes gave away her utter delight with the turn of events.

Lauren couldn't stop from beaming as she happily settled into her seat. "I think this is going to be one hell of a vacation."

As they traveled toward Dev's family home. Lauren was struck by the familial feeling that pervaded the back of the limo. Emma and Amy sat across from her and Dev. Ash was sound asleep with her head in Emma's lap, Christopher was slowly nodding off in Amy's arms, and Lauren looked down at the little boy in her own lap. She couldn't resist placing a tender kiss on Aaron's forehead as he slept in her arms. Even Gremlin seemed content to nap on the floor of the limo, only rolling over occasionally to offer a growl. He had taken to waiting for Dev to growl back, which she always did.

Dev reached into her pocket and took out a small bottle of pills. She dropped one into her palm and replaced the cap. Taking a bottle of water from the holder she was about to take a drink when she caught the look that Emma was giving her. "What?"

"Do you need that?"

"It's ibuprofen, Emma. Nothing serious." She glanced sideways at Lauren and felt compelled to offer an explanation. Her gaze dropped to the bottle where she fiddled with the lid. "Umm. This is not something that ever went public, but after Samantha was killed," she hesitated and then finished in a rush, "I had a small problem with sleeping pills." She chanced a look up at Lauren, whose eyes held no censure. "But I don't anymore."

"I'm glad you don't anymore," the writer said softly, gently bumping Dev's good shoulder with her own. Lauren grinned when Dev dropped her free hand down, wrapping long fingers around smaller ones. Devlyn was so different from anyone else she'd ever met. She was always brutally honest about herself. Even though this was something that she'd managed to keep in the family, she knew that if someone asked Dev about it, she'd tell the truth.

Yet Lauren had already promised herself that she wouldn't print a single word that would cause pain to Devlyn or her family. It didn't hurt that she really hadn't uncovered anything that could be truly damaging. She prayed she never would.

The writer watched as Dev closed her eyes and rolled her shoulders carefully. Then the President's head sagged forward. Lauren's face showed her concern. "Tired?"

"No. Praying."

Twin eyebrows disappeared behind fair bangs. "Praying?"

"Yeah. Praying that my dad doesn't let my mom cook for us."

"Amen," Emma and Amy said at the same time. Over the years, both women had been subjected to the culinary offerings of Janet Marlowe. The woman was sweet as could be. She loved her husband and Dev more than life itself and cooking was a hobby she'd enjoyed since childhood. Unfortunately, her skill level had also stayed the same as it was in childhood.

Dr. Frank Marlowe, Dev's father, had always had a cook. Luckily for Dev, that didn't change once he got married, but her mother still felt the need to jump in and "help" the cook every once in a while. Especially when she had guests.

"Oh, come on." Gray eyes rolled. "It can't be that bad." Lauren looked at each face. "No one is *that* bad a cook." *Okay, I am. But at least I don't make other people eat it.*

"Well, let's just say I'd rather eat some more of that shrimp from my ill-fated date with Candice Delaney than be subjected to my mom's cooking. I love my mom. Don't get me wrong but..."

"Oh, my God," both Emma and Amy finished simultaneously, shuddering with revulsion.

Lauren laughed, causing Aaron to fuss a little. She immediately clamped her lips shut and cuddled him closer to her. Kids weren't nearly so scary when they were unconscious.

Dev looked over at Lauren and grinned, lifting her pinkie and wiggling it at the writer.

Lauren stuck out her tongue in reply but she knew Devlyn was right. *Boy, am I wrapped by each and every member of the Marlowe family, or what?*

Two hours later and they were all standing in the entryway of the Marlowe family home. Lauren hung back with Emma and Amy, watching Frank and Janet welcome their daughter and grandchildren home. She desperately wanted to snap off a few photographs but she resisted the urge, not knowing how Mr. and Mrs. Marlowe would react. Lauren looked on uncomfortably as Janet Marlowe, who looked like a shorter, salt and pepper-haired version of Devlyn, wrapped her arms around her daughter and wept openly.

Frank Marlowe stood back with one grandson in each arm, wearing an indulgent smile for his granddaughter who was wrapped around his waist. He was tall and slim, with a thick head of white hair, a neatly trimmed beard and mustache, and generous mouth.

"Oh, baby!" Janet Marlowe put her hands on Dev's cheeks. "I'm so glad you're home." She frowned when she got an up close look at the fading scar on her daughter's face. "Are you really okay?"

"Mom, I'm fine. You know me, too stubborn to–" Dev stopped when she realized what she was about to say. She remained prudently silent while her mother stepped back and examined her from head to toe. "I swear to you, Mom. I'm totally intact."

"I'll be the judge of that, young lady," Janet snapped peevishly, but her eyes instantly softened. "You looked so tired when we called. I don't know why you wouldn't let us come up there and let me take care of you."

"I have a whole house full of people who–"

"*They* are not your mother," the small woman huffed, poking the President in the chest.

Lauren tried to stifle a giggle but failed.

Janet looked over and made eye contact with Lauren. *Ah, the infamous Lauren Strayer.* She lifted a brow.

So that's where Devlyn gets it. Lauren tried to look properly castigated as she lowered her eyes.

"Ah, Mom, Dad, you remember Emma and Amy." Dev directed her parents to their other guests. "David and Beth should be here in a just a few minutes. They wanted to make a quick run to the store first." *For antacids,* Dev mentally sniggered.

The greetings were quick and everyone's attention was soon back on Lauren. The younger woman began to visibly squirm under Janet and Frank's appraising, parental stares. She turned pleading eyes on the President that screamed, "help!"

Dev almost smiled at the look of unveiled panic on Lauren's face. "And this," Dev extended her hand to the writer and tugged her forward, "is Lauren Strayer. She's writing my biography, as you know. She's going to want to interview you both. So could you try not to tell her all of my embarrassing stories at once please?"

"But I wouldn't mind a few," Lauren jumped in.

"Oh, I'm sure I could come up with a thing or two about Stinky here," Frank offered with a wink. "Nice to meet you, Ms. Strayer. Welcome to our home."

"Please call me Lauren. And thank you, Dr. Marlowe." The writer was just dying to know where in the hell "Stinky" fit in here. She was definitely going to set aside some time to hear that story.

"Then you, young lady, should call me Frank." He smiled charmingly.

Lauren nodded and grinned back. Frank's Southern accent was even more pronounced than her own. "Thank you." She took a deep breath and faced the one she knew really counted here. "It's very nice to meet you, Mrs. Marlowe. Devlyn has told me a lot about you."

"It's nice to meet you, Lauren." The small woman took the writer's proffered hand. Lauren knew she was being sized up and she straightened her shoulders and made sure she gave a proper handshake. *Nothing wimpy would do for Janet Marlowe.* "And call me Janet. Mrs. Marlowe was my mother-in-law. God rest that evil bi–"

"Mom," Dev gritted out.

Janet smiled innocently. "God rest her soul."

David, his wife Beth, and Lauren were simply howling with laughter. Tears were streaming down their faces as their eyes darted between Dev's flaming cheeks and Frank's shit-eatin' grin. Janet was trying not to burst into laughter by busying herself with the coffeepot that had just been placed on the dinner table, but her slender shoulders were shaking.

Frank Marlowe looked properly satisfied as he leaned back in his chair. He had done every father's duty and regaled his audience with the time that Dev took off her diaper in the middle of a family dinner party.

Devlyn narrowed her eyes at her father and mumbled something from behind the napkin that she was holding firmly against her face. Lauren wasn't sure, but she thought she heard the words "air strike".

"So," Lauren sipped her water when her laughter finally died down. She fanned her cheeks. "Tell me, where did Stinky come from?"

Dev looked up, her eyes wide, and she clamped a hand over Lauren's mouth. She eyed her father warily. "You did not hear that. She did not ask that question. You did not hear that!"

Lauren licked the offending palm, causing Dev to jerk it free. The writer nodded wildly before Dev could recover from yelling "ewww" and wiping her hand on her jeans. "Yes, he did!"

Frank laughed low and evil. "Well, Devil here, was about, oh, fifteen I think–"

"Omigod! Kill me now, he's gonna tell her." Dev slumped in her chair and began to moan for mercy.

Frank snorted and then happily ignored his daughter. "Anyhow, she went out on this camping trip with a bunch of her friends. Seems our little Devil and a young lady friend of hers decided to go skinny-dipping in the pond."

Lauren's eyebrows nearly launched up off her forehead. She turned to Devlyn. "Skinny dipping? Oh my, Madam President. Who knew you had such a naughty streak?"

Dev glared at her father. "Well, if this makes it into my biography, the entire world will!"

Lauren patted Dev's knee and refocused on Frank. She made a quick gesture with her hands. "Go on. Go on."

"Apparently, everything was going along pretty well until one of the chaperones heard them splashing around and giggling in the pond and decided to check it out. The girls must have seen the flashlight, because they got out of the water, grabbed up their clothes, and started back to the camp, running buck nekkid through the woods..."

Dev groaned and slumped a little more. *Is it really possible to die of embarrassment?* David was pointing at her and laughing hysterically. *Yes,* she decided, *it really is.*

Lauren clamped her hand over her mouth. She tried to imagine Dev wet and naked, running through the woods. *Oooh...how much would I pay to see that? Hell, I'd take out a loan.* Her face suddenly colored and she shook her head slightly to clear it of its decidedly lascivious thoughts. "Gotcha. Nekkid," the word slipped out effortlessly, "teenaged Devlyn, streaking through the woods." She waited expectantly for Frank to continue, not sure which she was enjoying more, Frank's yarn or the mortified look on the President's face. "Is there more?"

"Uh huh." Dev's father nodded. "Her friend made it back okay and never got caught." He stared at Dev and pursed his lips. "Officially, that is." Then he laughed. "But Devil here, wasn't so lucky. Her nekkid a–" Frank stopped abruptly and cleared his throat. "Backside, I mean, stumbled into a den. A den containing one very protective mama skunk and four little baby skunks, all scared witless by the dripping wet human that had wakened them. You know what spooked skunks do, Lauren?"

Lauren burst out laughing. Then she wrinkled her nose at Dev. "Oh yuck, Devlyn."

Dev recovered long enough to scratch her cheek and flip Lauren the bird at the same time before she tossed a napkin at her father. "Thanks so much, Dad. There goes any shred of dignity I had left in Lauren's eyes."

David and Beth looked at each other. "We heard you puked on her, Dev. There was no dignity left."

Dev covered her face with her hands. "Was this visit really my idea?" she groaned.

"Yes!" the room chorused.

Frank continued undeterred. "It took two weeks, and thirty gallons of tomato juice, before we could be in the room with her without our eyes watering. And *that's* where the name Stinky came from."

Lauren felt a pang of sympathy for Dev who was still hiding her face. Once the writer managed to get her laughter under control, she reached out and gently rubbed Dev's back. Lauren leaned over and whispered, "If it makes any difference, I've always thought you smelled great."

Dev whispered back without moving a muscle, but Lauren could hear the smile in her words. "It makes a difference."

Sunday, June 13th

Lauren munched on a piece of toast and sipped her juice as she stood on the porch of the house in the morning sun. This was a beautiful place and the fact that the Secret Service had been ordered to set their perimeter several hundred yards away made it feel cozy and safe. She could only wonder what it would be like in the cabin they would go to later in the week. The writer liked the main house just fine.

Dev had let her sleep in this morning. Although to be fair, since the shooting she'd gotten to sleep till 6:30 a.m. while Dev was undergoing her physical therapy. What started as twice daily sessions had mercifully been reduced to three times per week and Julio had even given her this week off "for good behavior". Dev thought it was a therapeutic break for her muscles and Lauren decided she didn't need to be enlightened to that fact that it was just as much a break for poor Julio.

She had wakened to a soft summer breeze blowing in her window, the sound of children laughing and playing, and the smell of bacon cooking. *Oh, yeah.* Throw in sex and Lauren would swear she was in heaven not Ohio. She let that thought rattle around in her head until she had a dull ache in her lower belly and points more southernly. Lauren imagined Dev leaning over her and... *Enough!* She had forced herself out of bed and padded toward the bathroom. *Time for a shower. A very cold shower.*

After her shower, Lauren had towel-dried her hair and ran a comb through it before brushing her teeth and moving out onto the large back porch.

She leaned against the house, watching Dev's mother and father playing with their grandchildren. Gremlin was right in the middle of the chaos, romping, barking, and chasing a stick that Frank would toss out onto the lush green lawn every minute or so. *You little flea bag. You'd never fetch for me! Traitor.*

Amy and Emma were seated at a picnic table enjoying their breakfast. Lauren smirked. They were gossiping, by the looks of it. She'd catch up with them later.

Lauren had seen David and Beth walking hand in hand toward the woods. The only person that was missing was Dev. She slipped her hand into her pocket of her denim shorts and took another sip of her tangy, fresh squeezed grapefruit juice.

The blonde woman looked up when she heard a soft clomping sound coming toward her. Her breath left her lungs in a quick whoosh when she got a good look at the noise's source and who was riding him. Dev was sitting atop a beautiful quarter horse, wearing tight-fitting black jeans and chaps that were barely visible because they blended into the dark denim. A loose, light blue chambray shirt that matched the color of her eyes was tucked into the jeans and well-worn boots covered her feet. Her thick, ebony hair hung in a single braid that trailed down the middle of her back. Lauren sighed. It was truly enough to make any Tennessee girl swoon. *Okay, maybe not any girl.* But it did wonders for Lauren. To the writer, the President looked absolutely delicious. *I'm gonna need another shower.*

Dev rode slowly up to the porch and pulled her horse alongside. "Morning, ma'am," she drawled, sounding very much like her father.

Lauren couldn't stop her grin. She used her hand to shield her eyes from the morning sun as she looked up at Dev and moved to the porch railing. "Good morning."

"Sleep well?"

Lauren nodded slowly, not quite able to tear her eyes from Dev's. "Very well. How about you?"

"Oh, I was doing great until Dad came and got me up to go feed the horses."

The younger woman wrinkled her nose. "Lemme guess. 5:00 a.m.? Is that where you get it?"

"That's where I get it."

"How, by the way," Lauren motioned to the tall, chestnut colored beast, "did you get up on the tallest horse I have ever seen with your injured hip? You know you're not supposed to–"

Dev held up a forestalling hand. "Before you tear into me like Mom did," she grumbled, "I used a bale of hay and Dad helped me. I'm fine, I promise."

"It doesn't hurt?" Lauren asked skeptically.

"If I say it does, will you kiss it and make it better?"

Lauren began choking on her juice. "Who are you and what have you done with the President?" she coughed.

"Oh, that's still me. I guess I forgot to mention that I'm just much more relaxed at home." Dev laughed and took pity on her friend by changing the subject. "You get any breakfast?"

"Umm...yeah, the cook actually has a plate in the oven for me whenever I'm ready. I just grabbed a piece of toast to tide me over till I can bring myself to go inside and out of this beautiful sunshine."

Dev nodded again. "Yup, that's Dottie. Been the family cook

since I was a kid. And she's even successful at keeping Mom out of the kitchen. Mostly. No one goes hungry in the Marlowe house with Dottie around. If I'm really lucky, she'll make her special Devil cookies while I'm here."

Lauren smiled innocently and ran her hand up and down the rough wooden porch post. "You wanna tell me how you got the nickname Devil or should I ask your dad?" She allowed her head to come to rest against the post and took a deep breath of morning air, catching the scent of damp grass, the horse, and the faint aroma of Dev's soap and shampoo. She felt her knees go a little weak.

Devlyn shrugged. "It just comes from Dev. You know, like DEV-astating," she growled in a sexy voice. She leaned down towards Lauren who was nearly at her level because of the tall porch, her pale eyes sparkling with mischief in the morning sun. "And DEV-oted and DEV-our..." She grinned, giving the writer a truly evil smirk. "Just naturally popped up—"

Lauren's eyes raked over Dev. "Don't forget DEV-ine."

"Like you."

Lauren waited a beat, trying not to smile.

"Hey, that's not spelled right!"

"Call it artistic license."

Dev mulled that over for a moment. "Huh. Okay, I'll buy that from you. But only 'cause you're so cute."

My God, we're actually flirting with each other. Two more seconds of this and I'm gonna kiss her again. I swear I am. Lauren pushed off the post and leaned towards Dev until she could feel the combined heat of the older woman and her mount. She closed her eyes and their breath mingled—

"Hey, Devil!"

Lauren jumped back at the sound of Frank Marlowe's voice.

"Shit," Dev groaned, straightening in the saddle. "Later, Ms. Strayer." It was a promise.

Lauren adjusted her glasses and smiled. "Later, Madam President."

Tuesday, June 15th

Dev walked slowly towards the cabin where she, Lauren, David, and Beth would spend the next few days while the kids stayed with their grandparents in a tent out in the backyard.

Lauren had spent a solid day with each of Dev's parents and the tall woman suspected they now liked Lauren better than they did her. Dev chuckled good-naturedly. *I guess it was inevitable.*

Dev spied several Secret Service agents out of the corner of her eye. They were setting up in campers several hundred yards away. She wanted to give Lauren at least some sense of privacy. With everything that had happened, they all needed some rest. She glanced down when she felt an arm loop through her own. "Hello, Mother dear."

"Indeed, Devlyn Marlowe."

Dev knew that tone. It was her mom's "you are in such big trouble" tone. "What have I done now?" She sighed.

Janet kicked a stick from their path as they walked. "What is going on between you and Lauren?"

"Nothing."

"Don't you lie to your mother." She tugged on Dev's arm. "I've seen the way you two look at each other."

"And that would be exactly how?"

The shorter woman dug in her heels, bringing both of them to an abrupt stop. She reached up and caressed a tan cheek. "You haven't looked at anyone like that since Samantha. Are you sleeping with her?"

"No!" Dev pulled back a little. "You know I would never...I mean, I can't...I mean..."

Janet's blue eyes twinkled and she shook her head at her daughter. They began walking again. "I know. You always were horribly old-fashioned like that. You nearly drove Sam crazy. I thought the poor girl was going to spontaneously combust."

"I drove her crazy?"

"Uh huh. Before you two were married, she'd call me and ask me what she was doing wrong and why you weren't trying to get her into bed. Devlyn, in my day your actions would have been considered prudish. Now, it's just downright archaic. You need to chill out a little. It isn't as though one of you is going to end up pregnant." Janet chuckled at her own joke.

Dev stopped and put her hands on her hips. "Mother, are you suggesting I take Lauren to bed?"

"You love her, don't you?"

Dev hesitated. "I don't know."

"Devlyn Odessa Marlowe, don't you dare..." She waggled a finger in her daughter's face. "I can't believe you kiss me with those lying lips."

Blue eyes rolled and Dev nearly stomped her foot. "Mom!"

"Dev, you know I don't get involved in your life unless I think you're doing something really stupid." Janet's posture mirrored her daughter's. "I think holding back from Lauren is really stupid. She's good for you, honey. It doesn't take a rocket scientist to see that."

"Mom—"

"She's a very attractive woman. She's sweet and smart. Why I hardly knew she was pumping me for information when we spent the day together." Janet's voice was filled with honest admiration. "And in case you haven't noticed, your children adore her."

"Mom—"

"And she watches you with eyes that very nearly worship every move you make."

Dev's mind flickered back to the kisses they had shared on Air Force One. "She kissed me," she admitted quietly.

"Good for her! It appears that *her* parents did not raise a chicken."

Dev's jaw sagged. "Are you calling me a chicken?"

"If the feathers fit, dear."

"Funny."

"Did you kiss her back?" They turned a blind corner and were now facing a large wooden cabin with a small attached porch and a pile of split logs for the fireplace lining the front wall.

"I'm old-fashioned, Mom, not stupid. Of course I kissed her back!"

"Then what happened?"

"The plane landed. We came here and Dad told her the 'stinky' story. She may never kiss me again for all I know."

"Oh, I wouldn't be too sure about that." Janet elbowed her daughter lightly in the ribs. "I think if you give her any sign at all, she'll do a lot more than kiss you, Dev."

"Mom!" The President scrubbed her face hoping to remove some of the red from her cheeks.

"You've been alone too long, honey. Let the past remain where it belongs and look to the future. You need someone in your life. I know you. You don't fall quickly and you don't take these things lightly. But wake up and smell the coffee, Devlyn. You're in love with that girl." Janet helped Dev up the stairs. "There was a saying when I was a kid that I feel is most appropriate now."

"Shit happens?"

Janet snorted. "Hardly, dear. You snooze," she eyed her daughter seriously, "you lose."

David's wife, Beth, pushed herself off the cabin's sofa and plopped gracelessly onto the hardwood floor, causing her brown curls to bounce. Beth was a little shorter than Lauren, with wide hips and a scooped nose. She had a quick wit and a quicker smile and was a professor of early American history at Georgetown University. Beth and Lauren had instantly hit it off and the evening had already been filled with equal parts intellectual conversation, rambunctious laughter, and beer.

"Well," Beth said cheerfully, "why don't we play a game?"

"What kind of a game?" David wriggled his eyebrows and sank deeper into the soft sofa. "Strip checkers maybe?"

Beth laughed and reached over and slapped her husband's

knee. "Pervert."

"And you married him," Dev reminded. "What does that say for you?"

Beth took a long swallow of her beer while she pondered Dev's comment. "Good point," she finally admitted. She turned to Lauren. "I was thinking of something that could help us all get to know each other a little better."

"Beth." Dev's tone was warning.

Beth raised her amber colored bottle, its golden contents sparkling in the firelight. "We could play spin the bottle." She laughed again when her husband suddenly perked up. "But I don't want David to have a heart attack." Beth smiled sweetly at her husband, gleefully bursting his bubble. "He's right in the danger years."

"I am not!"

"Are too!"

"So what were you thinking about?" Lauren asked, curiosity finally getting the better of her. She set her third bottle of cold beer down on the floor next to her chair and dropped down onto the area rug beneath it, mirroring Beth. The writer tucked her legs beneath her Indian style, enjoying a light buzz from the alcohol and the aroma of oak from the crackling fire.

"We could always see how brave Madam President really is." Beth smirked at Dev. "How about Truth or Dare?"

"Bring it on, Beth! If I can handle a Republican controlled Congress, I can handle three measly Democrats."

Lauren snorted, nearly sending her beer through her nose. "Thanks a lot, Devlyn," she laughed. The blonde woman mentally cataloged her most embarrassing moments and most evil sins and then decided they would be worth sharing just to hear Dev's. "Okay, Beth. I'm in."

David yawned. "You know me, I'm game."

"You're all heathens, but I'll play along. I have a feeling I'm the good girl of the group."

Beth rolled her eyes. "You forget who you're talking to, Devil. Lauren might believe that BS, but don't try it on me or David. We've known you for too long." She took another drink and emptied her bottle. Then she clapped her hands together and reached into the ice-filled tub full of frosty bottles that sat among the four people. "Dev, you're so cocky tonight. I think you should go first. Truth or dare, Madam President?"

Three sets of expectant eyes turned towards Dev.

"Well, let's cut the President of the United States bullshit for the rest of the week. And I'll go with truth."

Lauren giggled when David made a loud honking noise, indicating that Dev had already made a tactical error with her selection of truth.

Beth happily picked up the gauntlet. "Truth: How many people have you slept with?"

There was a long pause. "I'm assuming you mean in a sexual sense?" Dev sipped her beer and shot Beth a look that screamed "Bitch!" "One," she said very softly.

Lauren dropped her bottle in her lap then cursed as the icy liquid seeped through her jeans. "Jesus – damn, that's cold." She turned wide eyes on Dev. "One. As in one, single, solitary person?" *Maybe she means one at a time. God, I hope she's not interested in more than one at a time.*

David and Beth burst out laughing.

"Yes," Dev huffed. "What else would it mean?" She grimaced when she realized her voice had taken on an indignant tone that sounded a lot like her Aunt Myrtle. "I know it seems kind of pitiful and pathetic but...umm...well–"

"It's not pitiful at all. It's really...err..." Lauren desperately searched for the right word, immediately throwing out "unbelievable" and "amazing". "Sweet." *There, that's a good word.* "One?" She mouthed the word silently, clearly in shock as she reached for another beer. *She's practically a virgin! Oh, please don't let them ask me that question. Please, please. Compared to "one" I look like a total slut! Pleasepleaseplease-please.*

Dev exhaled and considered who should be her first victim. She was tempted to pick Beth to exact her revenge, but was far more curious about the writer. "Okay, Lauren, truth or dare?"

"Dare!" Lauren blurted out, relieved she could avoid the question Dev had been asked.

The trio burst out laughing at how quickly the writer had made her decision. They knew this meant she had something to hide and now they could work as a team to figure it out. "Okay," Dev grinned. "Give me your bra." She laughed and gestured casually. "The one you're wearing."

Lauren's mouth dropped open.

Beth leaned over and clapped her hand over David's eyes, causing the man to protest loudly. "Hush up, David!" she scolded.

Lauren shook her head at Dev, loving the mischievous twinkle in the slightly glazed blue eyes. "You're drunk, aren't you?"

"No." *A little drunk.* "I'm...happy. C'mon, get to it." Dev snapped her fingers just to be annoying. "If you can't run with the big dogs, Mighty Mouse, just get up on the porch."

A single pale eyebrow lifted and Lauren sat up to her knees. She turned until she was completely facing Dev. "It was my bra, right?" She lifted her hands to the buttons of her lightweight denim shirt and Dev stopped breathing.

The suddenly stillness in the room alerted David that something was happening and the man began to squirm, trying to get a peek between his wife's fingers. They both laughed and Beth poked David in the belly. "No way!"

Lauren slowly undid the first button of her top, keeping her eyes riveted on Dev's.

Dev watched as Lauren paused briefly and then began to finger the second button. *Ooo, now I gotta put up or shut up. But if she takes her shirt off, I'm gonna die. My brain is just gonna ooze out my ears.* Dev knew she was grinning like a total idiot and blushing furiously, but she met Lauren's eyes and never wavered. "That's what I said. Of course, you could change your mind and go with truth."

Lauren's fingers stopped. "Do you want me to change my mind, Devlyn?" she asked softly.

David shook his head and was about to cry out "no" when his wife clamped her other hand over his mouth.

The President licked her lips and sipped her beer, knowing she had firmly hit the ball back to Lauren. "I want you to do what you want to do."

Lauren nodded slowly. *I want to ask you to come over here and do it for me. But since that's probably not a good idea – tonight – this will have to do.* The younger woman unbuttoned the second and third buttons, sliding her hands inside her shirt to find warm skin. Her bra happened to unhook in the front, and with a quick twist the cups fell away. Her bloused shirt and hands covered the most crucial spots. She grinned as Dev began to fan herself but didn't look away.

"Hurry up, Lauren," Beth called. "She said lose the bra, not perform a damn striptease!"

David whimpered at what he was missing. *This is so unfair.*

Dev finally bit her lip and glanced down at her beer just long enough for Lauren to pull away her hands and slip her bra out of one of her sleeves. She buttoned the third button but left the two highest buttons of her shirt undone, however. It was enough to show a fair amount of cleavage, but not enough to get arrested for. Then she crawled over to Dev on her hands and knees and held the lacy undergarment in front of her face. "I believe you asked for this?"

Dev took the black bra and looked at it. Then she mopped her brow with it before sticking it in the pocket of her pants. "Yeah." Her voice cracked like a prepubescent boy. "Thanks."

Beth finally removed her hands from David's face. "No more naked dares! How long do you think I can hold him?"

"Well, hell, Beth, you've held onto him for nearly fifteen years what's another fifteen minutes? Okay, Lauren, it's your turn."

Lauren didn't go back to her seat. Instead, she sat down next to Dev who had moved to the floor. The President lifted her bottle for another drink but just as the glass touched her lips Lauren snatched it from her hand and finished it off in one long swallow. "Ahhhh..." she breathed. "Thanks. It was getting hot in here."

"I'll say!" Beth pressed her bottle against her forehead.

David frowned and mumbled petulantly, "Not like I'd know."

Dev retrieved her bottle and held it up to the light. "You stole my beer. Man, you ask a girl for her bra and you gotta give her a whole beer? For a whole beer I should get the panties too!"

This time it was Lauren who blushed. *Oh, yeah. Dev's drunk. Nobody would believe I'm playing a teenager's game with the President of the United States.*

"Your turn," Beth reminded Lauren.

"Okay." The very tip of Lauren's tongue appeared as she concentrated for a moment. She pushed her glasses farther up on her nose. "David..."

The redheaded man sat up straight.

"True or dare?"

"Truth."

Lauren grinned wickedly. "What's the last horribly embarrassing thing that Devlyn did that you kept out of the press?"

"She went out with Candy Delaney."

"Hey! No fair," Lauren protested instantly. "I already knew that!"

Dev made a face at her Chief of Staff. "Besides, dumbass, that was your fault. You set me up with her. Personally, I think the fact that I got my speeches mixed up last week was pretty good. I mean, when was the last time the President started to give a speech written for The National Cattlemen's Association to the World Vegetarian League?"

Lauren sniggered. "That was embarrassing, but David really couldn't answer with that one." A beat. "Considering I read about it for two days."

"David!" Beth chastised. "You're supposed to nip that kind of thing in the bud!"

"I know you think I'm the great and powerful Oz—"

"You mean you're not?" Beth asked with devastating innocence, just as David leaned over and stole a kiss.

The tall redhead smacked his lips together happily when the kiss ended. "Okay, Dev, truth or dare?"

"Truth."

David grinned and grabbed a handful of popcorn. "How'd you break your pinkie finger, Devil?"

Dev choked on her beer and flicked the cap at David's head. "You know how I broke my finger, you prick."

"But I don't," Lauren pointed out happily. She grinned at Beth who grinned back. *Oh, boy. This should be interesting.*

Dev took a deep breath and then a big drink of her beer. "One night I got my hand slammed in a window." She pretended to take another drink, hoping that would be a suitable answer.

Lauren elbowed the President. "Annnd?"

"And it got broken when the window came down on it."

David wiped his fingers on his jeans. "The part she's leaving out is that she was naked and in the throes of passion when she did it. She grabbed the bottom of the window and pulled it shut on her own hand."

Dev reached over and punched him on the shoulder. "Thanks, pal!"

Lauren burst out laughing. She reached out and grabbed Dev's pinkie finger, holding it up for examination and giving serious consideration to kissing it. "And you know this how, David?"

"Because she was running for office at the time and they called me first to tell me the window was jammed with her hand stuck in it and Samantha thought they were gonna have to call the fire department. They wanted me to keep it from hitting the papers."

Beth began to howl. *God, I love this story! I knew David would be cruel enough to bring it up during the game. God, I love David!*

Lauren and David joined in until Dev, who was sitting with her arms crossed over her chest, pouting, finally had enough. "Okay, fine. Laugh it up, you rat bastards. Truth or dare, Strayer?"

Lauren jerked her thumb toward Beth. "It's her turn!"

"That's okay," Beth said. "Since no one has bothered to ask me a question, I'll be happy to let Dev take my turn. Have at it, Devlyn. And make it good."

Lauren stuck out her tongue at Beth. "Fine. I pick dare." *You're not getting me on that sex question tonight, Devlyn Marlowe.*

"I'm betting good money you have a tattoo somewhere. If you do, show it."

"No way! She is *not* the tattoo type. A hundred says she doesn't have one," David taunted.

"You're on!" Dev leaned over and they shook hands.

Gray eyes narrowed. *Shit!* "What makes you think I have a tattoo?" Lauren's words were tinged with as much indignation as she could muster. Which wasn't much, considering she did actually have a tattoo. Yet David was right; she wasn't the type. It was something stupid she'd done on a drunken dare when she was in college. Kind of like what she was doing right now.

"I know the type," Dev pronounced firmly. "Deceptively cute looking, all innocent like the girl next door. No, make that the 'All American' girl next door." She chuckled at the appalled look on Lauren's undeniably cute face. "You girls always have a tattoo because at some point in your life you bucked the system and either got a tattoo or dated a biker." Dev took another swallow of beer. "And you don't strike me as the biker dating type."

Shit, I hate it when Devlyn's right. And dating a biker would have been so much less permanent! Lauren looked nervously at David and Beth who were staring back at her, waiting with bated breath for an answer. She leaned close to Dev's ear and whispered, "Ummm...assuming just for a moment that I do have a tattoo, who exactly would I have to show again? Not everybody, right?" There was a hint of pleading in her voice.

Dev looked at David and Beth, giving a vague gesture. "You'd trust me to verify it and tell the truth, right Beth?"

Beth grinned. "Absolutely, Devil." David was about to protest but his wife beat him to the punch. "And so would David. We trust you implicitly, Dev."

Dev turned her silly, truly buzzed face to Lauren and wiggled her brows. "Just me then. You only have to show me. C'mon, Lauren," she crooned, barely able to control her laughter.

Lauren blew out a breath. "Just you?"

Dev nodded. "Just me. Where is it?" The tall woman's smile widened, she hadn't really believed the writer would have a tattoo. Lauren was far too straight-laced for that. *And someone got close to her with a needle?* "You were unconscious when you got it, weren't you?"

Lauren nodded. "You know it."

The blonde woman turned to Beth and David and made a circular motion with her index finger. The McMillians turned their backs, but not before a few more mumbled protests from David. She raised an eyebrow at Dev. "Promise you won't laugh?"

"No, I won't promise that." *God if I don't kiss her again soon I'm gonna die.* "When a girl gives you her bra before you've even ever bought her dinner, she totally gives up the right not to be laughed at," Dev teased.

"Bitch," Lauren mumbled as she rose to her feet and began undoing the button to her jeans. "It's on my..." A pause. "Hip. Sort of."

Dev swallowed hard, holding up her hand. "What do you mean 'sort of'?" *You drop your pants and I will die.*

"I mean sort of. It's well...I guess I'll have to show you. There really isn't a word to describe exactly where it is. But if you'd rather I stop−?"

"No, no, go ahead." *I just wish I were gonna remember this in the morning.*

Lauren bit her lip but nodded. "Stupid game." She positioned herself in front of Devlyn and glanced over her shoulder to find Beth and David making out on the rug and not paying the slightest attention to her and Dev. She unbuttoned her pants with agonizing slowness, then began to slide them over her hips.

Dev felt her heart pounding so hard she was sure that it was going to burst out of her chest at any moment. She whimpered pitifully when she glimpsed panties that matched the silky, lacy bra. Her vision suddenly became fuzzy and she felt lightheaded, and then everything went black.

Beth and David turned around at the sound of a loud thump.

Lauren pulled up her jeans and simply stared at Dev's prone body.

David jumped up. "Jesus Christ, Lauren, you killed her! Where the hell is that thing?"

Lauren pointed to Dev's body. "She's still breathing! I didn't kill her! She didn't even make it to the unveiling."

Everyone retired shortly after they had carried a snoring Dev to bed, which sucked, considering her room, along with Lauren's, was upstairs. Lauren went to her room, which was connected to Dev's via a shared bathroom. David and Beth had been awarded the master bedroom downstairs because of its larger bed.

Lauren changed into a pair of soft cotton short boxers and a threadbare T-shirt. She held her panties in her hand, wondering if Dev would give her back her bra or if the set would be lost forever. *Oh well,* she smirked inwardly, it was sort of kinky thinking of Dev with a piece of her lingerie. *God, how old am I again? Besides, she probably won't remember tonight. Those beers went right to her head, poor, evil thing.*

The writer placed her glasses on the nightstand and crawled into bed, sighing at the wonderful feeling of clean sheets and soft bedding. "Oh, this is nice." She nuzzled the comforter and closed her eyes, still a little wound up after the silly game. Her head was a little foggy from the beer, but she was certain she hadn't drunk enough to warrant a hangover in the morning. Just enough to feel incredibly...relaxed.

Lauren wasn't quite sure what woke her up. It took a moment or two for the sounds to register. She squeezed her eyes shut and crammed the extra pillow against her face. "I so do not need this," she mumbled into the thick feather pillow. One particularly low moan caught her attention and made her giggle. She wasn't sure whether it was Beth or David. "Somebody is a verrry happy camper right now." When the sounds continued, Lauren briefly considered stuffing a blanket or towel into the air vent that was carrying the erotic noises.

Finally, when she couldn't take it any longer, she headed for the bathroom, hoping that if David and Beth heard footsteps above them, they'd tone down their bed sports to a dull roar – in deference to those not so lucky.

She didn't turn on the light – a small nightlight provided more than enough illumination. Lauren used the facilities and washed her hands. She smiled into the mirror when she realized that she couldn't hear them in here. *I can sleep in the shower!* It wouldn't have been the first time, but it was a stall shower. So, with an unhappy groan, she quickly gave up on the idea. This couldn't go on all night. Hell, she'd been married for three years. She could attest to that fact!

Then another sound caught her ear. It was Dev. Lauren didn't hesitate to quietly open the door that led to Dev's room and check on her friend.

"Don't..." The President's voice was pleading again; apparently she was caught up in another nightmare.

Lauren stepped deeper into the room and moved to the edge of Dev's bed. She noticed two things right away. Dev was rolling around in her bed, twisted in her sheets, and she was naked as the day she was born. From the waist up at least. Her pajama top was wadded into a ball on the floor.

"Don't!" Dev thrashed again. Her breathing was coming in short, raspy bursts.

Lauren swallowed as a feeling of helplessness washed over her, leaving her nearly in tears. *Another nightmare? God, Dev, how often do you have these?*

"Please...please. Don't leave!" Dev tossed in the bed, fighting the covers and becoming more distressed by the second. Lauren knelt alongside the bed.

"Devlyn," she whispered. "It's just a dream, darlin'." Lauren carefully reached out to straighten Dev's sheets and tug something over Dev's naked breasts, which were bathed in silver moonlight. The sheet stopped just below what she was trying to cover. "Jesus." Lauren closed her eyes and tugged harder, cursing softly when the bedding wouldn't move. Dev's whimpers grew louder and when no amount of soothing seemed to work, Lauren tentatively crawled in bed alongside the older woman.

Dev let out a long hard breath, instantly curling up against Lauren and wrapping her arms around the writer's waist. She made a few more frustrated noises that were quickly followed by soft mewing sounds that eventually evened into gentle snores.

Lauren pressed her cheek against Dev's hair and returned the embrace. "That's it. Relax." She took a deep breath, catching the smell of fresh linen and Dev's skin. She exhaled contentedly. Lauren tried not to think of the warm, soft breasts pressing against her. *I don't want to move, even though I should. This feels too nice. Too right. What are you dreaming of, Devlyn?*

Wednesday, June 16th

Dev was caught up in that wonderful place between sleep and wakefulness, where the slightest push one way or the other is all it would take to get there. She was having the most wonderful dream: Lauren was in her arms, she could feel her, smell her, and if she lowered her lips just a hair, she could taste warm, soft skin. She shifted to hug her body pillow closer. With her next breath she was suddenly more awake than asleep.

Panic set in when she could feel her body pillow's gentle breath against the sensitive skin. *Don't panic, Marlowe! Too late! Okay, you don't remember anything after the tattoo thing. But that doesn't mean anything. Relax.* Dev could hear footsteps downstairs and by the angle of the sunshine cascading in through her window, she could tell it was at least mid-morning. *Wake her up, but don't do anything stupid. Tread softly.* "Lauren?"

"Hmm?" Lauren murmured, snuggling closer.

"Lauren?" It was all Dev could do to breathe and not bolt upright. "Come on, sweetheart. It's time to wake up."

Lauren shook her head and mumbled a grumpy "no". "Go 'way," she slurred even as she snuggled closer, shifting and pressing her face against Dev's chest. She sighed and began to lightly snore.

Dev whimpered. She bit her lip as the shivers worked their way down her spine and the gooseflesh broke out all over her shoulders. *I could stay like this for a while. What would be so wrong about that?* She ran her fingers through disordered, wavy blonde hair, loving its silken texture.

She was about to try again when there was a sharp rap on the door, just a split second before it opened. "Devil, breakfast is ready and I–" Janet Marlowe stopped dead in her tracks as Dev quickly pulled the covers over her half-naked body and the woman sleeping in her arms.

"Mom!"

Lauren's eyes flew open, only it was dark. She could feel something brushing against her cheek. Her mind desperately searched itself. "Oh, my God! A nipple!" she squawked loudly, squirming wildly as Dev held her down.

The President's face flushed bright red, and her mother began howling with laughter. "Well, Devil dear, it's good to know that she recognizes all the important parts." The older woman tossed her head back in renewed laughter. When Janet finally composed herself, she said, "Breakfast is ready if you two are the least bit interested." The woman continued to chuckle even as she pulled the door shut. "Frank, put a couple of plates in the oven – it may be awhile. Thank the Lord!"

Dev groaned, trying to decide what part of this was going to kill her first. She suspected it would be Lauren.

When Devlyn finally let go of her death grip on the sheet, the writer practically flew out of the bed, landing on the floor with a glorious, unceremonious thud. She looked around the room. *Dev's room?* Then the events of the night before came rushing back. "You..." Lauren swallowed. "You were having a dream."

Dev made no effort to move. She simply lay on her back with her arms out at her side. "Apparently." After a moment she added, "Do you, perchance, know where my shirt is?"

"I didn't take it off!" Lauren shot back defensively. Then she stopped and got a really good look at Devlyn's semi-nude body, which amazingly looked even better in the bright morning sun than it had in the moonlight. She stared. "Damn, Devlyn."

Dev rolled over on her side, pulling the blanket over herself, trying to hide her smile at Lauren's obvious appreciation of her body. "I didn't say you did. Can you get in that dresser behind you and get me a T-shirt? You'll know they're mine because they have the Presidential seal on them," she teased, hoping to lower Lauren's defensiveness.

They were here to relax and Dev was going to relax and get this sorted out without causing another problem between her and Lauren. More kissing, less problems. Was that so much to ask?

"Why are you so concerned about your shirt?" Lauren hissed. "I'm a girl too, you know." She ignored the fact that she had been staring at Dev's naked body like she was a sixteen-year-old boy. "We need to worry about your mother. She caught us...us..." Lauren waved her hands in the air, "in bed together!"

Dev took a deep breath and got out of the bed, looking around until she found her pajama shirt on the floor at the foot of the bed. She slipped it on. "First, I only wanted my shirt because believe it or not, I'm modest." *When I'm not drinking beer.* "And second, did my mother sound upset by the fact that she found us in bed together?" Dev tilted her head, finally getting a good look at Lauren in her cotton boxers and thin T-shirt. *Nice, very nice.*

"I dunno. I couldn't hear very well because one of my ears was pressed up against," she pointed at Dev and flushed a bright red, "you know!"

"Oh, yeah. I know." Dev sighed and took a tentative step forward. "Trust me. My mother was not upset. There's no reason for you to be, unless you're upset that you were in bed with me." *Which, you moron, she probably is. Jesus, Dev, what the hell did you do last night?* "I'm umm...I'm sorry if I did anything out of line, Lauren. I never meant to hurt you. To be honest, I'm not even sure how we ended up here together. But if I hurt you or upset you—"

Lauren raised her palms. "Hold it." *Dev's parents are not your parents, Lauri. Relax. She's not upset. Her mother didn't freak out. They won't be mad at her and nobody's going to come in here bran-*

dishing a shotgun. With effort, Lauren allowed some of her tension to slip away. "You didn't do anything. You were having a nightmare and I came in to see if I could help." She smoothed out the bottom of her T-shirt as she approached Dev. "I was worried. You didn't wake up when I shook you, so I climbed into bed and you calmed right down. I...um...I guess I fell asleep," she admitted bashfully.

Dev smiled. "You came in to help me with a bad dream? That was very sweet of you. I've been having trouble sleeping lately. Apparently you...well, we both slept like babies last night. Thanks for staying. I know it must have been hard for you." *Please tell me it wasn't. Please, please, please.*

Lauren looked up shyly. "Hard?" She laughed. "Ummm...that's not exactly how I would describe it, Devlyn." She reached up and fingered a lock of dark hair.

Dev took Lauren's hand, kissing it very gently. When their eyes met, a smile spread across her lips. "You know what, Lauren Strayer?"

Lauren shook her head "no" and gazed up at Dev from behind pale lashes. "What?"

"I really want to kiss you right now. Do you think that'd be all right? Or are you afraid my mom will come back in?" She gave the shorter woman a lopsided grin and inched a little closer, taking a deep breath and stroking Lauren's cheek with the back of her hand.

Lauren's eyelids drooped slightly when she felt the warmth of Devlyn's body come to rest against hers. Her heart began to pound and she lifted herself up onto tiptoes. "Whose mom?"

Dev slid her arms around the smaller woman and barely brushed her lips over Lauren's. Then, on impulse, she sighed and decided to show Lauren exactly what she felt. The kiss was slow and patient and as loving as she could make it.

Lauren whimpered quietly when Dev gently requested more, which she gave without hesitation. The writer felt Dev thread her fingers in her hair and pull her closer, deepening the kiss. *Oh, yeah, this is good in so many ways.* Lauren's thoughts slowly moved from how good the kiss was to what else might be worth trying. *Every blessed thing I can talk her into trying,* she decided, *as soon as I can figure out what that might be.*

When they finally broke apart, Dev smiled and brushed her thumb over Lauren's lips. "So soft. Now I have another question for you."

"Yes," Lauren sighed dreamily. "Whatever it is, as long as I continue getting kisses like that, the answer is 'yes'."

Dev straightened and gave Lauren a bright smile. "All right. If I'm going to take you out, then the least you can do is pick the place."

Lauren blinked. "Are you asking me on an honest to goodness, real live date?"

"Yes. And you can't back out now," Dev teased. "You already said yes."

A playful expression overtook Lauren's face. "Oh, I wasn't going to back out, Devlyn Marlowe. I'm holding you to your offer." She put her finger on her chin and pretended to seriously consider Dev's question. "Wherever we go, will there be a team of Secret Service agents lurking in every corner?"

"Yup. Unless you have some kinky fantasy that I'm not aware of that requires several agents."

"Ha! Wouldn't you like to know," Lauren shot back, stealing another small kiss. She hummed as they separated. "I should go get dressed." The smaller woman turned on her heel and moved towards the bathroom. "You don't have to take me anywhere, Devlyn. We can spend time together at home for all I care. So long as it's together."

"Actually, I would like to know," Dev called after her. "Now we get to go downstairs and face the family. Not to mention David and Beth. You ready for that?" *Home? Did she just say home? Go ask her, stupid. No. Wait. One thing at a time. Ask her later.*

Lauren turned around as she pulled open the bathroom door, the wood floor made her toes cold, but she felt warm inside. She cocked her head to the side. "We do it together right?"

Dev nodded.

"Then I'm ready if you are."

Thursday, July 1st

Dev rubbed her temples. The men and women in the Cabinet meeting waited for her to say something. Finally, she looked up and smiled. Even in a few months, this group had learned that this particular smile was not a good thing. "Fine," she said on a low and determined breath. "Since we don't seem to be getting anywhere talking to each other, let's try it the old-fashioned way."

"With a lot of screaming and yelling?" Secretary of Agriculture Montgomery joked, trying to relieve some of the tension.

"That's definitely another option." Dev smirked. "But I'm thinking more in the line of progress reports. These should be simple summaries of what you're currently working on. I want them from your sub-committees too. And do me a favor?" Dev pinned Transportation Secretary Diovanni with annoyed eyes. "Read over what your assistants are going to prepare for me to see *before* you send it. I'm holding you to the contents of these reports, ladies and gentlemen. I'm tired of trying to pry information out of you people. It's like trying to brush a tiger's teeth. I've already been shot; I'm not gonna lose an arm too."

David smirked, nearly choking on his juice. He raised a fist to his lips, coughing slightly as Dev turned her head to give him the "look".

Dev continued speaking as she glanced at her agenda. "Now that the peanut gallery has been heard from, are there any questions?" She looked at each face around the long table. "Comments, concerns? Criticism can be left with the woman who runs the shredder," she said wryly as she stood up.

"Seriously, ladies and gentlemen, we're doing good work here. But we need to open the lines of communication a little more. I'm not trying to purposely torpedo all your programs. But without the proper information, I can't make an informed decision. I'm assuming that our next meeting will be more fruitful?" She tilted her head and waited until her question was answered with a round of affirmative, if slightly grumpy, murmurs. "Good." She buttoned her blazer and handed her notebook to Liza.

The room cleared quickly, leaving behind the President, David, and Liza. Dev shook her head. "I swear," she mumbled, "you'd think I was working against them instead of with them. I can't believe I actually gave those people their jobs." She turned to her personal assistant. "How does my schedule look?"

"You're fifteen minutes ahead of schedule, Madam President."

"You're kidding? Let's fly to Paris for lunch!"

David laughed. "Madam President, are you always so sarcastic?" *Translation: do you have to be a smartass every second of the day?*

Dev smiled sweetly. "Is that a rhetorical question? Those are so annoying." Devlyn pushed in her chair and headed for the door.

Liza hurried after her. "The gift you ordered for Ms. Strayer's birthday arrived, Madam President. It's in your office if you'd like to go inspect it."

"Oh, good! God, I hope it's something she's going to like." Dev tugged on the sleeves of her blazer. "Not like I have time to return it and get something else."

"She's going to love it," Liza confirmed. "They're beautiful texts. First editions of Dickens aren't easy to come by these days."

"Tell me about it." Dev rolled her eyes as they turned the corner and headed down the corridor towards the executive offices. "Took me weeks to find mint quality and put these together. Let's just hope she likes them."

"She'll be fond of them because they're from you. Not just anyone gets birthday gifts from the President of the United States."

"The President isn't giving them to her." Dev looked at her assistant and wiggled her brows. "You coming to the party?"

Liza chewed her lip nervously. "Are you sure Ms. Strayer won't throw me off the balcony?"

"Nah. She's over that whole Casey thing."

"Really?" Liza asked hopefully.

"Umm...nope." Dev laughed. "But I'll keep her occupied." She suddenly stopped walking and glanced around conspiratorially. She leaned close to Liza. "Why did you set her up with a woman? How did you know she wouldn't freak out? Lauren hadn't ever mentioned a sexual preference that I'm aware of."

It was all Liza could do not to laugh. "Have you ever seen the way she looks at you, Madam President?"

Friday, July 2nd

Dev stood in front of the full-length mirror. She studied her reflection critically. "So what do you think?" The tall woman turned to face the four pairs of eyes that had watched her through the last three changes of clothing.

Emma clucked approvingly. "Devlyn, you look fine. Of course, you looked fine in the blazer, the skirt, the sweater *and* the blue jeans."

"Yeah, but I think the slacks are the best. Not too formal, not too informal." She smoothed the collar of her silk, rust colored blouse.

Emma snorted and rolled her eyes. "You're going to a movie in the private theater. You could go in your bathrobe if you wanted."

Blue eyes full of affection and exasperation glared at the nanny. "Do you mind if I want to impress her?"

Emma glared back. "I hate to break this to you, Devlyn, but if you haven't impressed her yet...what you wear tonight isn't going to make any difference at all."

"I didn't need to hear that! You're supposed to be giving me an inspirational pep talk!"

"Okay, look back at that mirror."

Dev dutifully complied.

"Now repeat after me: I'm good enough. I'm smart enough. And, doggone it, people like me!"

Dev whipped her head around and narrowed her eyes at the older woman. "Why do I put up with you again, Emma?"

"Because you love her," the children chorused the familiar answer.

"Oh, yeah," Dev mumbled. She noticed Ashley had moved from her sitting position and was now lying on her bed with her head on her arms. Her posture was undeniably dejected. The President walked over and sat down next to her daughter, rubbing her back. "Hey, Moppet?"

"Yeah?" Slightly sad eyes looked up at her.

"What's the matter?"

"Nothin'."

"Aww, c'mon. I know my girl better than that." She straightened her daughter's bright blue T-shirt. "What's wrong?"

"Does this mean you don't love Mommy anymore?" the little girl asked earnestly.

Dev's chest constricted painfully at the unexpected, blunt question. For a moment she had to remind herself to breathe. "No, I—" She swallowed hard and started again. "You know better than that. I'll always love Mommy, no matter what. But that doesn't mean I can't be very fond of Lauren. I want to see how she feels about me."

Christopher popped up next to Dev. "She likes you, Mom."

"Oh, she does, huh?" Dev asked, dropping onto the floor and kneeling down to her son's level.

"Uh huh." The boy nodded. "A whole lot."

"How do you know this, pal?"

He just shrugged one shoulder. "Dunno. She always won't let Gremlin eat you, and she smiles at you."

Dev snorted. "I may just eat him!"

"Nooo!" the kids cried, laughing hysterically when their mother turned her hands into claws and began licking her lips in an exaggerated fashion. "Maybe Lauren just thinks I'm silly. Besides, she smiles at you guys too."

Christopher grinned broadly and stuck out his little chest. "I know. She likes me a lot too."

"Chris is right, Mom!" Aaron climbed up on the bed next to his sister, propping his chin on his fists and adding his voice to the choir. "She likes you."

"Are you just buttering me up because you want me to ask Lauren about letting Grem sleep with you?" Dev teased, tweaking the nose of her youngest.

"Nuh uh!" Aaron laughed as he rolled away from Dev's pinching fingers.

Dev turned serious eyes back to Ash. "So, you don't like the idea of me and Lauren maybe seeing each other?" *C'mon, Ashley. Please don't be that way. This is hard enough for me without having to worry about how you guys feel about her. I know you're crazy about her!*

Ashley shrugged noncommittally.

Dev pushed off her knees and perched on the bed alongside the dark-haired girl. "Wasn't it you who said that I shouldn't be lonely?"

Ashley sighed. "Yeah."

"Well, what if Lauren could keep me from being lonely? That would be good, wouldn't it?"

The girl's brows furrowed. "I guess it would."

"Ashley, your mommy wouldn't want me to spend the rest of my life alone. And I really think that she'd like Lauren."

"Really?" Ashley seemed to brighten with this news.

"Oh, yeah." Dev nodded enthusiastically, knowing it was the truth. Sam would definitely approve of Lauren. She was an intelligent, beautiful woman who seemed to love her kids, and she wasn't afraid to challenge or support Dev, depending on what she needed. *What's not to love?* "Don't you agree, Emma?" Dev turned slightly pleading eyes on the nanny.

Emma smiled. "Most definitely." The older woman knew she was confirming this for Dev as much as she was for Dev's daughter.

Lauren pulled her hair back. She had finally settled on the fourth outfit she'd tried on: a pair of loose-fitting brown trousers, flats, and a sheer, crème colored blouse. She inserted two small, silver hoop earrings into her ears and set her glasses on the table. Then she dusted her cheeks with a light coating of earth toned makeup and carefully applied her lipstick. Now it was time to argue with the hair. "Up or down?" She turned to Gremlin, who was lying on the bed.

He lifted his head and looked, then flopped it back down on the comforter and closed his eyes.

"Thanks so much for that invaluable input, buddy."

The writer turned back to the mirror and let her hair fall free around her shoulders. "Down. Definitely down." She pulled it back once again and grinned. "Of course, up has its advantages too." Lauren turned back to the dog and presented her neck. "Does this say, 'I'm a toy; chew on me'?"

Gremlin yawned.

Lauren dropped her hair again and used her fingers to try to give some order to the wavy, fair locks. She glanced down at the clock, knowing Dev was due at any moment. *I wonder what we're going to do.* Lauren laid her hand on her belly and chuckled as what had to be thousands of butterflies danced inside her. "Why am I nervous?" she asked her reflection as she dabbed a touch of perfume behind her ears. "It's just Devlyn. I see her every day."

The blonde woman knew they wouldn't be leaving the White House, but she also knew Dev was a romantic at heart and would make their first official date together something special. "Now, as long as no one declares war anywhere, we'll be all set."

The knock on the door sent her stomach jumping, and she sucked in a deep breath. *Calm down! You've seen her nearly every day for the past seven months. You've even seen her half-naked.* A slightly lecherous grin twitched at the corner of her lips. *Okay, that's not what I should think about if I want to be calm.*

Setting her perfume back down on her dresser, Lauren took one last look in the mirror, reluctantly admitting to herself she really didn't have time to try a different outfit. "Okay." She nodded to herself. *I'm ready. Better answer the door before she leaves. Then again, it's not like I couldn't track her down. She only lives down the hall.*

Lauren opened the door and Dev stood before her. She held a single, pale rose, which appeared even more pristinely white as it stood out against her dark blouse. She held the flower out and gave Lauren a gentle smile. "Ms. Strayer? I'm Devlyn Marlowe, your date for the evening. By the way, I do *not* work in the morgue."

A million things ran through Lauren's mind at that moment, but the only thing she could think to say was, "That's the best damned pick up line I've ever heard." She took the rose and pressed the fragrant petals to her nose as she looked into Dev's eyes. "Hi," she said softly.

Effortlessly charmed, Dev smiled back. "Hi." She fought the urge to nervously shove her hands into her pockets. "I believe we're supposed to drop your furry little companion off with my children. They told me they're supposed to dog-sit tonight. For some reason they don't think that little...I mean, Gremlin, can spend any time alone now."

Lauren grinned knowingly.

"I think there may even be a petition to officially adopt him in the works. Sorry, it's out of my hands now."

The biographer laughed. She'd resigned herself to losing Gremlin to Dev's kids months ago. Not that she could blame him. She snapped her fingers and Grem jumped off the bed, but he walked over to her at a snail's pace. When he looked at Dev and bared his crooked, little teeth, but he couldn't even muster a growl.

Dev looked at the dog and pointed. "What's wrong with him? I should be fearing for the skin on my ankles right now."

Pale brows drew together. "I don't know. Ever since we came home from Ohio, Grem's been acting weird. Almost depressed." She held up the flower and smiled warmly. "Thanks. It's beautiful. You...um...you look beautiful."

"Thanks." Dev tried to act nonchalant, but knew her cheeks were tinged pink. "Just something I tossed on. You look," her own sigh interrupted her, "absolutely wonderful." Devlyn held out her hand and felt the warmth of Lauren's palm as she wrapped her fingers around the writer's. "Shall we?"

Gremlin followed slowly behind them as they moved down the hallway. The President glanced back at the midget canine and frowned. "I almost feel cheated because he didn't growl at me. And I didn't get to growl back." *I've been practicing, beastie.* "If he doesn't seem any better the first of the week, let's call in a vet." She glanced back again. "Or maybe a little doggie therapist."

"I think a vet would be best. Somehow I just don't see Gremlin responding well to therapy." She looked back at the ugly little dog. "Isn't that right, Grem?"

He grumbled in response, his head hanging low.

As they entered the family room, Grem seemed to perk up a little. He trotted over to the kids who were playing Chutes and Ladders on the coffee table.

Lauren looked at Dev again and let out a slightly nervous breath. She had wondered if going out with a woman would be much different than dating a man. With Casey, she had determined they could both be equally disappointing. With Dev, however, she was looking forward to their evening with a heady mixture of excitement and arousal. "So where are we going, Madam President? Are you my partner for Chutes and Ladders?" she teased, pointing at the game. "Frankly, I could use the help. Aaron kicks my butt every time."

Dev chuckled. "No, let's leave the kiddie games to the kiddies, shall we?" She opened the door and ushered Lauren out. "I have something entirely different planned for us."

They walked down the hall and were greeted by smiling faces every few paces. "Wow. I don't believe this." Lauren smiled back, a little confused. "I didn't even know that agents had teeth! Does every member of the Secret Service know that we're on a date tonight?"

Dev looked embarrassed. "Umm, I may have mentioned it once."

"Once?"

"Maybe twice."

"Uh huh," Lauren drawled skeptically. "Twice?"

"Or a few hundred times."

"Lord."

Dev ducked a swat as they continued through a series of hallways, stopping outside the private theater. She looked down at Lauren and smiled. "You know that new movie that's coming out next week? The one by that director you're so wild about?"

"Yeah." Lauren sighed. She knew she probably wouldn't get a chance to see it while it was still in theaters.

Dev pulled the doors open and the lights automatically came up. "Well, since I happen to have a house with a theater, I thought you might enjoy a sneak preview. But if it totally stinks, you're not allowed to leak it to the press. The director would come kill me herself," Dev joked.

Lauren's jaw dropped. "You got a copy of the movie before it was released?" She instantly held up a hand. "Wait. You're the leader of the free world. Sometimes I forget." She gazed at Dev in pure adoration. "This is so sweet." Lauren gently pulled the taller women into a hug, still mindful of her shoulder. "Thank you."

Dev returned the embrace, not giving a damn about her shoulder. In her opinion, this was the best therapy she could get. "Well, it's the least I could do since I can't really take you out on a proper date." Very slowly she released Lauren and led her to the front of the room.

The theater was larger than she remembered, having only seen it once on a whirlwind tour given by Michael Oaks. It was tiered like a regular theater and could very comfortably seat fifty people. But unlike most theaters, the floors weren't the least bit sticky and the chairs were full sized, overstuffed recliners. The drink and snack holders in between them were enough alone to make the room the envy of any movie or sports fan. The carpet was bright red. And the room still held the faint scent of popcorn from the last movie Dev had brought in for the children and some friends.

During the last administration, the President had the room outfitted with antique cinema posters that featured great silent screen actors like Rudolf Valentino, Clara Bow, and Robert Harron. Near the screen sat an organ, circa early 1900s, that had been used to accompany silent films in one of Washington's oldest movie houses. *Such a shame the public never sees most of these things,* Lauren thought.

Dev gently grasped Lauren's arm as they descended the stairs.

"And what's a movie without dinner?" A blanket had been spread on the carpet, and various chafing dishes had been set out on a low table.

Lauren hummed appreciatively; her belly grumbled when the spicy scent of hot tamales, Spanish rice, and black beans invaded her senses. "I guess I'm just a little hungry," she admitted sheepishly.

Dev refrained from commenting about Lauren's grumbling stomach. "So, shall we eat and chat or would you like to just cut straight to the chase?" She closed her eyes and shook her head. "I mean, would you like to watch the movie first or have dinner or–?" She stopped, drawing a deep breath. "I'm babbling now. I'll just shut up and let you tell me what you want to do."

Lauren chuckled softly and took Dev's hand. "I do believe, Madam President," she drawled, "that you are even more nervous than I am." She regarded Dev seriously for a moment. "Why is that?"

"Umm...well." Dev moved them to the blanket and began fiddling with the food. She prepared a couple of small plates and poured two glasses of wine. "You see, I've not been a very...God, this is awkward. I've only had one real experience with this whole dating thing." She sipped her wine, gesturing for Lauren to join her. "Samantha was the only woman in my life. And since she died, I haven't...I mean there hasn't been anyone else." She finally stopped when she realized she sounded totally stupid.

Oh, Devlyn. Lauren's gaze softened, her heart going out to her friend. They needed to have a talk about Samantha soon, but tonight was for them alone. "Don't be embarrassed by that. Maybe we can learn how to do this together." She looked into her wineglass. "I haven't been overly successful in the dating department myself. But...um..." The blonde lifted her head and looked into Devlyn's eyes. "I'm pretty sure we'll be able to muddle through if we really put our minds to it."

"I think we could muddle through anything if we put our minds to it." Dev leaned over and placed a delicate kiss on the smaller woman's cheek. She allowed her lips to linger for a moment before pulling away. "I think part of my nervousness comes from the fact that I've never been out with someone who already knows everything about me." She sipped her wine and closed her eyes tight. "Including some things I'm going to get my father for when he least expects it." She cracked her eyes open a fraction of an inch. "But if those didn't send you screaming into the night, then I'm damned lucky, and I'm really glad I met you."

Lauren suspected she'd barely scratched the surface of this complicated, sweet, beautiful woman. But she wasn't going to waste the chance. Her gaze dropped to Dev's lips as the urge to kiss the tall woman welled up within her. She leaned forward, smiling when Dev immediately leaned in to meet her. "I'm glad I met you too," she whispered and let her lips brush lightly against the President's.

Sunday, July 4th

Dev hung up the phone, looking to the clock on the wall. "Do people not realize it's 3:00 a.m. here?" She looked to David who was slumped in the chair across from her desk.

"With all due respect, Madam President, they don't give a shit."

"Ironic, isn't it? It's Independence Day here in the States, and I'm up in the middle of the night handling a possible missile crisis in China."

"And that's why you get the big bucks and the cool toys."

Dev snorted. "Yeah, right."

"Do we need to call in the Secretary of Defense?"

"No, not yet. But I suggest we haul the Chinese Ambassador's ass over here. His input will be very insightful."

"Lemme guess." David arched a rust colored eyebrow and slid his tie completely off. "Just because you can?"

Dev picked up the phone. "Pretty much. If I can't sleep, no one can." She reached across her desk and picked up a picture of Lauren and the kids that had been taken when they went on vacation. "Tell you what, just for grins and giggles, get the Secretary of Defense over here too."

David pushed himself out of the chair. "Yes, ma'am. I'll get the latest intel from the Situation Room too."

After several hours of tense negotiations, Dev had managed to get a satisfactory resolution to a problem that could have gotten completely out of hand with the simplest of missteps. "God, I need a shower and a nap. We've got the barbecue tonight and—" Her eyes went wide. "Oh, shit!"

David jumped back a step. "What?"

"It's Lauren's birthday. I ordered breakfast and flowers delivered to her room with a note saying I'd be joining her," she glanced at the clock again, "an hour and a half ago. Aw, she's gonna kill me." Devlyn opened the top drawer of her desk and pulled out a brightly wrapped box. "Let's hope she likes this."

She bolted out of her office and headed for the residence and a houseguest-turned-girlfriend whom she was sure was going to be supremely annoyed. "I should never have had breakfast delivered so early! She hates getting up early!"

"It's okay, guys." David called off the alarmed Secret Service agents who saw Dev sprint past them. "She's just...she's late, she's late..." *Awwww...go ahead and say it.* "For a very important date."

A few minutes later she stood in front of Lauren's door, running her hand through her hair. She took a deep breath and held it as she knocked on the door. "God, please don't let her be mad."

Lauren opened her door and pale brows lifted at the sight of a very disheveled Dev. She would have said something except for the fact that her mouth was full of an enormous bite of sweet roll. Instead, she grabbed Dev by the front of her shirt and tugged her into her room, kicking the door shut behind her.

"I'm sooo sorry," Dev began quickly. "I meant to be here when they woke you, but I had to deal with something that's kept me busy half the night. If I'd had time I would have called and told them not to do it. Or called you and told you to go back to bed or...umm...just called you, I guess."

Lauren waved a dismissive hand. "S'okay, Devlyn. Relax, I'm not angry." She motioned to the couch. "Can you stay for a minute?" She held out her roll and Dev ducked her head and took a bite.

"Umm...are there more of these?"

Lauren nodded and motioned her to the couch as she went to retrieve the plate of rolls and a pot of coffee. "So, what happened?" She hunted quickly for a second cup. "If you can talk about it, that is."

"I helped deter World War III this morning and I need a break. That's what happened." The dark-haired woman settled on the couch with a groan. She kicked long legs out in front of her. "Looks to me like they brought you a nice breakfast." Suddenly she remembered she had Lauren's birthday present. "Happy birthday!"

Lauren's face paled. "Oh, my God, Devlyn. Did you really stop World War III this morning?"

"Actually, pretty close." Dev closed her eyes and rubbed her temples. "I've been up all night."

Lauren joined Dev on the sofa and patted her knee. "I'm sorry." She looked down at the present that was thrust into her hands. "Wow, it is my birthday again. I swear they come quicker every year." She shook the package, trying to guess what was inside as she folded one leg beneath her. "Can I have a hint?"

Dev didn't answer. Instead, she jumped up and grabbed Lauren's glasses off the nightstand.

Lauren reached out and took them, wordlessly wrapping the wire frames around each ear. She stared down at the gift, trying to remember the last time she'd gotten a birthday gift. Her parents always sent a card, but they stopped giving presents when Lauren turned eighteen and became too old for such foolishness. Judd always gave her a gift on her birthday, but he was the only one. Ever. The writer pushed aside the bittersweet memories and held the box up to her ear, giving it another gentle shake. "Do you want me to open it now?"

"Please." Dev sat back down. "I'm afraid I'm going to have to go lie down before the barbecue tonight, so we won't get a lot of time together until then. I wanted a quiet moment to give it to you. I hope you like it."

"Okay, if you insist." Lauren was eagerly ripping open the paper and box even as she said the words. Out of the box she pulled three small, brown, leather-bound novels. "*A Tale of Two Cities. Oliver Twist. Great Expectations!* That's one of my..." Lauren paused and studied the books more closely, flipping open the first few pages. "My God, are these first editions?" she whispered reverently.

Dev released a very tense breath. "Yeah, they are. Do you like them?" she asked hopefully.

Lauren looked up with teary eyes. "I–" She had to stop for a moment. "I love them." She smiled, her chin quivering a little. "Thank you."

"Hey!" Dev reached out and caught a tear just as it fell from the corner of Lauren's eye. "My gift wasn't supposed to make you cry. No crying allowed!" She grinned. "Wait until you see what I ordered for you for tonight."

Lauren sniffed, only mildly embarrassed. She gave Dev a watery smile. "Will it make me cry too?"

"Gee, I hope not. You'll just have to wait and see." Dev suddenly felt an unexpected, stabbing pain at the base of her skull. "I just can't win. I've got a headache like you wouldn't believe. I'm going to go grab a couple of aspirin, call for a massage, and try to get some sleep." Suddenly she sat up straight. "It's Sunday, isn't it?"

"It sure is, Madam President." Lauren's expression sobered. "You work too hard sometimes, Devlyn. And you get headaches way too often. You need more sleep."

Dev grunted her agreement. "When I took the job, I knew what it meant." She sighed when she thought of the time. "I guess sleep is out of the question. The kids will be up soon, but maybe I have time for a massage."

Lauren carefully set down her books on the coffee table. "Umm. Devlyn, you know, I could give you a massage." She slid around behind the couch and began digging her hands into Dev's tense shoulder muscles, kneading them firmly. "Or, I could call someone for you?" she offered innocently, nearly laughing at Dev's deep moan of pleasure.

"Yeesss." Dev's head dropped forward, giving Lauren more room to work her tired, aching muscles. "I'll give you an hour to stop that. Okay, two hours. But that's my final offer."

Lauren chuckled and continued, feeling Dev relax even more. Abused muscles loosened. Before long the President's head fell to the side and she began snoring softly. Lauren enjoyed touching Dev for a few more moments before she slowly ceased her massage. She gently helped the exhausted woman to lie down, easing her onto the cushions and allowing her to stretch out. Lauren retrieved a blanket and tucked Dev in. She leaned over and kissed her on the cheek, absently wiping the faint lipstick smudge away with her thumb. "Sleep well, darlin'. Grem and I will be with the munchkins."

The biographer had just stepped out of her room when Emma met her in the hall. "If you're looking for Devlyn, she's in there taking a nap on the sofa. She was—"

"Up all night. I know." Emma shook her head in mild exasperation and smiled. "I'm glad she's getting a little rest. Here," she thrust a heavy package into Lauren's hands, "this came in Dev's personal mail this morning, but it's addressed to you. Looks like an early birthday gift to me."

Lauren examined the brown paper wrapping. The return address just said "home", but there was a Columbus, Ohio postmark. "Must be from Dev's folks."

Emma nodded. "I'm sure that's Janet's handwriting. But the only way to know for sure is to open it and see."

Lauren chuckled and tore into the paper. "Exactly." It was a book and when she finally pulled away the last of the brown wrapper both she and Emma turned as red as lobsters. "Oh, my God," Lauren whispered, feeling the heat in her cheeks.

Emma began laughing so hard that she had to step away from Lauren's door for fear she'd wake up Dev. "Oh, yes," she laughed. "That is most definitely from Janet Marlowe. Only she would do that, God bless her liberal soul. Dev certainly took after her traditional father, but you'll see a little of Janet peek out in her every now and then." Emma poked the white cover, tilting her head and seeing the darker pages at the end of the text. "At least she got you the paper and not the electronic version. I just don't think the illustrations would be the same on screen. Do you?"

"How would I know?" Lauren squeaked.

Emma rolled her eyes. "That's why she sent you the book, Lauren."

"Oh, yeah." Lauren shook her head and cracked open the cover. There was an inscription.

> *Lauren:*
> *You and Devil make a beautiful couple. I know you both insist that you're not sleeping together. But I still thought this would come in handy. SOMEDAY. Since you already appear to know what a nipple is, I'm quite certain you can skip all the way to Chapter Two.*
> *Happy birthday,*
> *Janet*

Lauren closed the book. What kind of mother sends the woman her daughter is seeing a copy of *The Joy of Lesbian Sex*? A smirk overtook her face. *A pretty damned good one.*

Dev rolled up the sleeves on her thin cotton shirt so they stopped just below the elbow. Tucking her shirt into her jeans, she looked around the room for her sneakers. She happened to be on her hands and knees with her head stuck under the bed when Lauren entered the room.

"Devlyn, the kids and I– Well, that's an interesting view." She chuckled, crossing her arms, taking the time to appreciate the denim-clad backside. In her hand was her camera and Lauren smirked as she clicked off a few photographs. Dev reached under the bed for her sneaker, grabbed it, and banged her head on the way out. "Ouch! Damn!" She sat on the floor rubbing the back of her head. "Hey! America does not need a close-up of my butt!"

"America might not." Lauren wriggled her eyebrows, her eyes sparkling with mischief. "But these are going in my personal collection."

"Pervert."

Lauren only laughed.

"Okay, what is it you and the kids want?" Dev winked at the trio as they marched into the room together.

"We're wondering if we have time for a movie with you before the barbecue?"

"Don't see why not." She continued to rub her head. "That hurt," she whimpered, hoping to get a little sympathetic TLC from the writer.

Lauren had to give Dev an "A" for effort. She was being treated to puppy dog eyes and Dev's most pitiful, pouty lower lip. The shorter woman laughed and gently stroked the back of Dev's head. "Poor, wittle baby," she teased.

"Oh, okay...I see. That's how it is." Dev huffed playfully, pulling on her shoes. "You'd think I'd get more sympathy than that...but nooo!"

"I can call in some staff members to coo over you, if you'd like." Lauren winked at Ashley and the little girl laughed.

"No, no, that's all right. I'll just sit here and be unloved," she paused for a melodramatic sniff, and then started singing a song Ash recognized immediately. "Nobody loves me. Everybody hates me. Going in the garden and eat worms..."

Lauren and Ash burst out laughing at Dev's little song. Ashley walked over and planted herself in her mother's lap, kissing her nose. "I love ya, worm breath." She hugged her mother tight around the neck and received a strong squeeze in return.

"I love you too, Moppet. Now, why don't you go back into the living room with your brothers and pick out a movie for us to watch? Lauren and I will be in in a minute or two."

"'Kay!" Ashley jumped up and ran back into the living room. "Mom said I get to pick the movie!" she called to her brothers.

"I did not!" Dev contradicted as she got to her feet. She turned to Lauren and opened her arms for a hug. "What about you? Can you love someone with worm breath?"

Lauren wrapped her arms around Dev and squeezed gently. She took the opportunity to nuzzle Dev's throat and sniff. "Ash is right. Definitely worms." *And I think I could easily fall in love with someone exactly like you.* Lauren exhaled explosively when Dev squeezed her hard for her comment. "Okay, okay. Lucky for you I like worms," she choked out.

"Guess it's just my lucky day then." Dev wrapped her arm around Lauren's shoulder, wincing slightly at the movement. She'd recently been taken down from three physical therapy sessions to two, because of the progress she'd made with her shoulder and arm. The pain, however, seemed to be a constant she was going to have to live with for some time to come. Then the sounds of children most definitely *not* behaving themselves drifted into the room. Dev closed her eyes as she propped her chin on Lauren's head. "Can I go back to bed?"

Lauren bit her lip to keep from saying "Only if I can join you!" She couldn't, however, stop the light blush that colored her cheeks from the mere thought. "Umm...maybe we should make sure the kids don't kill each other." The writer grabbed Dev's hand and tugged her towards the family room. "Can I ask you something?"

"You know you can. My life is an open book to you. No pun intended."

"Like I've never heard that before." She made a face. "Even Cardinal O'Roarke hit on that joke in the first six months." Lauren pinched Dev on the butt as they walked.

"Hey!" Dev protested, knowing full well that she was loving every minute of the teasing and banter.

"What I wanted to ask you was how you got to be so good with kids? Your kids, I guess. I know you don't have any brothers or sisters."

They made their way to the sofa, casually stepping over Christopher and Aaron who were sprawled out on the floor, wrestling each other. Lauren glanced down at the boys and smiled affectionately as she spoke. "Half the time they terrify me and the other half I'm worried for them. And they're not even mine."

"Hold that thought." Dev clapped her hands together, and the children's squeals came to an abrupt halt. "Why are we fussing?"

"Ashley is a stupid head!" Christopher offered, glaring at his sister, who had teamed up with Aaron against him.

"Am not!" Ash shouted back.

"Knock it off, or I know three midget humans who will not be attending the barbecue tonight."

"Mom!" the kids moaned together. "The fireworks!"

"I mean it." Dev's tone was firm. "Now, find a movie and agree on it, and we'll watch it together as a family. Otherwise, you can all go to your rooms and stay there for the rest of the day."

"Yes, ma'am," they grumbled with varying degrees of sincerity. Aaron led the way to the cabinet to claim his favorite disc and begin making his case to his brother and sister.

"You were asking?" Dev said wryly.

Lauren shook her head. "You solved the problem." She pointed to the kids. "No more fighting."

"Until the next time."

"I said you were good with the kids, not a miracle worker."

"True." Dev leaned back and faced Lauren. "I guess I've just had lots of practice." She grinned. "And as far as how you feel about them, your reaction sounds like a typical mom reaction to me. They terrify me half the time too."

Lauren's eyes widened. "Mom?" Sure, she occasionally spent time with the kids. With or without Dev. But that was mostly for the book. *Sort of.*

Uh oh. I'm scaring her. "Hey, it's okay. I didn't mean to imply...I meant that...well, I just think that being a mom will come naturally to you." She paused, a slightly sick feeling washing over her. She still had the niggling fear in the back of her mind that Lauren was planning on leaving the residence soon.

Dev was frankly surprised Lauren had lasted this long. And she was giving strong consideration to firing Michael Oaks outright. He and Lauren mixed like oil and water, and she knew that his continued presence as the White House Social Secretary, in what was supposed to be Lauren's home too, was a continuously aggravating factor for the writer. After all these months he was still angry that Dev had invited Lauren to stay in the residence over his objections. He made a special point of showing Lauren any bad press her presence drew, once even going as far as trying to attribute a drop in opinion polls to the fact that Lauren had accompanied Dev to a very public function.

"I'm not so sure about that, Devlyn," Lauren answered, breaking Dev out of her wandering thoughts. Her voice was very quiet. "Being a mother doesn't come naturally to everyone."

"I know." Dev smiled reassuringly. "But I'm sure about you. When you're ready, you can be fond of my kids without being tied down to them or anything. And someday, when you're good and ready, you're gonna be a great mom yourself."

Lauren felt confused and suddenly unsure of herself. She could hear the disappointment in Dev's voice. "Umm...thanks. But I doubt I'll have kids."

Dev thought about that for a moment. Lauren always chose her words very carefully. She hadn't said she didn't want children. Just that she didn't think she'd have them herself. "You never know. I have it on good authority that stranger things have actually happened."

A pale yellow eyebrow arched. "Brat."

"Am not!"

"Are too!"

Dev and Lauren suddenly stopped to find all three of the children staring at them in shock.

"Uh oh," Lauren mumbled. "Was that bad?"

"Nah," Dev whispered back. "They already know I'm a brat." The President reached out and tugged Christopher closer by the elastic of his shorts. "Isn't that right, buddy?"

"Yup," he giggled.

Aaron stepped forward. "But she's very, very sorry, Lauren. And she'll try to do better in the future." The little boy knew this speech by heart, having heard it applied to him on a nearly daily basis.

Dev shot Lauren a smug look. "We're a team."

Gray eyes rolled. "A team of troublemakers!"

The children cheered at this very accurate pronouncement. Dev lifted her arm to the back of the sofa, and, with a significant look at the small expanse of cushion between them, she invited Lauren to snuggle. "Even if you decide never to have kids, I still have three I can rent out from time to time."

"Do I get an employee discount?"

Dev mulled that over for a moment. "Absolutely! I am a President sympathetic to the plight of the little people, you know."

Lauren narrowed her eyes. "Was that a commoner or a short person joke?" she demanded with mock fury.

"Yes."

"I keep telling you, I'm not short, you're just tall!"

The kids finally decided on *Stuart Little,* and all three of them plopped down on the floor to enjoy the show. Dev's mind relentlessly probed the sore spot that was never very far from her thoughts. "We'd really miss you if you left," Dev whispered suddenly. She just couldn't go on wondering when the other shoe was going to drop. It was making her crazy. Realistically, she knew Lauren would leave at some point, but her heart was firmly entrenched in its state of denial.

Lauren felt a pang in her chest at Dev's words. "I'm not planning on going anywhere for a while, Devlyn. We had a deal right?"

"Right." She drew a deep breath and smiled. Dev wanted to question her further, but that "mother" comment had already spooked Lauren enough. Now wasn't the time to press her. "I'm really glad to know you're gonna be here for a while longer." She grinned and poked Lauren playfully. "It's nice to have someone to argue with."

Lauren smiled at Dev. "You argue with everyone, Madam President. I'm just one of the few people who will argue back."

"Yeah, you do, and I love...that. Sometimes it's the most intelligent conversation and spirited debate I get all day." Dev yelled for the kids to turn the TV down. "So, I, uh, know it's kinda last minute, Ms. Strayer. But do you happen to have a date for the barbecue tonight?"

Gray eyes twinkled. "What if I said yes?"

Dev hummed a little, tapping her chin as she thought. "Well, then I'd say whoever gets to take you is very lucky indeed."

The writer batted her eyelashes and drew out the already drawled words. "You mean you wouldn't have the CIA take him out?"

"Him?"

Lauren smirked, not taking the bait. "Or her."

"No. You're an adult. Free to make your own decisions. Free to date whomever you'd like. Even if it might be the *wrong* person. The *totally wrong* person. Which is, of course, everyone but me. Does the name Casey ring any bells with you?"

Lauren made a face. "You Yankees always did fight dirty!"

"Madam, might I remind you I am only half Yankee?"

Lauren slapped Dev in the belly with the back of her hand. "Yankee is Yankee," she pronounced firmly.

"Yeah, yeah. You're not answering my question. Do you have a date for tonight?" Dev turned a slightly predatory stare Lauren's way. "Hmm?" She drew her brows together as her body language suggested that maybe, if she didn't get the answer she wanted, Lauren might find herself being tickled senseless.

Lauren giggled. "Fine. Fine. I don't have a date. I'm completely dateless." She nudged her companion. "How about you, Devlyn?"

Dev laughed and pulled back. "No. I have a date. I just wanted to see if you did."

Lauren suddenly went very still. "If David set you up again, I'm going to—"

"Yeeesss? You're going to what?" A dark brow arched. *Really, now? Well, well, feeling a little possessive, are we, Ms. Strayer?*

The blonde woman's eyes turned to slits. "Why, I'll," she paused, realizing that she was being tweaked. *Ooo, Devlyn! Not nice.* She consciously lowered her voice and her body took on an air of unconcern. "Why, I'll graciously make myself scarce. In fact, now that I know about it, I'll see if I can't find an escort as well. That agent who always sits outside the Green Room is a cutie. And I didn't see a wedding ring."

"You don't have to go that far!" Dev held up her hand and wiggled her finger. "No ring here either. I'd love it if you'd let me take you tonight."

"I was counting on it."

Evening settled in as most of the senior staff joined the President and her family on the balcony of the White House overlooking the Washington Monument and the Mall. Tens of thousands had gathered for the Fourth of July celebration, totally unaware of the fact that a party was going on at the White House.

Lauren watched as Dev made the rounds, shaking hands and taking a moment to visit with each person. This didn't seem at all like the tired, slightly frazzled woman who had shown up at her door early this morning, after having been up all night. Dev never ceased to amaze her. The more she found out, the more she wanted to know. *One of these days I swear I'm going to get Beth McMillian alone.*

Eager eyes were looking over the beautiful spread of food that had been prepared, when she felt a certain tall, dark presence move in behind her. "Boy, that looks good," Dev whispered in her ear.

Lauren ran her finger across the piece of BBQ chicken she'd just placed on her plate. She brought the tip of her finger to her mouth and then licked off a speck of zesty barbecue sauce. "Ummm...it is." She looked over her shoulder and into the clearest, most beautiful blue eyes she'd ever seen. For a moment she was speechless. Lauren gave her head a small shake. "Did-did you get a plate yet?"

"I've just been sneaking little bites of the most delicious things."

Pale eyebrows disappeared behind windblown bangs. "Really?" Lauren glanced at the President's empty hands.

"Umm hmm." Dev leaned in, placing her mouth a hairs-breadth from Lauren's ear. "A nibble here. And a nibble there. You know how it is." She gave her earlobe a nip.

Lauren pulled away. She turned around to face Dev, painfully aware of the interested faces watching them. "What do you think you're doing?" she whispered harshly.

Dev stood up straight and mentally kicked herself for making Lauren feel uncomfortable. "I'm sorry," she said quietly. "I forgot for a second that that weirds some people out." There was a moment of almost painful silence, and it was Dev who awkwardly sought to fill the gap. "Are you having a good time?"

Lauren lowered her eyes and blew out a frustrated breath. "I'm sorry, Devlyn. I just..." She rocked her head back and forth and lowered her voice. "I've spent months denying that you and I were more than friends to nearly every person at this party. Now, I guess I feel...I," she hesitated, "I don't know how I feel." Lauren grabbed Dev's hand and squeezed, hoping it would give her a physical reassurance her words obviously lacked.

"I know. I didn't mean to make you uncomfortable on your birthday. But...um...make sure you save room for dessert." Devlyn quickly changed the subject. "It's something special. And it'll be here in about ten minutes."

Lauren nodded but didn't answer.

Dev waited until Lauren looked up into her eyes before she said, "I don't ever want to do anything that hurts or embarrasses you, Lauren. I mean that. If you're not ready for me to touch you in public, that's okay. You just let me know when and if you are, all right? I'll be here."

Dev's words were delivered in a calm, even voice, but Lauren could see pain lurking behind her eyes. "Damn, I'm sorry." She squeezed the hand she was holding again. "It's not like that, Devlyn. Really." With a gentle tug Lauren pulled Dev behind a large table and into the corner of the balcony, the most private spot she could find without going inside. She set down her plate. "It's not that I'm not ready," Lauren whispered. "It's that I feel like I've been lying to these people, and now I'm rubbing their noses in it."

"Lying?" Now Dev was totally confused. "Sweetheart, you haven't lied to anyone. What are you talking about?"

Lauren winced. "That's not true. At least, not completely." She turned and braced her arms on the railing, gazing out at the crowds in the distance who had packed the Mall area to wait for the fireworks. The view was truly breathtaking. "I've been thinking about you for months," she muttered cryptically.

"Thinking about me how?" Dev nudged her, starting to understand what Lauren meant. "Thinking about me, dating me, and sleeping with me are three separate things. All we have said to this point is that we weren't sleeping together, and we're still not doing that. And we've just started dating. You don't need to feel guilty or uncomfortable. And if you think Beth McMillian doesn't know that and hasn't passed that fact along to every person she can think of, you are a seriously deluded person. I love Beth dearly, but if you look up the word 'gossip' in the dictionary, you'll find an autographed eight by ten of her – smiling."

Lauren couldn't help but laugh. "You're right about that. Once I corner Beth alone, you're done for, Madam President. I'll be able to retire on the 'tell all' book." A bird caught her eye, and she followed it high into the early evening sky.

The writer let out a long breath. "I know it sounds silly. But for the last few months every time I denied the rumor that we were a couple, it felt like a lie." She shrugged one shoulder. "I guess it's all just catching up with me. I can't believe so much of what's happening." Lauren turned to face Dev. "And who it's happening with." Her eyes conveyed true regret. "I'm sorry if I hurt your feelings. I didn't expect you to be so," she searched for a word, "demonstrative, I guess. At least not in public."

"No. I'm the one who should be, and is, truly sorry. I've just always been 'out'. I figure that people know my preferences, and I'm just being me. But you're not exactly 'out'. I mean you're not even exactly...are you? Wait, it doesn't matter...I mean...okay, I'm gonna shut up now. Let me just say that I've been thinking about you for months too. And this relationship is a two-way street. I care for you a lot; more than a lot."

Before Dev could say another word a dessert cart that carried two huge sheet cakes on it was rolled out. One was decorated for the Fourth of July. The second was a special cake done for Lauren's birthday.

Lauren tried to peer around Dev to get a good look, but the taller woman clamped her hand firmly over Lauren's eyes. "I told you I ordered something special for you. You ready?"

Lauren nodded excitedly, anxious to move away from serious topics and relax and have fun. "Totally!"

"'Kay." Dev guided Lauren away from the railing and around the table, careful to make sure the blonde woman didn't trip. When the candles were lit, she peeled her hand away, showing Lauren the beautiful cake that had been crafted and prepared just for her by one of the top pastry chefs in the world, who also happened to work for the White House.

The cake itself was shaped like an enormous, colorful bouquet of wildflowers with her birthday candles strategically placed between confection petals and leaves. It was truly a sight to behold. Around the outside of the cake, and looking amazingly like clumps of dark potting soil, was a ring of Dottie's special Devil cookies. "Had those shipped in from Ohio just for you, Mighty Mouse. Happy birthday."

Lauren grinned as she looked down at the cake. "It's beautiful! I'm gaining weight just looking at all those Devil cookies."

The crowd that had gathered around them laughed.

Lauren's eyes suddenly widened and a slightly astonished look overtook her face. "Please tell me that isn't the correct number of candles!"

Sunday, July 11th

Lauren was heading for the library when she spotted a very tired President slowly padding down the hall towards her. An enormous smile lit up her face. "Welcome back!" Jogging the last steps until they met, she wrapped her arms around Dev and pulled her into a heartfelt hug. "How was Camp David?" *God, it's great to see you again. It's just not the same on video link.*

"It was rotten because you weren't there," Dev whispered into a pink ear. She pulled away, groaning at her own exhausted state. "It's great to be back." Her smile at Lauren was weary, but genuine. "C'mon, I need to make it to the living room before I drop dead right here in the hallway." Dev grabbed Lauren's hand and determinedly steered her in the opposite direction of the Carter Library. "I'm sorry I didn't get a chance to call more often. It was pretty crazy."

"Well, seeing as how it was all part of the continuing process to stop World War III, I don't see how I can really complain."

Dev snorted. "Well, I can complain. I missed you!" *God, I hate being called away at the last moment. Especially when you can't come with me.*

Hand in hand, they turned the corner and nearly ran into two agents.

"Welcome home, Madam President." The man straightened his tie and stood a little straighter.

"Thank you, Jack."

Amy nodded at Lauren, then addressed the President. "Good to see you again, Madam President."

"Good to see you too, Amy. I haven't made it back to the apartment yet. How's Ashley? Did you manage to keep her out of trouble while I was away?"

"All the kids are in bed early tonight, ma'am. They had a pool party at the Vice President's residence and were wiped out. And Ashley is hardly ever any trouble."

"Do you get paid enough to tell a mother sweet lies like that?" Blue eyes twinkled.

"Nope," Amy answered confidently. "The kids will be sorry they missed you tonight."

"Not as sorry as I am." A frown marred Dev's face. "Thanks, Amy." She tugged on Lauren's hand again to get them moving. She *needed* to kiss Lauren, and she wanted to do it in private. "Good night."

The agents both nodded. "Good night, ma'am," they called after her retreating figure. "Night, Lauren."

Lauren smiled and waved.

Dev picked up the pace.

"You're sure moving quickly for someone who's dead on her feet!" Lauren was having to jog every other step to keep up with

Dev's longer, powerful strides. "I can see firsthand that your hip has completely healed."

Dev guided her around a small, antique table that held a vase of dried flowers. Side-by-side portraits of Teddy Roosevelt and Grover Cleveland, both on horseback, hung above it. "When I'm motivated, I can do amazing things."

Lauren's eyebrows shot up. "Really, Wonder Woman?" she purred playfully.

Dev chuckled. "Oh, yeah." Merely waving hello to the agent posted outside the living room, Dev pulled open the door and yanked Lauren inside, nearly pulling her off her feet.

"Devlyn!" Lauren exclaimed. *Is it wrong that this is kind of turning me on?*

Dev kicked the door shut and pulled Lauren into her arms, forcing the smaller woman to tilt her head way back in order to look at her face. She didn't bother to say a word. Instead, she captured Lauren in a surprise, passionate kiss that left them both breathless.

"Hi," Dev said softly when their lips finally separated. Her heart was pounding so loudly she couldn't even hear the words when she muttered earnestly, "I *really* missed you."

Lauren sucked in a deep lungful of air and her eyelids fluttered open. She snuggled deeper into Dev's embrace, savoring her own body's reaction to her friend's closeness, and enjoying the solid, warm feeling of Dev's lanky form pressed tightly against hers. *Wow.* Lauren gazed deeply into Dev's eyes and sighed dreamily. "Hi. And I *really* missed you too."

"Ahem." From across the room, Emma cleared her throat. "I missed you toooo, Dev," she teased. Emma laughed so hard at Lauren's instant blush that her ample bosom threatened to take out one of her own eyes.

Dev made a face at the nanny. "Very funny, Emma. How is everyone?"

"Well, I'm fine. And the children are all in bed. Too much sun and fun at Vice President Vincent's did them in early, I'm afraid."

"Let's all have breakfast together tomorrow though, okay? I'll make sure Liza gets me back to the residence around 8:30 a.m."

"We'll be ready." The older woman shuffled past Dev and Lauren on her way out. "I'll see you two tomorrow."

"Good night, Emma." Lauren smiled.

Dev shed her jacket and tossed it on a nearby chair. She began untucking her blouse from her slacks. "Night."

Lauren plopped down on the couch and gazed at Dev affectionately as the dark-haired woman puttered around, quickly made herself as comfortable as possible, and put in a call for dinner. With a nod of the writer's head, dinner for one was turned into dinner for two.

Devlyn sat down next to Lauren and closed her eyes. "I'm so tired." She sighed and leaned towards the small fingers that began gently stroking her hair.

"Then you should rest."

"I'm hungry."

"Then eat, Devlyn," came the simple reply.

Dev smiled. "I'm so glad you're here with me tonight."

"Mmm...then you should definitely kiss me again."

Before Dev could comply, there was a light knock at her door. "No," she whimpered, grabbing a throw pillow and burying her face in it. "That can't be dinner this quickly. Whoever it is can just go away! I don't want to be the President any more tonight."

Lauren chuckled at Dev's minor tantrum. "You rest. I'll take care of it."

A dark head shook. "No," Dev sighed egregiously. "If they're knocking here, they're after me. I'll tell them to buzz off." She stood and gave Lauren a quick peck on the tip of the nose. "Save my seat."

Dev rolled her shoulder as she slowly moved to the door. It ached tonight. "This had better be good," she mumbled, pulling the door open. She was surprised to see Michael Oaks.

"Yes, Michael?" Dev inquired in a bored tone. Didn't the man have any life? They'd only been off Marine One for an hour. Didn't he have a home or girlfriend or pet rock somewhere? "And why are you still here?"

Michael blinked. "I had work to do, Madam President. But that's not why I'm at your door. Security is holding a man downstairs who wants to see Ms. Strayer. He claims to be her husband."

"What?" Lauren exclaimed from across the room.

"A Judd Radison."

"Ex-husband!" Lauren corrected.

"I see that she *is* here and not in her room." Michael's displeasure was clearly written across his face.

Lauren joined Dev at the door. "Judd is here?" She felt a dread building in the pit of her stomach. *Why would he be here?*

"Shall I bring your husband up to your room, Ms. Strayer?" Michael couldn't think of a single thing he'd like more than to throw a wrench into Devlyn and Lauren's budding romance. Lauren was an unmanageable annoyance that had somehow, and most certainly unjustly, gained the President's ear. It wasn't smart, it wasn't safe, and his dislike for the writer was only rivaled by the resentment he felt over his opinion on the subject being completely ignored by the President.

"Ex-husband," Dev growled, reminding Michael to get that straight damn fast. She turned to Lauren. "You want me to have him tossed out on his butt? I can do that you know."

"Michael?" she asked innocently, smirking as the black man's face darkened.

Dev wrestled the grin from her face. "No. Mr. Radison."

Lauren chewed her lip, sorely tempted to say "yes" and spend a few moments alone with her favorite person, but Judd hadn't contacted her in years. He wouldn't come here for nothing.

The writer laid her hand on the small of Dev's back. "I'd better talk to him in case it's something important." She turned to Michael. "You can have an agent bring him up to my room."

"Bring him here instead," Dev interjected. "If that's all right." She looked down at Lauren who nodded.

Michael quickly disappeared, ordering two agents to bring Mr. Radison inside the residence. He would personally escort him the rest of way.

Dev pushed on her door, but left it open just a crack.

Lauren crossed her arms over her chest. "I know how tired you are, Devlyn. Judd and I can go to my room and talk. I'm sure it will only take a few moments."

Dev's jaw worked. "I don't trust him."

"You don't know him."

A well drawn, sable eyebrow arched. "I know that he was married to you and lost you. Therefore, he is an idiot. I don't trust idiots."

"Dev." Lauren shook her head and sighed. "It wasn't like that. Judd and I just grew apart. Actually," she hesitated as she gathered her thoughts, "we were never really together, if you know what I mean. I thought I loved him. It was a mistake."

Dev clapped Lauren's shoulder, squeezing gently. "I'm sorry."

Lauren reached up and patted Dev's hand. "Don't be sorry. It just wasn't meant to be. I'm not even sorry," she admitted. "He wanted a wife and I wanted to have a career and a playmate. We just couldn't make it all work. Judd's not a bad guy. We just weren't good for each other."

Lauren was leaving out a lot, but what little anger or frustration she had over her failed marriage was long since gone. In truth, it had mostly been directed towards herself anyway. There was no reason to dig up old bones now.

The blonde woman nervously tugged on her glasses, glad to have Dev's close, supportive presence. "I just have no idea why he's here. Judd's not a social kind of guy. He wouldn't just drop by the White House at 8:oo in the evening on a Sunday night to say hello."

"You don't know for certain—"

Another knock indicated Judd and Michael were back. "Come in," Dev called.

Michael marched into the room with Judd Radison following somewhat reluctantly behind him. He quickly introduced Devlyn, who gave Judd a firm handshake, hoping her frank appraisal of the man wasn't as obvious as it felt.

Dev had to give him credit; he was a more handsome man than his photograph had made him seem. Judd was dressed in slacks with a neatly pressed crease down the front and a navy sport coat. He had short, curly, brown hair and dark green eyes that constantly flickered around the room as he walked, taking in the wonderful architecture and beautiful furnishings that characterized the White House.

Dev quietly dismissed Michael, making sure he left two agents immediately outside the living room, so that Mr. Radison would have an escort ready whenever he left. Which, despite his harmless demeanor, she hoped would be soon.

"Hello, Lauri." Judd smiled weakly at his ex-wife and gave her a tentative hug, which she returned just as awkwardly.

Dev blinked. The unease between the former couple was palpable. *They were* married *to each other? I'm less standoffish with my hair stylist!*

"Hello, Judd." The embrace loosened enough for Lauren to look at his face. She regarded him silently for a moment, and tears began to well in both their eyes.

Something was happening; Dev could see it. She felt confused and anxious at the same time. *I guess they do know each other.*

Lauren finally pulled away from Judd, the familiar scent of his aftershave lingering in the air. "Let's sit." She left her hand on his forearm as she directed him to the couch. "Tell me what's the matter," she said gently, feeling sick to her stomach. *Oh, God.* Something was very wrong. Judd's eyes never lied. Despite the fact that his lips could be significantly less reliable.

The man sat down and studied his shoes for a moment.

Lauren perched on the coffee table in front of the sofa and, with pleading eyes, wordlessly held out her hand to Dev.

Dev wouldn't have moved faster if she were on fire. With an enormous sense of relief, she stepped forward and took Lauren's hand.

Judd glanced up, surprised by the scene in front of him. His thick brows drew together as he focused on the women's linked fingers and the positions of their bodies. There was no space between them. "Are you two...um...?" He gestured vaguely and Lauren nodded. "Wow," he breathed, clearly in awe. "Not according to your dad."

The writer had always suspected that Judd and her father remained friends after the divorce. She'd just never had confirmation before now. Frankly, she hadn't been interested enough to ever ask. "It's a sort of recent development, Judd. Now, tell me what's wrong. I can see that something is. Are you in some sort of trouble?"

"No! It's not that. I...um...I moved to Falls Church, Virginia, last month, you know," he began awkwardly. "Took a job at a small architectural firm there. I guess we're sort of neighbors."

"Okay." Lauren drew out the word, rapidly losing patience. She'd forgotten about Judd's penchant for beating around the bush. "And you showed up at the White House to tell me that? C'mon, Judd."

"Your father called me an hour ago. I came right over." He looked at Dev, a little unnerved by her presence. But not enough that he wanted to drag this out any longer. "He wanted me to come and tell you in person, Lauri, so he wouldn't have to tell you on the phone." A deep breath. "Your mo–"

"She finally did it, right?" The color drained from her face as she said the words. "Oh, God," she whispered to herself. *She finally got what she wanted.* Her stomach threatened to rebel. She wasn't sure whether she should feel relieved for her mother or appalled by what she'd done. At the moment all she could feel was sick.

Judd nodded quickly, glad for the moment not to have to say the actual words. His forehead was sweaty and his hands were shaped in fists. "I'm so sorry, Lauri. Your dad, he...um...he wants you to call him as soon as you can. She died a couple of hours ago. He didn't want you to be alone."

"She's not alone!" Dev interrupted, her voice cracking with emotion. "She's not."

Lauren pulled her hand from the older woman's, despite the death grip Dev had on her fingers. Leaning forward, she wrapped her arms around her stomach in mute comfort. Her chin quivered slightly and Dev's chest constricted at the sight. "I don't...don't feel so well." Lauren's complexion was taking on a slightly green tinge and tears swam in her soft gray eyes.

"C'mon, sweetheart. I think we need to get you to the bathroom." Dev put her arm around Lauren and helped her up.

"I'm fine," Lauren insisted unconvincingly, but she didn't stop Dev from guiding her to her feet. "I need to call Daddy." Just then her stomach lurched harder, and she bent at the waist and groaned quietly. "God, I think I'm going to be sick." She'd forgotten all about Judd, who was still sitting on the sofa, wishing he were somewhere else. Her legs felt shaky.

"I know." Dev took charge of the situation, trying not to think about how she'd felt when Jane had told her about Samantha. "Let me help you." *I need to help you.* As soon as Lauren was far enough away from the coffee table for Dev to get a good grip on her, the older woman held her around the waist and quickly started walking them to the bathroom. "Please wait," Dev called back to Judd without looking over her shoulder. "I'll be out in a moment."

Her tone of voice made it clear that it would be wise for him to do as she asked. Judd nodded reluctantly.

When the bathroom door opened Lauren rushed forward and fell to her knees, retching violently into the toilet. Dev grabbed her glasses just before Lauren lost them. Quickly shoving them into her pocket, she held back Lauren's fair hair with one hand and stroked her back with the other, offering quiet words of comfort.

When she was finished, Lauren sat back on her heels. She was shivering a little, but she did feel much better. Dev handed her a cool glass of water and she rinsed her mouth out with the first sip, spitting it into the toilet and flushing it. Lauren greedily drank the rest of the glass down in one long swallow.

"Better?"

Dev's fingers were massaging her neck and she sighed at the coolness against her clammy skin. "Yeah. Much." Lauren grabbed a tissue and wiped her mouth. "Thank you so much." She exhaled raggedly. "This...it would be worse alone." Reaching behind her, she hugged Dev's legs.

"You don't have to thank me, honey. This is what friends do." *And you won't ever face anything like this alone – not if I can help it.*

August 2021

Sunday, August 1st

Lauren's fingers typed steadily across the keyboard as the kids played on the floor with Gremlin. A quick command had allowed her to disable the voice recognition input system. Now she was doing her work the old-fashioned way, but she didn't want to add to the noise in the room by talking over it. God only knew what the computer would do with the background noise – which ranged from quiet giggles to levels just above a jumbo jet, depending on what mood struck the kids and dog.

Right now, Gremlin was bouncing around them, yapping and barking and squirming between their legs as they played. To anyone else, his display would have seemed like that of a truly happy canine. But to Lauren's eyes, it was crystal clear that the pooch still wasn't himself. She was beginning to wonder if Dev wasn't right. *Maybe he did need a doggy shrink. But the kids do seem to make him happy.* If Lauren was sure of one thing in this life, it was that Grem was completely in love with the Marlowe children. She snorted inwardly. *You're not the only one, buddy.*

Since she and Dev had returned home from her mother's funeral, the writer found herself using any excuse to spend a little extra time with the children, not to mention their mother. Dev had been wonderful. And Lauren was quite certain that if it hadn't been for her constant support and comfort... She shook her head, forcing herself to stop considering the painful thought. Dev had been there for her every step of the way, exceeding the expectations she'd previously placed on a friendship, much less a romance.

Dev had pulled out all the stops, even managing to make sure that the family wasn't besieged by the press at the funeral and during the quick burial service in the graveyard. The President of the United States' attendance alone was an invitation for chaos. Dev had made it clear that she *would* stand by Lauren during this very emotional time and that no one would "suffer" because of her presence. Lauren's heart twisted in her chest when she heard the self-recrimination in Dev's voice. The press had been mostly absent and she wondered what favors Dev had called in just to make it happen.

It wasn't until they were back home in Washington, D.C. that a reporter caught Lauren and Dev on their way out of the White House and inquired as to the cause of her mother's death. To her dismay, Lauren had burst into tears. Dev's growled "No comment" coupled with a feral glare that would melt steel, had sent the reporter scurrying, and she hadn't been asked a question about it since.

Even with the constant pressure, Dev had been a total rock. When the President's popularity took a five point dive during her trip with Lauren to Tennessee, she'd brushed it off with her typical graciousness, assuring Lauren that the numbers would rebound when her tax cut package cleared the House.

Lauren felt the beginnings of tears, but they weren't sad ones. This time it was simple awe and appreciation over a relationship and a woman she'd come to count on and care about deeply that brought them to her eyes. She reached under her glasses and caught the tears on the tip of her finger. With a sniff, she wiped them away before they could fall and allowed a bittersweet smile to cross her lips. Despite the events of the last two weeks, Lauren had never been happier.

She glanced at the children, who were now settling down with Gremlin and arguing over which cartoons to watch. Dev was very careful about what her children were exposed to when she was away from the residence. The television set was firmly locked on channels appropriate to their ages. The writer also knew that Dev preferred that the children play games or read over watching television. Lauren clicked the off switch on her handheld computer, placed it on the table, and moved over to the floor with the kids. "Hi, guys."

They immediately stopped fussing when she joined them. "Hiya, Lauren!" Christopher grinned at the writer and scrunched up his nose as his face turned bright red.

Lauren smiled back. *You're too damned cute for your own good, Christopher. Just like your mama.*

Aaron simply scooted over closer to Lauren, slipping his hand into hers, then placing his head in the crook of her arm.

Ashley rolled over on her back, turning soft brown eyes on the writer. "How do you feel?"

Lauren was surprised at the question and blinked a couple of times. "Well, I'm...I'm okay, I guess."

"It's okay to be sad."

"You're right. It is," Lauren agreed quietly, knowing that Ashley had misunderstood her tears. She forgot sometimes that the children, even when they seemed as though they were off in their own world, were very aware of everything around them.

"Yeah," the little girl breathed. "I was sad for a long time when my mommy died."

Lauren's smile was bittersweet. "My mama was very sick. There wasn't much—"

Ash put her hand on Lauren's arm. "But it's still okay to be sad. Mom used to be sad all the time." Ashley's face suddenly brightened, and Lauren could not help but mirror her instant enthusiasm.

"What happened?"

"You came to live here."

"Oh, yeah?" Lauren fought the urge to cry again, knowing that it would only confuse the kids. Besides, she was tired of all the tears. "That makes me feel really good, Ash. Thank you for telling me."

Ashley shrugged, totally unaware of the significance her simple statement held for Lauren. "It was the truth."

"What was the truth?" Dev asked as she strolled into the room. She wore an enormous grin.

But Ashley was already focused back on television.

Lauren stood up to greet Dev. "It's not important." She narrowed her eyes. "Why do you look so happy and why do I have a feeling I'm not going to like it?"

Dev laughed. "I'd better watch myself. You're getting to know me far too well, Lauren Strayer."

"Uh huh. That doesn't answer my question, Madam President. Spill it."

"I just spoke with Julio and he gave me the green light to start jogging again. My hip is as healed as it's going to get. We're going out right now as a matter of fact. Hence, my lovely outfit." Dev gestured down her body with one hand. She was wearing a navy blue T-shirt, running shoes, and gray gym shorts.

The smile fell from Lauren's face. "Great," she said with a hundred percent false enthusiasm. "You know how much I love to jog."

Devlyn laughed. "Oh, I certainly do. But if you'd rather, I can just tell Michael Oaks that you're not up to it. You know how much he'd like to run right alongside me."

Lauren stepped close enough so that only Dev could hear what she said. "That was such a low blow," she teased. "Do you really think I can be baited so easily?"

"Yes."

"True."

Dev looked down at her shoes. "Actually, I was hoping to invite just you and the minimum number of agents that David will let me get away with." Dev's head was tilted downward, but Lauren could see the contemplative, serious look on her face. "It's been a couple of months..." she continued, talking about her hip and the physical therapy, and Lauren eventually caught a clue.

She's embarrassed about how slow she's going to be. Before, she could keep up with even the most fit agents. This is an easy one to help you out with, darlin'. "You know, Devlyn, for the last couple of months we've been working out in the gym and walking, but I really haven't been running. Do you think that maybe I could run up in the front with you, but that you could take it easy on me? Just until I get back in shape?"

Dev's eyes lit up. "Sure," she agreed enthusiastically. "I mean, if you really want me to, that is."

Devlyn had a healthy ego, but was truly egotistical about precious few things. Her fitness level, however, happened to be one of them. Lauren enjoyed indulging her friend where she could and was happy to do it here. That, however, didn't stop her from nearly having to bite her lip through to keep from smiling.

"If you wouldn't mind too much, it would really help me out if we could go extra slow for a while." Lauren gave Dev a hug and whispered in her ear, "I'm so glad your hip is doing so well, Devlyn." She held Dev a little tighter, the thought of the shooting sending a dull ache to her heart. "I don't know what I would have done if you hadn't been okay. I—"

"Hey." Dev felt a tremor run through the smaller woman and she tightened her hold, her mind racing to catch up with what had just happened. "It's okay." She pressed her cheek against the top of Lauren's head, hearing and feeling a series of unexpected sniffles. Dev didn't say anything for a moment so that Lauren would have a little time to get herself together. "You okay?" Dev finally burred.

Lauren nodded against her shoulder. "I didn't mean to do that. I think it's been building all day."

"It happens," Dev said quietly. "You're doing great. Better than I would under the same circumstances." *If my mother had hung herself in the living room...Jesus.*

Lauren snorted. "Somehow I doubt that." She lifted her head and looked at Dev's T-shirt. "I got you all wet."

"Like I give a damn."

Lauren gave Dev a watery smile. "Thank you."

"For what?"

"For everything. For being there when I needed you. For giving me the opportunity of a lifetime with this job. For just...just everything." Lauren exhaled in frustration, unhappy that she wasn't able to articulate what she wanted to say any better than that.

She's thanking me? When the mere thought of being without her makes me physically ill? "Don't be silly, Lauren. I didn't do anything anybody else wouldn't have done."

Gray eyes flashed. "Wanna bet?"

"Lauren." Dev drew out the word.

"You dropped everything to be there for me." Lauren shook her head. "No—Nobody—"

"Else is as *lucky* as I am," Dev finished for her. She lifted Lauren's chin with two fingers. "And I intend to keep it that way."

Lauren surged forward and kissed her soundly, willing Dev to understand every emotion she was feeling and just how much she cared for her. She broke away giggling when the kids began screaming "ewww" and "gross", and Ashley broke in with the kissing song.

"Aren't they romantic?" Dev asked drolly. "Little demons." She shot her offspring an evil look that still somehow managed to be smug.

Lauren blinked at Christopher, who was giving his mother a miniature version of her very own challenging, arched eyebrow glare. "Oh, boy." She winced. *Dev gets to take care of that little man.* "Okay, I need to go get changed if I'm going to let you torture me."

"You don't have to come." Dev smiled. Lauren was going to come, and she damn well knew it. Once she said she was going to do something, she never backed out.

"I know. But I will." She jogged back over to the sofa and picked up her tiny computer.

"We need to get you an office."

"I don't want an office," Lauren insisted. This was about the tenth time she had told Dev that since moving into the White House. "I like the view from the desk in my room. I just wanted to visit the kids today. Besides, the cherry blossoms were fabulous this spring. I looked out at them every day while I was supposed to be working." Her eyes twinkled. *Say it. You know it's the truth.* "I'm already looking forward to seeing them again next year."

Dev tried to hide the smile on her face by pursing her lips together, which didn't work. So then she bit the inside of her cheek, but that only held it at bay for a second or two. She had the nearly overwhelming urge to jump up and down like a little kid and scream, "Thank you, Lord!" Instead, she reached out and pulled Lauren closer and kissed the tip of her nose. The relief that flooded through her was almost enough to knock her off her feet. She needed something to hold on to. "You're not looking forward to it nearly as much as I am, sweetheart."

Thursday, August 12th

Dev knocked on the door with her elbow. She let out a disgusted breath even as she glanced at the heavy crate in her arms. Leaning the box against the wall, she lifted her hand to knock again, but the crate shifted and she decided she shouldn't risk it. The President set the box down and pounded on the door with her fist. "Come on, Strayer! I know you're in there. You and that little demon you live with can run but you can't hide!" She narrowed her eyes at a passing staffer whom she swore had sniggered at her.

Lauren pulled the door open and tugged her glasses from her face. "I was on the phone with Attorney General Sanchez. Did you know she thinks you're cute?"

Dev smirked. "I am cute. But would you like to see what is *not* cute?" She bent over and retrieved the box. "Well? Aren't you going to invite me in?"

"Oh, sure." Lauren stepped aside so Dev could fit past her. She cocked her head and looked at the crate. "What's up, Devlyn?"

"Where's that little monster you live with?"

"Grem?" She shrugged. "I'm not sure. He's around here somewhere." That was a lie, and she knew it. Lauren had seen him scoot his chubby butt under her bed an hour ago. She wasn't one hundred percent certain he was still there, but then again, she hadn't seen him crawl out either. The poor pooch had been so despondent lately, she just didn't think he was up to a showdown with Devlyn. "Why?" she asked warily. *What have you done now, Grem?*

"Because I intend to sue him for pupimony. Or pup support! Or, or, arghh...something!"

Ooo, there's that little pulsing vein in her forehead again. "What are you talking about?" Lauren chuckled.

Dev flipped the lid off the crate to reveal an enormous, bloated, miserably pregnant Pomeranian. The female lifted her tired head and whimpered softly, before letting it drop to the bottom of the crate in defeat. "You remember my mom's *prized, purebred show dog?"* Dev tapped her foot impatiently. *"This* is all that's left of her!"

Lauren burst out laughing and backed up a step from a glaring Dev. "I'm sorry! I'm sorry!" She continued to laugh.

"It's not funny! I'm in trouble with my mom. If she could reach my butt with her wooden spoon, it would be bright red by now!"

Dev's comments did nothing to curb Lauren's snorts of laughter. "Your mother will forgive you anything, and you know it. Besides, how do you know Gremlin did this?" she challenged uselessly, covering her smile with her hand. "He couldn't have been the only male dog in the area."

Dev lifted an eyebrow. "Look how unhappy she is." She pointed to the dog whose enormous belly forced her to lie on her side like a mutant pig. "Only sleeping with Gremlin could make a dog look that pathetic!"

Lauren rolled her eyes. When she peeked down at the former champion again, she couldn't help but wince. "Ooo...that's why I'm never having children." *Time to face the music, buddy. But I'd be more afraid of facing that Pomeranian than Devlyn.* Lauren turned her head and gave a soft whistle. "Gremlin, get your snaggle-toothed little ass out here."

The pudgy beast slowly crawled out from under the bed. Suddenly, he stopped and sniffed the air. His tail began to wag furiously and he broke into what almost resembled a run. Unfortunately, he wasn't very good at almost running and hit the crate head on, causing Dev and Lauren to jump back in surprise. But Gremlin's face was already basically flat, so he was completely unaffected. His chunky rear end wiggled wildly as he tried to use stubby back legs to climb into the crate.

The Pomeranian, "Princess", began to whine and her tail began to wag too, thumping rhythmically against the bottom of the crate.

"Ah ha!" Dev accused.

"That's not proof!" Lauren cringed when the rotund Pom tried to sit up to greet her now howling pet. "Okay," she admitted, "that's proof."

The writer took pity on Grem and hoisted him up into the crate, setting him gently next to Princess. That wasn't an easy task, considering that lifting Gremlin was like lifting a small torpedo and both dogs were shaking so hard it looked like they were having spasms. "Well, what do ya know?"

The dogs immediately started nuzzling each other, with Gremlin purring like a cat the entire time.

"He looks so happy now! They must have been missing each other." *Awwww...Grem you romantic devil, you. You were pining for your sweetheart all this time.* "Isn't that sweet, Devlyn?"

"Yeah," Dev agreed flatly. "Real sweet."

"Looks like Gremlin's gonna be a daddy." Lauren smiled at the President. "I guess that makes you an aunt."

"Wrong! They are all yours." Dev enunciated each word carefully. "Grem is yours, and *he* got her pregnant. Have fun, 'Grandma'. My mother has disowned the little tramp and I certainly don't want them."

But the sparkle in pale blue eyes gave Dev away. She wasn't too mad, and Lauren knew it. She moved closer to Dev, rose up on tiptoe, and gave Dev a tender kiss on the cheek. When she pulled away she could see a definite softening in the President's expression. "Don't be mad." She kissed Dev again, this time on the chin. "How can you be angry at true love? Please."

Dev fought to hold onto her indignation and anger, but they were melting faster than snow cones on the Fourth of July. "Tease," Dev grumbled petulantly. She made one last ditch effort to maintain her grumpy pose and failed miserably – again.

"Uh huh." Lauren's expression was unrepentant. She threaded her fingers together at the fine nape hairs of Dev's neck and kissed her in earnest.

For a long, breathless moment, both women forgot about the dogs at their feet.

Devlyn licked her lips when they separated. "Nice."

Lauren grinned. "Mmm hmm..."

Gremlin's happy groan drew both women's attention back to the crate. Lauren scratched her jaw speculatively. "Well, think about this, Devlyn. The kids can finally have their own dog."

"Oh, no!" Dev shook her head vigorously. "We're *not* taking even one of the demon spawn from Hell. Cerberus and his mate can just find homes for their evil seed elsewhere."

Lauren glanced down and made a face. "They are going to make some...er...ugly puppies."

"You're being kind."

"I know."

"My mom says any day now, so I hope you know something 'bout birthin' puppies, Scarlett. Now, if you'll excuse me, I have an appointment with the Secretary of Health and Human Services."

"That's great. Will you pick me up a food stamp application?"

Dev laughed and shook her head. "Spoken like a true Democrat, and, no, I will not. But I will gladly pay to get them sterilized."

Gremlin chose that exact moment to start howling even louder. Princess, however, remained conspicuously silent.

"Hush," Lauren scolded her pooch. Then she stuck out her tongue at Dev. "Spoken like a true Emancipationist."

"I prefer Emancipator."

"Oh, is that so?" Lauren grinned and crossed her arms.

"Oh, absolutely. Because, my lovely," Dev reached out for Lauren and spoke in her deepest, sexiest voice, "I can set you free."

Lauren leaned forward until her forehead was resting against Dev's chest. She sucked in a deep breath. "God, I love it when you talk dirty."

Both women began to laugh.

Friday, August 13th

Dev pushed herself away from her desk and tossed her pen down, clearly upset. *God, everything about this makes me sick.*

Special Prosecutor Miller leaned forward eagerly in his chair, causing it to squeak as he braced his forearms on the desk. His eyes took on a predatory glint. "We need to make a statement to the nation."

Dev's jaw worked. "How many times do I have to repeat that this isn't about the nation. It's about a fifteen-year-old *boy!*"

"A fifteen-year-old who tried to assassinate the President!" David closed his eyes and shook his head. He just knew Dev was going to react this way. "Madam President, I'm sorry, but I agree with Special Prosecutor Miller on this one."

"Better watch out, David. The A.C.L.U. is gonna want your membership card back for that."

Miller squared his shoulders. "This is a serious issue, Madam President."

Dev's face went stone cold. "You don't need to remind me of that, Mr. Miller."

David broke in, hoping to forestall an argument. "He was old enough to buy a gun on the street, plan the crime for weeks, sneak in the weapon without being detected by the Secret Service or any other damned security, and shoot you three times. Those aren't the actions of a child, Madam President."

"Our briefs are ready. Our position is strong. I'm certain we'll win," Miller said confidently.

"This shouldn't be about winning and losing. You're talking about putting someone who is too young to shave and spends more money on pimple medication than gasoline, into a maximum security federal penitentiary for the rest of his life."

"With all due respect, Madam President, my job is to *prosecute*." Miller braced his large hands on Dev's desk and stood. He'd had about all he could take. Every step of the way the President had insisted that he justify not only his office's investigation methods, but his tactical decisions as Special Prosecutor. He didn't need this shit. He was making three times the salary in private practice. If this was how Devlyn Marlowe was acting now, she'd be testifying for the defense by the time the case went to trial. The man stepped around the side of the desk, and Dev rose to her feet to meet his challenging stance. "My job *isn't* to do what's best for Louis Henry. He's got three attorneys who are safeguarding his rights very nicely, thank you."

"That's enough, Bill!" It wasn't that David disagreed with him, but he could see that Dev was about to boil over. Arguing wasn't going to get them anywhere.

"I agree that Louis Henry is dangerous and should be kept in jail for as long as possible. I'm reminded of it every time I look in the mirror." She reached up and traced the fine scar that ran along her left temple. "I just think that a federal penitentiary is the wrong place for him now. Certainly we can find something else."

"Would you excuse us for a minute?" David gestured towards the door with his head. "I'd like to speak with the President alone for a moment."

"Of course." Miller stepped away and marched angrily out of Dev's office.

Dev settled back in her chair, tapping her fingers on the soft leather arm. "You're gonna yell at me, aren't you, David? I can tell. The veins in your neck are all bloated, and your voice has that little squeak to it. Beth was right. You are in the heart attack danger years."

David grunted in frustration, not wanting to smile at his friend's joke. He did not want to say what he was going to say next. *Sometimes my job just sucks.* "It will make you look weak by not going after Henry with both barrels."

Dev drew in a quick breath.

The Chief of Staff held up his hands. "Hold your horses, Devil! And for once let me finish."

Her mouth snapped shut.

"Every political talk show in the nation has already speculated as to why we haven't made this move sooner. The Republicans started grumbling three weeks ago. Now, even the more conservative Democrats are joining in. You're pushing a crime bill that includes your DNA legislation right now. It's not the time to appear soft on crime!"

"David—"

"I'm not through. I know you don't like Miller. He's aggressive and arrogant, but he's very damned good at his job. But this time he's right, Dev. Louis Henry belongs in prison. Not some juvenile detention center. I really believe that, separate and apart from the political implications."

Dev crossed her arms over her chest and lifted her eyebrows. "Can I say something now?"

"Uh, yeah." David rubbed the back of his neck with his palm.

"If this is only about the boy, and not about my crime package, then why the little speech?"

David shrugged. "You pay me to tell you the political reality of things. This time, what's best for you politically also happens to be the best thing for the case. You need to trust your people."

Dev couldn't take David's brown eyes boring into hers, so she got up from her desk and moved over to the window, gazing out at the clear blue sky. She gave herself a mental kick in the ass and then spoke. "I just hate this, David. I can't stop thinking about my kids. It's like his prosecution has struck some sort of nerve or something. I can only imagine what Louis' parents must be going through. No, wait. I can't imagine that."

"And you feel guilty for going after him because right now it's going to help you politically."

"Yes." Dev turned to face her best friend, at a loss as to what to say. She knew that if she pushed matters, she could get her way on this, but she never brushed off David's recommendations. They were too valuable and almost never wrong. "You think I'm too close to this and it's affecting my judgment, right?"

"Yes."

"And that I should back off."

"Yes."

"And to let Miller make his motion and let the court decide whether Louis Henry should be tried as an adult."

"Yes."

"And enjoy the political benefits without guilt."

"Yes."

Dev sighed heavily. "These conversations are always so enlightening, David. Let's have one again real soon."

David chuckled. "I'm sure we will. Well," David clapped his hands together, "I suppose I should get him."

"I suppose." Dev smiled when, instead of heading for the door, David joined her at the window and put his hand on her shoulder. "David, you do realize that Liza is probably going to buzz me sometime in the next thirty seconds. I'm already running late for my next appointment."

"True."

"Well, it's not like you to waste even a few seconds when you could be picking my brain. So, what earth-shattering thing do you wanna know?"

A broad grin shaped David's lips. "Where exactly is Lauren's tattoo?"

Saturday, August 14th

Dev was grinning like the Cheshire cat when she offered Lauren her hand and gallantly helped her out of the limousine. "You know it's official now, don't you? The press will be all over us again." She linked arms with Lauren and, with exaggerated slowness, began walking her towards the White House steps. They stopped often and took a wide path to the house, letting the evening breeze rustle their hair and dresses.

Lauren leaned into Dev, gripping her bicep with her other hand. "After an evening like tonight, Madam President, the press can go to Hell. I don't care what they write about us."

Dev laughed at Lauren's spirited reply. "Don't go giving them carte blanche, or they'll be relentless."

"And they aren't usually?"

"Good point. When Sharon does a press recap about tonight, she'll mention that you were my date for the evening. There won't be any more denying it. Are you ready for that?"

The answer came more easily than she thought it would. "Absolutely." Her integrity as Dev's biographer would come under heavy fire, *but hadn't it already?* Devlyn would stand by her, and she knew in her heart that she was up to that challenge. What she felt for Dev, how she felt about herself when they were together...it was worth the hit her career would take.

Yes! Dev wondered if her cheeks would sustain permanent damage if her grin grew any wider. She was so proud at the moment it nearly hurt. She tucked the feeling away as one of the most important in her life. "Are you tired? Could I buy you a nightcap?" Dev wiggled her brows. "I happen to have an incredibly expensive brandy hidden in my room."

Lauren looked up at a sky full of a million twinkling stars, but tonight she didn't envy their position in the heavens. Tonight, things right here on Earth were pretty damned magical. They'd gone to dinner and the theater. The food had been fabulous, the performance had brought her to tears, and the company had been better still. The Secret Service had been there, as always, but ever since Dev's shooting she found it hard to resent their presence. Lauren laughed to herself. *Maybe I'm just getting used to this whole crazy life. No – not "getting used to", just doing a better job of accepting the realities.*

Despite the fact that this had been Lauren and Dev's first public event as a couple, when a normally reclusive rock star had shown up at the performance, he'd received most of the attention – much to Lauren and Dev's delight. Lauren suddenly wondered if that was really dumb luck, or the machinations of a certain lanky brunette who was known to pull a rabbit out of her hat at the most opportune times.

"I'm feeling nothing but wonderful right now, Devlyn." She bumped hips with the older woman. "I'm not tired at all. And I'd love to have a drink with you, but before I do, there's something terribly important that you should know."

"And that would be what, Ms. Strayer?" Dev removed the silk scarf from around her neck and draped it over Lauren's shoulders, allowing her fingertips to linger. "Don't tell me you have a jealous boyfriend who's going to show up tonight, and who I'm gonna have to punch in the nose?"

Lauren grasped Dev's hand and lifted it, examining her long fingers in the moonlight. "Have you ever actually done that?" she asked curiously. "Punched somebody, I mean?"

"Well, maybe once or twice...but I swear only when that person deserved it."

"Tch." Lauren's gave Dev's arm a little pull but didn't let go of her hand. "I don't know whether I believe that or not. I've never seen you so much as lift a hand to the kids. And you haven't pummeled the Secretary of Defense senseless, not that he has very far to go." While Devlyn did have the Devil's own temper when provoked, a gentle, even sensitive woman lurked underneath. Lauren wondered what it would take for Dev to get mad enough to resort to violence.

Dismissing such serious musings, the writer sucked in a deep breath. The late summer air was still warm and humid and the aroma of fresh flowers floated on the breeze. She almost regretted taking the last few steps into the White House and out of the evening air. "What I wanted to tell you was that I hate brandy. Always have. Don't suppose it would be possible to get something complicated, like a perfectly aged, frosty mug of root beer?"

"Hmm." Dev pretended to think. She nodded. "Yeah, I think I can handle that order. Or at least the kitchen staff can. Maybe we'll make it two, and I'll throw in a little ice cream in mine."

"Ooo...you've finally hit upon my idea of decadence, Madam

President." Lauren smiled her greeting to several cleaning staff members who were polishing the staircase railings with practiced hands and gossiping about their favorite soap opera couples. She lifted the hem of her dress as she ascended the stairs, easily navigating them in high heels but wishing she were in sneakers nonetheless. "Should I change first?"

"Hmm, tell you what. You come with me, and I'll loan you a set of very baggy, Presidential sweats if you'd like. That's what I'm changing into." Dev turned her head and whispered into Lauren's ear. "There's only one thing more comfortable."

Lauren shivered at the feeling of Dev's hot breath tickling her ear. "If you say something with the word 'naked' in it," she paused to fan her cheeks, "I'm going to jump your bones right here in the hallway. I swear I will, Devlyn."

"And this is a deterrent exactly how?" Dev laughed, tightening her grip on Lauren's hand. "You have such a dirty mind. So I guess I'll just have to make sure I don't say *naked* until we actually get to my room. Wouldn't want to give anyone a show."

"Liar."

"Now, now, Ms. Strayer." Dev's voice held a solemn but teasing note. "Have I done anything to make you think I would be anything but a very private and very passionate lover?" She waited until a lovely, pink blush crept slowly up Lauren's cheeks and greeted her words. *Damn, she's adorable. Wish I knew what she was thinking.*

Lauren swallowed hard. *Okay, you started this. Don't chicken out now.* "Honestly, Devlyn, I'm not sure. You haven't given me any clear signal one way or the other when it comes to," she bit her tongue, then whispered, "you know." *There. That was clear as mud.*

Over the past two months the women had kissed. A lot. A whole lot. But things hadn't progressed beyond that. For the most part, Lauren was grateful. It had given her time to come to terms with certain truths about herself and about what any romantic relationship with Devlyn would really be like. The taller woman was amazingly patient about the whole thing. Or absolutely terrified. Lauren couldn't tell which, but she was never rushed. Never pushed for more. The problem was, Lauren really wasn't nearly as patient as Dev and as her anxieties about a more intimate, physical relationship with Dev lessened, her libido began to squawk – loudly.

Then there was that damned book! There were only so many times a woman could read *The Joy of Lesbian Sex* before *needing* to try some of those things out. Lauren's mental picture of her and Dev doing what was talked about on page two hundred twelve was nearly enough to make her brain explode. *Oh, yeah.* She especially wanted to try that.

"What does 'you know' mean?" Dev tormented more. "No, no, I'm not sure what you're referring to at all." She chuckled wickedly as they turned down another corridor. "Skiing, knitting..." She opened the door to her private suite and turned a single standing lamp on. It cast the women in long shadows, but was more than enough to see by.

"Bitch."

"Is that any way to address the President of the United States? Tsk, tsk, little girl, I may just have to spank you for that." The door wasn't even shut yet, and Dev was kicking off her high heels. One sailed all the way across the room, hitting the wall with a dull thud. "Yuck. No wonder I never wear those. I don't know how you even stand those short ones you're always wearing. Ahhh, that's sooo much better," she moaned throatily as she closed her eyes and wiggled her toes.

The sound of Dev's low moan and the sight of her in that black, fitted dress, head thrown back, eyes closed, was more than enough to send every single drop of blood in Lauren's body stampeding south. "Sweet Jesus," she muttered, licking suddenly dry lips. "You really are trying to kill me, aren't you?"

Dev opened her eyes and marched over to the writer, who was now perched on the arm of the couch. She bent down and brushed her lips against Lauren's, teasing the tender skin around her mouth with nips and little licks. When they were both breathing raggedly Dev pulled back and swallowed hard, nearly undone by her own game. "Nope. I'm not teasing you at all," she lied blatantly, walking toward the dresser on slightly wobbly legs.

Lauren whimpered. "I repeat: liar." She smiled at Dev's responding chuckle. "I hate to do this to myself, Ms. Tease, but I'm afraid I'm going to need someone's help with these buttons. Emma was around when I got dressed earlier." Lauren shifted, showing Dev a row of tiny pearl buttons that worked their way from the top of her buttocks to her mid-back. "I can reach them all, but they're teensy tiny and murder on my nerves. Would you mind giving me a hand?"

It would be my pleasure! "Now who's teasing whom?" Dev moved in behind Lauren and very slowly began unbuttoning her dress. "But remember, my dear," she swept Lauren's hair off of her neck and leaned in to taste the skin there, "I don't lose gracefully." She gently undid each button, letting the back of her fingers graze over baby soft skin that hadn't been touched that way in far too long.

"Devlyn." Lauren groaned, her eyes growing hooded. Her blood pulsed hotter in her veins, even though she knew this was Dev exacting her revenge at her request to undo the dress. Unfortunately, her body didn't seem to care. "Be nice," she ground out. "You...um...said something about sweats."

"Sure did." Dev nuzzled the writer's neck for just a second more before giving it a little nip and undoing the last button. She ran her hand up Lauren's bare back before turning on her heel and heading for her bathroom. "You know where I keep them. Help yourself." *Oh, God, I need a cold drink of water – poured over my head.*

Lauren took a deep breath. She cracked open her eyes and watched as Dev disappeared into the bathroom. "Evil. Just plain evil," she whispered.

A big part of Lauren wanted to follow Dev into the bathroom. With the slightest push she suspected they'd end up in bed together. But Dev seemed content to play and tease, going forward steadily, but very slowly. Lauren could do that. She hoped. A moment of doubt assailed her and she laughed at herself, certain that once her body's blood flow directed itself back towards her brain, she'd be okay.

The blonde woman was rolling up the sleeves on one of Dev's sweatshirts when the President exited the bathroom wearing a navy blue, fleece robe. Gone was her dress, makeup, and jewelry. The hair around her freshly scrubbed face was slightly damp and she looked comfortable and content.

In the time Dev had been in the bathroom, Lauren's body temperature had managed to drop to normal. In fact, with the White House's powerful air conditioner, Lauren was surprised to find herself fighting off a chill. She dressed, smiling as the soft material warmed her skin. In truth, she plain enjoyed wearing Dev's sweats. For one, they were Dev's and smelled different than her clothes did, despite the fact that, like Emma and the Marlowe family, she used the White House's laundry service. The second reason was it really ticked Michael Oaks off when he saw her sharing things with the President. She smirked inwardly. *Bite me, you anal retentive prick.*

Dev looked at Lauren and told her with a gesture to turn around as she pulled another set of sweats out of the dresser. The writer dutifully turned and faced the door, but peeked over her shoulder just as Dev disrobed.

"Eyes front, Strayer," Dev teased while pulling on her pants.

Lauren squeaked as her head snapped forward, but she'd already gotten a nice look at an absolutely marvelous backside. Her mind strayed to their time in the Marlowe cabin in Ohio and the glimpse of Devlyn's naked upper body she'd gotten there. *Ooo...this is like a sexy puzzle that I get to put together piece by piece. And at the end...oh, my.* An enormous smile curled her lips at the delicious thought.

The strong hands on her shoulders startled her out of her thoughts. "Still want that root beer?"

"Uh huh." Lauren nodded, before turning around. *Chapter Six was all about how to use food...stop it! Just stop it! You'll drive yourself insane.*

Dev's bedroom was large and spacious, and they settled in a sitting area on a massive padded sofa, cuddled close together. They'd done this many times before, especially when Dev had something on her mind and just needed someone to talk to. Both women were comfortable with it, and it spoke of their growing camaraderie and intimacy as friends. Lauren pulled her legs up and leaned her head against Dev's shoulder.

She sighed as the familiar weight of Dev's arm settled around her. "The play was wonderful. Thank you for taking me out tonight."

"Oh, it was my pleasure. Trust me. I'm glad we've gotten to a point where we can go out in public. The press is going to go nuts, but I'm hoping it will be short lived. The conservatives will be up in arms. We'll take some heat and be called nasty names, but if we keep our heads down and stay low, the storm will blow over."

"I trust you, Devlyn."

"Glad to hear it, Mighty Mouse."

Lauren's eyes strayed to the mantel where a photograph of the Marlowe children was proudly displayed. She smiled at the sight. They had been so sweet, trying to cheer her up after her mother's suicide. Especially Ashley. They'd made her cards and showered her with drawings for her room. In her heart Lauren didn't really think it was fair of them to equate the loss of their mother with hers. She'd had thirty-one years to get to know her mother and failed. These sweet children were robbed of that chance all too soon. "Tell me about Samantha, Devlyn," Lauren was surprised to hear herself ask. "You don't talk about her much."

Dev tensed briefly and unconsciously pulled Lauren a little closer. "O-okay. She was a political science major when we met in college, and she was three years older than I was. David and Beth set us up, and we kind of fell for each other right away. We dated for about a year before I proposed. And soon after, we had a commitment ceremony." Dev stroked Lauren's arm with her fingertips.

She glanced at Lauren, who looked genuinely interested, so she reluctantly continued. "Eight years after that, as soon as it became legal in Ohio, we had a short civil service. We were already married in our hearts. We had three kids, and I loved her very much." A bittersweet smiled edged its way onto Dev's lips. "You two would have been great friends." She shrugged. "I don't think there's really anything else to say."

Lauren frowned and shifted in Dev's arms until they were facing each other and she could look into Dev's eyes when she spoke. "I think you're wrong. I think there is a lot to say about someone who was obviously so important in your life."

Dev shrugged again, dark brows drawing together. "I guess there is. I just wouldn't know what to say."

Quiet and unseeing, Devlyn stared at the far wall for so long that Lauren decided to change the subject. She opened her mouth to speak when Dev's low burr pierced the silence of the room. "Sam was the only person I ever trusted enough to give myself to completely. She held who I was in the palm of her hand and the core of her heart. She intrigued my mind, challenged my soul, and soothed my body and spirit. When she died, I was sure I had lost those things forever." She looked at the woman in her arms and smiled softly. "But I think I may have found them again."

Soothed her body and spirit? Jesus. I thought you didn't know what to say! Lauren tried to smother the bolt of jealously that lanced through her at those words. *You asked her, Lauri. Now suck it up and live with her answer. You knew she loved her like that.* But somehow, it was different hearing it from Dev's own lips. The smaller woman unconsciously pulled away from Dev.

"Oh, God, I'm so sorry." Dev closed her eyes. *Too much, fool! That was too much!* "I didn't mean...I mean...I didn't want you to be hurt or upset." *Fuck! Fuck! Fuck!* Dev moved forward as Lauren retreated not wanting to let her get away. "How can I make it right, Lauren? I don't want you to be jealous of Sam. She was a part of my life, yes. A part that is now over and long," she paused, feeling the beginnings of tears, "dead." She wiped her face. "I know I need to get on with my life and I want to get on with my life with you."

Lauren moved her hands through the shadows and wiped away Dev's tears with gentle fingers. "I didn't mean to upset you. I'm the one who should be sorry, not you. I want to know about her." She turned painfully open, gray eyes on her friend. "That was just a little hard to hear. It caught me off guard. But it was beautiful, and I'm so glad you had that...and have the kids." She smiled weakly and cupped Dev's cheeks. "I'm the one who asked you about her, right? So it's okay. I promise," she whispered. Lauren leaned forward and softly kissed Dev's wet cheeks, tasting the salty remnants of tears.

Thank God. "I don't want to make you feel any less special or important in my life. And I certainly don't want you to feel like you're competing with her, because you're not." Dev took a deep breath. *In for a dollar... Since we're already talking about Samantha, I might as well go all the way. If she's going to think I'm a complete idiot, she might as well have all the facts.* "Okay, I'm going to confess something that very few people know about me. Remember when Beth asked me that sex question during our game at the cabin?"

Lauren blinked, trying to follow what appeared to be a radical change in subject. She gave a slow nod. "Of course."

Dev shrugged, a little embarrassed. "Well, I told you that I'd only been with one person. So that was obviously Samantha."

Lauren nodded again, still confused. "I assumed that."

"Well, not only was she my one and only. Umm...we waited."

The writer looked at Dev questioningly. "For permission?" she hazarded wildly, not having a clue as to what Dev was trying to say.

Dev frowned. "Permission? Why would we need permission from anyone? We were both grown women. No, we waited until we were married. Well, I was waiting; she was complaining to Mom," Dev tried to joke. *I have never felt so incredibly ridiculous in all my life.* She rubbed her hands on her sweats, wishing she didn't sound so backward – so old-fashioned. Lauren was outgoing and adventurous. There was no way in Hell she could find this attractive in a potential partner. "I don't know why. I was young, and it's something I didn't...I...still don't...take lightly." Dev stopped and braced herself, praying Lauren wouldn't laugh.

She didn't. Instead, her mouth formed a tiny "O". "Wow," she finally muttered. Dev had just made several things very clear to Lauren, although she still wanted to shine a light on a few fuzzy parts. "So is it like a religious or a moral thing? I–"

"No. Just a 'Dev is a nut' thing. I don't just want sex, Lauren. I want it all. I want to make love and be in love with the person I'm with. I don't think I could fully enjoy the physical side thinking that there was nothing more to it."

Lauren sudden straightened. "Is that how you feel about us?" She blinked stupidly. "Like there's nothing more to it?"

"No!" Dev blurted out a little louder than she intended. "That's not it at all. I just wanted to explain. You know I like to tease and play and all. And I love that we can have fun that way, without pressure or expectations, but that doesn't mean there isn't more behind it. Especially when it comes to you, Lauren."

Lauren smiled tentatively, enjoying the fire behind Dev's words.

"My mother, of course, thinks I've lost my mind and all but told me to take you and ravish you." She smiled back at Lauren reflexively. "And don't think I haven't thought about it." Dev groaned, "Because I have. A lot. More than a lot." She swallowed hard. "I haven't tried anything more because my emotions for you run so deep that I can't bear the thought of taking advantage of you. Does that make any sense to you at all?"

Pale brows shot skyward. "No! What in God's name are you talking about? Taking advantage of me?"

Dev sighed. *Of course it doesn't.* "Sweetheart, I just wanted you to know that you mean so much to me that I want to be really careful. You and the kids are the most important things in my life and I don't want to rush or take chances with any of you." She dropped her hands into her lap. "My mom says I need to lighten up." She smiled self-deprecatingly. "I'm just not sure I know how. I want to go slow. I want to be careful. I care about you too much to do anything else. This is the way I've always been."

"There's nothing wrong with that way, Devlyn." Lauren gently reached out for Dev's hand and smoothly intertwined their fingers. "It's really very sweet." *And I am hopelessly in love you.*

"Face it. It's old-fashioned, and I know I sound like a complete fool. But I want you to know how much you mean to me." Devlyn gathered her courage and looked Lauren squarely in the eye. She drew in a deep breath. "Lauren, the reason I'm saying these things to you is that I want you to understand how important you are in my life." Dev swallowed again. "I care for you very, very much. Over the course of the last few months I've definitely realized that I'm totally in lo–"

An alarm rang out, causing both women to nearly jump out of their skins. "Madam President," a rapid, unfamiliar male voice spoke over the rarely used intercom system, "we need you in the Situation Room. Code One."

"Damn!" Dev leaned forward and kissed Lauren quickly. "I've got to go. We'll finish this as soon as I can, I promise." Dev was off the couch and to the front door before Lauren could say a word. As the door closed she could see Dev being surrounded by advisors and heard the word "bombing".

The Situation Room was buzzing when Dev pushed open the heavy door. The men and women in the room were in various states of dress that ranged from Michael Oak's khaki pants and pressed polo shirt to the Director of the FBI's jogging shorts and academy sweatshirt. Everyone who was seated immediately jumped to his feet. "At ease." God that was annoying, especially when she knew there were far more important things to deal with.

"When did the last one go off?" Blue eyes flickered to a large screen displaying a map of the United States with five areas lit up in bright red. To the left of the screen were five live holographic images of the sites with a city name hovering directly above them.

The Secretary of Defense and the National Security Advisor entered the room with David hot on their heels. Dev turned to face them. "Buckle up, ladies and gentlemen, it's going to be a wild night." She shook her head and pointed to the map. "Five bombings from coast to coast, all within the last hour."

"Military or terrorist?"

"My guess is terrorist," Secretary of Defense Brendwell jumped in. "Our military checks are already coming back negative. Though we've still got about twenty percent to go."

David ran a hand through his short, slightly disheveled hair. "Foreign or domestic?"

"We don't know yet."

The Chief of Staff glanced around the room. "How and why?"

He tossed his briefcase on the table and began rolling up his sleeves. When no one answered his question he barked, "Anyone?"

The Director of the FBI cleared her throat. "We don't know, sir. No one has come forward to claim responsibility."

"Yet," David clarified. "You don't know *yet*."

"Yes, sir."

Dev winced at the live image shots of several firefighters heading straight into the billowing flames of one of the buildings. "Get Press Secretary Allen out of bed and get her over here. We're going to need a lot of damage control on this. And where in the hell are the Directors of the DEA and ATF and the Secretary of the Treasury?" Dev yelled as another paper listing the exact bombing times and locations was placed in her hands. "And somebody find me a pair of socks or something!"

"Everyone is on their way, Madam President," came the answer from the back of the room.

"Okay, what do we have here?" Dev pointed to the screen, but looked at a young man to her left. He wore a U.S. Army uniform.

"In reverse order of attack: a post office in New York City, an IRS building in Atlanta, a federal courthouse in Dallas, a junior high school in Portland, and a shopping mall in San Diego."

She glanced up at the clocks on the wall, looking until she found the one telling her it was just after 11:00 p.m. on the West Coast. She cursed to herself; the stores would have just been closing about the same time as the explosion. "Injuries in the mall?"

"We're just starting to get casualty reports now, ma'am. But there are reports of dead or wounded coming in from each of the sites or adjacent buildings." The young man reached over and picked up the ringing phone next to him.

"David!" Dev whirled around to find her Chief of Staff in the jostling crowd. "Not good enough! We need this contained now!"

"We're on it, Dev!" his voice called back even though she never saw his face.

"Wake up every damned staffer we have if you need to. I want every piece of information available. Get me the mayors of the cities in question and the governor of each state on the phone."

Dev headed for the small room at the side of the larger one that was her own personal command center. Just before she entered she felt something being pressed into her hands. She looked down to see a fresh pair of white socks. Before she had a chance to even utter a small thanks, the person who'd handed them to her was swallowed up by the crowded room.

Monday, August 16th

The President rubbed her temples and took another sip of coffee. She eyed the omelet that had been placed before her. Dev wasn't hungry, but she could hear Emma's scolding voice blaring in her brain, "Eat! You won't be any good to anyone if you don't eat." She picked up the fork and cut away a small bite, placing it in her mouth and chewing slowly as she scanned one of the reports in front of her.

She wasn't a hundred percent sure, but she believed it had been at least thirty-six hours since she had stepped into the Situation Room. She'd only been out once, to give a brief prepared statement to the press. Since then, she'd been hunkered down at her desk, working like a dog, making sure the world knew what a safe place the United States was and how she would most certainly bring to justice the bastards that had called the nation's safety into question.

Among a million and one other things, this required phone call after phone call, video conference after video conference, sitting in on strategy sessions with her advisors and department heads, and continuing to deal with just as many of her normal duties as was possible. *God, there aren't enough hours in the day.* She was grateful, at least, that the children had Emma and Lauren, who she knew would spend a little extra time with them, just because she couldn't. That was one thing she wouldn't have to worry about.

"Don't," she grumbled to the staffer who was about to place a glass of orange juice in front of her. "Please. I hate the stuff. It gives me heartburn. Milk. A large glass of milk."

The young man nodded quickly. "Yes, Madam President."

They'd been lucky so far. Although Dev never thought the word "luck" was an appropriate one when it came to a situation like this one. Five bombs had gone off and only six people had been killed and twenty injured. *Only. It's not "only" when one of those people is someone you love.* By all accounts, it should have been so much worse in San Diego, but part of the explosive device had failed to go off. The junior high school in Portland had been nearly flattened, but even the janitorial staff had all gone home by the time the bomb had detonated. The community, however, was reeling.

While still wholly unjustifiable, Dev could almost understand the bombings in New York City, Atlanta, and Dallas. Those were all government buildings, always a favorite of terrorists. The two civilian targets, however, made no sense whatsoever, and this pissed her off more than anything.

When the door opened again, the Attorney General entered the room. She looked as tired as Dev felt. "Coffee's fresh." Dev pointed to the carafe in front of her.

"If I take another drink of coffee, it'll be oozing out my pores and my husband won't come near me for weeks."

Dev chuckled and rested her chin on her fist. "Nah, that's just a nasty rumor started by people who sell tea." Her good humor faded quickly, however, and she blew out a frustrated breath. "I need good news. Please tell me you have some good news."

"There's very little good news in a situation like this. But we have our top people deployed at every scene."

Dev nodded. "Do we know anything yet? Are they connected? If you feel the need to lie just so that I feel better, I won't resent it in the least."

"Well, that, at least, is something we do know. Preliminary reports show that the explosive devices in Atlanta, San Diego and New York were nearly identical. We're still waiting on the results from the other two cities. But, for now at least, it looks like the same person, or group, is responsible."

"Is that good news?"

"Most definitely. One group is easier to round up than two or three."

Dev leaned back and sighed heavily. "This is true. Well, there's some progress at least."

"Yes, ma'am. We'll get there."

Dev met the Attorney General's gaze head on. "Yes. We will." She laid her palms flat on her desk. "In your professional opinion, is this an all right time for me to get out of here for a little while so that I can take a shower and see my family?"

"Yes, Madam President. It would be a fine time." The older woman gave Dev a bittersweet smile. "You've had more challenges in your first eight months than most Presidents face in four years. You're facing these challenges in a way that makes me proud to be an American, a woman, and a member of your team. A lot of people think of you as a hero. I just wanted to take a moment to let you know that I'm one of them. It's an honor to work with you, Madam President."

For a moment Dev was speechless. "Wow," she finally mumbled. "That was one helluva pep talk. My kids' nanny could learn a lesson from you." Dev's expression turned serious. "You know I feel the same way about you, Evelyn."

Evelyn Sanchez squared her shoulders proudly as her cheeks took on a slightly pink tint. "That's just because I kick ass and take names."

Dev chuckled. "Why do you think I appointed you? That's my version of kicking ass."

Evelyn lowered voice. "We'll get them, Dev. I know it."

Dev nodded as she rose to her feet. She stretched, rolling her head in a slow circle to get out the kinks. "I'll be back in a few hours." Dev made a show of sniffing the air. "I think I tend to offend."

The Attorney General snorted. "Have you smelled the air in the

Situation Room? Why the hell do you think I'm in here with you?"

Heading into the residence, the first things Dev heard were the faint, but delighted squeals of two children; her brow creased as she wondered what had happened to her youngest child, whose voice was missing from the mix. As she made her way farther down the hall, she realized the sounds were coming from Lauren's room. She stopped and listened outside the ajar door.

"Is she okay?" Ashley asked worriedly.

"I think she's fine," Lauren answered with more confidence than she actually felt.

Dev rapped on the door. "Anyone home?" She pushed the door open a little further and stepped inside. "Is this a private party, or can anyone join the fun?"

"Mom!" Christopher jumped up and ran over to his mother, flinging himself into her arms.

"Hiya, pal." She groaned quietly as she picked him up. *Damned shoulder.* Blue eyes flickered around the room and landed on Aaron, who was on Lauren's bed fast asleep. She turned back to Ashley and Christopher. "Now, what's causing all this ruckus? I could hear you half a mile way."

"Puppies!" Ash grinned. "Princess is having her puppies!"

The tall woman leveled her gaze at Lauren, who was looking slightly green around the gills but otherwise in good spirits. "Oh, joy. How many so far?" She set Christopher down.

Lauren stepped out of the way to reveal Princess' bed. If Dev strained she could hear the faint whimpering sound of the mutant baby dogs. "Do you guys need a vet?"

"I don't think so. Then again, Princess has been silent on the subject." The writer stepped closer to Dev, leaving Christopher and Ashley leaning over the box Lauren had placed Princess in.

The little boy and girl cooed at the squirming puppies and gently stroked their longish, wiry hair.

Princess grunted and then let out a long-suffering groan.

"She's had two so far." Lauren winced. "But I don't think she's finished."

Dev couldn't disagree. Judging by the sounds coming out of the box, Princess still had a way to go. "Sucks to be Princess today."

"Oh, yeah." The shorter woman wrinkled her nose. "But on the bright side, I haven't thrown up or passed out yet."

A genuine grin stretched Dev's cheeks. "Wow. I'm impressed."

"You should be," Lauren teased back.

Dev peeked over Lauren's head and caught a glimpse of the puppies. "Oh, my God," she muttered.

"I know," Lauren giggled. "Poor things. They didn't inherit all of Grem's good looks. They look at least part Pomeranian." She mulled that statement over in her mind for a moment and then amended herself. "Or maybe part alien. One of the two."

"Grem's good looks?" Dev flicked Lauren a disgusted look, but chuckled when the tip of a pink tongue was the blonde's reply.

Of their own accord, Lauren's arms found their way around Dev's waist, and she placed a gentle kiss on waiting lips. "How goes it?"

"Not so well," Dev admitted quietly. "But we're handling it and starting to make some progress."

"Of course you are." Lauren cupped Dev's cheek with her palm and the President leaned into the comforting touch. "Anything I can do to help?"

Dev glanced at Aaron who was curled in a tight ball, snoring happily with a thin blanket draped over him. "You're already doing it, sweetheart. Thank you."

Slate gray eyes flecked with tiny bits of blue and green went round and innocent. "Well, I thought they should be here when the puppies were born."

Devlyn chuckled and lifted a droll brow. "Very sneaky. But we are not taking even a single one of Grem's babies. Speaking of my arch nemesis..." Dev's gaze narrowed as it crisscrossed the floor.

Lauren burst out laughing. "He's hiding under the bed. I tried to get him to come out earlier, but he's not budging."

Princess whimpered pitifully as another portly part-pug shifted within her.

Dev shook her head, cringing at the piteous sound. "Maybe he's smarter than I gave him credit for." Dev captured the writer's hand and gave it a kiss. "I'm on my way to get a shower and a change of clothes. I'll be back in a few minutes. I don't have a lot of time, but I'd love to spend what I have with the four of you. How about I meet you in the dining room for a snack in about twenty minutes?" *I think I can finally eat something.*

Lauren drew the tip of her finger down Dev's throat, lingering almost imperceptibly at her pulse point, then coming to rest on her collarbone. "What would you like?" She looked up at Dev from behind pale lashes.

Dev swallowed hard as a warm wave of desire washed over her. *Damn, she can flirt.* She growled and ducked her head for another quick kiss. "There are lots of things I'd like, but I guess I'll have to settle for food and good company." She winked at Lauren before heading towards the kids. Dev gave Christopher and Ashley a quick kiss on the tops of their heads, trying not to look into the crate again and risk traumatic blindness – again. *Aren't all puppies supposed to be cute?* "See you guys in a few minutes."

After a snack of fresh fruit and milk, they returned to Lauren's room to do a puppy check. Dev was dismayed to find that Princess had delivered not only a third, but a fourth puppy. "Holy cow!" she exclaimed, fending off Lauren's playful slaps. "They are so, so..." she searched her mind for an appropriate word.

"Cute!" Aaron provided helpfully, still a little dazed from his nap. He positioned himself in his mother's lap so that they could peer into the doggy crate together. "Now there's enough for us each to have our very own!"

And so it begins... "Aaron, we are not keeping these puppies."

Aaron's bottom lip immediately poked out. "Awww, Mom..."

"Aw, Mom..." Lauren echoed him cheekily.

"No." Dev glared at the writer. She put Aaron down and tried to look firm about her decision. "No. And that's final." She ignored Lauren's muffled snort.

Gremlin had finally gathered his courage and was standing on his hind legs, his front paws hanging over the edge of the crate as he peered down at his growing family. He looked at Dev and growled in warning, protectively baring his teeth. Dev only laughed. "Oh, don't worry about it, buddy. They are *all* yours." She started herding the children away from Princess and the squirming puppies so that the detachment process could begin.

All three kids began whining and dragging their feet.

Just as Dev was about to lose control of her brood, Emma poked her head inside Lauren's room. Upon seeing the impending disaster, she took charge, reining in the Marlowe children and escorting them out of Lauren's room.

"Thank you, Emma!" Dev called out to the nanny as the door shut.

When they were alone, Dev opened her arms and Lauren stepped into them without hesitation. She hummed her delight at having the smaller woman wrapped tightly in her embrace. They both stood in total silence. Devlyn needed the wordless comfort and Lauren was more than happy to oblige. "Don't suppose we can spend all day like this," she finally sighed.

The blonde woman tightened her grip on Dev. "I'm game if you are, darlin'."

Dev smiled into Lauren's hair, enjoying the light scent of her shampoo and the closeness of a friendship she'd come to cherish. "I need to get back there."

Lauren let out an unhappy breath. "I know. I haven't been able to keep up with much that's been happening. Between the puppies and the kids it's been crazy. I tried not to have the television going when we were together." She shrugged. "Ashley heard some people talking and had some questions that I thought you'd want to answer yourself." She stopped and rubbed her cheek against Dev's shoulder. "Were very many people hurt and killed?"

"One is too many, but, yeah, people were killed. I checked the numbers one more time before I left the Situation Room and the deaths had gone up to ten and forty-six injured. Initial numbers weren't as high as we suspected they would be, but they've been slowly climbing because of injuries in nearby buildings that weren't initially included in our figures or weren't reported. Some of the more seriously injured didn't make it." Dev stared at the far wall as she thought. "I'm going to be pretty busy over the next couple of weeks. I'll be doing a lot of traveling, meeting with governors, mayors, and community groups."

"I know." Lauren's voice took on a no-nonsense tone. "I'm coming with you. It's important for me to be there for you too. Like you were there for me at my mom's funeral. Not to mention that it's critical for the book."

Silence.

Lauren frowned, an uneasy feeling blossoming in the pit of her stomach. "Devlyn?"

Dev cursed under her breath and braced herself. "I'm sorry, sweetheart, but it's not safe for you to come on this trip."

"Oh, no! No, you don't!" Lauren tried to pull away, but Dev held her tight.

"No." She set her jaw. "I mean it, so there is no sense in arguing with me on this." *Even though you usually win our arguments.* "I'm not going to clear you for this trip, Lauren. It's too dangerous right now. Lots of people are scared and upset. And people who are scared and upset do stupid things. I won't risk your getting hurt."

Lauren's temper rose and an angry flush worked its way up her neck. "I won't be coddled! And if it's too dangerous for me, then it's too dangerous for you."

"I don't have a choice. I can't appear to be afraid to be seen in public. One of the points in going is to make sure that people see that this administration won't be bullied." Dev's eyes flashed with anger. "That *I* won't be bullied. This is my job."

"And what about my job?" Lauren snapped back. "The book—"

"Is not worth risking you over!" Dev consciously lowered her voice and grabbed hold of her emotions. She knew she was being overly cautious, but she kept thinking of what she'd already lost and what she wasn't willing to risk. The rational part of her mind told her that the Secret Service could keep Lauren as safe as they could keep her. Then again, she'd been shot three times.

"What happened to unlimited access?" Lauren demanded.

"This is not about that, and you know it."

Lauren finally pried herself loose from Dev's embrace. She couldn't get good and pissed off when the older woman held her in her arms. Lauren needed distance – even if it was only a foot or two. She crossed her arms over her chest and lifted her chin defiantly. "After the assassination attempt we still went places together. Why is this so different?"

"Because this is hot on the heels of something that has the public in an uproar. And half of them are insane on a good day! But when things like this happen, the crazy ones get even crazier and the extremists more extreme. That anger is directed at the piss poor government that they didn't like to begin with. People protest, people riot. Since yesterday there have been several credible threats made against me, the Vice President, and Air Force One." Dev threw her hands in the air. "Now is just not a good time! It's not forever, Lauren. I promise. God, with everything else that's going on right now, I just can't handle worrying about you. I couldn't stand losing you, too. Please."

Lauren went stone still. "How credible?"

"Even David is worried."

"Then you should stay!"

"I can't, but you can." Dev's eyes begged her to agree.

The President's words were soft but fierce, and the biographer felt herself caving in without wanting to. *For God's sake, not the "sad eyes". That's not fair!*

"Please, just this once give in. For me. Please," Dev whispered. This was far more than just business. She was playing on Lauren's affections, and she knew it. But this wasn't a game, and if Dev had to fight dirty, she would.

Lauren could see real fear in Dev's eyes and she exhaled explosively, running a slightly shaky hand through her thick, wavy hair. She looked away from Devlyn and bit her tongue to keep from continuing to protest. *Damn, you fight dirty.* She scowled at her options and when she turned back, intense, gray eyes bore so deeply into the President that she sucked in a surprised breath. "Swear to me that you'll do everything David says when it comes to security."

Dev blinked a few times. She wasn't expecting that. "Uh..."

"Promise, Devlyn! Or, so help me, I'll follow you around on a commercial plane if I have to, like some sort of damned groupie!"

Dev nodded, letting out a long, relieved breath. *Yes. Thank you.* "I promise."

"I can't believe I'm letting you get away with this." Lauren shook her head, then pushed her glasses higher up on her nose. "I'm going to worry about you the entire time you're gone."

Dev stepped forward and, seeing no resistance in Lauren's face, put her arms back around the smaller woman. "Thank you, Lauren. I know you think this is silly. But I swear to you it's not."

A pale eyebrow lifted.

"Okay," Dev conceded, "not completely silly."

"Just this once, Devlyn." Lauren sighed. "Next time I'm not letting you off the hook so easily. We'll duke it out like always."

Dev crossed her heart. "Next time you can pitch a fit for a long as you want...and then give in."

"Don't push it." But Lauren couldn't help but crack a tiny smile.

Dev smiled back and lifted Lauren's chin so that she was looking deeply into her eyes. She didn't stop to think about what she was saying, or the fact that she hadn't ever said it out loud to Lauren before. "I love you so much it hurts," she whispered fervently. The words dropped effortlessly from her lips. And in that instant, she wondered why in the hell she had waited so long to say them.

Lauren closed her eyes and buried her face in the crook of Dev's neck. Hot tears pricked her eyes and she let them come. Dev's arms tightened around her, and she sighed, absorbing the sweet pleasure of the moment. "You—" Lauren stopped and swallowed hard, collecting herself. "You are shameless and will say anything to win an argument," she teased weakly. She squeezed Dev hard and dropped a tender kiss in the hollow of her throat, and then pulled back to meet glistening blue eyes. Her heart swelled, and she promised, "I love you too."

David handed Dev the report as soon as she walked into the room. "We've got them, Madam President." He smiled triumphantly. "A militia group out of Oregon. They claimed responsibility about twenty minutes ago and what specifics they let slip about the bombings were enough to confirm that their claim is legitimate. We've already got a bead on their location. They've been under minimal surveillance for months. Although, obviously, we didn't know they were planning anything like this."

"Everyone involved in the decision making process, in the Oval Office now," Dev ordered, already heading for the room herself. She wanted to be comfortable when she heard this.

She settled in behind her desk while everyone else filed in. They all stood, waiting for David, who took a seat across from Dev. The next twenty minutes were spent briefing Dev about the militia group and the FBI's plan to go in and "neutralize" them. She asked every question she could think of and soaked up the intelligence information like a sponge. There were several minor clashes between agencies over exactly how this "neutralization" should take place, but Dev felt those disagreements helped to flesh out important considerations that shouldn't be ignored.

When the last briefing was over, Dev remained silent for several moments, absorbing what she'd been told, her mind running through the several scenarios that had been laid on the table for her consideration. Finally, she took a deep breath and said, "Ladies and gentlemen, I need you to step outside for a moment while I consult with the Chief of Staff." Dev's request was met with murmurs of agreement and the room cleared in a matter of seconds.

David studied the President attentively. "You know what has to be done, Dev." He sighed, and his gaze dropped to his hands. "We need to take them out before they do more damage."

"Women and children?"

The red-haired man chewed the inside of his cheek. "Yes." David looked at his hands again. "The Director of the FBI confirmed that there will very likely be women and children in the compound. Dev, they brought them in months ago as a 'fuck you' to you. The families are there to act as human shields against government invasion."

"We were just kids, David, but do you remember Waco?"

"I do, Madam President, but this is entirely different." His mind flashed to the television in his parents' living room, filled with images of flames, explosions, and body bags. "These people have struck out against the nation as a whole. They've *already* killed. They are large and organized. We got very lucky in tracing their location to this Oregon compound. They have 'hidden' camps all over the country."

Dev scrubbed her face with her hands. "Jesus Christ." She covered her eyes with her palms for a moment and then let her hands drop to the tabletop. "Can you call everyone back in?"

David nodded and moved quickly. He opened the door and motioned for the group to reenter the room.

Dev's expression was firm and grim as she waited for the last man to shut the door behind him before beginning. "So, are we operating under the theory that if we cut off the head of the snake, the body will die?"

The Attorney General set a new file in front of Dev. "Yes, ma'am, that is the current theory."

Dev pushed away from the table, rolling her shoulder to alleviate the slight ache that had developed. Her eyes flitted to each person as she spoke. "Is anyone here a student of Greek mythology? Does the word Hydra mean anything to you?"

The Director of the FBI nodded. "Yes, Madam President. The mythical creature had nine heads. Problem was, if you cut one of them, two grew back."

"Exactly." Dev waited and let that statement sink into the gathering of men and women. "One moment please." She turned her attention to the new file, carefully reading it over and processing. *The best choice was clear.* It made her stomach roil all the same. She closed the manila folder and tossed it back on the table.

Every set of expectant eyes trained themselves firmly on her and she met them head on. "Go get them, ladies and gentlemen. The first plan was the best. Go with that, but first incorporate the changes proposed by the ATF. And let's pray that we get every head of this particular Hydra, so we don't have to worry about any growing back."

"That's it!" David announced quickly getting to his feet. "I want the new plan, with those changes added in, ready for final review by the President in fifteen minutes. Let's call it," his eyes darted to Dev, then back to his audience, "Operation: Hydra." The room emptied quickly, leaving Dev and David alone. "You okay?" he asked in a low, concerned voice.

"I may have just ordered the deaths of innocent women and children. No, I'm not okay," Dev grounded out harshly. She stood and gathered the files she'd asked be left for her review. "But it was my call to make and I made it. Three hundred and twenty million people expect me to keep them safe. I had no choice. We have to move right now, before these assholes dig in deeper or bomb somebody else's building."

David didn't say a word. He knew this tone. This was her I-hated-every-minute-of-it-but-I-did-what-I-had-to-do tone. Her speech was quick and it was rough. This was a bitter pill for his friend to swallow, but he knew her well enough to know she'd take her medicine. Now Dev just had to live with her decision. Right or wrong.

"Tell them to get Air Force One ready to fly, David. And then call Beth and—"

"Tell her I won't be home for dinner?"

"For probably the next couple of weeks. We're going to Oregon first; I want to be there for the fallout. Then to the bombing sites. Jane and Liza will have a heart attack that I'm moving this trip up at the last moment." Dev shrugged. "But the time is right, and they'll live. That reminds me, based on the reports you showed me this morning, only absolutely crucial personnel are going with us this time. I don't want to risk anyone's safety unnecessarily." She moved for the door, but looked back over her shoulder before juggling the files and opening the door. "By the way, congratulations."

"For what?"

"You are now the proud owner of the ugliest puppy you will ever lay eyes on."

Tuesday, August 17th

"Ladies and gentlemen, members of the press, the President of the United States."

They had worked on her speech on Air Force One. And by the time her plane landed in Oregon, Operation: Hydra was over, and it was time to brief the nation. You could hear a pin drop as Dev took a deep breath and slowly walked to the podium. She looked directly at the camera and reminded herself to stay cool. "Ladies and gentlemen, thank you for coming today. As Press Secretary Allen said, I'll be making a short statement about the actions that were taken a few hours ago. At this time, I won't be taking questions; we'll set that up at a later date."

She paused for a moment, taking a sip of water. To the viewing audience her expression appeared concerned, but mild, but those who knew her well could tell she was troubled. "Early this morning, special tactical units of the DEA, FBI, and ATF, in conjunction with state and local law enforcement agencies, made an early morning entry into the fortified structures of the compound of the Brothers of Freedom militia group – a group that had been under observation."

She looked at the faces before her, making sure her eye contact conveyed that she had nothing to hide. "The entry into the compound was quick and decisive. It was well planned and timed to take place when the least number of people were expected to be awake and moving about. By timing the entrance for the very early morning, we hoped to limit the number of potential casualties, both for the people fortified inside this heavily armed encampment, and our own duly sworn law enforcement and military personnel."

Devlyn glanced at her notes very briefly, not wanting to lose an ounce of the trust and leadership she was trying to communicate by her words and confident demeanor. "While, overall, the entrance was a successful one, and many members of the organization were taken into custody, there were, unfortunately, casualties on both sides. Twenty-two members of the militia were killed and fourteen wounded. Our own agencies sustained losses and injuries to their personnel as well. Combined figures show losses to law enforcement organizations in this operation to be ten dead and five wounded."

She gripped the edge of the podium and increased the intensity of her voice to finish on a strong note. "The people responsible for the five terrorist attacks within our own borders, which took the lives of ten innocent men and women, seriously injured dozens more, and did millions of dollars in damage to government and civilian targets, have been placed under arrest and will be duly charged. A full investigation continues, and I assure you that everyone involved will be brought to justice. Everything that has happened over the course of this operation happened only after I had been briefed and had given my full consent. I am the only person who should be held responsible for finding the answers to any questions that might arise out of the actions taken under my direction today. As one of my predecessors said, 'The buck stops here.' I am your President, and I will be held accountable."

Dev knew that last bit was going to drive her entire staff right up the wall. It hadn't been a part of the original speech, but she didn't want there to be any doubt about who had made the decisions in this matter, and who would take the blame for any missteps. "Thank you, ladies and gentlemen."

She took the time to unbutton her blazer and collect her notes, then she turned and left the room. As she knew they would be, David and Sharon were waiting for her with both their mouths open. "Not a word right now. You can both yell at me later." Dev followed her Secret Service agents through the passages that led back to her hotel room. She did so silently, rereading a list of dead and wounded from the compound raid. She had highlighted the fourth and fifth names on the list; Lisa Lindsay, age eight, and Brian Lindsay, age six. Seeing the words made her sick to her stomach. These were two names she would never forget.

God help me, I got them killed. And now I get to live with that for the rest of my life.

September 2021

Wednesday, September 1st

Lauren glanced at her watch again and plopped down on her bed, scattering a handful of envelopes. She sighed and started to tear open another letter. Dev was supposed to have called more than an hour and a half ago and she needed something to do while she waited. So she was going over the last few days' mail, which was starting to form a messy pile on her desk.

"C'mon, Devlyn," she grumbled to herself. "Hurry it up. I've got an appointment in an hour." Lauren discarded several pieces of junk mail and began looking over some documents from her publisher. She laughed. Wayne always mixed some personal correspondence in with the business documents he sent. He was "old school" and insisted that his authors get paper copies of their books as well as contracts. Technology be damned. This meant that Lauren occasionally got an actual letter – in handwriting! Nobody would believe it.

Wayne had never believed that she and Dev were only friends. Even in the very beginning when it was actually true. But once she'd admitted to him that they were in fact dating, the man had become relentless, hammering Lauren for juicy details of her relationship and prodding her forward, telling her she'd been alone far too long. "You were damned right about that, Wayne." The writer looked at her watch again and frowned.

She was about to toss his letter in the waste bin next to her bed, when she felt something hard in the envelope. She peeked inside and found a small disc. "Ooo, a present! You might have said something, Wayne," she mumbled. "I almost threw it away."

Lauren hopped off the bed and checked her watch one last time. She shrugged. "Might as well kill a few minutes while I'm waiting on Wonder Woman. If she calls at all, that is." She moved to the entertainment center that was hidden inside an antique, cherry cabinet. Opening the door, she slid the shiny circle into her videodisc player, wondering what it could be. Not that she was complaining. She'd only seen one movie all year and that was when Dev had arranged for the special screening in the White House on their first date, over two months ago.

She scrambled back to her bed and nearly tripped over the crate that was filled with a sleeping Gremlin, Princess, and their puppies.

A three-dimensional image of a beautiful, middle-aged woman, wearing a white terry cloth bathrobe and sitting on a recliner flared to life, her dulcet tones filling Lauren's room.

"Starlight Publishing presents, the videodisc version of the best selling novel: Lesbian Loving: A Step By Step Guide to Satisfaction."

Lauren's mouth dropped open. "Why is everyone sending me instructions? Do I look totally inept or something!"

"I'm Angela Pickard. And this is my lovely partner, Judith." She made a "come hither" motion with her index finger, and a tall, stacked brunette suddenly came into view as she joined her mate.

"Oh, my God, Wayne! You are such a shithead," Lauren laughed, covering her eyes.

"Come with me and Judith on a journey of self-exploration, enlightenment, and sexual satisfaction."

Lauren uncovered her eyes and smirked. "But will you get naked?"

"Chapter One: Getting to know each other's bodies."

"Oh, my." Gray eyes widened. "We have naked."

Dev looked at Liza, who tapped her watch. The President had been in such a mood lately that her assistant hated to say anything. Then again, that was her job. "Madam President, you're incredibly late."

"Aren't I always?" Dev answered moodily as she circled her hotel suite, looking for the phone. She waved Liza off with an impatient hand. "I know. I know. But I just need five minutes. Please? I'm already late. What difference could five minutes make now?"

Liza sighed. "Ma'am—"

"I'll give you the state of Arizona."

Liza smiled. "I don't think you can do that, ma'am."

"Okay, I won't make you take one of the puglies." Dev crossed long arms and waited.

"You just bought yourself five minutes, Madam President."

"Wonderful!" Dev practically dove for the phone, which turned out to be on the nightstand by the bed. The President always traveled with her own communications equipment and her staff knew just where she liked things placed. Unfortunately, some hotel room electrical layouts weren't as accommodating to Dev's preferences as others.

Liza snorted softly and left the President to her call.

Before the brunette could give her access codes, David entered her suite without knocking. "Dev—"

"Go away!" She grabbed a throw pillow from the bed and threw it at him with deadly accuracy. "I'm calling my girlfriend." The words sounded strange and thrilling to Dev's ears and she smiled for the first time all day.

David grinned indulgently. Being in love suited Dev. "Liza said you aren't gonna make her take one of those hideous dogs." He threw the pillow back, hitting Dev right in the head, earning a glare as the President used a hand to straighten the shock of hair that was now covering her eyes.

"Go away!" she hissed. "I only have a few minutes and I'm already nearly two hours late. Lauren probably gave up on this call ages ago."

"Aww." David stuck out his lower lip. "Do you want to be alone so you can lie on the bed and coo and ahhh like a love-struck teen-ager?"

"No," Dev defended. "I'm going to sit up straight and do my best to look irresistible. Michael made sure this place had video link capability before we booked it. I hate being stuck without it."

David rolled his eyes, and then took on a more serious expression. "Listen, Dev, I know how much you want to talk to Lauren, but we're due at the Governor's mansion in fifteen minutes, and it's a thirty-five minute drive."

Dev glared at her friend and began manually entering her security access codes and dialing Lauren's number. She *was* calling Lauren. She needed to hear her voice. To see her smile. For once, the rest of the world could just wait. "Tell me, David, what is the Governor of Georgia gonna do to me if I'm late? Throw a rotten peach at me?"

David opened his mouth to speak and Dev held up her hand, forestalling any further comment. "If you don't give me five minutes alone, to speak with Lauren in peace, I'm going to march across this room and snap your scrawny neck."

"Scrawny!"

"David," Dev groaned. "Out! Or you're getting two of Grem's puppies!"

David's eyes went round and he threw his hands up in defeat. "No need to be cruel. I'll just call the Governor and let him know we're running a little behind schedule." He didn't wait for an answer; instead, he hightailed it out of the room just as the sound of the ringing phone in Lauren's room filled the suite.

Lauren's head jerked up at the sound of the phone. "Jesus," she gasped, surprised by the interruption in her viewing pleasure.

Angela Pickard smiled broadly. "You're doing wonderfully. I just know you are," she encouraged in a singsong voice. "And now it's time to move forward. Chapter Four: Multiple Orgasms – Making The Dream a Reality."

The writer jumped off the bed and began hunting for the remote control. Not finding it immediately, she headed for her videodisc player. She opened the entertainment center door and pressed the "off" button just as her phone rang for the second time. Nothing happened. She pressed it again. Still nothing. "Shit!" Lauren jammed her finger down hard on the button. She heard a light clicking sound as the button broke off and fell into the machine itself. Lauren blinked at the hole in the front of the machine then began cursing like a sailor called home early from leave. Her eyes frantically searched the machine for a volume control button, but she realized belatedly that the only volume control was on the remote.

Lauren screamed in frustration. The phone rang a third time.

"I'm coming!" Lauren called out uselessly as she tore at the covers of the bed looking for the remote.

Another ring.

"Coming!"

"Oh, yes, baby!" Judith threw her head back in ecstasy as the video's host, Angela, slid her hands up the brunette's naked body and began massaging ample breasts.

"I meant me. I can hear that *you're* coming," Lauren growled. She jammed the hole where the "off" button was again, grunting with abject frustration when nothing happened, and the phone rang a fifth time. She tried to lift out the disc player to yank the plug, but it was bolted to the cabinet, and she couldn't fit her hand behind it to reach the cord. Not wanting to miss Dev's call, Lauren finally began calling out her access codes as she darted to the side of the cabinet and tried to reach behind it for the power cord. With any other phone she could just answer, but not in the White House.

The phone dutifully processed Lauren's numbers and instantly said, in a clear, warm voice, "Video conference requested."

Lauren stretched out to reach the plug, but her fingertips could only graze its edge.

"Yes! Oh, Angela! Yes, give it to me! I want it!" Judith screamed.

Lauren's eyes widened when she heard the words. She pushed away from the cherry wood cabinet and desperately instructed the phone, "No. No video conference. Audio only. No! No! *No!*" But it was too late, and Dev began to materialize in front of her.

Lauren whirled around, and her jaw dropped at the vivid, three-dimensional image of the two women, now both naked, kissing deeply, and touching each other intimately. For a moment she just stared, mouth agape, until the phone snapped her out of her haze.

Angela pulled away from her partner and looked directly at Lauren. "I recommend direct stimulation."

"Oh, yes," Judith purred happily.

"Uh, Lauren?"

The blonde spun around at the very familiar voice and found

herself looking right into confused, blue eyes. "Hi, Devlyn," she squeaked, giving the President a weak wave.

A well-shaped eyebrow crawled up Dev's forehead and stayed there. "I know we've been taking things slowly–"

"Again! Again! Again!" Judith screamed at the top of her lungs, while Angela calmly described exactly what she was doing to earn such an enthusiastic response from her lover.

Lauren covered her face with her hands. "Sweet Jesus, just take me now," she mumbled into her palms. "Please. Right now. This very second."

Dev continued undaunted. "But, sweetheart, was it really necessary to start without me? I'm hurt," she teased, recognizing the slightly distorted scene before her as a video playing in the background. *A very interesting video. Who knew Lauren was so naughty?*

"Oh, Angela! Another one?" Judith squealed delightedly at the prospect. "But I can't." A pause. "Ohhh...I can! I can!"

Dev's second eyebrow joined its twin. "Hurt, but impressed. Very impressed."

Lauren opened her fingers and peeked out at Devlyn, who was wearing a bemused grin. She dragged her fingers up into her hair, forming an interesting, Mohawk-like hairstyle. "I can't make it stop, Devlyn!"

"You lost the clicker again, didn't you?" Dev asked knowingly.

"Again, Angela? No, I can't." the stacked brunette was nearly sobbing.

"Judith, love, you can, baby. I know you can."

"Yes!" Judith screamed again. "I can!"

Lauren could only whimper and pray a lightning bolt would miraculously strike her directly in the forehead and put a stop to this wretched, endless torture.

Dev shook her head and chuckled. The color of her friend's face was a sight to behold, the vivid, red tint making Lauren's pale eyebrows appear nearly white. "Did you try the nightstand?"

Gray eyes scanned it. "Not there."

"The bed?"

A shake of the head. "Already tried that."

Both women suddenly glanced down when they heard the pitter-patter of tiny, scampering feet. "The puglies!" they shouted in unison. And, sure enough, the remote control/chew toy was lying on the floor under the bed.

Lauren retrieved it with a mumbled prayer of thanks. And, with a quick press of the button, Angela and Judith disappeared.

Dev smirked at her blushing friend. *God, she's pretty.* "So, Lauren–"

"Don't ask."

"But–"

"If you love me, you'll drop it."

Devlyn began to pout. "Pleeease." She batted long eyelashes.

Throwing her hands in the air, Lauren looked up beseechingly and spoke to a cream colored, plaster ceiling. "What exactly did I do to deserve this?"

Friday, September 3rd

"Grandma! Grandpa!" Ashley screeched. The little girl flung herself at Frank Marlowe, winding her arms and legs around him like a vine that had attached itself to a tall tree. He leaned down and scrubbed his soft beard against Ashley's cheeks, laughing as she squirmed and giggled with delight

His gaze dropped to Christopher and Aaron. "Hi, boys." The white-haired man continued to torment his granddaughter as he spoke to his grandsons. "We've missed you. You're growing like God da–"

A sharp glance from Janet silenced him.

"Like weeds," he finished sheepishly.

"We missed you too!" Aaron chimed in from his position in his grandmother's embrace.

Christopher nodded his head wildly, agreeing with his brother Aaron as he waited impatiently for an open spot with a grandparent.

Janet Marlowe extended her free arm, and Christopher joined them.

Letting go of Ashley, Frank looked up and smiled at Lauren, who was standing quietly in the wings, enjoying the family reunion. "Nice to see you again, Lauren," he drawled slowly, his eyes twinkling at the young woman.

"Same here." She turned to Janet. *I will not think about the book she sent. I will not!* "Did you have a nice flight?" The writer nervously tugged at her glasses.

Janet just rolled her eyes. "Well, come here! I talked to Dev on the phone before this horrible bombing mess. You can't pretend you're not a couple anymore," she announced firmly. She shot Lauren a look when she started to protest. "And that means I get a hug."

Lauren laughed and happily joined Christopher and Aaron in giving Janet a good squeeze.

Amy and Emma hovered in the background, and the nanny directed the porters carrying the Marlowes' luggage to the Lincoln bedroom. "Well, now," Frank boomed, once everyone had said hello, "Devil's going to be sorry she missed this, but how's about we get McDonald's for lunch?"

The children cheered and Emma laughed and picked up the phone, already knowing what everyone's orders would be. They were the only household in America that had a hotline to the local McDonald's.

Janet looked around the room slowly shaking her head. She still couldn't believe her little girl was President. Sometimes it was truly incomprehensible. She watched fondly as the boys tugged their grandpa by the hand back to their room to show him their latest drawings. Ashley was hot on Frank's heels, exacting his promise to go to her room next and see the Barbie that Grandma had sent her and the new, much improved hairdo she'd graced her with.

The room quickly emptied leaving just Lauren and Janet. The younger woman stood by somewhat awkwardly. Dev wasn't due back to the White House for several more days and Lauren was dying to use this time to get to know her parents better. Dev loved them and she knew it would be important to the President that she establish at least some sort of relationship with them. She rocked back and forth on her heels, suddenly a little nervous. She hadn't exactly had raving success with her own parents. "Well, I guess I'll leave you—"

"Good Lord, get over here and say hello. I don't bite, dear. Despite what Frank might say after a few beers."

Lauren giggled, then made a face when the comment fully registered. *Ewww...* "No offense," she mumbled, taking a seat next to Janet on the sofa, "but let's not go there."

"You're thinking 'ewww', aren't you?" Janet accused. "I can tell." She looked mortified. "I'm not that old!"

"Oh, no," Lauren quickly corrected. *Uh oh.* "It's not that." Her head swayed back and forth as she searched for the right words. "It's just...just...good grief! You're somebody's mother!"

Janet was dumbfounded. "And mothers aren't sexual beings?" She snorted and eyed Lauren in disbelief. "Maybe I needed to start you off with a more basic book, dear. I didn't think the cabbage patch theory of conception was popular with young people these days."

"That's not what I meant, and you know it!" Lauren groaned in embarrassment, but it soon shifted into laughter with Janet joining in. The blonde woman's earlier tension was all but forgotten. It was hard to remain formal or even the slightest bit uncomfortable around Devlyn's brash, uninhibited mother.

"Just remember, Dev is *three* somebodies' mother." Janet wriggled her eyebrows and Lauren saw a flash of Devlyn in the gesture. "And I'll bet you think things about her that make the stuff in Chapter Eight look tame."

"Bu-bu," Lauren sputtered helplessly. Her eyes widened. "You *read The Joy of Lesbian Sex* before mailing it to me?"

Janet waved a dismissive hand in the air. "For research purposes, of course." Then she winked. "Why, if I showed that book to

Frank, I'd never get out of bed. Well, you've been married, you know. As a matter of fact, one time..."

"Oh, my God," Lauren whimpered and covered her ears with her hands. "This is just wrong. Wrong. Wrong. Wrong."

Janet laughed harder.

Lauren fixed a hard stare on Dev's mother. "Now I know where your daughter got her evil streak."

Janet only shrugged. "Frank could have told you that, dear."

Wednesday, September 8th

Dev's long strides carried her down the hallway of the White House and towards her family and Lauren. She'd been gone for more than three weeks touring the bombing sites and participating in endless community rallies and meetings with community leaders. The tall woman was so glad to be home, she nearly cried when Air Force One touched down at Andrews Air Force Base.

Her parents and Ashley met Dev in the hallway, where they all shared a round of hearty hugs and Devlyn endured her mother's scolding over the fact that she'd lost some weight. Weight she didn't need to lose. "I'm okay, Mom. I swear. I've just been busy." Dev smiled indulgently. "You need to get Dottie to send up Devil cookies more often. I haven't had any since Lauren's birthday."

Dev's eyes scanned the hall and her brow furrowed. "Speaking of Lauren...where is she? And the boys?" She didn't say it, but Dev was disappointed Lauren hadn't greeted her along with her parents and Ashley. She'd thought about the writer for days on end and was so anxious to see her it was giving her a slight stomach ache.

The small group was silent for a beat, and Dev's demeanor instantly turned wary. She stood up straight and her alert eyes snapped in the direction of Lauren's and the boys' rooms. "Where are they?"

"Now, honey, this is nothing to worry about." Frank put his arm around his daughter's shoulders. "They'll be completely fine in a few days."

The blood instantly drained from Dev's face.

"Good Lord, Frank! You're scaring her to death. And to think you're a doctor," Janet scolded, fixing her eyes on Dev's face. "They've got the chickenpox, honey. That's all. The first spots showed up yesterday. It's nothing serious; that's why nobody called you."

Dev closed her eyes and willed her heart to stop pounding. "Chickenpox?" she questioned on a ragged exhale. *Wait. Chickenpox? That can't be right.* "But I thought nobody got−?"

"You thought we'd beaten those nasty buggers?" Frank answered. He ran a hand over his beard and scratched his chin.

"Not so, Devil. Not this strain anyway. It's resistant to the standard vaccination. Now, it's not nearly as common as the old classic was because it doesn't appear to be quite as contagious. It popped up in isolated spots all over the country a few years ago and now it seems to be visiting the capital." He snorted. "Apparently, some children at the kids' schools have it as well."

Dev frowned, still not placated. They began walking towards their rooms. "But they're okay, right, Dad?" The President held her mother's and daughter's hands as she went, nodding her greeting to several agents who'd remained behind with her family.

"Absolutely," Frank assured her confidently. "Miserable, but okay."

"They're spotted like freaks!" Ashley added enthusiastically.

Dev raised an eyebrow. "And just how did you avoid this, when your brothers and Lauren—"

"And Emma," Janet added, wincing.

"Ooo, and Emma," Dev amended, "weren't so lucky?"

Ashley shrugged one shoulder. "Grandpa said it's a crap shoot. And they stepped right into a big pile of—"

"Ahem," Frank interrupted. "I'm sure your mama gets the idea." He pretended to be oblivious to the evil glare Dev leveled at him.

They reached the boys' room first. Dev had laid her hand on the knob when her private physician stepped out of Lauren's room just down the hall. Blue eyes flickered sideways and Dev jogged across the carpet, catching the man before he could turn the corner.

"Hold up, doctor!"

The doctor straightened and tucked his stethoscope into his coat pocket. "Madam President, welcome back. How's the shoulder?" He reached out to touch the body part in question, but Dev pulled away annoyed. She didn't want to talk about her damned shoulder.

"How is everyone?"

"They have the chickenpox, Madam President. I just checked on the boys. They're sleeping and seem to be doing well."

"And Lauren?" Dev leaned in a little, awaiting his response.

He shifted uncomfortably, tempted to say Lauren was nearly as big a pain-in-the-ass patient as Dev when she was ill, but the man wasn't an idiot. "Chickenpox is always a little more difficult on adults than children, Madam President. That seems to be especially true with this new strain, but I'm sure she'll appreciate that you were concerned. I'll tell her you came by to check on her."

"No, that won't be necessary. I'll be in to see her as soon as I get changed. I only need five minutes."

The doctor looked aghast. "Oh, no, Madam President, you can't go in there." His tone was as authoritative as it was unyielding.

"She's still contagious and will be for several more days."

Dev put her hands on her hips. "I really don't care, doctor. I *will* be going in there." Her hand shot out and she grabbed him by the wrist, checking the time on his Rolex. "At about four thirty-five, as a matter of fact."

"That goes contrary to my best medical advice as your chief physician. You simply cannot–"

Blue eyes flashed. "If you try to keep me out," she said, dropping his wrist, "I'll call in the Marines to clear the path."

The short man gulped audibly, and Dev could see beads of perspiration suddenly dot his bald head. *God, she was the most difficult patient I've ever had!* "It's my duty to inform you that it is not in your best medical interests to be around Ms. Strayer, your sons, or Ms. Drysdale for the next several days." He puffed out his chest and stood his ground. "I'm afraid I'll have to insist. I'm certain that Mr. McMillian would back up my–"

"You can insist until you're blue in the face, doctor! This is not David McMillian's house. It's mine. And I don't intend to be kept from my family when they need me most. My own father, who is an extremely competent and well-respected physician himself, says that getting this strain of the chickenpox is a crap shoot. I think I've been through enough crap this year, don't you? My chances of catching it are slim, but if it'll make you feel better, I'll wear one of those silly, little masks." Dev pointed the mask still hanging around the doctor's neck.

"Well, um, yes." He gave a short nod. "That would greatly reduce your chances of infection." He nodded again, wishing he had thought to suggest that to begin with. "Other than staying completely away from them, which is something I can see you won't do," he finished in a rush before Dev could begin arguing with him, "the mask would be best, Madam President." He was mollified for the time being, now that the President was at least starting to see reason. "I'll see that you get one immediately."

"You do that," she said, already heading back towards her room. "I'm going to put on some blue jeans." *And then visit three spunky blondes that I've been missing with all my heart.*

True to her word, five minutes later Dev had changed out of her suit and was now wearing jeans, sneakers, and a short sleeved denim shirt. Her mother had talked Frank and Ashley into a visit to the Rose Garden, luring them away from their prospective checkers match with the promise of ice cream later. The older woman had smiled indulgently at her daughter, knowing she needed a few moments alone with Lauren to say hello. *Besides, what kind of people stayed indoors when it was such a beautiful day?*

The boys' nurse was sitting outside their bedroom door, reading a magazine, when Dev approached. The young woman quickly explained that the doctor had given them each a shot earlier and that it had not only brought down their slight fevers, but put an end to their itching. The only reason they were napping now was that as soon as the medicine began to take effect and they started to feel better, they had begun wrestling with each other like there was no tomorrow. They were simply worn out.

Dev's doctor had found the nurse only moments before and grumpily given her a paper mask to pass along to the President. She handed Dev the turquoise colored mask and chuckled when the President rolled her eyes but dutifully put it on.

Devlyn thanked the nurse and quietly crept into the boys' room. They were snuggled together in Aaron's bed, wearing only their underwear. The bedding was in a pool around their feet, their pillows were on the floor, and they were both drooling. *God, I wish Lauren were here with her camera.* Dev moved quietly over to the bed and perched on its edge. Ashley was right. They were spotted freaks. But they were her spotted freaks. And that made all the difference.

She softly stroked the top of each fair head before pulling up the sheet and tucking it around them. "Good rest, boys. We'll catch up at supper."

Dev left instructions with the nurse to let the boys know she was home when they woke up. With butterflies in her belly, she made her way to Lauren's room. *I should have brought flowers or something. Or candy. She likes chocolate. Damn! Why didn't I bring chocolate? I'm much more charming with the help of chocolate.* Dev had almost talked herself into going to get some at this very moment when she found herself standing in front of Lauren's door. A Secret Service agent walked past her with an odd look on his face, but the dark suited man said nothing.

She frowned, giving him a look as he walked by. *What's with him?* Then she realized she was still wearing the surgical mask and must look a little odd. "Oh, well," she mumbled, reaching up and knocking lightly on Lauren's door.

Her knock was greeted by a loud thump as something hit the door.

Lauren yelled out, "I told you to go away! And don't even think of coming near me with that damned harpoon you call a needle! Don't make me sic Grem and his demon litter on you. They're meaner than they look!"

Blue eyes went round. "Oh, boy." *I'll bet she's been giving the doctor hell. Heh. Good girl.* "Laur–" Dev paused and slipped off her mask, stuffing it into her pocket. "Lauren, it's me."

"Devlyn?"

"Yup. Can I come in?" Dev had just begun to turn the handle when Lauren's voice stopped her.

"No."

Dark eyebrows lifted. "What do you mean 'no'?" she asked impatiently. "I want to see you!"

"No. Go away." The next time Lauren spoke her voice had softened. "I'm not fit to be seen, darlin'. And you might catch it."

Dev narrowed her eyes at the door, wishing she had X-ray vision. "I don't give a damn what you look like. I want to come in!" She leaned her forehead against the cool wood. "Don't make me order an air strike."

Lauren chuckled, but sobered quickly. *Could this be a trick?* "You don't have a needle with you, do you?"

Dev rolled her eyes. "Gee, I knew I was forgetting something. Ever since I got over that pesky crack habit, I've been fresh out."

"Very funny. Okay."

Thank God, Dev thought as she began to turn the knob.

"You can come in as long as you don't laugh."

Dev stopped, then bit her lip. *I will not laugh. I will not laugh.* The President opened the door, took one look at Lauren, and burst out laughing. "Oh, God, I'm sorry."

Lauren's wavy, shoulder length hair was sticking up wildly in all directions. She was wearing a pair of old, gray sweats and an oversized T-shirt that swallowed up her compact body, making her look like a little girl. Her skin was slightly pale except for the speckling of bright red dots that covered every inch of exposed skin. One hand was roaming her body, scratching as furiously as her fingers would allow. She was wrapped in a sheet and wearing the absolutely most pathetic face Dev had ever seen. Well, when she walked in it was pathetic; ever since she'd laughed, Lauren had just looked pissed.

"Kill, Gremlin!" Lauren shouted. "Attack! Eat her!"

Gremlin was lying on the floor at the foot of Lauren's bed. To his credit, he did look up at the President in response to his mistress' command. Unfortunately, all he could muster was a weak growl and a big yawn. Fatherhood was even more taxing than the activity that got him in that position to begin with.

Dev took the time to shoot the pooch a disgusted look before smiling sympathetically at her sick friend. "I'm sorry, sweetheart. You just look so adorable, I couldn't help but laugh." The murderous glare in Lauren's eyes let Dev know the writer wasn't buying it, and she sat down on the edge of the tall bed, close to Lauren, but not touching her. "I missed you. I love you," she said softly.

Lauren's gaze immediately softened and she sighed. "I love you too." She shook her head sadly. "You're going to continue to make it impossible for me to stay angry with you, aren't you?"

A satisfied smile worked its way across Dev's lips. "Basically." She reached up to smooth back a lock of golden hair only to have Lauren duck out of her way.

"Devlyn! You can't touch me!"

"Wanna bet?"

Lauren blew out an exasperated breath. "I don't want you to get sick."

Dev shrugged one shoulder. "And I can't *not* touch you. Not anymore."

Lauren's heart melted at the words. She looked up into honest eyes and felt herself fall a little bit more in love with this amazing woman. "I'm so glad you're home," she whispered.

"Me too."

They stared at each other for a long moment and Lauren could see something lurking behind Dev's eyes. She knew Dev was upset about the people who had been killed when the FBI raided the Brothers of Freedom compound. David had told her that Dev had taken the deaths of the children especially hard, which didn't surprise Lauren in the least. It was a horrible waste. These months of getting to know and love the Marlowe children had driven that point home.

With a morbid streak that surprised even Washington insiders, the press had relentlessly harped on that aspect of events during Dev's tour of the bombing sites. They assigned the blame to Dev and the Attorney General and the nation followed right along with them. The tall woman appeared to take it all in her stride, patiently answering question after question about every detail of the raid, and every decision she had made concerning it. Even on television, Lauren easily spotted the lines of tension that etched Dev's normally open face and the wariness surrounding her usually unguarded personality. Especially when a reporter would mention Lisa and Brian Lindsay.

"Are you okay?" they both asked simultaneously. They smiled.

"I'm okay, Lauren. It wasn't a fun trip. But it needed to be done. I'm just glad it's over."

Lauren ached to hug her friend and felt her frustration building over the fact that she couldn't. Then an idea came to her. She scooted down by Gremlin and picked up a small blanket that had been tossed across the foot of her bed. The shorter woman grabbed it and shook it open.

"What? Phft! Phft!" Lauren threw the blanket over Dev, covering her upper body completely and cutting off her words. Before she could say anything else she felt strong arms wrap around her and squeeze her tightly. Dev closed her eyes in pleasure, instantly returning the comforting embrace. "Damn, I needed that."

"So did I."

Dev frowned at the unusual heat she could feel coming from Lauren. "You have a fever," she pointed out flatly.

"A little one. Yes." Lauren shifted in Dev's arms as Dev's fingers grazed her back. *Ooo...Jesus, that feels good!* She moved again, this time pressing her shoulder into Dev's and wiggling it.

Dev looked a little alarmed. "Uh, Lauren?"

Lauren threw her head back. "Ooo, yeah."

The President sucked in a breath, immediately aroused by Lauren's low groan. When Lauren's movements grew more frantic, Dev finally caught a clue. "Oh, no, you don't! I'm not a scratching post." With firm hands she pushed the smaller woman away.

"Pleeease," Lauren begged. "I'm itching everywhere!"

"No." Dev shook her head from under the blanket before pulling it off. "I can't."

"Yes, Devlyn," Lauren said seriously. She pinned the President with stone hard, gray eyes. "You can. For the love of God, scratch my back. I *need* you to scratch it."

Dev tried not to think about how sexy and cute Lauren looked when she begged. She loved her; she could overlook the bright red dots. "I won't." *And I'd die before I put one scar on your beautiful skin. Well, normally beautiful.*

"Puuuhleeez," Lauren whined pathetically. With a loud moan, she flopped backwards on the bed and began moving around like a fish out of water, trying to get to a spot between her shoulder blades.

"No." Dev rose to her feet. "Get the shot the boys got and you'll feel better," she explained reasonably.

"Shot? A needle stabbing into my flesh, and a foreign liquid forced into my body?" Lauren made a face. "Are you insane?"

"Most likely. But that's not the point." Deciding it was safe to be near Lauren, just not on the bed with her, Dev knelt in front of the bed. Shivering in revulsion as she caught a glimpse of one of the puppies that had wandered out from under the bed, Dev scooted closer. "I just want you to feel better, sweetheart."

"I want that too, Devlyn. But you know how I feel about needles."

Dev smiled affectionately. "I know, but it will just be a small one."

Lauren regarded her skeptically. "How small?"

"Tiny. Barely noticeable."

"And it will stop the itching?"

"Or your money back," Dev finished lamely.

Lauren's head swayed back and forth as she considered her options. Three more days of itching until she went insane. Or the shot. This was a really tough call.

"You know," a leer transformed Dev's face, "once you start feeling better, I'd love to scratch an itch of a *different* kind."

Dead silence.

"Call the doctor."

Sunday, September 12th

"So?" Dev settled down on a bench in the White House Sculpture Garden. The afternoon was sunny and crisp. A gentle breeze blew across the lawn, bringing with it the scent of wet grass. Dev raised her arm in a familiar manner, inviting Lauren to snuggle into her. The movement still caused a dull pain in her shoulder muscles, but the President considered the closeness of the position well worth the discomfort. "Are you feeling better?" Her eyes lighted on a delicate metal windmill sculpture that moved with every gale. "You look great, Lauren. I'd never even know you'd been sick."

Lauren didn't care that they were outside, and instead of snuggling next to the tall woman, she laid her head in Dev's lap, stretching out on what was left of the bench. "I feel sooo much better. The doctor gave me a clean bill of health this morning. No more fever, no more itching. I'm even glad I had that shot," she admitted somewhat sheepishly. "It made the last few days bearable."

Dev gently combed her fingers through Lauren's hair, rolling its silken strands between her fingertips. "I'm glad you're feeling better." Dev frowned. "I've discovered that I hate it when you're sick, and there's nothing I can do about it."

"Nothing you can do about it?" Lauren snorted quietly as she absorbed the warm sunshine and Dev's interested gaze with idle pleasure. "Yeah, right. And I suppose everyone has Bethesda's best doctor making house calls for the chickenpox."

"Well, I..." Dev's face colored and she looked off into the distance. "I just wanted you to be okay."

"You're sweet." The writer tangled her fingers with Dev's free hand. "So," she gave the hand she was holding a little tug and let out a slightly nervous breath. "Now that I'm feeling better, and we're allowed to talk about the tough stuff, how are you really doing, Devlyn?"

Dev remained very still, then shrugged a little. "I'm okay."

A slender, pale eyebrow arched. "Don't, Devlyn," she said with quiet finality. "After all these months, I know better."

The President looked down and regarded Lauren seriously. She was met with a direct gaze. "You do, don't you?"

"Yes." A tiny smile curled red lips. She gave Dev a playful poke, drawing her out. "So tell me. How are you doing?"

Dev sighed so deeply it was nearly a groan. "How am I supposed to be doing?" she bit out harshly. "I got innocent women and children killed. I hurt like hell."

Lauren chose her words carefully. "You didn't get anyone killed."

"I did!" Dev insisted. "I sent in the FBI. I gave the order." She swallowed hard. "I knew they were in there. I knew those bastards had women and children in there. And, God help me, I did it anyway. Two babies died that morning. The little boy, Brian, was caught in the crossfire and shot in the chest. The little girl, Lisa, died from smoke inhalation when the west wing of the compound caught fire."

Dev's chin began to quiver and Lauren felt her heart break. She sat up and looked at Dev, meeting watery blue eyes with her own. The younger woman gently cupped Dev's cheeks with both hands, dropping a feather-light kiss on her lips, before slowly gently pulling back, waiting patiently for her to continue.

Dev swallowed again, nearly undone by Lauren's tenderness. "They found the girl curled up under her bed with her dolls and her backpack." Dev laughed without a trace of humor. "Apparently, she was hiding from the big bad government invasion."

"Jesus." Lauren closed her eyes and squeezed Dev's hand. The exact cause of death for individual militia members and their families hadn't been released to the press yet because of the ongoing investigation.

"They were nearly the same ages as—" Dev stopped, the churning in her guts threatening to send up her last meal.

"That wasn't your fault, darlin'," Lauren whispered. "Stop blaming yourself. You're not eating." Her fingers grazed dark circles that had become a nearly permanent fixture under Dev's eyes over the past few weeks. "You're not sleeping."

"But—"

"No!" Lauren lowered her voice. "No. Those people had to be stopped. We both know that. You did what you had to so that could happen. That doesn't make you responsible for the children's deaths. Their parents became responsible when they put them in harm's way. Not you."

Dev nodded miserably. "David has been saying the same thing, but I just feel so damned responsible for it all, and I should. That comes with the job." She exhaled wearily. "In my heart of hearts, I know there are horrible things happening everyday that I can't control, no matter how much I want to. But this...how do you live with this?" Her eyes pleaded with Lauren for an answer, but the biographer held her tongue, letting Dev finish. "I hurt for everyone who died that day. On both sides. But to have the names of those two innocent children weighing on my heart, knowing that if I personally hadn't said 'Go in there', they'd still be alive..." Dev looked away. "That's hard to deal with."

"I know," Lauren muttered quietly, gently guiding Dev's face back around with the palm of one hand. She tenderly stroked a prominent cheekbone with her thumb and tilted her head slightly to the side as she spoke, sending soft, pale hair tumbling over one shoulder. "I'm so sorry that you're hurting. You're a caring woman, Devlyn, and I wouldn't expect anything less from you." Lauren smiled softly. "You made the best choice under the worst of circumstances. You told me so yourself. Don't second guess that now. You did the right thing." She opened her arms. "You look like you could use a hug."

Dev smiled, slipping into Lauren's outstretched arms. "From you? Always. Never doubt that." Dev felt much of the tension of the past weeks melt away under Lauren's comforting touch. She closed her eyes and allowed herself to be held. "You've got the touch." she murmured, sinking deeper into the embrace. *Soothing my soul.* "I love you."

Lauren pressed her cheek against Dev's, feeling its softness and warmth. She squeezed her tightly, praying to convey even a fraction of the love and concern she felt for her. "Any time, Devlyn. I love you too."

Dev rested there for a long moment, listening to the birds, finding a surprising amount of solace and peace. She blew out a long, slow breath and did her best to just let the worries and guilt go. It would take more time, to be sure, but she had that. And she wouldn't be alone.

When Dev finally pulled back she was ready for a change of subject. "Now I want you to tell me something." She quirked a dark, playful brow, indicating that the deep thinking part of the conversation was over.

"Whatever it is, I didn't do it." Lauren grinned charmingly, irrationally pleased that she could help to lighten Dev's load.

Dev chuckled. "Oh, I'm sure you didn't. You're totally innocent, right?"

"Oh, yes," Lauren dutifully replied, batting golden lashes.

Dev nodded. "I see. So, tell me, sweetheart, what kind of videos are you watching while I'm away?" *Okay, I pretty much know what kind. But it's still fun to watch you squirm.* Blue eyes twinkled. "Even more importantly, what kind of books are my mother sending you?"

Lauren's face immediately turned bright red. That was the last question she expected, and her mind reeled for a moment as she searched for a good answer. "Why?" she squeaked. *Oh, yeah, I'm brilliant with words. Big time writer, my ass. She mentally rolled her eyes.*

"Because just before my parents left, my mom said she sent you a book that would help you identify all the parts, despite your good head start." She grinned and bumped shoulders with the shorter woman. "Did she give you a book on the care and feeding of your very own lesbian or something?"

Lauren burst out laughing, feeling a little dizzy from her blush. "Umm...something like that." She wriggled her eyebrows. "It's got pictures."

Dev's own grin widened. She had missed this with Lauren and needed it just as much as she had needed the talk. She loved teasing her friend and gave her another slight nudge. "What kind of pictures?"

"Wouldn't you like to know?" *And now that I'm feeling better, I think it would be a very good time to show you.*

Saturday, September 18th

It had been another magical evening for Lauren. In her wildest dreams she had never imagined herself in this place, either emotionally or physically. Part of the magic was undoubtedly the setting, the White House itself, whose walls held unimaginable secrets and whose rooms were as interesting and unique as they were beautiful. Even after nine months of living there, she found herself utterly fascinated. Then there was her dinner partner, the most powerful person on Earth. Not too shabby there either. But the biggest factor was Dev herself – not her influence or position, but the woman underneath, whom Lauren had come to adore.

"I can't believe I just had dinner with the King of England." She laughed a little, taking Dev's hand as they strolled through the Rose Garden.

The President pulled away in mock annoyance. "Is there no woman in my life *impressed* with the fact that *I* am President of the United States?" *So it doesn't sound as cool as "King". Can I help that?*

"Yes." Lauren rolled her eyes and laughed. *Only you could pull off that ego, darlin'.* "If it makes you feel any better, I was horribly impressed with you the first time I laid eyes on you." Then she paused and started to laugh. "No, that's not quite true. When I first saw you in person I nearly dropped dead on the spot. But obviously I'd seen you on television a gazillion times before that."

"A gazillion?"

Lauren nodded. "At least."

"Wow. My PR people rock." Dev made a motion for Lauren to continue as they passed in and out of the shadows created by the softly glowing lamps that lined the garden path and a full moon.

"I wasn't *really* impressed with you until I took the time to go beyond the sound bites that saturated network television. But once I did...wow!" Lauren quirked a playful grin. "Or maybe it was the fact that I was drugged out of my mind at the time."

Dev nearly stumbled. "Excuse me?"

The blonde woman scrunched up her face and smiled brightly, crinkling her nose and the corners of her eyes. "It's not what you think," she laughed.

Dev accepted Lauren's answer easily, but not before offering a tiny snort. She kicked a stone from her path. "So is that why you didn't vote for me? Because I was overexposed?"

Lauren stopped dead in her tracks, tugging Dev to a halt with her. "How do you know I didn't vote for you?" Her hands automatically went to her hips and she shot Dev a meaningful look.

Dev scratched her cheek and smiled ruefully. "Oh, that." She winced inwardly. *Me and my big mouth.*

"Yes, that," Lauren demanded.

"Well, umm...Michael was a little overzealous in the materials he requested for your background check." Dev's eyes conveyed regret and a good dose of embarrassment. "That information is private. I swear it is. But that doesn't mean, if you ask the right people, that it's not easy to find out. I'm sorry."

"Bastard."

"Are you mad at me?" Dev braced herself.

"Yes."

"Really mad?" Devlyn tilted her head to the side and peered into eyes that looked nearly translucent in the muted light.

Lauren dropped her hands from her hips. "I should be." She tugged on the stems of her glasses, bringing them a little higher on her nose, and sighed. "But I'm not, I guess."

Dev smiled. "Thank you." But the smile slid away quickly, her frustration leaking into her voice. "Why didn't you vote for me?"

"Oh, God." Lauren rolled her eyes as the women resumed their walk.

"What?" Dev waved a frustrated hand in the air. "I want to know."

Lauren laughed. "I know you do."

"Why are you torturing me?" Dev growled in mock frustration.

"Because it's fun."

"Well, there is always that."

A long arm wrapped around Lauren's waist as they slowly walked, the easy rhythm of their strides matching perfectly. *So, this is what being in love is like,* Lauren thought with equal parts awe and gratitude. *God, was I stupid before. If I'd only known.* Now she understood what Dev had been talking about. Making sure that it was real...that it was right. She glanced sideways, admiring the way the moonlight washed over Dev's hair, bathing her in a rich, white aura. At that very moment, Lauren realized that nothing in her whole life had ever felt so completely right.

She had, in her own way, loved Judd, but there had always been something missing. A connection that was absent from their marriage. Lauren never felt as if part of herself was missing when they were apart. Even in the best times she had never longed for his touch or laugh or smile. Never bled when he was cut.

With Dev it was so different. If, for some reason, they couldn't talk, which they did most evenings when Dev was finally finished for the day, Lauren would lie awake in her bed and listen for the President's distinctive footsteps and the sound of the door opening just down the hall. No matter what she was doing, or whom she was talking to, she always found her eyes or thoughts straying to Devlyn. And when miles separated them, she felt truly alone.

They walked on in silence, but it was a comfortable silence. A gentle peace stole over Lauren.

Dev stopped and faced the shorter woman, pulling her into a tight embrace. "I'm so very much in love with you, Lauren. You have no idea."

"No." Lauren shook her head emphatically. "You're wrong. I do. For the first time in my life I honestly do understand. More than that, I finally understand what you were trying to say to me in your room that night. About having it all." She reached up and cupped Dev's cheek, peering into eyes that shone silver in the moonlight.

"I think we do." Dev slowly leaned in and gently kissed the writer. Their lips separated, but only a hairsbreadth, and Devlyn whispered, "It's been worth it, hasn't it?" *Believe it like I do, Lauren. With your whole heart.*

"Oh, yeah," Lauren sighed, immediately feeling the loss when Dev pulled back far enough so that she could look her in the eye and gauge her reaction. Something suddenly clicked in Lauren's mind, and she thought of the fresh roses that had been placed in her room every morning since her very first day at the White House. She smiled, utterly charmed. "You've been courting me from the very beginning, haven't you, Devlyn Marlowe?"

Dev felt a heat flood her cheeks. But the blush went unnoticed in the dim light. The tall woman leaned in until Lauren could feel the heat of her body and whispered in her ear. "That's the point of courting, Lauren. You fall in love so slowly that it becomes a part of you without your knowing it." She brushed her lips against Lauren's ear, feeling the tremor left in the wake of her tender touch. "You do realize that at this very moment the marksmen on the roof are probably watching us," Devlyn teased a bit. "Didn't your little sex video tell you that this is a big turn on for most males of the species?"

Lauren groaned. "The video pretty much ignored men altogether, which was sort of the point, smarty pants. And you're never going to let me live that down, are you?"

"You're not the one who had to explain to her Chief of Staff why there were erotic sounds coming from your bedroom when I called you. He thought we were having phone sex, for God's sake!"

The breeze blew a lock of Lauren's hair into her eyes, and she reached up, absently tucking it behind her ear. "I'm so sorry. That was a bit of a surprise for me too. A joke from Wayne, I think. Or maybe it wasn't a joke. I'm not exactly sure." She leaned into Dev as they began heading back towards the White House. Another gust of wind caused her to shiver and shift closer still to her warm-blooded companion.

"Cold, sweetheart?"

"Mmm hmm. A little."

"Then I know of a certain fireplace and two cups of cocoa that have our names on them."

"Marshmallows?"

Dev kissed the top of Lauren's head. "As many as you'd like."

Lauren wiggled her toes in front of the fire, grinning from behind her mug as Dev pulled on fleece slippers. "Wimp," she muttered, getting a lovely view of Dev's tongue as a reply. She gestured at Dev's feet with her chin. "This is truly heaven. Take those off and let the fire do the work."

"Nuh uh," Dev grunted, picking up her own mug and joining Lauren on the floor. "Hate being barefoot. Have since I was a kid."

"Any particular reason why?" Lauren leaned back, staring into the glowing embers as the wood let off an occasional pop or hiss.

Dev thought about that for a moment, rolling a swallow of hot chocolate around in her mouth. "None that I'm aware of. But maybe I had a traumatic, barefoot incident when I was little."

"Maybe subconsciously you're afraid you'll have to make a mad dash through the woods naked," Lauren taunted. If Dev could find every excuse to bring up the video, the least she could do was to return the favor.

Dev laughed softly. "I admit it wouldn't be on the top of my list. I had scratches in delicate places that itched for weeks."

Lauren snorted, having to clamp her hand down over her mouth to keep from losing her cocoa. "No comment." *Ooo, wait. Wasn't there talk of scratching a particular itch when I was sick? God, I itch!*

Dev reached over and pushed a lock of blonde hair behind Lauren's ear. "That's my line."

Lauren looked confused. "God, I itch?"

"Huh?"

Lauren shook her head, realizing what Dev meant. "Never mind."

"Are you okay?" Dev questioned softly. "You seem a little distracted." When Lauren nodded in an uncharacteristically shy fashion and smiled at her, Dev's face instantly mirrored the gesture. She was glad to know she wasn't the only one who could be thrown off track by the simplest of looks or touches or phrases. She drew her fingers lightly up Lauren's neck and threaded them into silky, pale hair. The touch was soft and intimate and meant to garner the writer's complete attention.

It did.

Lauren found herself holding her breath without knowing why.

Dev set down her mug, then deftly relieved Lauren of hers, though neither woman's eyes strayed from the other's. The President lifted her other hand to Lauren's face, tracing a pink cheek with her thumb and silently drawing Lauren closer. She didn't stop until their faces were almost touching.

"I think you should know, Madam President, if you don't kiss me, I'm going to die." Lauren's voice was an octave below normal and it resonated all the way to Dev's bones.

"Me too," Dev breathed.

Their lips met, slowly, gently, brushing together in an explosion of sensation that caused both women to moan and shiver. Nothing was ever rushed or hurried with Devlyn. Lauren wasn't sure if she should be singing her praises or cursing her name. Whichever it was, it would have to come later; right now her body was otherwise engaged. She was set on a sweet, low burn when the kiss deepened, and warm, wet tongues began gently tasting and exploring.

Dev was nearly done in by the soft moans that escaped Lauren as their lips eagerly brushed together again and again. In the garden, in the moonlight, bewitched by a pair of shining gray eyes, Dev had already decided that tonight she wouldn't stop unless Lauren asked her to. The writer's gentle touch, and the heady smell of her skin and hair, only served to strengthen Dev's resolve. She was nervous as hell, but her body shared none of her mind's trepidation and was responding in hot flashes to Lauren's touch and taste and the heat of the moment.

"Oh, God," Lauren gasped softly when they parted for much needed air.

Dev groaned and her eyes fluttered open with exaggerated slowness. "That was, um..."

"Wonderful."

"Oh, yeah," the President agreed quickly. "But your kisses always are." She smiled, wondering if she looked as aroused as she felt.

"Can we," Lauren paused to wet her lips. "Can we do that again?" she asked quietly, giving Dev an adorable grin that she knew the older woman found totally irresistible.

Dev nodded nervously. "Actually, why don't we move someplace where we can be more comfortable?"

The blonde woman glanced down, flushing a little at the suggestion. She was pretty damned comfortable right where she was. "Like?"

"The couch?"

Considering the couch was all of six inches away, Lauren had no reason to object. "The couch could be good." She sucked in a slightly ragged breath and slid up to perch on its edge. Lauren glanced down at Dev, who was rising to her knees.

Dev placed warm hands on Lauren's thighs and the smaller woman adjusted her legs so that Dev could kneel between them. This was different. Mixed in with the desire she'd seen so often in her friend's eyes was a good dose of fear. Lauren could think of only one reason that Dev would be afraid right now, as opposed to all the other times they'd kissed in front of fire...after a wonderful evening together, sitting so close together they could feel the heat of each other's bodies through their clothes. *Oh, God.* Lauren suddenly became very aware of her own heartbeat and the sensitivity of her skin.

Devlyn swallowed hard and reached out to take Lauren's hands. "I'm very nervous, just so you know. I'm not trying to...I mean," she stopped again and frowned, clearly unable to articulate exactly what she wanted to say. "I'm just...I'm–"

Lauren pressed two fingertips against Dev's lips, feeling their incredible softness. "I understand." She removed her fingers and replaced them with her lips, giving Dev a gentle, almost chaste kiss. "Don't worry," she whispered against Dev's mouth. "Nervous goes both ways."

Blue eyes widened a little. "It does? You don't seem–"

"I am."

Dev licked her lips. "Okay. Just didn't want you to think that I wasn't. Because I so very am," she admitted.

Lauren shrugged a little. "But we'll be that way together, right?" She searched Dev's eyes for her own reassurance and was instantly rewarded by a stupid, lovesick, lopsided grin that threatened to melt her into a puddle right on the spot.

The President took a deep breath and let her hands slowly slide up Lauren's thighs, then hips. Her palms found their way under Lauren's sweatshirt, stopping the moment she felt the hot, bare skin of her belly.

Lauren sucked in a quick breath and her body jerked in response.

Dev almost pulled away, but small hands covered hers, holding them firmly in place. She flicked a questioning gaze at Lauren's face and was held there by intense, dilated eyes.

Lauren leaned in, enjoying the feeling of Dev's hands on her naked skin. They felt as good as she'd imagined they would – warm, soft, and strong.

Dev moved closer and dropped her mouth to Lauren's slender neck, nuzzling the hot, slightly damp skin and tasting its saltiness with gentle lips and tongue. Her hands traveled slowly up around the younger woman's torso, to her back, where she began a gentle massaging.

"Oh, that's nice," Lauren moaned as she wrapped her arms loosely around Dev. "Very nice." Of its own volition, her head rolled to the side.

Devlyn responded without hesitation, moving up Lauren's throat to the slight hollow behind her ear, nipping softly as she went.

Lauren gasped when Dev hit a particularly sensitive spot.

For Dev, it was an experience she was sure would kill her before the evening was over. *But what a way to go.* Lauren felt so good, and it felt so right to be touching her, that she couldn't even fathom stopping. Not now. "I'm thinking," Dev whispered as she took Lauren's earlobe into her mouth and sucked gently, "I dunno...bed?"

"Yes," Lauren breathed. She was pretty sure if this torture didn't end soon, she'd find herself on the other end of a federal prosecution for hurting the President of the United States.

They stood on slightly wobbly legs and walked slowly towards the large four poster bed along the back wall. At the foot of the bed, Dev stopped. She cupped Lauren's chin with her palm and gently tilted her head upward so she could look deeply into her eyes. Despite the butterflies in her belly, Dev smiled and spoke with a quiet certainty. "If you want to stop, you just say the word."

Lauren gave a quick nod, frantically trying to remember how to form a coherent, verbal response. She finally settled on, "Okay." *Like that's gonna happen!* her mind snorted incredulously. Nothing short of a nuclear attack *on the United States* was going to stop what was happening in this bedroom tonight. She drew in a deep, but ragged, breath when she felt her sweatshirt being tugged up her body. *Yes. Too many clothes.* The idea was more than welcome and Lauren lifted her arms over her head to assist in its removal. Her jeans and panties were next in line and when Dev trailed her fingers down her thighs, as she swept the material off her body, Lauren felt as though she might faint. Thin, satin bra straps were lowered one at a time, and kisses left in their place. Lauren closed her eyes and moaned softly.

Devlyn took in the sight before her and licked very dry lips as Lauren's bra fell from her boneless fingers. "Beautiful," she whispered reverently. "Absolutely beautiful." She slowly reached out and allowed her fingers to make contact with smooth skin that glowed slightly in the faint light of the room.

The way Dev was looking at her sent a flood of blood to her belly and a rush of heat between her legs. She felt as though she were being worshipped by those incredible blue eyes and wasn't nearly as nervous about her nakedness as she thought she would be. Any remaining uneasiness was fading fast as her body reacted to Dev. Lauren took in the rapid rise and fall of the taller woman's chest and the flare of her nostrils, as she stood open before her, exposed and inviting.

Dev's breath caught as her hands slowly slid over more soft skin. She leaned in and placed a tender kiss on Lauren's cheek. "I love you."

Lauren turned her head and captured Dev's lips in a sweet kiss. She laid her hands on Dev's hips and gave a gentle tug, bringing their bodies together all along their lengths. When their lips separated, she pulled back a little and smiled. "I love you too, Devlyn. Very much," she said softly. "With all my heart." Her gaze quickly dropped back to the full lips she already wanted to taste again. Lauren threaded her fingers through long, dark hair and she went back for more, offering herself to Dev in every way she could convey with a heartfelt, passionate kiss. She was rewarded with a deep moan and a rush of breath as the kiss turned hungry, and she gave herself up to the passion of the moment.

A hot path was cut across flesh now slightly damp from anticipation and desire. Dev's fingernails caused a tingling sensation up and down Lauren's back as the President grazed her skin. A tremor tore through Lauren as a rush of arousal hit her so hard she felt her knees go weak.

The writer's hands soon found themselves working their way under Dev's shirt, pushing it up as they sought silky skin.

Dev ducked as Lauren pulled the material over her shoulders, then her head. She felt her shirt slide down her back as Lauren simply dropped it the second it cleared dark tresses.

Lauren's gaze burned a path from Dev's face to her chest. She grinned broadly, fully appreciating Dev's braless condition. "Definitely a nipple." Lauren chuckled as Dev lowered her arms.

A dark, elegant brow lifted. "Mom was right. You do recognize the important parts."

"Umm, Dev?" Lauren questioned, never taking her eyes off Dev's breasts. She licked her lips and swallowed.

"Yes, sweetheart?"

"We're about to make love, right?"

"God, I hope so," Dev breathed. "I'd hate to have to go swimming in the Potomac."

"Then leave your mother out of this."

"Deal." Dev laughed, but it quieted quickly when she felt Lauren's fingers begin to work the buttons of her jeans.

The smaller woman instantly dropped to her knees and began sliding off Dev's jeans and panties at the same time. Where Dev's fingers had trailed down her thighs, Lauren used her lips to tenderly pay homage to every inch of newly exposed skin. She worked her way down one leg, then back up the other, as she slipped off Dev's fleece slippers then pants and panties. By the time she returned to Dev's hip, both women were visibly shaking. She placed one last kiss on Dev's hipbone before rising to her feet.

It felt as though fire was rushing through Devlyn's veins and her furiously pounding heart was threatening to escape the confines of her chest. She wrapped her arms around Lauren and slowly began leaning back towards the bed. Both women moaned loudly at the first exquisite feeling of skin on skin as their bodies met again. Dev prayed nothing would interrupt them. She was sure if they had to stop now, she would simply die. "Oh, God," she groaned as Lauren came to rest on top of her, and soft breasts pressed into hers. Their legs tangled together, igniting a new fire in her soul.

For Dev it was an expression of absolute love, trust, and devotion to the woman now in her arms and bed. To touch her like this, to finally add a physical dimension to the deep love they shared, sent her spirit soaring and set her body aflame.

Dev savored Lauren's tentative touches, which were growing bolder by the second. This was where she wanted to be. Always. She didn't give her heart easily, but once she did, she held nothing back. Anything she had, anything she was, was Lauren's for the taking. *I want her for the rest of my life.* For an instant, the thought surprised her, then she felt Lauren's breath caress her neck as she left a gentle trail of kisses on her neck and shoulders. "Lauren..."

The younger woman smiled when she heard Dev say her name. She had never heard it said with such passion and urgency before, and her own body responded with enthusiasm. *God, it's never been like this before. So good. So right,* her mind thrilled. There was no denying her reaction to the combination of soft skin, toned muscle, and womanly curves beneath her. She admitted to herself that she should have given into some of her curiosities years ago. But when Dev whispered her name in her ear, and sure hands drifted from the small of her back to her bottom, pulling them closer together, she knew it was more than gender. It wasn't just a woman making her feel this way. It was Dev. And that made all the difference. There was no way on the planet that her blind date, Casey, would have evoked these sensations or emotions. It was the person. This person. And she was hopelessly in love with Dev.

Remembering that she was the one who had done this before, Dev rolled them over and slowly began kissing her way down Lauren's body, the blonde woman's soft whimpers and moans urging her on.

Every muscle in Lauren's body went rigid with pleasure and she heard herself moan loudly just as her very sensitive nipple was enveloped by a hot, wet mouth. Her hands found purchase in Dev's hair and she gasped, pulling Dev tightly to her breast, desperate to be closer still. "God, yes, Dev," she encouraged, shifting her body and making more room for her lover to take her places they'd never been together.

Dev hummed her approval into Lauren's breast, her own body pulsing in time with the gentle ministrations of her lips and tongue. She knew it wouldn't take much before she would simply explode from the pleasure she was giving and receiving.

They crested together as a couple and again as individuals. When their bodies finally came to rest, the room was filled with soft whimpers and labored breaths. They cuddled together, pulling the sheet up over their damp bodies.

Lauren snuggled close to Dev and hummed quietly, waiting for her to say something. She kissed the hollow of Dev's throat, feeling her lover's ribs expand against her as Dev drew in a deep breath and let it out slowly, ruffling Lauren's hair.

Dev kissed the writer on the forehead. "I love you, and I'm keeping you, Mighty Mouse."

Lauren laughed and poked Dev in the side, drawing a muffled squawk. "I love you too. And you certainly gave a new meaning to Wonder Woman."

Now it was Dev's turn to laugh. "And here I was afraid I'd lost my touch."

"Oh, no, darlin', your touch is just fine." Lauren closed her eyes, feeling the irresistible tug of sleep. "Trust me, it's juuust fine."

Sunday, September 19th

Dev woke automatically at 4:45 a.m., only this time the warm body curled up next to her gave her a very good reason to stay in bed. She rolled over and wrapped her arm snugly around Lauren's waist, spooning their bodies together. Without waking, the writer laid her hand on Dev's arm. Dev sighed happily. *Yup. I am staying right here. Not moving a muscle. Besides, it's Sunday, and Lauren would kick my butt if I got up this early.*

A few more moments ticked by, and Dev gave into temptation. She grinned and swept back Lauren's hair, placing several soft kisses at the nape of her neck. Dev was greeted with a long, steady growl she was pretty sure wasn't Gremlin. "Mornin', sweetheart."

"Sleep." Lauren captured her hand. "Dark. Nighttime. Sleep."

Dev chuckled. "You're cute when you're monosyllabic."

"Nighttime has two syllables, you damned Yankee. Go back to sleep," Lauren mumbled. She rolled over, burrowing into warm arms.

"Yes, ma'am. Anything you say." Dev kissed Lauren's forehead.

"But when you do drag your backside out of bed," Lauren teased, reaching out a fraction of an inch to kiss just blow Dev's collarbone. "I'll have two poached eggs, toast, coffee with cream, two sugars, and a glass of milk."

Dev's eyebrows jumped. "Oh, you will, huh? What? You think this is a fancy hotel or something?" The President couldn't wipe the stupid grin off her face. Hell, she couldn't muster the willpower to even try. She had wondered many times what a "morning after" would be like with Lauren, and she was delighted to find it was pretty much what she had expected.

Lauren groaned, more awake than she wanted to be. "Well, last night you were trying to impress me. Taking me out, buying me root beer floats." She sighed and let her fingernail graze over a nipple that was too close to ignore. Dev jumped a little and squealed in surprise, causing Lauren to laugh. Immediately contrite, she covered the spot of her attack with the warm palm of her hand. "I just kinda figured I'd get breakfast too."

"Would you like me to cook it for you?" Dev grabbed Lauren's evil hand and brought it to her lips, kissing her palm soundly.

"Oh, that'd be wonderful," Lauren uttered softly as she buried her face between Dev's shoulder and the pillow, already tumbling back towards asleep.

"Okay, then I will."

"What?" Lauren lifted her head but quickly let it drop back to the pillow.

"Unhand me, wench!" Dev struggled and broke free of the laughing woman's grasp.

"Where are you going?"

Dev stalked across the room, naked as the day she was born.

Lauren pulled Dev's pillow to her face and nuzzled it as the tall woman slipped into a robe.

"I'm going to the kitchen to make you breakfast."

"You are not!" Lauren shot up a little too quickly and had to give herself a second to stop seeing stars.

"Yes, I am." Dev wiggled her feet into her slippers.

"The President of the United States is not going to the kitchen to make me breakfast."

Dev leaned over and kissed her nose. "You're right, the President's not, but Dev Marlowe is."

"Do you even know where the kitchen is?" Lauren moved towards Dev and tugged on the belt of Devlyn's bathrobe.

"No, but I'm sure someone around here can direct me." Devlyn put her hands on Lauren's shoulders and pushed gently, guiding her back to bed. "You just stay right here. I'm going to go fix you breakfast."

"God, I love you." Lauren snuggled back down into the covers and rolled one eyeball in Dev's direction.

"You're not so bad yourself." The President winked.

"When you get lost trying to find the kitchen, I'll send Gremlin to find you." She heard Dev make several mumbled, derogatory comments about her dog as she walked across the room. "But not for a few hours," Lauren added softly just the bedroom door, and her eyes firmly closed.

Monday, October 4th

"Come here, you little..." Dev ground out as she struggled to get further under the bed to retrieve several more puppies. "Your time here is over, beasties. Now you get to go and terrorize other parts of the world."

Lauren came back in from the bathroom where she had had to lock Gremlin and Princess before Dev could even get near the puppies. She covered her ears at the sounds of Gremlin's and Princess' howls. "God, I feel like a kidnapper!"

"Don't think of it as kidnapping, sweetheart," Dev offered. Lying flat on her belly, she reached under the bed, cursing as the puppies scooted away. She rose to her knees and looked at Lauren. "Think of it as liberation day." Dev gestured towards the bed. "I could use a hand here."

Lauren flinched as two of the puppies poked their noses out from behind the comforter, bared their teeth at the President and growled. "You'd better count your fingers when this is over, Devlyn. Because they don't seem to want to leave." The writer cautiously moved forward and picked up two of the more docile puppies; they were nearly asleep, despite the commotion their brothers and sisters were causing.

"Oh, sure, take the easy ones. I was hoping you could coax out the ones that were growling at me." She gestured to the two Lauren was putting in the box. "I could have done that. And if I get bit, you have to kiss it and make it better."

A lascivious grin twitched at Lauren's lips. "I'll do that anyway, darlin'."

Dev quirked an eyebrow. "You have a dirty mind. Just like my mother. No wonder she loves you." She looked back under the bed where the snarling puppies had once again taken refuge.

"Watch out, Devlyn. I've discovered I have a thing for older women."

"Hey! I'm not that much older! Besides, you," Dev strained, trying to get under the bed again, "couldn't handle my mother. She'd kill you." Dev laughed recklessly, waiting to see what kind of a response that would get. Before she got an answer one of puppies nipped her finger. "Ouch! Dammit!"

The baby dogs all began to bark and whine.

"Hey." Lauren's eyes snapped. "Quiet!"

The puppies instantly went silent.

Lauren dropped to her knees and gently began examining Dev's finger. *Please don't let it be bleeding.*

"I'm okay. He missed. Mostly." Before Lauren could get a good look, Dev pulled her finger away and began wiggling it in front of her face. "I still have all ten, and there's nothing broken or bleeding." She smiled at the sound of Lauren's relieved sigh. "You know why they don't want to leave, don't you?"

"You're sure it's okay? You don't need a Band-Aid or anything?" Lauren wanted to see for herself, so she captured Dev's finger. She studied it carefully, finding only a small red scratch, which she promptly kissed. "They just like sleeping under my bed 'cause it's so nice and quiet."

A sexy smirk overtook Dev's face. "I can change that right now, sweetheart."

Lauren rolled her eyes and laughed, feeling a sudden heat in her cheeks. "Sorry, Devil. I've got a meeting with Wayne in fifteen minutes. And you've got one with the Secretary of Transportation in ten. I'm surprised Liza hasn't been here looking for you already. Not that I'm not tempted. Because I am." *More than you know, darlin'.* Her eyes twinkled.

Dev poked out her lip, then smiled when Lauren leaned in for a kiss.

"But," Lauren diverted her kiss at the last second, denying Dev's lips and giving her a playful peck on the cheek instead, "can I have a rain check?" She laughed again at the look of shocked outrage on her lover's face.

"Brat."

"Later," Lauren promised, earning an instant smile. She turned back to the puppies and gazed at them affectionately, even the ones who had inherited Gremlin's dislike of the President. "Let's get this over with, so I can stop feeling like Cruella DeVille."

"Well, then get your little fanny under there, Mighty Mouse, and dig the little beasties out. I think you'll fit more easily than I will." The President sat back on her heels. "Then I can take them and make the coat."

"That's not even close to funny, Devlyn." But Lauren giggled anyway as she scooted her upper body under the bed and pulled out two reluctant puppies. "Hello, my little demons." She lifted them both up and gave them sloppy kisses, receiving an enthusiastic face licking in return.

"Well, eeewww!" Dev grimaced as she watched the scene unfold. "Hurry up and put them in the box, and I'll take them to their new vict...I mean owners. Heh, that's another perk to being President. You can give away really ugly puppies, and people have to take them." Dev wrinkled her nose and pointed at Lauren's mouth. "And if you think you're gonna get another kiss from me, you'll need to, at the very minimum, brush your teeth. With bleach."

Lauren jerked her chin towards the door. "Out! Before I decide to keep them *all*," she drew out the last word, watching with satisfaction as blue eyes widened perceptibly.

"Going," Dev squeaked as she shuffled towards the door, trying to keep hold of the jiggling puppy crate.

Lauren puttered around her room for a few moments before taking Wayne's video call. She pulled out some handwritten notes as her publishing agent's secretary brought Wayne on the line.

"Hiya, sweetheart," he said affectionately.

Lauren smiled. "Hi, Wayne. How's life in the Big Apple?"

"Eh." He moved his hand in a teetering motion. "Could be worse. Could be Cleveland. How are you?" He wriggled eyebrows liberally dosed with gray. "Been doing anything lately you'd like to tell your old buddy Wayne about?" He gave Lauren his best wishing look.

Which had never worked on her anyway.

"God, Wayne, why do I work with you again?" Laughter bubbled up inside Lauren when the man patiently began listing all his virtues, which, in actuality, didn't take very long. "Okay. Okay." She held up her hands in defeat. "I get the picture."

Wayne continued unaffected. "And when you're finished slumming with the *President of the United States*," he grunted, "don't forget to give *me* a call. Some people still appreciate a charming yet rugged man."

"Wow. Rugged *and* charming?" Lauren crossed her arms over her chest and tried not to laugh as both eyebrows edged their way up her forehead. "Uh huh. I'll be sure to call you, Wayne," she drawled.

Wayne blew out a disgusted breath. "No, you won't," he clutched his heart, "but I'll love you anyway." His face grew serious. "Even when you mess with a winning formula."

Lauren worried her lower lip. She'd figured this was coming. "You didn't like it?"

"Oh, I liked it." He threw his hands in the air. "Hell, I loved it. But it's not a good idea, Lauren."

Her eyes went round and innocent. "What's not a good idea?"

"Lauren." Her name came out a low, raspy growl.

"You need to quit smoking."

"Don't change the subject." He shook his head ruefully. "It's dangerous ground. Your Adrienne Nash books are bestsellers, for Christ's sake. Why you would jeopardize that now, is beyond me. Well? I read the draft. I can't stand it and I have to know!"

Lauren's eyes widened a little. *Geesh.* "Well, I don't think I'm exactly jeopard—"

"No. No," Wayne said irritably. "Not that." He rested his chin on a fist. "Are they or aren't they?"

Ohhh... "Adrienne Nash and her new partner are friends," Lauren replied a little defiantly.

"That's obvious. I want to know if Adrienne is shaggin' her lovely, new sidekick. Sometimes I think yes, sometimes I think no."

"That you think at all is beyond me," Lauren mumbled.

"Well?" he insisted.

Lauren sighed. "I'm not sure." Her face grew pensive. "Let's just say I'm strongly considering it."

"Well, don't," he said flatly. "I've got the numbers right here, and the gain isn't worth the risk."

"I sent you the first rough draft five days ago. And you've already done market research?" she asked incredulously, slipping off her glasses and setting them in her lap.

"Please." He rolled his eyes. "Ye of little faith. When Adrienne still had no boyfriend after your second novel I ran the stats." Wayne picked up a stack of computer printouts and waved them in the air. "You've got an eighty-nine percent female following. Of that number, a third would pray for your immortal soul and stop reading outright if Adrienne took a female lover."

"They can go to Hell," Lauren snorted.

Wayne tossed the papers back on his desk and "tsked" the writer's shortsightedness. "But only *after* buying the book." He pointed to the stack. "A third of the readers say they don't give a shit who Adrienne sleeps with, as long as she's getting some. Then again, they also indicated that if Adrienne came out as a lesbian, they weren't sure whether they'd keep reading. By the way, they want the bad guy from your first book to come back."

"Come back?" Lauren's brows drew together. "I drowned him. He's dead. He can't come back!"

"Fiction," Wayne reminded in a singsong voice.

Lauren slumped back in her chair, looking completely bewildered. "My readers are idiots?"

"Ahem!" He shot her a pointed look, and she reluctantly quieted. "The last third approve of the idea, but insist on graphic sex scenes. Our research shows that their attention will wane if they don't get one at least every sixty-three point four pages."

Lauren's face dropped into her hands. She closed her eyes and groaned. "Oh, God."

"That's a start, sweetheart!" he praised. "But how about adding a 'Take me now!' right after that?"

Sunday, October 10th

They entered quietly, going wholly undetected; three sets of socked feet tiptoed stealthily across the floor. The Secret Service could take lessons from the Marlowe children. This morning, the game plan was to pounce on their unsuspecting mother before she woke up. On the rare occasions when they were out of bed first, this had become a tradition of sorts. They usually ended up in her bed for a while, telling stories or discussing their upcoming day. It was a fun time that both mother and children enjoyed.

Ashley noticed immediately that something was different this morning and shushed her brothers as she pointed at the extra lump in their mother's bed. She stopped and studied her mom, who was snoring lightly. Then she moved to the other side of the bed to find Lauren. A wicked grin curled the little girl's lips and she dropped to her knees. Ashley crossed her arms and rested them on the edge of the bed. She propped her chin on her wrists and kissed Lauren's nose, barely touching the skin.

Her brothers fought hard to stifle their giggles.

Lauren's nose twitched as she was slowly drawn from a blissfully deep sleep. Another kiss and the blonde woman scowled, instantly aging features so youthful in slumber. Pale eyelashes fluttered open to find an unexpected pair of brown eyes staring back at her from only a millimeter away. "Holy!" Lauren's eyes popped wide open and she bolted upright, sending the sheet into a puddle around her waist. Her heart was pounding a mile a minute and she stared wide-eyed at a smiling Ashley.

Still half asleep, Dev rolled over to see what was causing the commotion next to her. "Lauren? Sweetheart?" She pushed a stray lock of dark hair from her eyes, trying to focus. "What's wrong?"

Lauren snatched up the sheet to cover her nakedness. She was only partially successful, and her befuddled mind couldn't quite understand why Dev's children were all standing in front of her giggling hysterically. "I-I don't know. I woke up, and these eyes were right in front me!" Lauren rubbed her own eyes in confusion, her voice still hoarse from sleep.

"Uh huh." Dev pushed up on her elbows and glanced past Lauren, quickly figuring out exactly what had happened and not buying her children's "Who me?" looks for a moment. "Yup. Morning raid." She sighed. "I probably should have mentioned those before." Dev glanced apologetically at Lauren and helped tug up the sheet again, this time covering the crucial areas.

"All right, you little monsters." Dev glared at her children. "Everyone turn around and look at the wall. Lauren and I need a minute to wake up."

"Aww, Mom!" Three whining voices joined forces.

"Don't 'Aww, Mom' me. Do it." She made a spinning motion with her hand, then nudged Lauren's shoulder once they were no longer being watched. "You okay?" she asked quietly.

"I guess." Lauren suddenly realized that the children had just caught her naked in bed with their mother and she flushed from head to toe, her red skin causing her fair eyebrows to stand out in vivid relief. "Oh, God, Dev, this is bad, right?" she whispered, clearly upset as she unconsciously tightened the sheet around her. "This is bad. Bad. So not good," she babbled, pulling up the comforter as well. "I should have gone back to my room last night. I fell asleep–"

"Sweetheart, this is not bad; at least not for them. I promise. True, we need to get you some–"

"Pajamas."

"Right." The older woman nodded. "But they're fine. They adore you and this won't kill them." Dev wanted to hug Lauren, but she didn't think this was a good time to get physical with her. "They come wake me up once in a while and we all snuggle. From now on I'll make sure they know they have to knock."

"But, Devlyn–"

"But nothing," Dev said seriously. "I love you and won't sneak around to be together. I'll have a talk with the children." She softened her voice. "You know I love it when you stay with me at night." Unable to stop herself, Dev reached out and grazed Lauren's bare shoulder with the back of her hand. She sighed at the feeling of soft, warm skin. "We'll make some changes so this doesn't happen again, okay? They have to learn to respect your privacy, too."

Lauren glanced uncertainly at the children who were talking among themselves. They giggled and punched each other periodically, and she thought she heard the words "boobie" and "naked". *Oh, God!* she groaned inwardly. Lauren turned back to Dev and gestured between them with a quick hand. "Isn't this the kind of thing that turns kids into serial killers and stuff?" She was half teasing, but this was painfully awkward for her and she fought the urge to simply bury herself under the blankets or bolt from the room. A grown up she could have dealt with. Hell, what could be worse than Dev's own mother walking in on them at the cabin? It didn't matter that it was purely innocent. Janet didn't know that. But this...this was different. These were kids!

Dev had to bite her lip to keep from laughing as she reached to the end of the bed to fetch her robe. "No." She handed it to Lauren. "It's a lack of honesty about things like this that turns them into serial killers. Lauren, they've seen me naked before." Dev decided to tease Ashley, so she raised her voice. She waited until Lauren had slipped into the robe before she said loudly, "I was naked and in a swimming pool when I gave birth to Ash, for heaven's sake." She grinned when the little girl whirled around and narrowed brown eyes at her. Dev shot the small brunette a "serves you right" look and ordered all the children to turn around and apologize to Lauren.

"We're sorry," they muttered, pointedly looking at Dev and not

Lauren.

Dev tilted her head towards her lover and turned up the heat in her glare. "What was that, kids? And to Lauren, not me."

"Sorry, Lauren." This time the voices were clear and the blonde woman was presented with three contrite faces.

Christopher bravely spoke up. "We didn't mean to scare you."

"S'okay, kids." Lauren smiled to make sure they knew she wasn't angry with them and was instantly greeted with three relieved sighs. "It just takes my brain a few minutes to wake up." Her gaze flicked back to Dev. "And let's not talk about giving birth, shall we?" She shivered at the thought of all that gore. "I'm still traumatized from watching Princess have those puppies."

"And Ash was probably just as ugly!" Christopher exclaimed, to his brother's delight. Both boys began laughing.

"Was not!" the little girl shouted back, punching Christopher hard on the arm.

"Ouch!"

"All right, guys, that's enough," Dev snapped. "Go into the living room and give Lauren and me a minute or two. We'll meet you out there."

"'Kay." Ashley rousted her brothers towards the door, but ran back to Lauren's bedside before leaving herself. "I really didn't mean to scare you. Sorry." She grinned tentatively. "We like it when you're here. You can have slumber parties with Mom as much as you want."

Lauren couldn't help but smile. She reached out and smoothed Ashley's sleep-tousled hair. "Thank you, honey. I'll remember that." She cupped the little girl's chin and tilted her head so that they were looking eye-to-eye. "And I'm sure you were a cuter baby than Grem's puppies." She stuck out her tongue and scrunched up her face. "Barely."

Ashley giggled and gave Lauren a hug, "Mom says I was the most beautiful girl baby. And she never lies."

Lauren gazed fondly at Ashley. "I know, sweetie."

Ashley pulled away when Dev cleared her throat and jerked her thumb towards the door, reminding her eldest that she was supposed to be vacating the room. "Gotta go." Ashley giggled as she ran out to meet her brothers. "You were uglier than me, Chris! There are pictures to prove it."

Lauren laughed and shook her head, thinking that she should have guessed Devlyn would have such a precocious daughter.

"Oh, yeah," Dev sighed, leaning back against the headboard and opening her arms to Lauren. "It's happening."

"What's happening, darlin'?" Lauren sank back into Dev's embrace, sighing contentedly. Surprisingly, she already felt a lot less embarrassed. She would make sure it didn't happen again and

Dev seemed okay with it. The kids seemed to consider it more funny than traumatic. Of course *she* was a little traumatized, but she'd get over exposing herself to three munchkins.

"You're turning into a mom," Dev said with an air of finality. She brushed her fingers through Lauren's hair. "You'll know the process is complete when you're cleaning 'fudgesicle-face' with a napkin wet with your own spit."

"Ewww!" Lauren moaned. She buried her face against Dev's warm skin, then laughed. "That particular aspect of motherhood is something I will never experience, Madam President."

"And the other aspects?" Dev felt her heart skip a beat. "I'm sort of a package deal, Lauren." She held her breath and waited.

Lauren pulled back to look at Dev's face. "I know, honey." She smiled reassuringly and laid her hand over Dev's heart. The pounding under her fingertips sent a pang through her own chest. "Everything else I take one day at a time."

"It scares the hell out of you, doesn't it?"

"Pretty much," Lauren admitted readily. "But not as much as it did before." Her gaze softened and she found herself wanting to kiss Dev in the worst way. Lauren leaned forward and gently brushed her lips against Dev's, savoring their warmth and her lover's tender, heartfelt response.

The darker woman hummed into the soft mouth pressed against her own, returning the kiss with her whole heart. "Things are going to be great, Lauren," she muttered softly, taking a final nip of Lauren's lower lip before pulling away. "You'll see."

Lauren licked her lips and grinned happily. "Things are already great."

Dev knelt down, tugging on Aaron's jacket as she zipped it up. He was about to protest again when she raised a finger to silence him. "It's chilly out today. You're wearing a jacket."

"But–"

"Or you can stay home today while Lauren and your brother and sister and I go to the zoo. You choose, son."

He lowered his head, then looked back up. "Yes, ma'am. I'll wear the jacket."

"I kinda figured." She nodded and gave him a quick kiss on the cheek. She glanced up at Lauren, who was standing next to her wearing a grin. "And where's your jacket, missy?" A playful brow quirked. "I'll be happy to take you to your room to get it, if you need me to."

Lauren wrapped her arm round Dev's waist as the President stood to her full height. She lowered her voice. "You just want to get me alone in my room, Madam President." *And I want you to get me alone my room,* her mind declared happily.

"Do you blame me? We always have so much fun there. Besides, you want me to get you alone in there too." She winked. *Oh, yeah. I read your mind.* "Sorry to disappoint, but right now I have a much more wholesome motive. I just want to make sure you're warm enough. You're just getting over being sick." She held up her hands to forestall any interjection. "Yes, I know it was last month. But you see, in mom and girlfriend time, that would be 'just getting over being sick'. Humor me."

Lauren rolled her eyes, but couldn't keep from smiling. "Okay, Mom," she teased. "I'll grab one on the way out...just like I was planning on doing anyway." She rose up on tiptoe and kissed Dev softly on the lips. "But it's nice that you care." Another tender kiss. "It's sweet, like you." *And makes my heart feel like bursting.*

"I'll give you 'Mom'." Playfully, Dev swatted Lauren's behind as the entire troop headed down the hall towards the waiting motorcade. "I'll remind you of that little wisecrack tonight, when you want to be tucked into bed." She chuckled.

"Ewww." Lauren made a face. "Why must you keep doing that? You need help, Devlyn."

"Ah, probably true," Dev agreed unrepentantly as they stopped outside Lauren's room. "It comes with the job. I think my brain cells are dying faster now." She tapped on the door as the kids giggled and romped all around them. "G'wan. Go get a nice warm jacket."

Lauren ducked into her room, grabbing a lined denim jacket from the closet next to the door and her camera from the top of her desk. "Is this good enough?" She held it for Dev's inspection with one hand and looped the camera strap around her neck with the other.

Dev nodded her approval and freed Lauren's hair from the strap around her neck. Another few seconds and Lauren was wearing the jacket. Dev blinked in mild surprise when Ashley and Christopher each took one of Lauren's hands the very second they popped through the jacket's sleeves and led her biographer down the hall without a backwards glance. Dev looked down at her youngest. "You're stuck with me, buddy. Will I do?"

He nodded and smiled, reaching up with both arms so Dev would pick him up.

Dev looked at him doubtfully. "You think I can actually lift a chubby thing like you, do you?"

His grin broadened, putting dimples in his plump cheeks. "Yup."

Dev pursed her lips. "Lucky for you I work out." She scooped up her husky son easily and settled him against her good shoulder as they moved to the door.

As usual, the press was waiting outside, snapping pictures of the First Family as they walked. Out of reflex, Dev shielded Aaron's face and was pleased to see Lauren using her own body to block their view of Ashley and Christopher. Several members of the Press Corps had been invited to the zoo in order to take photos. They, however, knew better than to be too obtrusive. Dev had been very generous with press access and none of the Corps was anxious to do anything that might harm that relationship. As they settled the children into the car, Dev leaned over to Lauren and whispered, "Thank you."

"You're welcome," Lauren whispered back, her expression turning sour. "I don't know how you do this year after year, Devlyn. Sometimes I think if I have to deal with one more of those bast–" She finished the mumbled word with Dev's palm clamped firmly over her mouth.

Dev shook her head and grinned. "Careful there, Mighty Mouse. You almost slipped in front of my innocent," she glanced at her children and contorted her face into the silliest pose she could come up with, "impressionable kids."

The children all giggled, looking at Lauren and saying in unison, "But she's very, very sorry, Mom. And she'll try to do better in the future."

With wide eyes, Lauren nodded and crossed her heart. "I'll try to do better in the future," she dutifully repeated when Dev removed her hand.

"That's a good girl. My father is a bad enough influence. But I love you anyway," Dev said fondly, ignoring her children's groaned protests over her mushiness. She took a moment to look at the notes Liza had given her earlier in the morning. "Did you know I'm delivering a speech at the zoo today – at the monkey house? I'm dedicating it." She nudged Lauren. "Do you think someone is trying to tell me something about my administration?"

"I hope not." Lauren intentionally kept her voice light as she carefully studied her lover. She knew Dev was apprehensive about this. It was her first local appearance since the shooting. Lauren wrapped her fingers around Dev's, feeling an uncharacteristic chill. "Hey," she whispered softly, her gaze straying for just a moment to find that the children were playing with the activity books Emma had sent along for them. She looked back to Dev. "Are you okay?"

"Umm...well..." *Oh, boy, Marlowe, she's got your number.* "I'm a little nervous, you know? I can't seem to help it."

Lauren leaned closer to the President, worry coloring her tone. "Is there any reason to be worried? More than normal, that is?" She knew Dev didn't really believe there was a high level of danger. Otherwise, neither she nor the kids would be coming along. Still, when Dev had mentioned giving her speech, a tiny, worried crease had appeared in her forehead.

"No, of course not. The zoo is actually only open to government employees today. And while that doesn't mean everyone there loves me, it does make things a little more secure than usual." She turned and caressed Lauren's cheek. "Besides, you know I'd never allow you or the children to be put in harm's way. I've just got butterflies." Dev swallowed and licked suddenly dry lips. Her voice grew even quieter, so that the children wouldn't hear. "Sometimes I can still hear the shots." She gazed out the window, her eyes unfocused. "I guess it's going to take longer than I realized to get over that."

Lauren squeezed the hand she was holding, part of her wishing she'd been there that day to help Devlyn, the other part relieved beyond measure that she hadn't. *I'd have gone crazy seeing her like that.* The writer forced herself away from the dark thoughts and smiled gently. "It's okay to talk about it, whenever you want."

Dev nodded, but said nothing.

Lauren exhaled slowly. *Later, Devlyn.* She smiled tentatively, her eyes searching for Dev's. "You're going to be great today, darlin'. You always are. And I know David will have security as tight as a drum." A smile shifted into a full-fledged grin. "And after your speech you can hang around with us and eat junk food all day long."

Dev couldn't maintain her solemn expression when faced with such a delightful prospect. "Ooo, a woman with a plan. I like that." She leaned in for a quick kiss, which inspired another round of giggles from the munchkins across from them. Dev turned her head slowly and smiled at them. "And, of course, should they realize they're short three monkeys at the zoo, I'll be more than happy to make a donation."

The motorcade stopped at the private entrance the President and her family would be using to enter the zoo. Dev had to put her arm out to hold back the mad rush for the door. "Easy, kiddos," she laughed. "The doors on this car are eight inches thick. Let's let the guys outside open them so you don't rupture anything." Ashley dropped back onto her mother's lap with a sigh. She turned her head and they rubbed noses. "What's up, Moppet?"

"Can we see the penguins?"

"Absolutely. We're here to have a good time and see all the animals today. I only have this one little thing I need to do this morning and then I'm yours for the day."

Lauren couldn't help but smile when the limousine was filled with wild cheers. It had been a while since they'd gotten a full day with Dev. While she, Emma, and Amy did their best to fill in, it just wasn't the same as having their mom with them.

Christopher plopped down in Lauren's lap, wrapping his little arms around her neck, while Aaron stood between them. "What animal do you want to see?" Christopher asked.

"Yeah," Dev's head turned slowly and she raised an evil brow. "Which animal do you want to see, Lauren?"

"Well," she looked at each child in turn, "I already see a baboon, hyena, and wildebeest on a daily basis. How about something different?"

Three little voices all shouted together once they realized Lauren was actually talking about them. "Hey!"

Ashley turned to her mom and whispered indignantly, "You gonna let her talk about us like that?"

"Why not? It's the truth. I just can't believe she didn't peg one of you as an enormous, stinky warthog."

"Mom!"

"Only if you're good today. Otherwise, I'm pretending I don't know you," the President teased as the doors were opened from the outside.

Dev helped the kids out of the car and into the custody of their respective Secret Service agents. Before getting out herself, she leaned over and leered at Lauren. "And in case you're wondering what I'd like to see most, it's a tiny, incredibly precious tattoo of a leprechaun, right on your—"

"Oh, God." A bright blush turned the tips of Lauren's ears scarlet, and she buried her face against Dev's chest. "You'd better hush up, Madam President. Or I won't be responsible for my actions. I might have a tiny tattoo, but you've got the cutest dimple right on your lovely—"

"Why, Ms. Strayer," Dev's eyes went round. "I didn't realize that you were taking inventory of my dimples." She smirked. "I have three, you know." Dev exited the car and then reached back in to help Lauren out.

Lauren stepped out of the limo, shielding her eyes from the bright morning sun with her hand. She could tell that Dev was much more relaxed and was a little shocked by how much it bothered her when Dev was anxious and worried. She leaned in close to Dev and whispered, "Believe me, darlin', I now know every square inch of your body."

Dev sighed with contentment and zipped up her jacket. "Yes, you do. And my body thanks you." She wiggled her brows at Lauren, who grinned back as the agents prepared for them to enter the zoo.

Dev met up with Liza while Lauren went with the kids. The President rolled her shoulders, wishing Lauren were there to rub them. She had learned where her muscles kinked the worst and the best way to work out the pain that settled there far too often now. Dev wondered if that was because of the job or the shooting. Or both.

She felt a hand brush her arm; turning, she found Liza slipping her last minute note cards into her pocket. "Thanks." Dev cleared her throat, hoping she didn't look as nervous as she felt. This was a real trial by fire for her. Some of the people in this crowd had been present when she was shot. They had seen her taken down. They had seen their President crumble and fall like a mere mortal.

For Devlyn Marlowe this was the closest thing to a panic attack that she had ever really experienced in her public life. She looked at her hands and realized they were shaking. She rubbed them together, took a deep breath and walked out on the stage.

Lauren stopped at an exhibit and allowed the kids to point and talk to the animals while she turned around to observe her lover. Because the spot she had chosen gave her an excellent view, she didn't look like she was hovering. Which, of course, she was. *But I'm worried, dammit.* Lauren lifted her camera and began to focus, zooming in on Dev. *Jesus. She's shaking.* She almost left the kids with the Secret Service and went up there, but before she could move, Dev strode to the podium.

Devlyn smiled and licked her lips, once again shoving down her nervousness. Her gaze moved rapidly over the crowd. The applause she was hearing was barely audible in her world as her eyes landed on Lauren. The smile that she had on her face softened and became one that was reserved for Lauren alone. *There's your strength, Marlowe. Latch on to it.* "Good morning, everyone. They tell me I'm here to talk about monkeys this morning, but since I don't like to tell stories about my Chief of Staff, I guess they mean the real thing..."

Dev didn't have problems tracking her family like everyone else who got separated in a situation like this. She was being guided along quite nicely by the Secret Service detail, who knew exactly where every member of the Marlowe family was at all times. Right now, Dev was being escorted to the seal exhibit.

She did take the time to shake a few hands and sign a few autographs for the crowd, hoping that would help her later in the day, when she would be less social as she spent time with her family.

Devlyn slowed her pace as she approached her four favorite people, a huge smile brightening her face. She wrestled it away immediately, glancing around to make sure there wasn't a drinking fountain anywhere nearby. There wasn't. Dev shoved her hands in her pockets as she closed the remaining distance between her and her family. She stopped alongside Lauren, who was kneeling in front of Aaron. They appeared to be in the midst of a very indepth conversation. Dev still had to fight to keep the grin off her face as

she watched Lauren cleaning something from her son's face, oblivious to her presence. "Umm, Lauren?"

Lauren glanced up. "Oh, hi. You're back." She smiled affectionately. "We missed you. And why are you looking at me like I grew a
mustache while you were gone? Do I have something between my
teeth?" Lauren immediately swirled the tip of her tongue across
pearly whites, searching for the offending piece of food.

A small laugh bubbled up that Dev was helpless to control. "No.
Your teeth are fine." She looked pointedly at Lauren's hand. "I was
just wondering how exactly you wet the napkin you're using to clean
his," her gaze drifted to her son and she grimaced, "filthy face."

"Huh?" Lauren looked down at the wadded up, chocolate ice
cream covered napkin in her hand. She frowned. "Well, there was
no drinking fountain or bathroom nearby, and it was all over his little face, and it wouldn't come off, and I couldn't stand it. So I–"
Gray eyes widened to an almost comical degree. "Oh, my God."

The look of pure, unadulterated shock on Lauren's face was
priceless, and what had started out small was now a full-fledged
belly laugh for Dev. The dark-haired woman wiped tears from her
cheeks as she leaned back against a rail and offered Lauren her
hand so she could pull her up.

Lauren hadn't even made it all the way to her feet, before she
was pulled into a heartfelt hug. She grinned against Dev's chest as
she felt the older woman's silent laughter. "Very funny." She
pinched her hard in the belly for the teasing, drawing a muffled
squawk that ruffled her hair.

"Welcome to the club, sweetheart," Dev finally said. "It's been a
wild year for you, hasn't it?"

Aaron looked between the women. "What club?"

"The one where they clean your sticky old face with their spit,
stupid-head," Christopher added helpfully.

"Oh." Aaron just shrugged. What did he care?

"I-I," Lauren stuttered, still a little wide-eyed. "I didn't even
think about it."

Dev shrugged casually as she found something terribly interesting about her shoes and kicked at a non-existent pebble. "Yeah,
comes pretty naturally to us mom types."

Lauren was speechless and Dev took pity on her friend, giving
her a moment to compose herself. She looked up and found Aaron's
Secret Service agent lurking close by. She motioned the young man
over and in a few quick strides he was ready for his orders. "Could
you please take Aaron to the men's room and give him a little clean
up? Even though clinical research has proven that 'mom spit' and
hydrochloric acid are exactly the same thing, I think a little soap
would come in handy for this job." Dev reached down and cupped
her son's chin, so she could get a good look at the damage.

"Eww...now I gotta go wash my hands!" She arched an eyebrow at her son. "You're a slob, buddy."

Aaron blushed.

Ashley, who had finally pried herself away from the railing where she was watching the seals, joined her brothers. Her voice took on a sage quality. "Grandpa says if it isn't on your face, you're not enjoying it properly."

Dev's eyes went round as an entirely X-rated thought popped into her mind at Ashley's innocent statement. She felt a sudden, burning heat sting her cheeks.

Lauren looked at Dev quizzically. "Why–?" Her jaw sagged with her realization and she blushed so fiercely she felt lightheaded. Lauren covered her eyes with her hands. "You're such a pervert, Devlyn Marlowe."

"What?" Ashley questioned. "What? And why are you guys all red?" She hated being left out of the loop.

Lauren narrowed her eyes at Dev, who stared back at her with devastating innocence. "No wonder your parents call you Devil."

Dev just wriggled her eyebrows.

Ashley put her hands on her hips and waited.

Lauren looked down at the girl. "It's nothing you need to worry about, sweetheart." The blonde's gaze flicked back to Dev, and she glared at the grinning woman. "Your mom was just making a very *private* joke."

Lauren reached out and took Dev's hand. "C'mon, you; we're leaving the kids with their agents for five minutes so I can buy you some ice cream." In a much lower but still teasing voice she added, "And keep you from traumatizing them with your wicked ways."

Dev felt herself being tugged away. She waved at Christopher and Ashley, who had already hooked up with Amy and were heading towards the alligator exhibit. "Keep an eye on your brothers; we'll be back in a minute. Be good and don't give Amy any trouble."

The little girl threw her hands into the air. "Do I ever?"

"Yes," Dev called over her shoulder. "I've got an FBI file on you an inch thick. Be good till we get back."

"Yes, ma'am."

Once the women were a few feet away, Lauren eased up on their pace. She leaned closer to Dev and spoke quietly, concern coloring her tone. "Your speech was wonderful, Devlyn." She looked for a tactful segue, but in this instance there didn't seem to be one. Lauren let go of Dev's hand and gently rubbed her back as they strolled along at a snail's pace. "You okay?"

The President nodded slowly. "Yeah, I'm fine. I just needed to get back out there and do it. Kind of like falling off a horse for the first time. You just have to get up and get back on before you lose your nerve." She smiled wryly. "Funny, when I was on tour after the bombings, being out there didn't bother me, but this, here at home, where it happened – this shook me up." Dev felt her guts begin to churn when she thought of the shooting and she quickly pushed the thoughts away, focusing on the here and now. "I don't understand it, but I survived it, and that's all that matters."

Unexpected tears pricked Lauren's eyes and she felt her throat close.

"Hey." Dev stopped walking and wrapped her arms around the shorter woman's waist. "None of that, okay?" She tilted her head in entreaty. "Today's supposed to be fun."

Lauren nodded and drew in a deep breath. "You're right. I'm sorry." She smiled weakly and they resumed their trek.

"It helped having you here today. Keeping watch over me, were you, Mighty Mouse?"

Lauren laughed lightly. "You know it, Wonder Woman. Somebody's got to keep you out of trouble."

Dev's hand let go of Lauren's waist as they maneuvered around a popcorn stand and a large family. "Get any nice pictures?"

"Hmm. Absolutely. A bunch of the kids and several great ones of you. Not that just about any picture of you isn't great."

"Right," Dev snorted.

Lauren rolled her eyes at the suddenly bashful look that had overtaken Dev's face. "Trust me, Devlyn. You and the camera are carrying on a love affair that should make me green with jealousy. You're gorgeous, and you damn well know it."

Dev's mouth opened, but no sound came out.

Lauren laughed in earnest, retaking her lover's hand and twining their fingers together. She wanted to talk more about how Dev felt about the shooting. Dev needed that. But she also sensed that the President wasn't quite ready. She needed more time, and that was okay by Lauren. She could be patient when she had to be, and she had no intention of going anywhere anytime soon.

The women approached the front of a brightly bannered concession stand that smelled so good Lauren was sure she had gained five pounds just by being within sniffing distance. *Thank God we work out so much.* There were no lines, and the blonde walked right up ahead of Dev, taking a spot at the counter. "Pick your poison, Madam President," she said brightly. "I'm buying."

Dev sighed happily. *God, she's wonderful. I'm keeping her.* Taking a deep breath, she wrapped her arms around Lauren from behind, and rested her chin on the shorter woman's shoulder as she considered the menu. She pressed her lips against Lauren's ear and in a sexy purr said, "Fudgesicle."

Ooo... Lauren nearly swooned on the spot. She held her fingers up for the vendor, who was openly staring at his most famous customer. "Make that two."

Wednesday, October 13th

"She looks nervous." Dev elbowed David, who was perched next to her on the edge of her desk in the Oval Office. "Don't you think she looks nervous?"

David nodded. "Oh, yeah. She's nervous." The man winced. "And that was just the promo."

Lauren was about to be interviewed by the nation's number one, live, early morning talk show, *Wake Up, America*. It was a "feel good" program that eased millions of Americans into the day. The show's anchor, the irrepressible and ever-so-palatable-before-breakfast, Debbie Charles, was a personal friend of Dev's, who had interviewed her several times over the years, first as Governor of Ohio and then as President-elect. The woman was fair and likeable and knew how to stick to relevant topics, never letting her questions drift into areas that were too personal or gossip-laden.

Dev's face grew pensive. "Lauren will be fine, right?" She glanced sideways at David just as the promo for the show ended and a coffee commercial took its place. "I mean, she's done tons of personal appearances to promote her biographies. She told me so herself. This is just like that."

"Were they televised?" David asked absently, wishing he had a big, jumbo mug for his coffee like the incredibly happy looking man on television.

Dev chewed her lip as she thought. "Umm...now that I think of it, I guess they wouldn't have been. There was no video disc included with her background check. If she'd done TV it certainly would have been there." Dev chastised herself for being so busy the last few days that she hadn't really bothered to find out how Lauren felt about the interview. "She seemed fine with it, right?" Other than the younger woman's mentioning it earlier in the week, during breakfast, the subject had never even come up.

"Well, she was a little reluctant to do it when she found out it was going to be televised nationally. Especially since it was live." David frowned, resigning himself to his own, now obviously inadequate, coffee mug. "But once I explained how good publicity that showed her in a professional, rather than personal, light would be – and how it would go a long way towards keeping the party dogs off your back about your relationship," he shrugged, "she didn't seem to have a problem with it."

Dev sprang to her feet, knocking a folder containing the day's agenda to the floor in the process. "You said what?"

David looked up in surprise. "What?" His eyes widened at the look on Dev's face. "It's the truth, Dev. Lauren's a big girl. She asked me if this would help you, and I said yes."

"I don't care if it is the truth." Dev's gaze hardened. "I don't want you pressuring her."

"And I didn't!" David defended, slightly miffed.

Jane and Liza, who were sitting on a sofa that had been pulled over next to Dev's desk so that they could have a better view of the television, both looked at each other knowingly. If David and Dev didn't have at least three good disagreements a day, the world as they knew it might come crashing to a halt.

The commercials ended and the music for *Wake Up, America* started. Lauren and the show's co-host, a young, clean cut man in a cable knit sweater, were now sitting in side-by-side chairs, chatting quietly over their morning coffee. "Jesus Christ." Dev pointed at the image. "Does that freakin' coffee company own the world or what?" She reached behind her, picking up her steaming mug of that exact brand and sighed with pleasure as both she and Lauren took sips simultaneously.

David narrowed his eyes enviously at Lauren's enormous, super-sized mug. *I don't care if it is nothing more than mug envy. After the show, I'm calling Beth.* Beth knew the proper store for everything and its exact location.

"Wow. She looks good on TV," Jane commented appreciatively. "I don't see that extra ten pounds TV people are always complaining about."

Liza squinted. "Me neither."

"Shhh!" Dev leaned forward eagerly.

The man sitting next to Lauren turned to the camera and smiled brightly, his blindingly white teeth fairly sparkling in contrast to his tanned skin. "And next, Traci Corbin will be filling in for Debbie Charles, who called in sick with...if you can believe it...the chickenpox! Our very special guest this morning is Lauren Strayer, biographer to the President."

Jaws dropped in the Oval Office.

"But first," the young man continued, "the weather." A large map of the United States appeared and *Wake Up, America's* much beloved weatherman materialized right along with it.

"David!" Dev growled, her entire body shaking.

"I'm on it!" Liza thrust a phone into the Chief of Staff's hand, and he frantically began calling to find out whose head was going to roll and how they could stop this interview before the portly weatherman worked his way to California.

Lauren shifted uncomfortably in her chair, running a nervous hand through her hair the second the camera panned over to the weatherman.

Traci Corbin brushed past the show's male co-host, who was on his way for a makeup retouch before his interview with the Washington Redskins' quarterback, which was going to take place in the next segment. She took the seat opposite the writer and extended her hand. "I'm Traci Corbin. Sorry I didn't get a chance to introduce myself earlier."

Lauren grasped the chilled palm and gave it a companionable squeeze. "Lauren Strayer. It's a pleasure to meet you."

Traci looked slightly harried. "I just got the call they needed me to come in an hour ago and I had to make a mad dash for the studio." The forty-something woman needed all the time in makeup she could get. "I made a few notes while they were fixing my hair." She smiled. "I hope you don't mind if my questions are a little rough."

The older woman's friendly demeanor instantly put Lauren at ease. "No...I..." She blushed slightly and forced her hands to stop twitching. "That's fine. As long as you don't mind a slightly nervous guest. I don't really do TV interviews, so this will be something of a first."

Traci nodded and gave Lauren's arm a sympathetic squeeze. "Live TV is always a little nerve racking. You'll do fine."

A man suddenly appeared a few feet in front of Lauren and Traci, but well off camera. He held up five fingers. Then four, three, two, one. Traci smiled. "Welcome back to *Wake Up, America*. I'm Traci Corbin, filling in for Debbie, who is home sick today. With us this morning, we have Presidential biographer, Lauren Strayer." She turned to face Lauren. "Good morning."

"Mornin'."

"That's quite a job you have, Ms. Strayer! Following around after President Marlowe. Is it as exciting as it sounds?"

Lauren smiled as just a little more of her nervousness floated away with the simple question. "Sure. Sometimes. The White House is a whirlwind of activity. Always. And sometimes it's just a lot of hard work. I spend most of my time experiencing what the President does throughout her day and the rest of my time doing research and organizing what I learned, so that, in the end, I'll be able to distill four years into a single book that's an accurate portrait of President Marlowe."

"Interesting." Traci tapped her chin as though she were truly considering her next question. "So how do you produce an," her fingers fashioned quote marks in the air and her eyes took on a slightly predatory gleam, "'accurate portrait' when you're sleeping with your subject?"

Dev's face dropped to her hands as she groaned. "Oh, my God."

The sounds of the President's groans were nearly drowned by the other moans echoing around her.

Dev peeked between her fingers so she could continue to watch the interview. "Come on, Mighty Mouse; don't let that bitch fluster you. You're better than that, sweetheart."

Lauren blinked at the interviewer, momentarily stunned by the blunt question.

Traci stared back at Lauren and a tiny, almost imperceptible smile twitched at her lips. *I just got my Associated Press quote. Fuck* Wake Up America! *I want my own show. And Marlowe can kiss my ass.*

Dev had denied Traci's repeated requests for a one-on-one interview. Traci had been persistent. Too persistent, actually. And she'd gotten a little visit from the Secret Service, who not so politely asked her to tone it down or risk prosecution under D.C.'s stalking laws and a host of other federal statutes enacted to protect the President. They'd even revoked her press credentials for a short while, placing her on a probationary status. *Me! Traci Corbin!*

"Ms. Strayer?" Traci reminded, absolutely loving the long seconds of stunned silence that were ticking away.

For a split second Lauren was confused. She'd been promised this interview would be about her work and wouldn't venture into private matters like who she slept with. Then she caught a glimpse of the look on Traci's face. Her eyes narrowed at the sight as a flash of understanding passed between the women.

Dev paled. "Uh oh. She's pissed."

David finished yelling into his phone. He furiously snapped the cover closed and threw it to the floor at his feet and stomped it. Twice. *"Wake Up, America* claims they didn't know that her press credentials had been pulled earlier this year. Apparently, the show's other correspondents refused to do the interview with Lauren. They didn't want to look unprepared. The show has used Traci in the past and she was the best they could do on an hour's notice." David glared at his phone as though this were all its fault. He stomped on it again.

Lauren shifted in her chair, meeting Traci's gaze directly. "That's a good question, Ms. Corbin. And, to be truthful, I don't think I can be totally objective."

Traci smiled triumphantly. "You don't?"

Dev, David, Liza, and Jane all grimaced.

"No. But then again, no writer is one hundred percent objective, is she?" Lauren picked up the gauntlet and ran with it. "Everyone brings her own life experiences to bear on what she writes, despite the best intentions. We're only human, after all." *Unlike the members of certain professions!* Lauren warmed to her topic. "I think the keys to being as accurate and honest as possible are good editorial support, meticulous research, and a heartfelt commitment to serve your readers."

Traci's smile began to slip.

"You can still maintain those things no matter what your relationship is with your *subject,*" Lauren drew out the last word with evident distaste. Not that she hadn't used it herself in the past. She had. But she was sure she'd never said it in a way that conveyed that the people she wrote about were laboratory rats...to be dissected. Lauren grinned sweetly. "Did that answer your question, Ms. Corbin?" she asked innocently, knowing full well she'd just rained on the interviewer's parade. *Bitch.*

"That's my girl!" Dev shouted gleefully.

"Go get her, Mighty Mouse! Ask about her boob job and nose jobs!"

All three women stared at David.

"What?" he complained. "I'm Chief of Staff. I know things!"

Traci glanced down at her notes. "Um...yes, actually, it does." She looked up and smiled at the camera.

Dev shivered.

"Ah...yes. Now, Lauren—"

Lauren bit her lip to keep from asking, "Who in the hell said you could call me by my first name?" Instead, she tried to look interested, wondering how long a three-minute interview could possibly last.

"President Marlowe is the first female President."

Lauren nodded, fighting hard not to roll her eyes. *And you said you didn't have time to do research.*

"She's also a very attractive woman, wouldn't you agree?"

Lauren's eyebrow twitched. "Anyone with eyes would agree, *Traci.*"

"They sure would! Can you tell America what President Marlowe thinks about being named the world's most *eligible* woman?"

The temperature in the studio dropped ten degrees. *What? She is not eligible, and you know it!* "I'm not sure what Devlyn thinks about that." Lauren's hands shaped into fists, though her face remained impassive.

"Don't take the bait, Lauren," Dev said to the image in front of her. "I'm *not* eligible!"

Jane nodded. "Off the market."

"Totally taken," Liza agreed fervently.

Lauren leaned forward in her chair, looking at the magazine Traci had suddenly thrust in front of her. Dev was pictured on the cover with her arm wrapped around Hollywood's newest starlet, Takesha Vasquez. It was clear that the picture was doctored and merely intended to show how good the two women looked together. Which, Lauren admitted reluctantly, they did. "This is total and utter crap," she announced crisply, tossing the magazine down on a small table that sat between her and Traci.

Dev's eyes widened and she sucked in a nervous breath. "Don't kill her on live TV."

"I could fix that," David stated confidently.

Everyone in America waited for Lauren to blow a gasket. Instead, she smiled charmingly and said in a soft, Southern accent,

"I happen to know that President Marlowe prefers blondes."

Several members of *Wake Up, America's* crew chuckled. Traci joined in reluctantly.

Off camera, a man held up his hand and began counting down on his fingers.

Traci dutifully read the teleprompter. "Thank you, Lauren. Join us in our next segment where America gets to wake up and meet Redskins star quarterback, Elvis Simpson."

On the television in the Oval Office a commercial replaced Traci and Lauren's images. Dev turned to David. "She did okay, right?" *No bloodshed. Yet. I'd be running if I were you, Ms. Corbin.*

"Oh, yeah, very professional." *Thank you, God!* "She was wonderful. And she only looked like she was going to hit Traci for a minute there."

"Too bad she'll never hear those compliments, pal," Dev said wryly.

Liza and Jane turned sympathetic glances towards David.

The red-haired man frowned, but took the implication seriously. "She's going to kill me, isn't she?"

Dev nodded and slapped her best friend hard between the shoulder blades. "I regret that you have but one life to give for your country...and that my girlfriend is going to snuff it out when she gets home."

Traci marched off the set in a huff, upset she hadn't gotten more of a reaction out of Lauren. What could have been a lead story on the nightly news had been reduced to a meaningless sound bite that wasn't sensational in the least. She stopped dead in her tracks at the sound of a hard voice coming from behind her.

"That wasn't very nice." Lauren stood three paces behind the slender, older woman, her facial muscles twitching with the force of her pent up anger and frustration. She'd taken enough shit from the press over the past ten months. But now...now there was finally a face attached to that malicious, big mouth.

Slowly, Traci turned to face the woman behind her. "I'm a news correspondent, Ms. Strayer. I'm paid to get a story, not to be 'nice'. If I wanted to be 'nice', I'd write biographies for a living."

Lauren took another menacing step forward. "I don't think you were trying to get a story at all. You were trying to get a reaction." *And you almost did.* "Those were nothing more than cheap shots. And something I'd expect more from the tabloids than a supposed 'news correspondent'." Another step forward. "It takes skill and talent to write for a living, Ms. Corbin. Don't kid yourself. Your obvious inadequacies are the reason you can't do it."

"Ooo, ouch!" The reporter gave Lauren a less than sincere

smile. "I can die happy now. The President's girlfriend has told me off. Are you finished having your little tantrum, Ms. Strayer? Because I'm going home. Besides, I'm sure you're due back at the White House to do a little Chief Executive back scratching."

Lauren's face turned an angry shade of purple. She calmly slid off her glasses and tucked them safely into the pocket of her jacket. "Oh, there's going to be scratching." The writer's eyes glittered with rage. "But I was thinking more along the lines of bloody streaks down your face." Lauren smiled a cold smile, enjoying the look of shock and poorly masked concern on Traci Corbin's face. "Though I'll be sure to give Devlyn your regards tonight."

"Hi, Lauren!" A nervous and very familiar voice interrupted their conversation.

Lauren didn't even turn her head; she just continued to burn holes through a wide-eyed Traci with her withering glare.

Oh, shit. David was right. Thank God I was so close to the studio. David's frantic call had reached his wife when she was only two blocks away from the studio on her way to a downtown meeting. She could be there more quickly than anyone else, and by the tone of David's voice she knew she needed to hurry. Beth rushed forward and stepped into the small space that remained between the women.

"Hi, I'm Beth McMillian." She reached out and took Traci's hand, shaking it vigorously. "And if I were you, I'd leave now, before my friend Lauren claws your eyes out and my husband has to find a place to hide your worthless," her gaze dropped to Traci's chest, "silicone-filled body."

"Oh, the cavalry!" Traci leaned in and stage whispered to Beth, her bravado returning now that it appeared she wasn't about to be pounded within an inch of her life. "And just in time too. I would hate to have damaged blondie's 'all American' good looks." She took a deep breath and looked over Beth's shoulder at Lauren. "Give the President my best, won't you?" Traci smirked.

Lauren finally snapped and lunged forward, but Beth turned around more quickly than anyone would have thought possible for a basically sedentary history professor. She used her greater weight to hold Lauren back by the shoulders. The younger woman looked as though she was going to spontaneously combust if she didn't kill someone.

"Let. Me. *Go!*" The writer watched angrily as Traci took this as her cue to leave.

"Lauren, don't do it," Beth soothed. "The legitimate media will tear you and Dev apart. Take a deep breath and think of Dev and the kids."

Her words had an immediate effect and Lauren stopped pushing against Beth hands.

Beth nodded her approval. "That's it. She's not worth it."

Lauren blew out an unhappy breath and tried to calm herself. "Bitch," she seethed in a whisper, feeling hot tears spring to her eyes. "It's always something. They're always lurking and lying and distorting. And they never stop, even when you try to play their game!"

"No, they don't." Beth sighed, glad that when Lauren finally had this meltdown she was away from the White House. Beth had seen it building over the past few weeks as Dev's popularity slipped further in the polls. In addition to the furor over the bombings and subsequent FBI raid, Dev's own party, along with the Republicans and several conservative Democrats, had begun to question the President's morals. After all, she was shacked up with her girlfriend in what was considered by most people to be a public residence. "If you intend to have any kind of a relationship with Dev, you're going to have to learn to ignore most of this."

"Easier said than done," Lauren admitted. She brought shaking hands to her eyes to wipe the tears away, then to her temples, where she was developing a horrendous headache. *God, what is wrong with me?* She let out a ragged breath, more upset by her lack of control than Traci Corbin. "You're right, Beth. Let's go." The two women began walking towards the exit. "I'm not even going to ask why or how in the hell you got here not thirty seconds after that joke of an interview ended."

Beth laughed. "My loving hubby called me on my cell phone and cleared the way with studio security." She shrugged. "I just happened to be nearby. He told me that if I didn't get over to this studio a.s.a.p. he was never coming home again because he'd be busy trying to explain how a simple interview turned into a homicide."

Lauren nodded. "David is a smart man. Too bad he has to die for talking me into this." A small grin edged onto Lauren's face. "He knows the early morning hours are when I'm most likely to commit murder."

Beth chuckled, linking her arm through Lauren's. "I suggest we let him live and just torture him for the rest of our natural lives. It's far more fun that way. Never let them see you sweat and never let them forget it when they do something stupid. Now, how about I buy you breakfast?" *I'm never going to make my meeting anyway.*

Lauren laid a hand on her churning belly. She'd been too nervous to eat anything and had already been up for nearly three hours. "Will there be alcohol?"

"Absolutely. Nothing wrong with a Bloody Mary at," Beth glanced at her watch, "7:30 a.m."

"Mmm hmm...or Mimosas."

"Or Screwdrivers."

"Or beer," they both said together, bursting into unexpected laughter as the tension surrounding them plummeted. They pushed through the front doors of the building and were hit with a blast of moist air.

Beth suddenly stopped walking and stared out at the street lined with cars and rain puddles. "Uh...you're going to have to drive."

"Sure." Lauren shrugged, her eyes tracking Beth's gaze. "What are you looking at?"

"The empty space on the road behind that car in the handi-capped spot," her shoulders slumped, "where my car used to be."

"Oh." Lauren grimaced and wrapped her arm around Beth's shoulders, steering her towards her own car. "Sorry." Her brows drew together as she thought. She glanced at her friend as they stepped down off the curb. "Do you think Dev could have Traci Corbin deported?"

Beth laughed. "I'm sure David's looking into it as we speak."

Friday, October 15th

"Gentlemen." Dev leaned back in her chair, allowing her gaze to sweep over every Emancipation Party member present. She closed her eyes briefly in a silent bid for control. "I don't give a good God damn what you think on this issue. This is my private life you're prying into!"

Party Chairman Bruce Jordon loosened his necktie with thick fingers. He was only a few years older than Dev, but had silver hair and a deeply creased, hangdog face. "No offense, Madam President, but when the Party agreed to hire Lauren Strayer to write your biog-raphy, we didn't realize that you'd be getting into a—" he momen-tarily fumbled over his words, torn between what he wanted to say and what was appropriate. "Ahem... We...ah...we never seriously contemplated a physical relationship between the two of you."

"Good." Dev crossed her arms over her chest. "Because neither did I." She looked at David, but he just shrugged. Dev was on her own here. When he heard about this meeting, Geoff Vincent had gone to the White House to show his support for Devlyn, only to be turned away by David. This had to come directly from the Presi-dent's mouth and no one else's.

Dev refocused on Party Chairman Jordon. "What happened between Lauren and me happened just like it would have for any other couple. Over a period of months, by working together and helping each other through some rough spots, we developed a close friendship which, in turn, blossomed into love."

She stopped and drew a deep breath, resenting the hell out of every second of this. She pointed directly at the main source of her antagonism. "It wasn't you, Bruce, in the hospital holding my hand after I got shot. And I don't recall your being the one to go in and help soothe my children's fears when they thought their mother might die." Dev wanted to shout at the top of her lungs that she didn't have to justify her actions to the Party or any other bastard on Earth. But that wasn't totally true, and she knew it.

"Dev," the man sat up a little straighter in his chair, "look, you know I have a great deal of respect for you. I have no problem with your...lifestyle. What I do have a problem with is that *National News Magazine* is about to release a nearly twenty-page cover story about you and Lauren. They've got pictures of the two of you out together."

"Yeah, well since we've been out together in public, I'm sure they do. What is the real problem here?"

Chairman Jordon slammed his palms against the table, the resulting bang causing nearly everyone in the room to jump. Dev didn't move a muscle. "Don't screw around with me, Dev. You know damned well that you got elected by being honest about your sexuality, but not by rubbing people's noses in it. Samantha—"

Dev's face turned to stone and her voice dropped to a dangerous level. "Don't you dare bring her into this. Not one God damned word about her!" she boomed.

Mentioning Sam's name was taboo, and the Party knew it. After her death, they'd wanted to exploit public sympathy for Governor Marlowe and they'd nearly lost Dev because of it. If it hadn't been for David's cooler head, Dev would have broken with the Emancipation Party then and there. Since then, however, they'd always been able to work through their differences. Until now.

Bruce Jordon threw his hands in the air and let out a disgusted grunt. "Not this time." He jutted his jaw defiantly. "I'm not catering to your ego for one more second! We've got problems that won't go away by ignoring them. Half of Washington is calling your morality into question. They've got *big* problems with the fact that Lauren Strayer is living in the White House, under the same roof with you and your children, while you're carrying on an affair with her. They believe that your children are being exposed to something less than decent, and that by continuing to pay her, the Emancipation Party is encouraging this amoral behavior."

"And the Party would rather not be subjected to that kind of publicity?"

"Exactly."

"Yet the Party doesn't have a problem when some half-assed gossip magazine calls me 'The World's Most Eligible Woman'?"

Mr. Jordon looked confused. "Dev, that's true." *And it was good publicity. There is a difference.*

"Like hell it is. One, I'm not eligible. Two, the article in *National News Magazine* is accurate. I saw a copy of it last week and I have no problem with it. Three, if people want to talk about my morality let's discuss the fact that before Lauren, I spent the last four years alone. It's all well and good that then I wasn't 'rubbing the public's nose' in anything," Dev sneered. "But I had no one in my life. *No one.* I served my term as Governor, and then ran for President, *by myself.*" She enunciated her last two words with excruciating precision, letting everyone know just how she felt about that time. "For God's sake, Bruce, you've been with Olga for over twenty years and now you've got the nerve to criticize me for finding someone who makes me happy?"

"It's not the same thing."

"Bullshit. I'm in love with a woman who loves me and adores my children and suddenly I'm immoral? I feel like I'm going backwards in my life! It doesn't make sense."

"If you were married to her it would be different." Chairman Jordon shifted in his seat. "But this living together—"

"Wrong!" Dev sprang to her feet. "You seem to be conveniently forgetting that same sex marriages still aren't legal in almost half the states in this country! We've made strides, yes. But—"

"But!" The Chairman jumped up, joining Dev. "It *is* legal in your home state." He squared his shoulders and sucked in his stomach, throwing his chest out in the process. "Or is she just a distraction and a quick roll in the sack that you have no intention of getting serious about? Because if she is—"

"You son of a bitch!" Dev turned on the man and advanced, her hand curling into a tight fist.

David was between them in an instant. *What is it with Dev and Lauren this month? Time for another vacation!* "Don't do it. It's not worth it." He held his hand firmly against Dev's chest and his eyes met hers. "You and I both know you're in love with Lauren. He's just pissed and scared." He lowered his voice and pleaded with his friend, knowing he couldn't stop her if she really had a mind to punch Bruce. "Don't let him get to you."

David looked over his shoulder. "Mr. Chairman, I think it would be in your best interest to leave right now. We can continue this at a later time when heads are cooler and the facts are clearer. Let us run some numbers—"

"Screw the numbers, David! I will *not* let a damned poll tell me who I'm allowed to love and who I'm allowed to invite into my home." Dev pushed against his hand, still trying to get closer to Chairman Jordon as the rest of the party leaders quickly shuffled out of Dev's office.

David and Dev were left alone to look over the scattered coffee cups and meeting agendas that were left on the table when the Party members fled the room. Each of them took a chair and sat quietly, wondering how the hell things went so wrong so fast.

Saturday, October 16th

"This last one is from me." Christopher thrust a package into his sister's hands. "Happy birthday, Ash."

"Thanks, Chris." Ashley grabbed the box and tore open the paper. "Wow! Scientist Barbie with her laboratory! Thanks, Chris!"

The little boy smiled brightly and adjusted his glasses. "You're welcome." He leaned in and whispered conspiratorially, very aware that Lauren, his mom, and Emma were listening. "Can me and Aaron play too? Even though it's a girl toy. We can blow up the laboratory and kidnap Barbie!"

Ashley was about to tell her brother to keep dreaming when she got a warning glare from Dev. She relented with a tiny huff. "Sure, Chris. C'mon." Ashley picked up the disc containing the Nancy Drew Mysteries that Lauren had given her, the tickets to *The Nutcracker* that were from her mom, the sweatshirt from Emma, and the glow-in-the-dark necklace from Aaron. She turned to follow her brothers, who had already run from the room, when Dev's voice caused her to turn back.

"Aren't you forgetting something?" Dev reminded gently. Ashley had already politely thanked Lauren and Emma. But it never hurt to say it again.

"Thank you, Lauren and Emma," the girl dutifully repeated. Then a genuine smile creased her cheeks. "I love my stories and sweatshirt. I'm going to show my friends at school!"

Lauren chuckled. "I'm glad you like it, Ashley. I was just your age when I started reading those. Only I used the actual books."

Ashley made a face. "Wow. You're really old."

Dev and Emma dissolved into laughter.

"Gee, thanks, kid." Gray eyes twinkled.

"You're welcome," Ashley answered sincerely as she ran for the door.

Dev called out another "Happy birthday" to her eldest, and Ashley skidded to a halt. She ran back to her mother and hugged her fiercely. "Happy birthday to you too, Mom. It's so cool to share a birthday. Are we really going to go to the ballet – just the two of us?"

Devlyn closed her eyes and squeezed her tightly, feeling a nearly crushing guilt over the lack of quality time she could lavish on each child individually. "I promise, Moppet. Just you and me. A special afternoon for the two of us." Dev felt her chest constrict and decided if she didn't think about something different, and fast, she was going to cry. "How does it feel to be so big? Eight years old!" She sighed wistfully. "I can hardly believe it."

Ashley beamed. "It's great! Bye." This time when she ran out of the room she didn't turn back.

"Well, now, Devlyn," Emma said, "I think I'm going to go relax and call my son, Tommy." The matronly woman smiled tiredly. "It's been a busy day." And it had. Ashley had had several girls from her class spend the afternoon at the White House and then had another smaller family party that was just wrapping up.

"You do that, Emma. And thank you so much for everything." Dev smiled wryly. "I don't pay you nearly enough."

Emma snorted. "Isn't that the truth?" She padded slowly towards the door. "Night, ladies."

"Night, Emma," Lauren and Dev called back.

"Wow." Lauren shook her head in admiration. "She did a great job this afternoon. I could barely hear all those screaming second graders from my room today. With my door shut. And my headphones on. And my head buried in a pillow."

Dev rolled her eyes. "Wimp."

"True," Lauren chuckled. She liked her quiet time, and life at the White House certainly was never that. At least not with the Marlowes in residence. "So..." Lauren sidled up to Dev and molded her body to the President's lean, lanky form. She dropped a kiss on Dev's throat. "What does the big birthday girl want today?"

Dev growled as she captured Lauren's lips in a passionate kiss. When she heard the younger woman moan softly, she deepened the kiss, reveling in the taste and scent of her partner. When she pulled away, Lauren looked a little dazed as she slowly licked her lips. "Does that give you a hint?"

Lauren swallowed. "Uh huh." She grabbed Dev's hand and began leading her out of the living room. "We're going to my place. And I'm not letting you out until morning."

Dev was willingly led along as far as her front door. Then she pulled Lauren to a stop.

"What?" Lauren asked in exasperation. "I've been waiting my turn all day!"

Dev smiled. "I know, sweetheart. But couldn't you just stay here? What if the kids need something, or David could–"

"Nope. It's all arranged." She tugged hard on Dev's hand, nearly taking her right off her feet.

"But–"

"God." Lauren rolled her eyes, laughing when Dev didn't get a chance to close the door behind her before she was dragged out into the hall. "Emma knows. David knows. And probably the entire Secret Service knows that I'm having," she unceremoniously pushed open her door and ushered Dev inside, "a sleepover tonight."

"Is that what you told them?" Dev chuckled, scanning the floor for Princess and Gremlin. She was always wary of surprise attacks and since coming to the White House, Princess had taken on Gremlin's decidedly unpleasant disposition. Well, unpleasant to Dev. Everyone else, except for Michael Oaks, who Dev suspected hated

Santa Claus and his own mother, seemed to adore both dogs.

"Yup. That's exactly what I told them." Lauren finally stopped her march when she stood in front of her couch. She lifted Dev's hand and kissed it softly. "Sit. It's time for me to give you my present now."

"Heh." A lecherous grin raced across Dev's face. "Do I get to unwrap it?" She reached out and slipped her hands under Lauren's University of Tennessee sweatshirt, resting her palms against a warm, firm belly.

Lauren smacked Dev's hands away and pushed her down onto the sofa, pausing to kiss her soundly. "Yes, you do. But not till later."

Dev threw out her lower lip, and Lauren couldn't help but laugh. "Sit tight for one second so I can get your present, okay?"

Dev nodded indulgently. "Yes, ma'am."

"Thank you." Lauren patted Dev's shoulder as she disappeared behind the President and headed for her desk. She retrieved an envelope from its shiny surface, surprised by her own nervousness. *Relax. This was a good idea. She won't think it's stupid.* Lauren winced inwardly. *I hope.* The blonde woman dropped down on the couch next to Dev, sitting Indian style.

Dev's gaze drifted to Lauren's hands. She waited a few more seconds before her curiosity got the better of her. "Aren't you going to give it to me?" she prompted.

"Uh...of course I am." Lauren shook her head in dismay, suddenly wishing she'd gotten Dev a more traditional gift. But knowing it was too late now, she screwed up her courage and slowly passed over the thick envelope. "Happy birthday, Devlyn."

Dev smiled brightly. "Thanks." With a gleam in her eyes she tore it open, blinking at what appeared to be a contract from Starlight Publishing. She glanced up in question at Lauren, who simply gestured back to the papers.

"Read it. You went to Harvard." The writer's eyes crinkled with her smile. "I know you can understand a simple contract between Lauren Gallagher and her unnamed co-author. The co-author for her next Adrienne Nash novel."

"I," Dev's face grew pensive. "I don't understand."

"I know how much you enjoy my Adrienne Nash novels. I thought you might like to help me with the next one." She worried the inside of her cheek. "I start planning the next when I'm about three-fourths finished with the one I'm working on." Lauren shrugged one shoulder. "That's where I am now. The contract is a 50/50 royalty with me and my yet to be named co-author. Nobody ever has to know about it but you, me, and the IRS." She grinned.

Blue eyes widened. "You want me to work on your book?" Dev whispered.

Lauren nodded slowly, not sure how to take Dev's reaction. "Only if you want to," she clarified quickly. "I-I – oh, crap. It's a stupid idea, right? I should have gotten you a sweater or something. I mean, you're only the busiest person on Earth, and there's no way you'd–" Her words were cut off by an incendiary kiss, the force of which nearly sent her off the other end of the sofa.

"It's great," Dev muttered against Lauren's lips. "Next to Ash coming on my birthday, it's the best birthday gift anyone's ever given me. It's another wonderful reason to spend time with you." Dev paused to slowly draw her tongue along Lauren's top and then bottom lip, earning a deep growl from her lover that sent shivers down her spine. "Even though being crazy in love with you is more than enough reason for me." She pulled the rumpled contract from between their bodies and dropped it to the floor, moaning softly as Lauren's hands slid under her shirt and around to her back, where they began teasing the sensitive skin between her shoulder blades. "Lauren?"

The writer was quickly getting lost in a sensual haze, which caused Dev's muttered words to roll right over her. She pulled Dev closer, moaning as her fingers threaded into soft, dark hair, and she felt Dev's entire body come to rest solidly atop her.

"Lauren?"

"Mmm?" she breathed faintly.

"Can I unwrap my other present now?"

"Oh, yeah." Lauren's eyes slid shut as her shirt was nudged over her breasts and then her head. "God, I love your birthday."

November 2021

Thursday, November 4th

"What in blazes is taking so long?" Dev complained.

"Don't worry so much. Whatever happens, we'll be fine." *Right?*

"But—"

"Darlin', it's only been thirty minutes," Lauren reminded as she crossed, then uncrossed, and then crossed her legs again.

"I can see that you're not worried."

"Very funny."

The two women were sitting in side-by-side, wingback chairs, clutching throw pillows that had large, gold, Presidential seals embroidered on their centers. They were in one of Dev's sitting rooms, the Treaty Room, where more than one historic agreement had been signed.

A large, low, dark wood table held several dozen historical mementos and photographs of various Presidents and foreign dignitaries shaking hands and signing documents, commemorating the auspicious occasions that the room was named for. The room had a traditional, very masculine feel to it, with its heavy furniture and wine colored wallpaper. Dev and Lauren waited anxiously to find out whether if by the end of the day Lauren would no longer be the President's biographer.

Things had come to a head last month when the Emancipation Party officially called for Lauren's resignation. Privately, Dev had been told that if her girlfriend didn't resign by Thanksgiving, Lauren would be fired outright. Dev's response, which was that if Lauren were fired she would break with the "bastards" for good, could be heard at the opposite end of the White House. It had been a shout fest of epic proportions that even David couldn't smooth over.

Wayne and two lawyers from Starlight Publishing had arrived in D.C. yesterday. They were now in a meeting with Party Chairman Jordon, the Party's lawyer, and David, who, with great difficulty, had convinced Dev and Lauren to wait in the Treaty Room and leave the negotiating to the lawyers.

"You know," Dev began, pitching the pillow across the room and jumping to her feet, "they can't make you leave. They can't!"

Lauren exhaled wearily. "Devlyn, think about this for a moment. My credibility has taken a serious hit. They have a right to be upset. No matter what now, they're not going to get the biography they paid for."

"Bullshit! But you can still stay here, whether you're doing the book or not."

Lauren tightened her grip on her pillow, her soul aching. "I don't think that would be such a good idea," she said so softly that Dev barely heard her. The writer turned away, unable to look Dev in the eye.

"What?" Dev marched back to Lauren and dropped to her knees in front of the younger woman's chair. She felt a surge of panic tear through her. "Wh-what did you say?" *No! I did not hear that. I didn't!* She waited patiently until Lauren couldn't avoid her gaze for another moment.

The look in Dev's eyes sent a stabbing sensation straight to Lauren's heart, and she found her mouth refusing to repeat the words. "This is hurting you. I'm hurting you," Lauren finally whispered, fighting back tears. "The polls—"

Dev rested her palms on Lauren's knees, a determined glint in her eyes. "I don't give a damn about the polls! This is still my home, Lauren. I won't be told who can stay with me and who can't. I love you and I don't want you to go anywhere."

"I love you too," Lauren insisted. "But if my staying here is ruining your career, then I should leave." It was the last thing she wanted to do, but she'd be dammed if she would take Devlyn down with her.

"Polls go up and down. I'm higher in the numbers than I was last month, and things are already looking better. It was the bombings that really hurt me in the public eye, sweetheart. Not you. And despite the Party's complaints to the contrary, most people couldn't care less who I'm in love with and where she lives. This is just the bastard conservative wing flexing its muscles. And the head bastard, Bruce Jordon, is posturing and trying to gain a better foothold for himself within the Party. If they can get me to ask you to leave the White House, it will be a great show of strength. If I refuse, then they'll just wave their 'superior morals' in America's face and blame every ill in government on our relationship. This *is* the ugly side of politics, Lauren."

"There's an attractive side?" A small smile twitched at Lauren's lips.

Dev shook her head in amused exasperation. "I'm sort of partial to the power, doing things to help mankind, shaping the future..." She shrugged. "Little things like that."

Lauren tugged on Dev's jacket lapel fondly. "You would be, Wonder Woman."

Dev relaxed a little. Lauren was teasing her. That was a good sign. "For some reason I can't fathom, they can't seem to get it through their thick skulls that I would never ask you to leave. *Never.*"

Lauren opened her mouth to speak, but Dev pressed two fingers against her lips to forestall her words. She needed to clear this up once and for all. Because she, for one, knew she could never live with the doubt. With her free hand, Dev gently fingered the ends of pale hair that barely brushed Lauren's shoulders. "Do you want to leave?"

Lauren shook her head vigorously.

Thank you, God. "Are you happy living with us here?" There was a second's hesitation, while the events of the past year raced through Lauren's mind like wildfire. The battles with the press. Dev's shooting. The loss of a great deal of her personal freedom. Never being truly alone, but never being lonely. Dealing with idiots like Michael Oaks. The increased responsibility and fear that came along with loving Dev and her children. She quickly nodded. Lauren had never been happier.

Dev let out a shuddering breath and licked dry lips. A single second had never seemed so long. "Okay, then," she muttered, "good." The President drew back her fingers and kissed Lauren gently on the lips. "Then no matter what happens with the job, you'll stay, right?" Her eyebrows lifted in entreaty. "Promise?"

Lauren smiled, giving in to what she really wanted in the first place. She had faith that Dev would be able to fend off the political attacks that her presence here would bring. With her next breath, Lauren reached out and grabbed onto the life that Dev was offering. "I promise. They'll have to bomb me out."

Dev's heart started beating again. "It's about time you gave up on that selfless crap and got with the program, Mighty Mouse."

They both laughed, but the sound died quickly when there was a knock at the door; David opened it and poked his head inside. "Ready?"

Dev pushed herself off Lauren's knees and stood, offering her hand down to her lover. When they were both on their feet, Dev nodded to him and David opened the door, allowing the small group of men and women to file into the Treaty Room.

Lauren held her breath as her eyes darted to Wayne. He gave her a smug smile, and she almost ended up in a heap on the floor from the sudden release of tension.

David was the first person to speak. "Madam President, I think we've come up with a solution that we can all live with."

Dev crossed her arms over her chest and glared at Bruce Jordon. "Is she fired?" She stepped closer to Lauren, raising her eyebrow in challenge.

The silver-haired man crossed his own arms and jutted out his chin. "One way or the other, Ms. Strayer will no longer be employed by the Emancipation Party." His defiance was obvious and Dev felt her temper begin to flare.

The President lifted her arm from Lauren's shoulders and took a step towards Chairman Jordon. Her hands twitched, wanting to form fists. "You mother—"

But David slapped her on the back — hard — causing her to cough and sputter, and cutting off Dev's snarl mid-sentence. "You really ought to see to that cough, Madam President."

Dev turned murderous eyes on her best friend.

David cleared his throat, figuring he'd better get to the heart of the matter before Dev had a stroke or killed him. Or both. "As I was about to say, this is the arrangement that, with Ms. Strayer's consent, we'll implement immediately. Lawyers from the Party, as well as Starlight Publishing, agree that, should the matter go to trial, there is a reasonable likelihood that Lauren's romantic relationship with you, Madam President, materially alters her ability to perform in a manner that is consistent with the terms and reasonable expectations of her contract. In other words, she may be found to be in breach. Though, at this point, all parties concerned want to avoid litigation." Lauren threw up her hands and rolled her eyes.

"What in the hell does that mean?" Dev roared. "Speak English, not lawyer."

David pursed his lips. "Here's the deal, Madam President." But he glanced at Lauren as well. "Starlight Publishing has offered to buy out the remainder of Lauren's contract with the Emancipation Party. In addition to taking over her salary for the next three years, they will compensate the Party for the salary she's already been paid over this past year. Starlight will also pay a reasonable fee for the biographical information Ms. Strayer gathered while working for the party."

"If you can call two million dollars reasonable," Wayne snorted.

David ignored him. "In return, Ms. Strayer will deliver a biography as planned. However, she will be under the direct employ of Starlight Publishing, who will receive all profits."

Lauren finally joined the fray. "So, I can continue to do my job, write the book, live here, and the only thing that changes for me is that I report directly to Starlight and sever any ties with the Emancipation party?"

Wayne winked at Lauren. "That's the deal, sweetheart. You can thank me later."

"Where do I sign?"

There was a knock on the door. "Madam President, I have the contract that Chief of Staff McMillian requested," Liza called from the outer office.

"Come in, Liza, and thank you," David answered as the President's tall assistant brushed past the attorneys and Wayne and presented David with three copies of the contract they'd just negotiated.

Wayne handed Lauren a pen. "I think this is where you sign."

Starlight Publishing and the Emancipation Party's attorneys

each took a moment to give the document a quick once-over before their solemn nods declared that it was, indeed, an accurate reflection of the deal they'd struck.

Bruce Jordon signed first, then Wayne, and finally Lauren, who launched herself at Wayne and gave the flustered man a firm kiss on the mouth for his efforts. When he figured out what was happening, he pulled Lauren into an affectionate hug, laughing when she squeezed him so hard he could barely breathe. "Thank you, Wayne," she whispered in the stocky man's ear. "You don't know how much this means to me."

"You don't have to thank me, sweetheart. A bestseller will be thanks enough."

Lauren laughed then gave David a hug as well. "I know this was mostly your doing, David," she said softly, her face and voice conveying her true gratitude.

David's already ruddy skin took on a darker shade of red. He shrugged lightly. "Just doing my job." But his warm brown eyes glittered with pride over a job well done.

Lauren looked at him skeptically. "Uh huh."

"What about my hug?" Dev griped playfully. "I'm last on the list?"

Lauren grabbed the President's hand. "*You* rate a full-blown celebration, Madam President. Liza," she said, never breaking eye contact with Dev, "how long until the President's next appointment?"

"Twenty-three, nearly twenty-four minutes," Liza answered without hesitation, causing Wayne to raise both eyebrows. The woman was a human organizer and alarm clock all rolled into one. He wondered whether she was single.

"Good." Lauren smiled at Dev. "Would you like to take a walk with me?"

Dev's face instantly mirrored the happy grin. This was turning out to be a great day. "Lead the way."

Lauren and Dev padded slowly to the door, hand in hand. The writer opened it for Dev, who was just about to walk through when she felt Lauren let go of her hand.

Lauren spun around and stomped back to face Bruce Jordon. "Mr. Jordon," Lauren squared her shoulders, "you are an asshole of the highest order. And it will be my supreme pleasure to let America know that fact in *Starlight Publishing's* biography of the President." She smiled insincerely and spoke in her sweetest Southern drawl. "Have a nice day."

With that, Lauren marched past Devlyn and out the door.

Dev looked back to the Party Chairman with a smirk so perfect David wished he had a camera to capture it. "What she said." Then she ran to catch up with Lauren, who was already halfway down the hall.

Sunday, November 7th

"C'mon, Daddy. Pick up the phone. You're *always* home after dinner." Lauren punched the speakerphone and video functions and waited, hoping tonight would be the night he would answer. She'd dutifully called her father once a month since her mother's death, just as she had since leaving home thirteen years ago. Only, since Anna Strayer's suicide, Lauren's father was suddenly never home when she called.

The generally stolid, retired plumber had told his daughter in no uncertain terms that when she chose to go back to Washington, D.C. after Dev's shooting and while Anna was still in the hospital, she was choosing "that woman" over her own mother.

Lauren hadn't disagreed with her father. Though the circumstances weren't quite the way he had made them sound, Lauren knew in her heart that if there was a real contest, she would always choose Devlyn.

His attitude had softened immediately following his wife's death, however, and when Lauren came home for the funeral, he welcomed her with open arms. But it only took hours for bad feelings to rear their ugly heads again and for Howard to assign blame for his loss to Lauren. If she'd only stayed to help. The stress of reading about her daughter having an affair with the President was simply more than the fragile woman could be expected to take. If she'd only sent Anna to different doctors... The list went on and on, and Lauren found that she couldn't leave Tennessee fast enough.

That was four months ago and though they'd never been close, she'd never gone this long with no contact at all. While she was quite certain that she'd never have the kind of relationship with her father that Dev had with Janet and Frank Marlowe, she still loved him and wanted to know that he was okay.

Lauren was about to give the verbal command for her phone to hang up when her father picked up. A flashing green light on Lauren's phone let her know that there was no image available. She remembered that her father had always hated that part of the phone and only allowed a visual link to please her mother. Now that her mother was gone, he must have disabled everything except for the simple voice transmission.

"Hello."

"Daddy?"

Click.

Lauren blinked at the sound of the buzzing dial tone. "Oh, that went well. Guess you figured out how to turn off the caller ID. Still mad at me, by any chance?" she muttered sarcastically. But she was hurting, despite the fact that she tried to brush it off.

The blonde woman snatched up Gremlin and Princess' leashes from the top of her dresser. Both dogs magically appeared from nowhere, beating Lauren to the door. "How do you do that?" she asked the short pooches, feeling herself slipping into a full-fledged bad mood. She bent over and snapped the leashes on the collars and grabbed her jacket from the coat rack.

When she opened her door she was surprised to find Ashley standing there. "Hi, Ashley." Lauren peered down the hallway, looking for, but not finding, Ashley's brothers. "I was just on my way out to walk the dogs. What can I do for you?"

Ashley dug her toe into the carpet. "I dunno." She reached down to pet Gremlin and Princess, who were howling, their bodies shaking in utter delight at the sight of their friend.

"Okay," Lauren drew out the word. "Well, we could talk when I come back, or you could join us? Grem loves it when you walk him."

Ashley smiled and reached for the leash. "I was coming over to see if he and Princess could play. I'm bored."

"Ahhh...I see," the writer stated seriously, trying to remember what she had done for fun at Ashley's age at, she glanced at her watch, 7:30 p.m. Somehow she didn't think throwing rocks at the abandoned house at the end of the street, putting pennies on the railroad tracks so passing trains could flatten them, or staring mindlessly at the television for hours on end would be high on Dev's list of approved activities. "Wanna borrow a jacket of mine?"

Ashley's eyes lit up. "Sure!"

Lauren chuckled softly. "Okay, you can have this one." She held up her worn jean jacket for the girl's inspection. "Or," she put the end of Princess' leash between her teeth and grabbed a second jacket from the rack, "Dhis un."

The girl selected the buttery-soft, suede jacket and shrugged it on. It swallowed her whole and Lauren gave her a fond look, helping her push up the sleeves before she shut the door to her room.

Lauren said to the first agent they passed in the hallway, "We're going to the South Lawn to walk the dogs." A few seconds more, and the agent normally assigned to Christopher joined them at the top of the stairs, remaining several respectful paces away. Lauren glanced down at Ashley. "Amy's night off tonight?"

"Uh huh."

Gremlin could tell they were getting near the door, and he began pulling Ashley along.

The dark-headed girl was trying to pull him back into line, but failing miserably.

"Gremlin!" Lauren barked.

He slowed for a moment in response to his mistress' cross use of his name, but soon began to tug on the leash again.

Ashley laughed; her arm was fully extended, and she was skipping every third step. "He really wants to go out!"

"Apparently." Lauren shook her head. "Let's trade." She took Gremlin's leash, giving it a sharp tug to slow down the pug and then handed Ashley Princess'.

The Pomeranian show dog was acting like, well, a show dog, prancing quietly down the hall like royalty. She was the very picture of serenity and obedience. "Why do I think instead of you getting better behaved, you'll just drag Princess down?" Lauren asked Gremlin flatly, more to hear Ashley laugh than to scold her beloved pet.

They opened the doors to the South Lawn and were greeted with a blast of chilly autumn air that smelled heavily of wet leaves and soil. "Brrr!" Lauren shivered as she stuck her hand in her pocket. "We'd better make this a short trip."

"Okay," Ashley agreed, snuggling deeper into the warm suede.

"You going to tell me what's wrong?" Lauren asked casually. Ashley was a chatty, bright child who wore her emotions on her sleeve for the world to see. It didn't take a rocket scientist to figure out something was up with her. "You didn't seem too happy when you came to my door."

"You didn't look too happy either," Ashley shot back.

"You're too smart for your own good." Lauren snorted. "Your mama has that same problem." She moved to the left, guiding Ashley and the dogs around a large, muddy puddle. "Well, you gonna tell me?"

"You first."

That earned Ashley a raised eyebrow, but Lauren didn't refuse. "I tried to talk to my daddy on the phone and he hung up on me."

Ashley frowned. "That's not very nice."

"No." Lauren sighed and pulled the collar of her jacket closer around her neck. "It's not."

"Is he mad at you?"

Lauren nodded. "I think so. Mad and disappointed, I guess."

Ashley made an unhappy face. There was nothing worse than having a parent disappointed in you. "How come?"

Lauren exhaled wearily and glanced down at Ashley, considering how much to tell her. She decided she was old enough to understand the simple truth. "He's disappointed because I didn't stay in Tennessee to help my mama this summer." There was a pause. "When she was sick." They approached a bench, and Lauren motioned for Ashley to sit down.

They both took a seat. "Let's let 'em run around for a while," Lauren said as she unhooked first Princess' then Gremlin's leash. "They're already going to need baths."

"How come you didn't stay home then when she was sick?"

Lauren winced at the complicated situation being distilled into a child's simple question. "C'mere," she held out her arm, and Ashley scooted closer, pressing tightly against Lauren. "I didn't stay home because, in my heart, I didn't think there was anything I could do for my mama. But *your* mama needed me, and I thought I could make her feel better." She shrugged. "My heart told me I needed to come home...this home."

"When she got shot," Ash recalled.

"Uh huh. So that's why my daddy is mad at me."

"That doesn't seem fair." The girl hugged Lauren. "I'm sorry."

Lauren leaned down and kissed the top of Ashley's head. "I'll be okay, sweetie. It just makes me sad. We'll work it out eventually." *Or not.*

They were both quiet for a moment as they watched Gremlin and Princess playing in the yard and splashing through the leaf-strewn puddles.

"Mom didn't come home for dinner tonight," Ashley commented very softly. "She's working late."

Ahhh...so that's it. "I know. She's in a meeting tonight with some people from Mexico."

"She couldn't come to *The Nutcracker* with me last week. It was my birthday present; it was going to be just the two of us. Emma took me, but it's just not the same."

"Oh, honey." Lauren closed her eyes and tightened her hold on Ashley. "She wanted to go with you. Your mama felt terrible about that." *She was nearly in tears that night when she told me.* "But it was an emergency and—"

"And she had to work late," Ashley finished glumly. "She always does."

Lauren let out an unhappy breath. She had no good answers for this. Ashley didn't give two shits about the global economy. "You know she has a very important job that takes up most of her time, right?" she began rhetorically.

"Yeah." A dark head nodded. "I know."

"But when she has to miss out on being with you and your brothers, it's not because she thinks y'all are less important than what she's working on."

Ashley's eyes widened a little, and she looked up at Lauren's face to see if she was telling her the whole truth. "It's not?"

"No way, Ash. Nothing is more important to your mama than you guys," the writer announced firmly. She cupped Ashley's chilled cheek. "But the stuff she's doing is very important, and she knows that the people who love her will cut her some extra slack when there just aren't enough hours in the day to get everything done. Nobody except her family will do that."

"They won't?"

Lauren shook her head gravely. "No."

Ashley's face turned contemplative. "I didn't know that."

"I know. It's a hard thing for even grown ups to understand. And it's not fair to you or your mama. But she's doing the best she can, Ash. If she could, she'd spend all her time with you guys."

An enormous grin broke out across her face. "She would? Really?"

"Of course!" Lauren squeezed her again, sharing her warmth. "She's very proud of you and loves you like crazy. Besides," she pressed her forehead forward against Ashley's, "I happen to know she got tickets again for this week, so you guys can still go to the ballet."

"I know. It's still going to be just the two of us." Ashley tugged on Lauren's coat a little. "That's okay with you, right?"

Lauren smiled indulgently. "Absolutely. You'll both have a wonderful time, and you can tell me all about it. And maybe, if something comes up, and your mama absolutely can't make it...even though she wants to more than anything...maybe we can go?"

"Sure!" Ashley blurted out. "I would miss Mom. But that would be fun too." Impulsively, Ashley kissed Lauren on the cheek. "Thanks, Lauren."

"You're welcome, sweetie."

"I love you."

Lauren swallowed hard and closed her eyes. "I love you, too."

Tuesday, November 9th

"We're finished for the day, right?" Dev shifted on the sofa anxiously.

"Sure," Lauren answered slowly. "If you want to be." She sat down her notebook on the coffee table, a little put out that Dev wanted to end their interview so soon. This hour had been set aside all week. *Then again, it's not like we're getting anywhere.* It had been thirty minutes of pure frustration, with Lauren having to pry every single word out of her normally talkative partner. Dev had been nervous and withdrawn, her gaze finding the antique grandfather clock, which had been an October addition to Lauren's room, every few minutes. Dev's sudden restlessness left Lauren confused and on edge herself.

The blonde slipped off her glasses and began gnawing on the tip of one earpiece. "Do you have a hot date or something tonight?" she asked teasingly, but her words were laced with annoyance and insecurity.

"No. No." The President waved her hand dismissively. "I've got nothing going on." Dev groaned inwardly. *Shit. That was convincing.*

Five minutes into their work, while Dev was thinking about how much she loved Lauren and how much she wanted to be married to her, she'd suddenly remembered she had an evening appointment with a jeweler to pick out a ring. Ever since then she'd been a nervous wreck, just thinking about how she was going to make a quick exit in the middle of their scheduled meeting without arousing Lauren's suspicions. *God, I'm helpless without Liza and Jane to keep my schedule.*

The jeweler had also asked for Lauren's approximate ring and hand size, stating unequivocally that this was crucial information if Devlyn wanted to pick out a truly flattering piece of jewelry. Personally, Dev thought that was a load of crap, but where Lauren's happiness was concerned, she wasn't taking any chances. "Nothing is going on," she repeated when it looked like Lauren was waiting for her to elaborate. She reached subtly for Lauren's hand, only to have it pulled away.

"I see." Lauren sprang to her feet, easily detecting Dev's lie. She picked her notebook up as she rose and walked back to her desk, setting it down carefully. The clock chimed seven times, and Lauren wondered if Dev might be hungry. Lauren spoke with her back to Dev as she gently tossed her glasses alongside her computer. "Would you like to have dinner together? I'm sure the kids have already eaten."

Arrghhh. Yes! "I'm not really hungry."

"Okay." Lauren's own appetite disappeared. *Stop being such a big baby. She doesn't have to spend every evening with you. Maybe she just needs a little time to herself.* She consciously kept her voice light. "I'll see you tomorrow morning then."

Dev was on her feet and at Lauren's side in an instant. "How about a late supper? I'm sure I'll have an appetite in...say...two hours?"

"Are you okay, Devlyn?" Lauren searched her face. "You don't seem yourself tonight."

"I'm fine," Dev blurted out more harshly than she'd intended. She let out a muffled curse and glanced at the clock. "I'm just not hungry, that's all." And that was the truth. Dev couldn't even think about food right now. Casually, she reached for Lauren's hand again, only to be denied. Dev cursed again.

"What is wrong with you? And don't you dare tell me nothing." A slender, fair eyebrow lifted. "You're acting all anxious. And why do you keep trying to grab me?"

"I'm not trying to grab you, I'm trying to hold your hand and talk to you." Dev's voice took on that deep tone she normally reserved for when things weren't going well in a meeting.

"You are trying to grab me!" Lauren's temper snapped, and she held her hand up in front of Dev's face, snatching it away just as Dev reached for it again. "See!" An angry flush began crawling up her cheeks. "And you're not 'talking' to me. You're lying to me."

"I am not lying to you!" It was like a slap in the face and Dev took a step backwards, stung by the accusation that was technically true, though she knew this wasn't the sort of lie Lauren meant. "I've never lied to you." She chewed on her lip as her own temper reared its head. "Thanks so much for thinking so highly of me. I am *not* a liar."

"Then why do you keep looking at the clock every ten seconds, but insist you don't have any place to be?" Lauren shot back. She stepped forward and poked Dev in the chest with a rigid finger to get her attention. "You don't have to spend every minute with me, Devlyn Marlowe. But don't tell me you don't have someplace to be when it's not the truth. I'm a big girl. If you've got other plans, just say so!"

"Okay, fine," Dev put her hands up in defense. "You're right! I have someplace to be. I have an appointment tonight. There. Are you happy now?" She crossed her arms over her chest and waited.

A large part of Lauren's anger deflated, only to be replaced with genuine hurt. "No, I'm not happy. All you had to do was say that in the first place." She turned her back on the President and her voice dropped to a whisper. "Judd lied to me whenever it suited his purposes. I won't put up with that again, Devlyn." *Not from someone I love.*

"That's nice." Dev purposely ignored the barely detectable slump of Lauren's shoulders. "Thanks. Thanks for comparing me to the slime ball, cheating ex-husband, who was screwing his girlfriend and lying to you about it. Excuse me if I happen to have a meeting I can't really discuss." She stopped and grabbed her jacket off the couch, nearly taking the arms off as she pulled it on.

Lauren whirled around, gray eyes flashing. "How did you know about that?" she spat. "I know I never told you that."

"How in the hell do you think I knew that?" she huffed, buttoning her jacket. "I did the damned math when the FBI gave me your background file." Lauren opened her mouth, but Dev kept right on talking. "And before you go and get all pissed off at me for that too, you don't really think the Party would have hired you without doing a complete background check first? Or that I would invite you into my home, with my children, without doing one! Goddammit, Lauren! I've always been straight with you. This *one* time I have something I can't talk about and you act like it's the end of the world. Well, it's not. It's just something I can't talk about."

Lauren's face contorted in anger as she ground out, "Get out!"

"Fine!" Dev turned on her heel and marched towards the door. "You know where to find me when you come to your senses."

"Why should I bother to find you? I'm sure you've got your

spies watching every move I make. You can come to me!" Lauren rushed past Devlyn and flung the door open for her. It slammed so loudly against the wall that a picture hanging in the hallway outside crashed to the floor.

Dev took a deep breath and stepped calmly out of the room. She picked up the picture and hung it back on the wall, glancing back at Lauren when she was finished. "I don't have anyone watching you. I love you. But I won't be treated this way either. I'm not out to hurt you, and you know that." She felt the tears in her eyes and forced them back. "But apparently you can't afford me the same courtesy." Dev took a deep breath. "Good night, Lauren. Sleep well. I love you." She fussed with the picture for another few seconds before turning and slowly walking away.

A band tightened around Lauren's chest at Dev's words. She nearly went after her, but her stubbornness and anger won out, causing her feet to stay firmly rooted to the ground. After all, she wasn't the one who had lied. Why should she chase after Dev to apologize when she hadn't done anything wrong? Lauren snorted derisively, completely disgusted with herself. She knew that one more look into those watery blue eyes, and she'd be saying she was sorry whether she wanted to or not. "Damn. Damn. Damn," she muttered to herself, before quietly closing her door.

Gremlin and Princess poked their heads out from under Lauren's bed now that the loud, unpleasant lady was gone. With dark, beady eyes, they watched Lauren shut the door and then lean against it for a long moment with her eyes closed.

"You can come out now, you cowards." Lauren sighed dejectedly, wondering how in the hell things had got out of control so quickly. "She's gone." Lauren flopped gracelessly onto the bed and hugged her pillow. She blinked rapidly, sending a scattering of hot tears cascading down her cheeks.

Gremlin jumped up onto the bed and snuggled alongside his mistress, who pulled him close and kissed him on the top of the head.

"Thanks, buddy," she whispered to her pet. "You were right. I definitely needed a hug."

Dev entered her private office in the residence to be greeted by a smiling David and the jeweler. Her jaw was clenched shut like a steel trap as she tried to shake off her hurt and anger. She shrugged out of her rumpled jacket and hung it crookedly on a coat rack near the door. As soon as Dev let go of it, it slipped off the wooden hook and fell to the floor. The tall woman remained frozen, not giving a damn about the blazer. She stood that way, staring at the wall, for a long moment before taking a deep breath and turning around to greet her guest.

"Good evening," Dev said, still not leaving her spot by the door. "I'm," she stopped and cleared her throat, coughing a little. "I'm sorry I'm late. I was unavoidably detained."

One look at Dev's face and David made his way across the room as quickly as he could without alarming the jeweler. "Are you okay?" he queried under his breath, reaching down for the jacket and settling it on a hook.

"Maybe we should wait on this, David." Her voice cracked. "Now might not be the time."

David blinked rapidly as his mouth worked for several seconds before any sound came out. He lowered his voice. "What do you mean now is not the time?"

"Lauren and I just had a huge argument." She bit her lip. "Maybe I was wrong. Maybe I'm rushing things."

"What?" David hissed, gently grabbing Dev by the forearm and leading her out of the room. He glanced over his shoulder at a waiting Alvin Cartier. "We'll be just one moment. Please sit down." Once they were safely in Dev's den, David put his hands on his hips. "What happened?"

Dev paced for a moment and then turned to her friend. "I forgot about the appointment tonight, and when I remembered I got so nervous Lauren picked up on it and asked me what was wrong, and then it all just went downhill from there." It had all come out in a rush, and she took a deep breath and sighed. "We had an argument; she accused me of lying to her and of being like her ex-husband and—" She rubbed her temples. "I'm not like that. I know she was upset, and it was a silly argument, but..."

Dev felt confused and suddenly very tired. All she wanted to do now was go to her room and shower and go to bed. She knew that tomorrow it would probably all be over, but right now it just hurt.

"But do you really think you're rushing it? Because if you do, then I'm marching out there right now and telling that Mr. Cartier to go home and keep his mouth shut." David squeezed Dev's shoulder comfortingly. "This one is your call, Madam President." The red-haired man didn't think for one second that Dev would take him up on it, but it was in the "Best Friend and Chief of Staff Handbook" for him to offer anyway.

She closed her eyes and took a deep breath. "God, I must be out of my damned mind. No. I'll take a look. I love her too much to let her go. She's not getting away from me that easily. I'll just have to show her what this Yankee is made of." She grinned. "And then use the guilt I'm going to be able to milk this for – for the first two years we're married."

David let out an explosive breath. "You had me worried there for a minute, Devil. I thought you were going to do something stupid over one argument." He smirked. "Not that it would be the first time." His face grew serious. "And what in the hell did you do to rate a comparison to Lauren's ex? I've never even heard her mention him."

"You know," she shook her head, "I'm not sure. She said I was like him because he lied to her, or something like that. But I know deep in her heart she doesn't believe that. At least I hope she doesn't. She was just mad because I'm an idiot. I'm so nervous over this whole thing I'm not handling myself very well right now. I'll have to figure out a way to make it up to her."

David rolled his eyes and shook his head, knowing Dev would be one of the Devil's own until she made up with Lauren. "How about you start by going out there and picking something really special? You can grovel later. I've always found that particularly effective with Beth."

Dev laughed, already feeling a little better. "Nice to know I can get groveling lessons from an expert." She slapped her friend on the back. "Now let me go find the perfect ring for my lady."

Wednesday, November 10th

Dev had completed her stretching routine three times, waiting for Lauren. She finally realized that the writer wouldn't be coming this morning. "She must really be pissed off at me."

"Ma'am?" Jack, an excellent running partner and an agent Dev was particularly fond of, stepped to her side. "Are you okay?"

She blew out a breath, sending her bangs into disarray. "Yeah, I'm fine for an idiot. C'mon. Let's give the boys and girls a good run this morning."

After the shooting it was Dev's shoulder that gave her, and continued to give her, the lion's share of her physical problems. Her hip had fully recovered and she was pretty much back to her old self as far as jogging was concerned. Despite that, it was her hip that ached whenever it rained or it was particularly cold. Since it was both on this crummy, pre-dawn November day, they were relegated to running laps in the gym. Dev was angry...with herself and with Lauren. She took out that anger on the track, and, by extension, on the agents who ran with her. Her blistering pace caused two of them to fall out, leaving them panting on the floor.

Jack was keeping up, but it wasn't easy. He could tell the President was working through something in her mind, and he hoped to God that she would find the answer soon, before the entire detail was reduced to a gasping, heaving mess. But he had to admit it; there was something kick ass about having a President who could give the most fit agents a run for their money.

By the time Dev was finally finished running, nearly an hour later, she was limping slightly and her hair, shorts, and T-shirt were soaked with sweat. She walked the track a couple of times to cool down, before grabbing a towel from her bag and wiping away the sweat that was pouring down her face. As she lowered the towel, Liza entered the gym.

"Good morning, Madam President."

"Not really, Liza," Dev groaned as she waved goodbye to the men and women who had run with her this morning. She received several barely veiled dirty looks as the agents filed out of the gym. The run had done Dev good, giving her time to set her resolve. "But I have hopes that I can salvage it."

"Ma'am?"

"Nothing. What's on the agenda for today?"

"That's what I wanted to talk to you about. I have some good news for you."

Dev smiled a pathetically grateful smile. "Wonderful. I could use it."

"The Secretary General of the United Nations called this morning. He regrets to inform you that he will be unable to attend lunch with you today. He is currently snowed in at JFK and the storm is keeping everything grounded." Liza gave a little grin as she looked at her organizer. "I assured him that we could reschedule next week and then I managed to make your afternoon appointment with Secretary Wisecroft a lunch meeting. So after your meeting with Press Secretary Allen, you have lunch with Secretary Wisecroft, and then you're free for the rest of the day."

"You know," Dev's smile grew larger, "you're a good kid, Liza. I may just have to adopt you."

Liza laughed, genuinely glad that she had made her boss happy. "My parents might protest, but I appreciate the thought, ma'am."

"Okay, then," Dev began as she exited the gym and headed towards the residence with Liza hot on her heels, "I have a couple of things I need you to do for me, then you can take the rest of the day off too."

Skipping their usual run rather than facing Dev before she was ready to talk, Lauren had spent the day alone in Georgetown, shopping and trying not to think about the way they'd left things the night before. The time away today had done her good; she felt as though, once she was able to step back, she could put things in perspective. *Better late than never.* Lauren was still confused about why Dev thought it necessary to lie to her, but at least now that she'd had a chance to calm down a little, she felt as if they could talk about it. She hoped.

Lauren discovered that she needed a day away from the White

House, Secret Service, and especially the press, more than she'd realized. She'd never understood what a valuable commodity privacy was until it was in short supply.

When it became public knowledge that she and Dev were a couple, the two women had had a huge argument over Lauren's turning down the Secret Service protection that Dev was determined to pay for out of her own pocket. It wasn't just the money. Dev and her family were very well off and it wouldn't have affected their standard of living in the least. It was the principle more than anything. Lauren couldn't stand feeling like she was under lock and key.

She had just been fooling herself, of course. Just today, Lauren had been recognized twice by total strangers. Once by a middle-aged construction worker who was working on the building next to where she'd parked her car. When he saw who she was, he began screaming something about taxes, alimony, and President Marlowe. Lauren didn't stick around for an in-depth discussion. Instead, she picked up her pace.

Next, a clerk at a toy store had recognized her when she was purchasing David, Liza, and Dev matching hot pink stress balls. Lauren was surprised when the frizzy-haired teenager asked for her autograph. She was about to ask the girl which one of her biographies she'd read, when the clerk started peppering her with questions about the relationship between her and Dev. What kind of shampoo did Dev use? What was it like living in the White House? Were the President's eyes really as blue as they looked on television? Lauren actually answered that one, laughing out loud as the girl nearly swooned when she confided that somehow, impossibly, they were even better in real life.

Lauren had to face the bitter truth. While she had achieved moderate success in her own right, her private life had never been public. Not like it was now. Even though her patience had been pushed to the limit time and time again since she'd moved into the White House, in her heart she believed Dev was worth every moment of it.

Now, after having her bags full of Christmas presents for the Marlowe children searched and X-rayed, she was back in the East Wing and ready to search out Dev and try to settle things between them before they got any further out of hand. The writer's brows knitted when she found a note taped to the front of her door. Fumbling with her bags, she pulled off the note and managed to open the door and stumble into her room without dropping anything. "Okay, next time, when the porter asks if I want help, I say 'yes'," she muttered.

Gremlin appeared from behind the sofa and began whimpering with joy as he wound himself around Lauren's legs. She laughed. "I love you too. Gimme just a second and you can slobber on me all you want."

She gently dropped the bags on her bed and perched on its edge. Gremlin jumped up next to her and laid his face on her lap, where he received an immediate scratching behind his ears. "Pleasure hound." Grem's tail, had it been able to reach the bed, would have begun to thump wildly against it, as he let out a happy moan. "Yeah, yeah, I'll take you for a walk in just a while. Let my feet rest for a minute, will ya? Should we see what's in the envelope?"

Lauren slid her nail under the flap of the envelope and it opened with a tiny pop. She pulled out the note card, her face creasing into a brilliant smile before she even started reading. *Devlyn's handwriting.* Taped to the note was a piece of milk chocolate, wrapped in bright silver foil. "Mmm..." Lauren let out a sensual groan at the aroma, as she immediately opened the wrapper and popped it into her already watering mouth.

Gremlin whimpered.

"Sorry. No chocolate." She petted him sympathetically. "I could never be a dog."

Lauren allowed the rich chocolate to melt in her mouth, pooling on her tongue as she read.

> *Sweetheart,*
> *I'm sorry.*
> *I didn't mean to hurt you or lie to you. I've been a little preoccupied by something very important these last few weeks, and I had a meeting last night that brought me a step closer to my goal. I'm afraid I can't talk about it right now. Just this once, you'll have to trust me.*
> *I wasn't thinking, and I made a poor choice. I know none of this makes sense to you. But I'll explain the best I can if you let me. Just know that I love you, and I don't like it when we argue. I thought of you all day today.*
> *There's something I'd like to share with you. All you have to do is follow the trail I left for you.*
> *With all my love,*
> *Stinky*

She laughed at Dev's signature. *Always the charmer, Devlyn. I shouldn't have thrown you out of my room before we could work things out.* It was immature, and Lauren knew she'd simply let her anger get the best of her. Now, however, she was more than ready to talk. *The trail I left for you?* She scratched her jaw then jumped off the bed, sending Gremlin scampering over to Princess, who was sleeping on her back at the foot of the bed in her favorite doggy position. *Trail?*

Lauren opened the door and peeked out into the hallway. Sure

enough, there were chocolates sprinkled down the hall in the opposite direction from where she'd just come. *I need to look down*
every once in a while.

Closing her door, she moved a few paces down the hall and
picked up another foil-wrapped chocolate. A few more feet, and
there was another. And so the trail continued, with Lauren scooping
up the candy, until she was led right to the door of the President's
formal dining room.

The writer paused at the door to chew and swallow, having
popped no less than four pieces of chocolate into her mouth on the
way there. She wiped the corners of her lips with her fingertips,
realizing that she was a little nervous. "Relax. It's just Devlyn," she
whispered to herself. They'd argued occasionally over the past
eleven months. But rarely did it reduce either one of them to tears
and this time it had done just that to both of them.

Lauren took a deep breath and screwed up her courage, ignoring the sudden churning in her belly. She lifted her hand to knock
but noticed that the door was just a crack open. The blonde woman
hesitated with her hand still in the air, not sure whether the open
door was an invitation or an oversight on the part of the President.
Deciding that Dev made very few mistakes, Lauren pushed open the
door and made her way inside.

The Presidential dining room was one of the younger woman's
favorite places in the magnificent house. It had a light, airy feeling
that was aided by its high ceilings and floor-length, mint colored
drapes. A delicate crystal chandelier hung high over the dark wood
table, and a pristine, white marble mantelpiece surrounded a fireplace. The chairs were upholstered with a green, pale yellow, and
rose floral print cloth, whose colors were repeated in the beautiful
bouquets of fresh flowers that adorned the tabletop and mantel. It
was elegant without being excessive.

Dev looked up from her seat at the dining table that was set for
two. The lights were low but several candles were lit and the curtains were open, allowing the last remnants of daylight to spill
through the window. Devlyn quickly jumped to her feet. She'd been
waiting for over an hour, hoping that Lauren wouldn't just toss her
note in the garbage can. She tried to find her voice as she gestured
to the table. "Would you like to have an early dinner with me?"

Lauren let out a relieved breath and nodded quickly, crossing
the floor to stand in front of her lover. "Absolutely," she said softly.
The biographer reached up and affectionately raked her fingers
through Dev's slightly askew bangs. *God, I think I'd forgive her*
anything. "I'd-I'd love to."

Dev smiled. She reached out to take Lauren's hand, but stopped
herself. There was no way she was going to invade her personal
space without her permission, despite the fact that Lauren was still,

seemingly absently, running her fingers through Dev's hair. "I'm so sorry," she said sincerely, pulling out a chair for Lauren.

Lauren didn't say a word. The look of indecision on Dev's face, when she began to offer her hand but quickly withdrew it, pierced Lauren's heart. She reached out and took Dev's hand, wrapping strong fingers around Dev's longer ones. She tugged the taller woman towards her and surged forward herself, pulling Dev into a desperately tight embrace. She buried her face in the crook of Dev's neck, smiling when long arms immediately wrapped around her, returning the heartfelt gesture. "I'm sorry too," Lauren said on a slightly ragged exhale.

"I hate it when we argue," Dev whispered back. She tightened her arms around Lauren. "Let's not do that again anytime soon, okay?"

Lauren nodded against Dev's shoulder. "Deal."

The viselike grip on Devlyn's chest eased, and she said a small prayer of thanks as her world began to right itself.

Lauren greedily drew in a breath that brought with it the warm, clean scent of Dev's skin. She found it comforting in the extreme and didn't want to move from this spot. But after a moment she did, knowing they weren't quite finished yet. Apologies were one thing, but this particular argument called for explanations as well. She licked her lips and leaned back in Dev's embrace, tilting her head so that she could watch Dev's face as she spoke. "Can we talk about what happened?"

"I think two reasonable adults can sit here over a wonderful dinner and talk about it, if you'd like." Dev began to move towards the phone, but Lauren held her firm.

"Later. Please."

Dev turned back to Lauren, swallowing hard. "Okay. I...but I need to know if you really think I would ever intentionally lie to you." Dev sat down in her chair and gestured for Lauren to sit in hers. Then a bleak thought entered her mind. *Oh, God, what if she says yes?*

"No, darlin'," Lauren reassured quickly, seeing the pleading look in Dev's eyes. She sat down and scooted her chair closer to Dev, not stopping until their knees were touching. "I don't. At least not that you'd plan."

Dev's gaze dropped to the floor.

"I can understand your having a private meeting," Lauren paused here, treading very carefully as she reached out and grabbed a fork from the table and restlessly ran her fingertips over its prongs. "You've gone to lots of private meetings concerning security issues or whatever. I've tried hard not to make myself a nuisance." A wry smile curled Lauren's lips. "Which is no easy task, considering I start missing you like crazy after a few hours."

Dev dared to glance up and meet Lauren's steady gaze. A stupid, happy grin creased her cheeks. "You don't know how many meetings I've sat through where you were the main thing on my mind. I don't just miss you when we're apart. Hell, I start missing you before you're even gone." Dev laughed quietly. "I actually anticipatorily miss you."

Lauren blushed slightly, but continued. "I wasn't upset that you had to go. I was upset because when I asked you whether or not you had plans, you said 'no', even though that wasn't the truth." She stared at Dev with a painfully open expression. "Why would you do that, Devlyn?" she asked quietly.

Dev nervously twisted the napkin she'd picked up while Lauren was talking. "Lots of reasons, I guess." *And they all suck.* "I'm dealing with something now that is downright nerve-racking for me. I had a very important appointment last night, which I nearly missed because I scheduled our time together to work on the biography right over it. I forgot all about my prior commitment until a few minutes into our time together."

Devlyn shrugged her shoulders. "Then it sort of hit me between the eyes, and I panicked. I was embarrassed by my mistake and didn't want to make you feel bad or," she winced, admitting this to herself as well as Lauren, "look foolish by having to cancel our meeting. So I tried to end it as quickly as possible. To make matters worse, I tried to cover for the rotten decision I'd just made."

Lauren let out a slightly shaky breath. "That's it?" When Dev instantly nodded, she couldn't help but roll her eyes at herself. She'd been imagining all sorts of horrible things. She liked Dev's simple explanation much, much better. The blonde woman set the fork back down and reached out to still Dev's nervous hands. "It's okay," she promised.

Dev let out her own ragged breath as relief coursed through her.

Lauren lifted Dev's hand and brought it to her lips, tenderly kissing a sensitive palm. "I guess we sort of pushed each other's buttons yesterday, huh?"

Dev nodded and took a sip of melted ice water. "You really hit both of mine by comparing me to Judd. I've told you things about myself that no one on this earth but you and I know. And I trust you to protect them implicitly. I've been honest with you even when it would have been easier to omit or color the truth. So when you compared me to your ex-husband, who I knew had cheated on you..." A breath. "That hurt a lot."

Lauren's stomach twisted at the thought of causing Dev pain. "That's not what I meant. At least not completely. I was trying to tell you that when you lied, it made me feel like I felt when Judd did it, which was lousy."

The writer studied their linked hands. *Time to open up a little yourself, Lauri. It's your turn.* "By the time Judd had started having an affair, for all intents and purposes, our marriage was over. I couldn't muster enough concern over our relationship to even begrudge his looking for happiness...or sex, I guess, elsewhere. But even though we weren't lovers anymore, I still considered him a dear friend." Lauren's voice was soft, but Dev could hear the frustration leaking into her words. "When I asked him outright if he was seeing someone else, he denied it. And he did it over and over again." Lauren shook her head, not quite understanding it herself. "I know it sounds funny, but in my mind that, and not the affair itself, was the real betrayal."

Lauren felt Dev squeezing her hand, and she returned the comforting pressure. Her face took on a slightly lost expression. "God, Devlyn, the thought of our drifting apart like that and not even caring...and..." She stopped and swallowed around the solid lump that was forming in her throat.

"That's not going to happen to us, and you know why?" There was a fierceness in Dev's eyes that Lauren found oddly comforting. "Because we can do this after we argue. We can sit down and talk about it and make it better." Devlyn caressed Lauren's cheek with her thumb and smiled. "Let me tell you this. What I'm working on now is absolutely the most important thing I have ever done. The moment I can talk about it, you will be the first to know."

Lauren smiled a broad, genuine smile for the first time all day. "Fair enough." She leaned forward and brushed her lips against Dev's, pulling away only a hairsbreadth. "Thank you for inviting me to dinner," she whispered, kissing Dev again. "I love you. All of a sudden I've decided that I'm incredibly hungry."

A soft moan was Dev's reply.

Saturday, November 13th

It was beginning to look and feel like the holidays at the White House. Everyday Dev was amazed to see more and more early Christmas decorations – some antique, some new – going up. It was kind of like going to Disney World as a kid. She started, realizing that soon all her children would be old enough for that particular family trip. *Maybe next August, before school starts.*

Right now, however, she needed to have a chat with Lauren about one of the most cherished Marlowe family traditions. Dev prayed that her plans regarding Lauren's inclusion would be well received. She shifted the box she was holding under her arm and knocked on Lauren's door.

The door opened and an arm shot out, nearly pulling her off her feet as she was yanked inside by her collar. Then there was the kiss that followed. *Wow!* Devlyn grinned when the writer finally let her go. "Hi."

"Hi. I missed you today." Lauren smiled at the slightly flushed look on Dev's face, feeling the heat in her own.

"Me, too." Dev reached around behind her and shut the door. "How was your day?"

Lauren tucked a strand of hair behind her ear and took off her glasses. "It was okay. I got a lot done." She gave Dev a little smirk. "Found a couple of your high school yearbooks."

Dev's smile disappeared and was replaced by a petulant frown.

Lauren reached out and tugged on the protruding lower lip, keeping it up until Dev laughed and slapped her hands away. "Jane also came by and brought over a couple of boxes of her own personal mementos." The blonde woman winked. "I guarantee you don't know some of the stuff she's got in there. I had no idea she's known you since you were in college. And she's got photos to prove it."

Dev covered her eyes. "Oh, God. This is what my secretary does on her day off?" The President groaned as she took a seat on Lauren's couch, giving it a pat so the younger woman would join her. "The new bio is going to have a more extensive picture section, isn't it?"

"You know it." Lauren smirked, dropping down on the sofa next to Dev. "Your mom has already donated baby pictures. Wayne is just wild about the picture of naked baby Devlyn on the bearskin rug, by the way."

Dev's head dropped, but Lauren could see her shoulders shaking with silent laughter. "I'm gonna kill my mother."

"Wayne offered me an extra five percent on royalties if I could produce a current photo in the same pose for a 'now and then' comparison."

"In his dreams," Dev growled.

"And mine." Lauren wriggled her eyebrows. "Okay, what's up? I didn't expect to see you until tonight."

Dev sobered. "We need to have a little talk. You have a minute?"

Lauren's brow furrowed. She didn't like the suddenly serious look on Dev's face. "I came to the door, didn't I? Shoot."

"Okay. Every year at Thanksgiving the Marlowes set up candles that burn through the holidays, for our family and friends. White candles for those who are with us. Blue ones for those who aren't. We put them on the mantel." Dev glanced at Lauren, who was listening interestedly. "There are two reasons I'm telling you this. First, there is a set of candles for Samantha and her parents." Dev's gaze softened. "If they make you uncomfortable, I won't put them up."

Lauren laid her hand on Dev's knee and gave it a gentle squeeze. She smiled weakly at her friend. Her feelings about Samantha were so mixed up. Part of her admired Devlyn's wife. By every indication she had been a strong, funny, interesting woman in her own right. A wonderful, loving partner to the young, ambitious politician, Devlyn Marlowe. Another part of Lauren felt helpless and angry. There was no competing with the memory of Dev's first love and the woman who gave birth to Christopher and Aaron. But Lauren realized these were her own insecurities, and they existed despite the fact that Dev had never done a thing to encourage them.

The blonde woman swallowed. "Devlyn, darlin', that's not necessary." Lauren mustered a little more of a smile. "Samantha doesn't disappear just because I'm in your life now. Not for you, or the kids. Don't get me wrong," she snorted a little, ready to admit her own shortcomings. "I'm not above petty jealously. But this is a beautiful tradition that must be important to you and the children. I don't see a reason to change it."

Dev's posture instantly relaxed. "Thank you." She leaned over and gently kissed Lauren on the lips, allowing the contact to linger and then deepen. Dev didn't pull back until she felt the rise and fall of Lauren's chest begin to grow uneven, and her own breathing was ragged.

Lauren groaned softly when the lips against hers disappeared. "Have I ever told you what a great kisser you are?"

Dev smiled roguishly. "No. But feel free to do so. In great detail. You are a writer after all."

Lauren's eyebrows crawled up her forehead and disappeared behind pale bangs. "No, thanks. I was just checking."

"Brat." Dev stuck out her tongue.

Lauren chuckled, then poked the box. "So what do we have here? Something for me?" she hinted.

Dev repositioned the box on her lap. "Well, actually, with your permission, I was planning on making an addition to the family tradition, which is the second thing I needed to ask you about. Here, this is for you." Dev handed the box to her lover. "It's sort of an unofficial welcome to the family."

"Whoa." Lauren jaw dropped open in surprise at the weight of the box. "You didn't have to–" She stopped when she lifted off the lid and released the rich aroma of vanilla into the air. Inside the box were two white candles and one blue, each about four inches in diameter and ten inches long. Carefully, Lauren moved aside the candles to find the source of the bulk of the weight: three sturdy, silver candleholders. "They're beautiful," she whispered, picking one up. "Anna Gallager Strayer" was engraved in bold letters across its front. She sucked in a surprised breath, feeling tears spring into her eyes so quickly that she was helpless to stop them.

Dev reached out slowly and pulled Lauren close to her. "I love you. I want to put those up with the rest of my family. Is that all right with you?"

Lauren sank into Dev's embrace. "I love you too," she breathed softly, then sniffed. The writer pulled away and cupped Dev's cheek, tenderly brushing a prominent cheekbone. "Are you sure, honey?" she whispered emotionally. "I'm not really–"

The President placed her finger over Lauren's lips to quiet her protests. "No, this is a tradition to celebrate the lives of the people who have touched us. The people who love us. And the people we want to remember. You belong there now. You belong there just as much as David and Beth do, or Emma, or Amy. We're adding one for Liza this year, too."

A blonde head nodded once. "Thank you," she whispered when Dev's finger dropped from her lips. Lauren smiled affectionately at Dev, wishing she could put into words how special it made her feel to belong to Dev's clan, whom she loved more than she would have believed possible. She sniffed again. "I-I don't know what to say."

Dev hugged her close and scooted down to get comfortable and make it clear she intended to stay there for a while and hold her lover. "You could tell me that you'll get that baby picture back from Wayne," she teased, placing a kiss on soft, fair tresses.

Lauren laughed and pinched Dev's belly. "Nuh uh. It's too cute not to share. Suffer, Madam President."

Monday, November 22nd

"Good morning, Madam President. Good morning, Lauren." Liza handed Dev a file and her mug of coffee. They were in the Oval Office, Dev sitting behind her massive wooden desk, with Lauren sitting several paces away in a high-backed, leather upholstered chair. They were together, but lost in their own work as Lauren prepared questions she had for an interview later that afternoon and Dev mentally went over a short speech she was giving that morning about the new healthcare reforms she intended to officially propose in January 2022.

"It's a light day today, Madam President," Liza continued. "First, you have to pardon a turkey."

Dev looked up from her folder and Lauren snickered, taking a quick shot of the surprised look on the President's face. "Excuse me?" Dev suddenly paid closer attention. "Did I hear you say that I was pardoning a turkey?"

A soft click and muffled chuckle indicated that Lauren had just captured the surprised look on Dev's face on film again.

Liza grinned, but refrained from asking Dev if she had ever bothered watching anything any of the past Presidents did. She didn't think it would be a wise career move. "Yes, ma'am, it's a

Thanksgiving tradition," Liza explained patiently, somehow looking at and speaking to Dev while entering something into her handheld organizer. "The President always pardons a turkey; then it's sent to live at the zoo."

Dev tossed her pencil down and retrieved a pen, opening the file Liza had given her. "Liza, if I pardon the turkey, what will I be having for Thanksgiving dinner?"

"Turkey, of course; just not the one you pardon." Liza struggled for words, not sure how to explain this rather bizarre ritual. She finally settled on saying, "It's just a tradition. Vegetarians and children love it."

"Not my kids," Dev snorted. "They're carnivores and not ashamed to admit it."

"Especially Aaron," Lauren chimed in. "That boy could eat an entire turkey himself. I swear he's going to be a sumo wrestler when he grows up."

Dev sighed and took a sip of her coffee as she read through the rest of her agenda. "So, basically, it's become tradition for the President to give the country the bird on Thanksgiving?"

Liza and Lauren both rolled their eyes, but still burst out laughing at Dev's lame joke, as the President searched her desk for something.

Dev's assistant recovered first and glanced at Lauren, who just shrugged. "I guess you could say that."

"But don't say it in front of a live microphone, Madam President," Lauren suggested, taking a few more pictures, including a very nice one of Dev and Liza together looking over something on the desk.

"Picky, picky." Dev snorted without looking up. "You're starting to sound more and more like David everyday."

"David is a very wise man," Lauren teased.

"How much did he pay you to say that?"

"Nothing. But he did get on my good side by donating a photograph of your college dorm room. Now I know where Aaron gets his slob tendencies."

"Very funny." Dev looked up from the document she was reading. "Take note that *two* people shared that room, and one side of it was neat and clean, while the other was a vile pigsty. Then go have a good look at David's office and tell me which side of the room was mine. Those are his sweat socks lying on the floor in the picture."

Lauren rose to her feet and put her hands on her hips. She narrowed her eyes. "How did you know there were sweat socks on the floor in that picture?"

"Because the entire time David and I roomed together, there were sweat socks on the floor. And what's really scary is that part of me believes they were the same pair."

Lauren and Liza both went "Ewww" at the same time.

Dev shivered. "I know."

David strode into the room, his face buried in a file as he did so, causing him to run right into Lauren. "Oh, sorry." He tucked the file under his arm as he looked around the room at the grinning women. David began chewing his mustache nervously. "Uh oh. Those smiles are nothing but trouble. I've seen my wife, mother-in-law, and sister-in-law, all in the same room together, smiling just like that. The next day our den was painted lavender."

"You're right, David. You should be afraid of us all." Dev didn't let Lauren's sniggers deter her. "But in this instance," she looked up, tapping her pen on the desk, "we were discussing turkeys, and your name just naturally popped up."

David gave a fake laugh, complete with raised upper lip. He lifted the file folder. "If you're not nice to me, I won't tell you what Santa got you for Christmas."

"I already know what Santa got me for Christmas." A satisfied grin curled Dev's lips. "It's the same thing I got for my birthday," she informed David casually, her eyes never straying to Lauren, who blushed a bright red.

David looked between the women for an explanation, but gave up quickly. "Yeah, okay. But his elves also just delivered the Republican and Democrat-suggested amendments to your DNA Registration Act."

Dev jumped up from her desk and joined David, peering down at the file. "What did it cost me?"

"Just the first-time offender clause. *And...*" David paused, looking so completely pleased with himself that Dev thought he might burst. He couldn't help but puff up his chest. "We also managed to rewrite it so that it has the full support of the NRA and all of the major law enforcement advocacy groups. The carefully worded amendment that funded DNA-coded locking mechanisms on firearms was the key. Good job with that particular addition, Devil. You, Madam President, are a very popular person at the moment. Your latest numbers just came in, and it looks like you've finally gotten past that bombing mess. Christmas is going to be good to you, Dev. Lots of people will be wanting to ride on your coattails."

Dev scowled. "And I thought my coattails were short and unpopular."

"Ha!"

Dev jumped back, her eyes widening at David.

The Chief of Staff placed his hands on his hips and puffed out his chest like a comic book superhero. "That's why I'm here," he declared with exaggerated gusto. "I make them *long* and *popular*."

Lauren regarded David carefully. "Just what did Beth put in your cereal this morning, David?"

Dev rolled her eyes. "Don't pay any attention to that. He always falls in love with himself every time he does a good job." Dev gave her Chief of Staff a ghost of a wink.

Liza glanced at her watch. "Shall we go pardon a turkey, ma'am?"

Dev stood and retrieved her jacket. By rote, David moved forward and took it from her hands, helping her shrug into it and smoothing the sleeves. "Wonderful job, David," Dev said softly, all teasing gone from her voice.

The tall man picked a piece of lint from Dev's navy blue jacket. "You deserved this one, Dev," he answered back equally quietly. "It's a good piece of legislation."

Dev nodded and cleared her throat, breaking the intimate moment between friends. "By all means, let's go save a fowl, little life." She looked at Liza and Lauren whose faces remained impassive. "Oh, come on, that deserved at least a little groan." She encouraged them by making a "hurry up" motion with her hands until she got the desired response. "Thank you. Now that didn't hurt, did it?"

Lauren found Dev in the music room that had been added and decorated during Bill Clinton's administration. It displayed instruments donated by some of America's most respected musicians. The walls were adorned with an eclectic combination of gold records, sheet music signed by Broadway's great composers, photographs of artists who had visited or performed at the White House over the years, and painters' renditions of singers and musicians ranging from Louis Armstrong to John Denver to Kathleen Battle. Dev had it outfitted with the latest electronic equipment, and the room was now a music lover's and a techno-geek's delight.

The writer entered quietly, enjoying the soft sounds of Vivaldi that drifted through the air. It wasn't until she was nearly on top of Dev that she realized the woman was sound asleep in a large, padded recliner.

"It's been a busy life, hasn't it, honey?" Lauren asked softly, gently brushing her fingers through Dev's hair. The President had been running herself to near exhaustion trying to wrap everything up as best she could, just so she could start all over again on January first.

Lauren smiled down at her lover, and gently increased the pressure of her fingers moving across Dev's forehead. "Devlyn?" she cooed in a hushed voice. "Darlin'?"

"Hmm?"

"Your mom and dad are due in about an hour from now."

Dev's eyes remained closed as she reached for Lauren and

tugged her onto her lap. She wrapped her arms around the smaller woman and nuzzled a sensitive spot behind Lauren's ear. "I'm not speaking to my mother," she said softly, her voice rough with sleep. "She gave you that nasty little picture."

"That is a perfectly charming, bare-naked baby picture. I love it."

"My mother is a troublemaker."

Lauren waggled her finger at Dev. "Your mother is a wonderful, kind, sweet woman."

A single blue eye opened very slowly and looked into the smiling face that Dev adored. "Do you have a fever? Are you delusional?"

"Dunno; maybe you should check."

Dev's hand worked its way under Lauren's T-shirt. "Ooo, that's nice and warm."

Lauren wrapped her arms around Dev's neck, which started a mini make-out session that neither one wanted to end anytime soon. Dev groaned and threaded her fingers in Lauren's hair, crushing her lips against hers.

"Oh, yeah, they got it all figured out, Frank." Janet clapped her hands together. "I knew that book was a good idea!"

Lauren's head snapped up. Suddenly the arms around her were gone and she was toppling backwards. The dark-haired woman tried to grab her, but it was too late, and Lauren's bottom hit the floor with a glorious thump that was immediately followed with a not so glorious, "Ouch!"

Dev grimaced as she leaned over and helped Lauren to her feet, "I'm sorry, sweetheart."

Lauren rubbed her backside, mumbling something about Janet learning to knock. "S'okay."

Dev gave Lauren's bottom a little pat. "Weren't you the one who, not two minutes ago, called her a wonderful, kind, and sweet woman?"

"How nice of you, dear." Janet Marlowe beamed at Lauren and opened her arms to the blonde for a hug. "I knew there was a reason I liked you so much."

Lauren moved over to Janet and gave her a hearty hug. "Welcome back, Janet. Dev was just saying how thrilled she was that you dug up those old photographs." Gray eyes danced with mischief. "I hope you brought the other ones we talked about."

Janet winked. "And more."

"Oh, yippee," Dev groaned, watching Lauren give her father a hug. Dev fell in after Lauren and gave both her parents hugs. She elbowed her father. "I'm so doomed."

"You sure are, Devil. But it's a good kind of doomed." He leaned in close and whispered in Dev's ear, "That's a fine young woman you've set your sights on. Or your mother wouldn't think so highly of her."

Dev pulled back and looked into her father's eyes, soaking up the acceptance she'd always seen in their blue-green depths. "That means a lot, Dad, knowing that you and Mom like her."

"She's a sweetie, and your mom adores her."

"Good." Devlyn glanced over at Lauren and her mother who were chatting conspiratorially. She looked back to her father. "I'm going to propose to her on Christmas Eve." Dev raised her finger to her dad. "Don't you dare tell Mom," she whispered urgently. "There is no way she could keep from spilling the beans. David and I are having a hard enough time keeping it from Beth. And the fact that I'm so nervous I'm ready to swallow my tongue isn't helping at all."

"Devlyn, that's wonderful. And I promise, not a word to your mother." He wrapped his arm around his daughter's shoulders and led her out the door. Frank had grandchildren to spoil, after all.

Lauren and Janet looked up to find they were alone in the room. Bewildered, they glanced around for a few seconds, then shrugged and sat down on the sofa, laughing and continuing their conversation.

Frank nudged his daughter. "Your mom will have a wonderful time planning a wedding. Thank God our stock portfolio is healthy."

"It's more than healthy, and you know it," Dev snorted. "But I sure hope Mom wants to do something, because there is no way I'll have time." She sighed again. "If I had to do it, we'd end up getting married in front of a Justice of the Peace. Hey," she nudged her father back, "you weren't due for another hour or so, and how did you find us?" Dev looked around, noticing for the first time that her parents didn't have a Secret Service escort.

"Lord, you know your mother. She told that sturdy, young agent who wanted to walk us around the halls to go find someone else to guard, that she wasn't going to steal the china."

Dev laughed softly. "Sounds just like something Lauren would say." She shook her head. "No wonder they get along so well."

Frank scratched his neatly trimmed, white beard. "Could be. I have noticed a few subtle similarities." He winked at his daughter. "Lucky you. But, to answer your question, we caught a tail wind and arrived early. I personally think it was divine intervention."

Dev stopped walking. "What?"

"I know that other passengers were praying that the flight would be over soon before your mother talked them to death."

This time the President burst out laughing. She linked hands with her father and looked behind her, surprised not to see Lauren or her mom following. "Should we–?"

"Now, Devil, let's not be too hasty. They'll notice we're gone. Eventually." Frank patted the hand he was holding. "Besides, don't forget, I was on that plane myself."

December 2021

Friday, December 3rd

Lauren didn't even bother to remove her jacket or shoes before she collapsed, face down, across her bed. Gremlin and Princess both hopped up on the bed and were studiously licking her ears when she heard the knock on the door.

"Enter at your own risk," she called across the room before dropping her face back onto the soft mattress.

Dev stepped inside, took one look at her lover, and an indulgent grin immediately broke out across her face. "Poor baby," she offered with sincere sympathy, crossing over to Lauren and kneeling near her head.

Princess had already jumped down and scurried under the bed, where she became uncharacteristically brave and growled at the President.

Dev just snorted.

Gremlin, on the other hand, was bolder. He remained standing on the bed, backed up a step and planted his butt directly on Lauren's head, where he could guard his mistress and take a stand against the President...sitting down.

Lauren was too tired to care, but she managed to raise her head just a hair to nip the tail that was tickling her nose.

Gremlin gave a surprised yelp, then resettled himself, baring tiny, spiky teeth.

Dev wondered when the portly beast had learned to narrow his eyes at her.

He barked.

Dev barked back, and Grem scampered off Lauren's head, falling onto the bed with a high-pitched yelp before jumping down to the carpet to join his mate. Dev rolled her eyes when his growls grew fiercer once he was safely under the bed where she couldn't reach him. "Chicken," she taunted.

Turning her attention back to Lauren, the President gently stroked long fingers through blonde strands of hair, trying to coax their owner into looking up, and doing her best not to think about how Gremlin's butt had just been there. "Sweetheart?"

"What?" came the muffled reply.

"How was your day?"

Lauren rolled over with a groan, throwing her arms out to her sides. Her voice was a pitiful whine. "It was awful. Just awful."

"Uh huh." Dev stood up and walked around the bed. Reaching over, she pulled the smaller woman upright. Lauren slumped forward like a rag doll while Dev removed her blazer and then blouse, leaving her clad in a crimson-colored, silk bra.

A tiny grin danced across Lauren's face as she fell back onto the comforter and sighed. She loved every second of the attention Dev was lavishing on her, and Lauren happily abandoned herself to it.

"So tell me about it then," Dev encouraged. She gently removed one of Lauren's earrings, then the other, rubbing her earlobe with her thumb before setting both earrings on the bedside table.

"Hmm?" the writer groaned, feeling her shoes being slipped off and the room's cool air tickling her toes as strong fingers began an attentive massage. She instantly forgot Dev's question and closed her eyes in pleasure. "Oh, God, that's good."

Dev smirked. "Your day? Tell me about your day."

"Oh, right." Lauren let out a satisfied grunt at Dev's ministrations. "Well, I knew it was going to be one of *those* days when my alarm didn't go off this morning. I need a new one. And not one of those obnoxious talking ones. I hate those."

"So that's why you were AWOL from our workout this morning." Dev settled down on the floor and continued to rub slender, achy feet. She glanced down to see two black doggie noses, one tiny and delicate, the other large, flat, and covered in drool, poking out from under the comforter. They snarled and Dev snarled back. She watched smugly as the noses promptly disappeared.

Lauren was going to scold Devlyn for teasing the dogs, but the thought was swept from her mind when Dev flexed Lauren's toes, stretching them one at a time. "Sweet Jesus, that feels good."

Devlyn waited a moment for Lauren to go on. When she didn't, Dev prompted, "Lauren?"

"Yeah?" the blissful woman replied dreamily.

Dev stifled a laugh. "You were going to tell me about your day."

Lauren flexed her toes in Dev's very attentive hands before continuing. "I was?" She lifted her head a little and forced her eyes open to be greeted by a sharply raised eyebrow. Her head dropped back to the mattress. "Oh, right. Yes, that's why I missed our workout. Then I put my thumb through two perfectly good pairs of hose while I was hurrying to get dressed."

"Gotta hate it when that happens."

"Uh huh. So, I made a mad dash to my appointments this morning. And I got a flat tire in Georgetown. Lucky for me, my first appointment was for breakfast with Beth. But she forgave me for being forty-five minutes late and called Triple A."

"Why didn't you just call them on your cell phone?"

"Because I dropped it on the sidewalk and watched it shatter into about a million pieces."

Disbelieving but playful blue eyes pinned her.

"Okay, it was only three pieces," the writer conceded with a sigh. "But it was still broken!"

Twin dark eyebrows rose. "Go on, sweetheart."

Lauren sighed and removed one foot from Dev's hands, only to replace it with the other. "After breakfast, where they got my order wrong, but I was running too late to send it back, I finally arrived at General Brendwell's office with two minutes to spare. Then that son of a bitch kept me waiting for nearly an hour longer than I had expected he would."

"How long did you expect he would?"

"Half hour."

"The bastard."

"Exactly. *Then* he had the nerve to get mad when I cut his interview short in an effort to keep my schedule intact. You know, he is a total prick."

"I agree. But he's also very highly respected and has a brilliant military mind. He was the right choice for Secretary of Defense." Dev smiled when Lauren groaned with delight as she pushed her thumbs up the center of her foot from heel to toes.

"After that, I locked my keys in my car and forgot the override code. Just a little harder. Ahh...right there. That required another call to Triple A. After that, I got trapped on Dupont Circle." Lauren raised her head briefly, narrowing her eyes at Dev. "Surely you can do something about that."

Dev shot Lauren a regretful look. "Sorry. I'm not on the street zoning and planning commission, but I'll send a memo."

Her head dropped back down to the bed. "You do that."

Dev stood up, hearing Lauren's mewing protests that her massage was over. She reached back down and unzipped Lauren's skirt. "Lift."

The writer lifted her hips as her skirt and hose were pulled off in one deft motion. A single eye popped open, watching as Dev moved across the room to her dresser and opened her second drawer.

"Aha!" Dev swung around and pointed an accusing finger at Lauren. "I wondered where this set of sweats went."

"Oh, right," Lauren snorted softly. "Like you'd even notice if a pair went missing. You have a hundred sets of sweats."

Dev began rummaging through the drawer. "And my socks, too! You little thief." She laughed. "Can't you just steal the towels like everyone else?"

The President returned to the bed and knelt down long enough to put the socks on Lauren's feet. She realized she'd forgotten to get something out of Lauren's dresser and ran her fingers around Lauren's hip to gave her bottom a pinch. "Commando?"

"Ugh, no panties?" She shrugged weakly. "Sure. You only live once."

"That's my girl." Dev worked the sweatpants up her legs.

"Devlyn, darlin', I don't mean to criticize, but you're doing this all wrong."

"No criticism there."

"Aren't you suppose to be undressing me?"

"Later."

Lauren wanted to protest, but it really didn't matter how Dev touched her. Just as long as she did. Besides, later was good too. "Okay."

"Lift."

Lauren lifted her hips once again and felt the sweatpants pulled all the way up, warming her legs. Then a hand circled her wrist and pulled her upright.

"Bra on or off?"

A blonde brow lifted faintly. "You need to ask?"

Dev chuckled and lovingly removed the undergarment.

Lauren groaned softly. "Later?"

"Absolutely. Later." Dev tossed the bra on the pile with the rest of Lauren's rumpled clothing. Lauren helped Dev put on her sweatshirt by lifting her arms. Dev couldn't resist allowing her hands to drift under Lauren's sweatshirt and move across warm skin.

Lauren sucked in a surprised breath when Dev used her knuckles to graze the silky skin on the underside of firm breasts. Before the blonde could utter a word, Dev's thumbs ran lightly across her nipples, causing them to instantly go painfully erect. "Devlyn," Lauren warned in a low growl, "be nice."

Blue eyes went round and innocent. "That was nice. Mean would have been if I'd lifted your shirt," which she did, "and lowered my mouth—"

"Stop!" Lauren pulled back and shook her index finger in front of Dev's face. "You got me dressed again for a reason. So unless 'later' has arrived, don't start something we can't finish." She pulled down her shirt. "What's the plan?"

Dev frowned, but quickly got over the fact that Lauren's shirt was now back in place. "You, me, the kids, Jr. Monopoly in the living room? Emma baked cookies and made cocoa."

"Wonderful." Lauren sighed contentedly, feeling much better than she had moments ago. She leaned in and gave the tall woman a heartfelt kiss that she just barely resisted the urge to deepen. "So how was your day?" She wiped a tiny lipstick smudge from the corner of Devlyn's mouth.

Dev shrugged. Standing, she tugged Lauren to her feet and wrapped her arm around her lover's trim waist as they slowly walked towards the door. "Flew to New York this morning to give a speech in front of the United Nations."

"Show off."

Saturday, December 18th

Dev's gaze flickered down to her meeting agenda, which was resting next to her notepad, then to the clock on the wall. She covertly rolled her eyes at the young man at the end of the table, who had just initiated what had to be the fortieth holographic visual aid explaining crop destruction. She knew she should be paying attention to what he was saying, but she couldn't help it. Dev had already decided she was going to back the request for aid to the farmers, whose infant winter wheat crops had fallen victim to this year's unusually early and harsh blizzards. To Dev, this young man was "preaching to the choir", as her dad would say. She didn't need to be convinced.

Besides, it was Saturday, she had a hot date, and he had already talked a *lot* longer than expected. Her thoughts had wandered to Lauren's newest Adrienne Nash novel. Though her pseudonym would appear as co-author, she was leaving the actual writing to Lauren and confining her contribution to plot and character development ideas. What she couldn't understand was why Lauren had decided to bring in a beefy character named Dirk. And, worse yet, why Dirk had to have the hots for Adrienne! Dev scowled and put a line through the circle that contained Dirk's name on the agenda. "Better be a damned redshirt, meant to bite the dust before he gets anywhere near Adrienne!" she mumbled, glancing up sheepishly when she realized she'd said that aloud.

"Madam President?" The Deputy Secretary of Agriculture, the toothy young man making the presentation, looked at her with round eyes, terrified that she might actually have a question.

Dev gave him a regretful smile and a little wave. "I'm sorry. I wandered there for a second. Please, go on."

He nodded, and gave the voice command for the hologram to project a new picture. This one was of two stalks of wheat. One was clearly damaged, while the other was not.

Dev glanced at the other faces in the room, and, after confirming the Secretary of Agriculture was still awake, let her eyes travel back to her notepad. *You're gonna screw up the perfectly good subtext, Lauren. God, it will be just as horrific as it had been on* Xena. It had been twenty years since that show ended, and she was still pissed off that the writers were forever inserting the boyfriend of the week. *Xena and Gabrielle loved each other. End of story.* Her attention wandered to the pages they had worked on the night before. Dev had *not* been happy with the way Lauren had ended that chapter. She drew a picture of "Dirk", complete with noose around his neck, on her notepad. "I'll kill the rat bastard!" she growled and every pair of eyes turned in her direction.

The Deputy Secretary's eyes bulged and he gulped audibly.

"Okay, ladies and gentleman." David reached over and patted

Dev's arm, smoothly taking charge of the meeting. "I think we're all set. The President has another meeting she's late for, so..."

The Secretary of Agriculture was the first on his feet, looking as relieved as Dev felt. He wasn't sure why the President was about to commit homicide, but he most certainly didn't want to be the target, and while his Deputy Secretary did have a propensity to drone on and on, he was fond of the young man and didn't want to lose him either. "Thank you for your time, Madam President. Can we count on the support of the White House?"

David nudged Dev, who looked up from her drawing, which now included something that looked like a gun to Dirk's head. "Absolutely!" she said, even as she slammed closed her notebook and rose to her feet. "You'll have everything you need from my office first thing Monday morning. Isn't that right, David?"

"Yes, Madam President." He stood and buttoned his jacket. "I can finish up here, ma'am, if you'd like to get to that next meeting." He motioned her to the door.

"Right. Thank you, David. I'll see you Monday."

Dev did her absolute best to hold back her laughter until she was well within the residence. She ended up in front of Lauren's door, and used her forehead to gently knock against it. When the door opened, she smiled at her lover who was holding her glasses in one hand and her camera in the other.

"We need to talk about Dirk."

"Dirk?" Lauren was truly confused. "From my books?"

"Oh, yeah. Because of Dirk, the Deputy Secretary of Agriculture now thinks I want him dead."

Thursday, December 23rd

Lauren lay on her belly on her bed. Scattered around her were dozens of papers, outlines, reference books, and even a few world maps. Her chin was propped up by one hand, and she was turned around so that her head was at the foot of the bed. The writer had a pen between her teeth, which she pulled out occasionally so she could scratch some notes on one of the several tablets of paper.

She had scrubbed her face and brushed her teeth for bed, and she was supremely comfortable in a threadbare, University of Tennessee T-shirt and a pair of thin, dark gray sweatpants that were so worn, if you held them to the light you could see through the knees.

Dev sat alongside her, back propped against the headboard by several large feather-filled pillows. The area around her was free of her own mess, though Lauren's had spilled over into her work area and now covered the entire bed. She held a single note pad and a pencil, which she alternately chewed and tapped against the paper restlessly. Devlyn's hair was slightly damp from a quick shower

she'd taken nearly an hour before. She wore soft, red flannel pajamas and thick sweat socks that didn't quite manage to keep her toes
from being chilled.

Although the temperature inside the White House rarely varied
more than a degree or two, the rest of Washington, D.C. was in the
throes of a blizzard. The relative silence of the room was periodically broken by the howling wind that scattered dry snowflakes
against the tall bedroom windows.

Gremlin and Princess had taken up refuge on the sofa and were
snoozing happily on opposite ends. Lauren had speculated earlier
that the dogs must have had a lovers' quarrel since Princess usually
slept right on top of Gremlin and the portly pug didn't seem to mind
a bit.

Tap. Tap. Tap...tap. Tap. Tap.

Lauren swung her head around and peered with obvious irritation over the top of her glasses to see Dev nervously tapping her
note pad with her pencil again. The President seemed to be obliviv-
ous to her actions and Lauren bit her lip to keep from saying something rude. She let out a slightly impatient breath and slowly turned
her eyes back to her own work. Lauren had just about figured out
how Adrienne Nash, intrepid explorer, could escape from her latest
capture when she heard, *Tap. Tap. Tap...tap. Tap. Tap.* She closed
her eyes briefly, schooling herself in patience before turning her
head and glaring at Dev, who was deep in thought. "Do you mind?"

Dev's head jerked up. "Huh?"

Lauren sat up a little so she could reach back and lay her hand
over Dev's, effectively putting an end to the tapping. "You're making
me insane."

Bewildered, Dev just looked at her. "What are you talking
about? I'm trying to think of ideas for Adrienne Nash. I'm not doing
anything to you!"

Lauren groaned inwardly. Dev was used to working in the constant background noise of her endless meetings. She, on the other
hand, while in attendance at most of those meetings, would slip
back to the silence of her room to really get things done.

"Okay. You're right. I'm sorry. That tapping was just breaking
my concentration. Go back to your thinking." Lauren patted Dev's
thigh and lay back down, spreading out her papers even more and
jotting down an idea that suddenly came to her.

Dev glanced down at Lauren and frowned. "We need more
light."

"No, we don't."

Dev balanced her notepad on her thighs. "Yes, we do. Working
in low light is bad for your eyes."

Lauren set her own pen down and turned around again. "That's
not true. Not unless you have to strain to see. I work at night all the

time. The light is fine. I can see perfectly."

Dev snorted.

"Don't you say a damned word about my glasses, Devlyn. My vision 'issues' have nothing to do with poor light, and before you start up again, I am *not* having anybody poking my eyes with needles or lasers or whatever they use," she huffed, going back to her work, now thoroughly distracted. After a moment of dead silence she added. "And that's final. No how. No way."

"Baby." Dev stuck out her tongue and petulantly kicked at the papers surrounding her feet. "God, you're messy." She picked up a paper containing nothing but Lauren's doodles and crumpled it into a tight ball. She aimed for the waste bin by the desk across the room and, in perfect free-throw style, took the shot. Which she promptly missed by several feet.

Lauren's eyes flickered up from her outline. "Dev," she whined in frustration, "what if that was important?"

"It wasn't," the President announced firmly, silently vowing to retrieve it from the floor later just in case Lauren was right. *Better safe than sorry.* "The bed is a pigsty." Dev's kicking grew a little more vigorous. "How can you work like this?"

Lauren was about to snap back with a smartass reply but got a good look at the maps and papers and reference books that were covering the bed. She let out a grumpy breath, cringing inwardly. *Okay, so it's just the tiniest bit messy.* Without a word, Lauren grabbed Dev's big toe and used it to lift the long leg. With her other hand, she scooped out the papers that were underneath.

"Hey!" Dev squawked indignantly, her eyes wide with mild outrage.

"Hush." Lauren let go of the toe, causing Dev's leg to drop back to the bed with a dull thud, bouncing once. She tugged on Dev's socked foot affectionately and went back to her papers.

"Grab my toe..." the words trailed off as Dev mumbled under her breath.

Lauren began to rhythmically wiggle her own foot as she thought. *Adrienne could escape on horseback. Oh, yeah, folks would love that.* The blonde woman pulled over a map, wondering if this particular island would have horses. *I'll check on-line tomorrow.* Unconsciously, she continued to move her foot back and forth.

Dev glared down at the offending body part, trying her best to ignore the shaking bed. Lauren's foot suddenly stopped all movement and the President sighed in relief, her thoughts drifting back to her own project. *Dirk the jerk. Dirk the dick. Dirk must die. He's only in the way. Why can't Lauren see that Adrienne would be so much better off with that hotty redheaded sidekick of hers? What does Lauren mean she's "thinking" about getting them together? What's to "think" about? They're perfect for each other. Don't worry, Adrienne. I'll straighten out this mess.* Dev smirked. *So to speak.*

The bed began to shake again with what was now a full-fledged bouncing of Lauren's entire leg. Dev was jolted out of her plans and she fixed her gaze on the source of her annoyance, watching in dismay as it continued to bounce, and bounce, and bounce, and bounce. "Stop shaking the bed!" she blurted out when her patience had dwindled to nothing.

"Sure, honey," Lauren answered absently, patting Dev's calf. She was so fully caught up in her newest idea that she didn't bother to turn her head as she spoke.

Dev rolled her eyes when the movement stopped for all of two seconds then continued, albeit at a less forceful pace. Trying to get more comfortable, she scooted down further in the bed, inadvertently bumping Lauren's elbow and causing the younger woman to draw a black line right across the notes she'd just completed. "Oh, sorry," Dev said quietly. But she didn't move her foot. "Can you—?"

"Yes!" Lauren scooted over, putting at least two feet between her and Dev to give the President more room. "Better?" she mumbled.

"A little."

A few minutes more and Lauren heard the *Tap. Tap. Tap...tap. Tap. Tap.* Again. "Arghhh!" The blonde woman dropped her head, letting her forehead hit the bed. She ground her teeth together.

Tap. Tap. Tap...tap. Tap. Tap. ... Tap. Tap. Tap...tap. Tap. Tap.

Lauren hastily sat up and scrambled to the head of the bed to join Dev. She reached out and plucked the pencil from Dev's fingers, tossing it across the room with a quick flick of her wrist.

Dev stared at her in mute shock as the pencil bounced off Lauren's computer screen and fell to the floor.

Lauren smiled sweetly. "That's *much* better. Thank you."

"You," Dev gestured angrily with hands, "you-you just can't do that!"

Lauren nodded her head wildly, her lips forming a tight, white line. "Oh-oh, yes I can, Madam President!"

"Fine." Blue eyes narrowed. "If that's the way you feel."

Lauren threw her chest out and crossed her arms over it. "Oh, yeah," she growled. "It's the way I feel."

A slightly predatory grin flashed across Dev's face and Lauren's eyes widened at the sight. Casually, Dev swung her feet over the edge of the tall bed and pushed off, landing on the floor.

Lauren's brows drew together. "Devlyn, where—?"

Dev reached down and grabbed the comforter. She raised the edge of the thick, soft cloth and brought it back down in a lightning-fast move that sent most of Lauren's papers sailing straight into the air. For a split second, they floated around Lauren's head and legs, then drifted down to the comforter like large, rectangular pieces of snow. "That," Dev smoothed the comforter back into place, "is the way *I* feel." *Take that, messy...messy...err...foot shaker!*

"Ooo!" Lauren's face turned bright red, and she launched herself at her lover, wrapping her arms around Dev and swinging her back onto the bed with a loud grunt. "I can't believe...uuff...you...did that!"

Dev instantly rolled over, pinning Lauren down with her body weight. "Believe it!"

Lauren's nostrils flared. "Get off me!"

"No! You're making me crazy!"

"Me? Ha!" Lauren pushed against Dev, trying to dislodge her. "You're the one driving me crazy!" the writer choked out forcefully, her face turning even redder.

The veins in Dev's throat and one in her forehead, bulged as she pushed back against Lauren with all her might, refusing to release her captive. "I'm not letting you up! You'll just make more mess and bounce, and bounce, and bounce." Dev bounced against Lauren to emphasize her words, causing the headboard to slam against the wall with her every movement.

Lauren exhaled explosively, and perspiration beaded her upper lip as she threw her entire body into her escape attempt.

"And then you'll nag," Dev grunted, fully realizing for the first time just how much strength Lauren's compact body contained as the shorter woman nearly wriggled free.

"Nag? I think not, Queen Nag!" Lauren was finally able to sneak her arms out from between their bodies, but her wrists were quickly caught by Dev, who held them over her head and pressed them into the soft pillows. "Dammit! Get off me so I can kill you!"

"Never! Never! Never!"

Their eyes locked and they held each other's defiant gazes for all of two seconds before they both burst into helpless laughter.

Dev let go of Lauren's wrists, and this time it was their giggles that shook the bed.

Lauren let out a deep breath, shifting slightly so that Dev wasn't pressing so firmly against her rib cage. She wrapped her arms loosely around her partner, feeling soft, dark hair slide between her fingers. "I think we've both officially lost our minds. The pressure has finally caused us to snap." But she was smiling the entire time she spoke and truly couldn't think of a nicer spot on Earth than right where she was.

"Uh huh," Dev agreed. She leaned forward and brushed her lips against the soft ones only a few inches away, parting them easily with her tongue and deepening the kiss.

Lauren moaned softly and pulled a leg out from under Dev,

immediately wrapping it around Dev's legs, holding the older woman in place. They were both breathing heavily and perspiring from their roughhousing and the unexpectedly intense kiss they'd just shared.

"We're fussing and nagging like an old married couple," Dev murmured, placing another small kiss at the corner of Lauren's mouth before pulling back slightly and loving the intimate way their bodies were now twined together.

Lauren nodded. She cocked her head to the side speculatively as she truly considered Dev's words. "We do sound married, don't we?"

Dev laughed. "Oh, yeah." The writer's body felt hot against her skin and, unable to resist, she nuzzled the smooth, hot skin of Lauren's throat.

Lauren gasped as attentive lips and teeth found a sensitive spot along her jugular. "So why don't we then?"

"Why don't we what?" Dev's lips tenderly began working their way around Lauren's throat, and the blonde arched against the touch.

"Get married." The words were out before she could stop them or think about what she was saying.

Dev's lips halted mid-kiss and her body went deadly still. Her eyes slid closed for several heartbeats as her mind raced. Then she pulled back slowly and opened them. "Did you just propose?"

Lauren blinked. *Oh, my God. That's exactly what I did! I didn't mean to do that, did I?* A bolt of sheer panic raced through her, but she was surrounded by the reassuring weight of her lover, who grounded her in more ways than one. And with every breath came the comforting scent her mind would forever tell her was Dev. Her anxiety passed almost as quickly as it had appeared, replaced instead by an unyielding certainty she hadn't even known herself capable of. Even if she hadn't intended to say it, deep in her heart it was what she wanted. "I—" She licked her lips, unable to gauge Dev's response by the look on her face. "I guess so." Lauren steeled herself for...she wasn't sure what. "Yes, yes I did." Firmer this time.

Dev couldn't help but smile. Part of her wanted to choke Lauren for completely ruining all those weeks of planning. All the worry and fear she had put herself through were for nothing! But a bigger part of her was thrilled senseless. So senseless, in fact that for just a moment she forgot to answer Lauren's question until she felt the increased thudding of Lauren's rapid heartbeat against her own chest. "Yes." She smiled and quirked a brow.

Lauren studied Dev's face carefully; her own tentative smile appeared and she released a slightly shuddering breath. But Dev had taken so long to answer she wasn't sure they were even talking about the same thing anymore. "Yes, what?" Lauren held her breath, her heart skipping a beat at the sudden twinkle in Dev's eyes.

Dev shot her a mildly exasperated look. "Whaddya think? Yes, I'll marry you, ya goof."

Lauren was speechless. "Wow," she finally breathed, hugging Dev with all her might. "This is so great." Lauren buried her face in Dev's hair. "I love you so much."

Dev tightened her hold on Lauren. "I love you too, sweetheart."

Pale brows drew tightly together. "Can we even get married here?" *God, Lauri, you might have checked before you asked.*

Dev smiled at the sudden worry that colored Lauren's voice. She propped herself down on one elbow and traced the writer's cheeks, then fair eyebrows. "Every state, including D.C., will recognize another state's marriage. But not every state will perform the ceremony." Dev's eyes conveyed true regret. "Tennessee won't. I'm sorry, honey."

Lauren shrugged. It hadn't crossed her mind to go back there anyway. "But I bet Ohio does, right?" she asked innocently, batting fair lashes and waiting for the response she knew she'd get.

A brilliant smile broke out across Dev's face, causing tiny creases around her eyes.

Oh, yeah. That was the right thing to say.

"It sure as hell does!" Dev blurted happily, rolling off Lauren and onto her back. "My folks will be thrilled." She turned her head and regarded her companion lovingly. "I'm thrilled," she whispered, her voice cracking.

Lauren rolled onto her side to face Dev. Her smile mirrored the dark-haired woman's. "Me too, darlin'." She slipped off her glasses, and, without turning her head, reached behind her and set them on the nightstand.

"You just don't want to be part of the spectacle of a White House wedding," Dev teased.

Lauren chuckled softly and rolled on top of Dev, settling heavily there. "I just want to make you happy." A slender brow quirked. "And if we happen to be able to piss off the press in the process..." Lauren could feel Dev's silent laughter.

"No wonder I love you. You're evil. Who could resist that?"

"Uh huh," Lauren agreed, leaning forward and tasting the soft skin just below Dev's throat. She reached up and unbuttoned the top button of the President's pajamas so her lips could drift lower. "Really evil," she agreed softly, unable to resist opening a second button and releasing more of Dev's shower-clean scent.

Dev sighed softly and pushed her hands underneath Lauren's thin T-shirt, trailing them up her naked back.

The smaller woman murmured her approval at Dev's gentle touch.

A third, then fourth button was slowly undone as Lauren

worked her way lower still, exposing more warm, slightly salty skin to her lips and tongue. When the last button was freed she reached up and pushed the flannel shirt open and nuzzled the silky underside of Dev's left breast. "Mmm...God, Devlyn," she groaned, her tongue darted out, tracing a hot path from the underside of Dev's breast to the center breastbone, "you are so soft."

Dev gasped and her eyes slid closed, a flood of warmth spreading down from her belly and settling between her legs at Lauren's sensual touch. She sat up, taking the smaller woman with her, and covered Lauren's mouth with a passionate kiss.

Lauren swept the pajama top from Dev's strong shoulders, hazily marveling at the combination of sleek muscles and smooth skin beneath her hands as the President continued to kiss her senseless. Her hands moved into thick, dark hair, where her nails grazed Dev's scalp. She deepened the kiss further, swirling her hot tongue around Dev's as she swallowed her lover's moans.

Reluctantly, Dev pulled away. "You too," she encouraged raggedly, her chest heaving.

Lauren's eyes fluttered open and she looked at Dev blankly for a several seconds as the words tried to penetrate her brain.

"You too. I need to touch you, too." Dev tugged at the hem of Lauren's shirt.

Lauren lifted her arms high over her head, and her T-shirt was pulled off in one swift motion and tossed to the floor. Their movements slowed, as they traded kisses and tenderly whispered words. Next came flannel, sweats, and panties, until at last they fell together in a tangle of arms and legs, groaning at the flawless contact of naked skin on naked skin.

"I want to kiss and taste you everywhere," Dev murmured against Lauren's chest. A low but enthusiastic moan answered her, and she turned her head to the side to nip and lick against a sensitive nipple.

"Oh, Dev," Lauren whimpered, her body jerking slightly at the delicious sensation. "You enjoy teasing me, don't you?" Then she felt she couldn't draw in enough air as Dev began doing anything but tease.

As she used her mouth to entice the woman in her arms, Dev's hands slowly traced hot paths up the sides of Lauren's slightly damp body. She moved from knees to shoulders and then back down again, soaking in the exquisite feeling of soft skin under her hands.

The sensation of short, well-manicured nails gently grazing her back and shoulders sent shivers through her own body, causing a moan to escape Dev's throat. The President never realized how much she ached for this woman's touch until she was receiving it. Lauren simply had a way of eliciting every emotion that Dev was capable of feeling.

They made love slowly, passionately. Taking the time to truly enjoy each other, to caress and gently kiss, experiencing the best of what each offered the other. Sensual hums of delight mixed with low, throaty groans.

A smile curled Dev's lips when her ears picked up the soft but nearly constant moans that spoke of Lauren's arousal and love, with just a little impatience thrown in, as the smaller woman tried to get her body closer to Devlyn's. Dev had come to recognize these as the signals of her lover's impending climax.

She held Lauren closer, wanting it as much as Lauren did, her body reacting strongly to the sights and smells and sounds surrounding her.

Dev whispered words of love and devotion as their bodies instinctively found a sensual, perfect rhythm. When Lauren threw her head back and cried out softly, Dev followed right behind her. The sight of her lover's face as she released, the feeling of Lauren's sweat-slicked body bucking beneath her, and the fingers that had become talons digging into her shoulder blades, were more than enough to bring her to her own precipice and beyond.

Heaving chests slowed and pulses calmed, as they relaxed, nearly melting together. Lauren slowly ran her hand down the smooth skin of Dev's back and tiredly pulled up the comforter, which had somehow ended up half on, half off the bed, around their entwined bodies. She kissed a damp shoulder, eliciting a contented hum from deep in Dev's chest and a murmured "I love you."

Lauren couldn't have been more contented herself as she felt more than heard Dev's breathing even out and her heart slow further as sleep overtook her partner. "I love you, too," she whispered softly. Gray eyes fluttered closed and she smiled faintly as Dev's arms tightened around her.

Saturday, December 25th

"Lauren?"

Silence.

"Lauren?" The whispered voices were more insistent now.

"Go 'way," the writer slurred, pulling the pillow over her head.

Three sets of giggles nudged Lauren closer to wakefulness. "It's time to get up," Aaron insisted. "Santa came!"

Lauren whimpered softly and lifted her bedraggled head from her pillow. She was in Devlyn's bed, but the President was nowhere to be found.

"Santa came; we get to open presents. C'mon!" Christopher grabbed one of Lauren's hands and Ashley grabbed the other and they literally dragged the writer out of bed.

"Okay, okay, I'm coming," Lauren laughed, letting go of Ashley's hand long enough to grab her glasses. She looked over at the clock. 3:30 a.m. *God, no wonder I'm tired. I only went to bed three hours ago.* "Do you always get up in the middle of the night for Christmas?" she asked Aaron as she fumbled for her glasses.

"Uh huh. As soon as Santa comes, we can open presents. That's the deal," he crowed excitedly, tugging at Lauren's T-shirt as the woman stumbled out of bed, yawning.

"Where's your mama?" Lauren's voice was still hoarse with sleep, and she stuck her fingers under her glasses to rub her eyes.

"She's in the living room. C'mon, we'll show you!"

Lauren looked wistfully at the bathroom as she was tugged past it and out into the living room.

"Here she is," Ashley announced, her voice still a whisper.

The room was pitch black except for the twinkling of the white Christmas tree lights, which illuminated Dev's sprawled form. She lay on the floor in front of the tree, with Ashley's new bike assembled and waiting, Christopher's halfway there, and Aaron's still in the box. A wrench was still clutched in one hand and the trail of drool leading from her mouth to the carpet was glistening with every blink of the lights.

Lauren bit her lip to muffle a chuckle. It was exactly where she had left Dev several hours ago, with the President promising she'd be coming to bed soon and that she didn't need any help; that this would only take a few moments. *Good grief, Devlyn. What am I going to do with you?*

Christopher stared at his mother curiously. "How come Santa's elves didn't put the bikes together? Isn't that their job?"

Lauren's eyebrows jumped up into her hairline as her mind scrambled to come up with a suitable answer.

Ashley looked at her brother impatiently. "You're so stupid, Chris. The Secret Service probably made the elves leave the packages downstairs. The elves couldn't very well put them together in the North Pole, because 'put together' bikes would take up too much room in the sleigh."

Gray eyes widened as Lauren listened to Ashley's explanation. *With an imagination like that, we may have another writer in the family.*

"So Mama had to do it here," Ashley continued in a clear voice.

"Oh." Christopher nodded, finding his sister's explanation completely believable. "Of course."

Aaron tugged on Lauren's hand and she peered down at the small blond boy. "Can we wake her up? It's Christmas!"

Lauren smiled. "Sure, honey. Go ahead and wake her up."

The words were still hanging in the air when Christopher and Ashley let go of Lauren's hands and all three children ran over to their mother, happily shaking her awake.

Lauren watched with amusement as Dev sleepily tried to fend them off for a few futile seconds before waking up enough to realize what was going on. The President exclaimed, "Merry Christmas," pulling all three children into a group hug that went on longer than any of the kids could stand.

"Okay, ya little monsters." Dev released her captives and frowned as she wiped her drool away with the back of her hand. "Have at it. And help Aaron read the names on the packages."

Three shrill cheers rang out, causing Dev to jump back a little. Ashley quickly grabbed Aaron's hand and they both ran to the stockings with Christopher hot on their heels. Each child grabbed his own and plopped down in front of the fireplace to examine the booty it contained.

Dev padded over to Lauren who was still watching quietly with a grin plastered across her face. "Mornin'. Sort of," Dev whispered, placing a soft kiss on Lauren's lips. She wrapped her arms around the smaller woman.

"Mornin', darlin'." Lauren squeezed Dev back, sinking deeply into the warm embrace.

"I fell asleep."

Lauren laughed. "I know. I'm sorry. I crashed myself, or I would have come and gotten you."

"Did the kids ask—?"

Lauren shook her head and led Dev by the elbow to the couch, where they both dropped down with twin groans. "Ashley blamed your being passed out under the tree like an old drunk on the Secret Service."

Dev laughed, then smacked Lauren's arm playfully. "I was asleep," she whispered loudly. "That is not the same thing as passed out!"

Lauren stuck out her tongue.

"I need coffee," Dev whined.

"Me too. I'll get some coffee for us and some juice or something for the kids."

"You don't have to do that." Dev's protest was halfhearted. "We just sat down. I can wait."

"Please." Lauren rolled her eyes knowingly. "You're the biggest coffee addict I know. And besides, if I don't get some caffeine soon myself, I'll die. And I hear that sort of thing is a real downer on Christmas morning."

"Thank you." Dev wrapped her arm around Lauren's shoulders as they both stood. "I love you."

Lauren bumped hips with Dev. "I love you, too."

"It seems strange without Emma around," Dev commented, not quite ready to let Lauren go.

"True," Lauren allowed, smiling at Ashley's squeal of delight when the little girl discovered some brightly colored nail polish in her stocking. "But the woman does deserve a vacation. I can't believe you sent her and her sister on a cruise. That was so sweet. It's all she's talked about the last two weeks."

Dev shrugged and found something interesting about her feet. "She deserved it."

"I know." Lauren smiled indulgently and gave Dev a little shove. "Go on, take some pictures and start passing out presents. I'll be right back with some coffee. Maybe I can bribe a couple of agents into taking Gremlin and Princess for a quick walk, too."

"A couple? Why not just one?"

"They're still not talking to each other."

Dev looked confused. "The agents?"

"No, Grem and Princess."

Dev snorted.

Lauren winked at her lover then lifted her hand to gently rake her fingers through dark, disheveled bangs that were sticking out in several directions. "Then we can find out what Santa left for you under the tree."

Dev leered at the blonde, wriggling her eyebrows. Her voice dropped to a purr as she pressed her lips to Lauren's ear. "I thought I got my present last night."

Lauren blushed, then burst into embarrassed laughter. She glanced towards the kids who were lost in their own world of chocolate, toys, books, and clothes. *What could be better? Last night!* her mind crowed. "Well, I consider that the gift that keeps on giving."

"If I'm lucky."

The biographer smacked Dev on the bottom and turned for the kitchen. "Trust me, Devlyn," she said, smiling over her shoulder. "We're both lucky."

David knocked on Dev's door for the third time. It was nearly 11:00 a.m., and Dev was expecting them. The agent outside the door could only shrug. He'd heard movement in the apartment very early this morning, but since walking Gremlin several hours ago and taking him back to the President's apartment, he hadn't heard a blessed thing.

"Good Lord, David, just open the door!" Beth moaned. Her arms were full of gifts, and the puppy Dev had given them as a "gift" was jumping anxiously at their feet. "The kids will be up; it's not like we'll catch Dev and Lauren naked on the couch or anything."

"Of course not," David snorted. Then he paused and started to truly consider what his wife had just proposed.

Beth rolled her eyes and pushed passed David. "Keep dreaming, pervert. But it will never happen." She juggled her packages and turned the knob. "Hello?" She stuck her head around the door and peered into the room. "Awww...we should have brought a camera."

The living room was strewn with bright colored wrapping paper, and Bing Crosby was softly crooning about a "White Christmas." The lights were off, except for the tree, and the fragrant scents of pine, burning oak, and chocolate filled the air.

David and Beth moved quietly farther into the room and Beth let down the puppy and unhooked his leash. The little dog immediately toddled towards the Christmas tree, where he carefully navigated his way between the piles of open boxes and paper. He found a large stuffed bear and plopped down next to it, closing his eyes. The puppy had seen Dev and fully intended to bare his teeth in a ferocious growl. He was saving it for after his nap.

The McMillians looked at each other with huge smiles on their faces. Dev was sound asleep on the sofa, wearing a Santa hat and a sweater that still had tags hanging from its arm and neck. Tucked safely in her arms was Lauren, who was snoring softly and clad in a worn T-shirt, pajama bottoms, and new snow boots.

All three children were asleep in various parts of the room. Aaron was half under the tree, and Beth had to duck down to see the little boy's face. He was asleep in a pile of candy wrappers with chocolate staining most of his cheeks and lips. Christopher was slumped in a chair, a half completed puzzle in his lap and a racing car at his feet. He wore a crisp Hawaiian print shirt, complete with tags, over his navy blue, footie pajamas. The small brunette was stretched out on her belly in front of the fire, which had burned down to bright orange coals. Ashley was snoring louder than Lauren and wore a pair of sunglasses and a white baseball hat that proudly proclaimed "Tennessee Volunteers" in bright orange letters. She held a Barbie loosely in one hand and a comb in the other. Barbie's blonde mane was standing straight up.

Gremlin was snuggled up against one side of the little girl with Princess snuggled up to the other. Doggy estrangement was an odd thing.

Blue eyes opened wearily, and Dev gave a little wave to her guests, careful not to jostle Lauren. "Merry Christmas," she mouthed silently, tightening her hold on the woman sleeping in her arms before closing her eyes.

Beth and David deposited their packages on the ground in front of the tree. David held a hand out to his wife as they wandered over to an empty loveseat. They sat down quietly and snuggled together closing their eyes. It had been a solid month of formal parties, visiting dignitaries, tuxedos, banquets, champagne, gowns and speeches. Both David and Beth let out long, contented sighs. They always did like the Marlowes' idea of a quiet family holiday.

It was late, and together Dev and Lauren had tucked the children in before returning to the living room. Dev jammed her hand in her pocket, feeling for the ring box nestled deep inside. She wondered for the hundredth time if she should just go ahead and give it to Lauren. *So what if I wasn't going to be doing any asking?* She'd still gotten it for Lauren. Dev was old-fashioned enough to want her wife wearing a wedding ring from her. To her dismay, she wasn't sure exactly how Lauren would feel.

Dev had been totally thrown when Lauren proposed to her. Thrilled, but thrown. All those weeks of worry and planning had gone up in a glorious poof of smoke in the wake of Lauren's natural tendency to cut straight to the chase. It was a characteristic that Dev adored. But, in this one instance, it left her not quite knowing what to do with herself or the ring in her pocket.

The writer's face crinkled into a smile and she sucked in a deep breath of pine-scented air. The presents were gone from beneath the tree, but Dev had insisted it would remain up until New Year's. To take it down even a day early was to risk bad luck for the entire new year. Lauren shook her head at the surprisingly superstitious custom that came from such a reasonable, down-to-earth family.

The President took a calming breath and screwed up her courage. Just because Lauren wanted to get married didn't mean she'd wear the ring. She sighed and tightened her hand around the box. "Lauren?"

It had been years since Lauren had a Christmas tree, and it was downright embarrassing how happy the simple but comforting tradition made her feel. "Mmm...nice." She turned to Dev and extended her hand, wrapping her fingers around Dev's, which were slightly chilled, and pulling Dev down to join her in front of the tree. "What's up?"

"Ahhh..." Dev's mind went blank for a moment and the muscles in her face twitched nervously. It was stupid, she knew, since she wasn't actually proposing. But still...it was as close as she hoped to ever come again. She licked her lips and cleared her throat a little. "You remember when I told you that I was working on the most important thing I had ever done, and that as soon as I could talk to you about it, you'd be the first to know?"

"Sure." Lauren leaned forward, her curiosity brimming. Thoughts of that evening and their nasty argument caused her to wince internally. Then and there, despite the fact that it was still a week before the New Year, Lauren made her resolution early. *Well,* she admitted privately, *it's more of a vow than a resolution, but it will have to do.* She'd been given an extraordinary chance at happiness with Devlyn and her children and she was going to do whatever it took to hold on to it. She'd never had so much to gain and so much to lose at the same time. And she promised herself that when things got scary, and she knew they would, she would hang on tight and ride the storm out, secure in the knowledge that what awaited her afterward would be more than worth the sacrifice. *Wow. Who knew being in love would make me so profound?*

Dev turned over the hand she was holding and placed the box in the center of Lauren's palm, curling small fingers around it. "Well...I love you. And this is it." Dev wasn't sure how to explain, so she babbled nervously as Lauren's gaze darted from the box to Dev and back again. "I had it made for you." She bit her lip as Lauren cracked open the black velvet lid. "That's what took so long. I...um...I hope you like it."

Lauren blinked stupidly at the ring, too shocked to really take in its detail, as her mind processed exactly what it symbolized. *The most important thing she'd ever done. Oh, God.* Her gaze jerked up to meet Dev's very serious looking face. "You were going to propose?"

Dev nodded. "Yes," she said quietly.

Lauren felt a sinking sensation in her belly. "And the night we quarreled, and you left for an appointment you couldn't tell me about?"

The President laid a hand on Lauren's leg. "Oh, sweetheart, that's not important." She gestured towards the ring with her chin, her eyes hopeful. "Can I put it on your finger?" When Lauren didn't answer, Dev began reaching for the box.

Lauren grabbed Dev's hands, stopping their motion. Her voice was low and harsh and startled Dev with its sound. "I'm so, so sorry."

Dark brows drew together as Dev searched Lauren's face, not quite understanding whether she was declining or accepting the ring. Her heart began to thud in her chest when she saw tears in Lauren's eyes. She immediately brushed them away with gentle fingertips. *Damn! She's trying to let me down easy. If she had wanted to exchange rings, she'd have given me one, right?* Dev's jaw worked silently, and she forced herself to continue, pushing down her disappointment. "Sorry for what?"

"For the argument. Things got so out of hand. If I'd only known—"

"Stop," the President interrupted, taking a few seconds to let out a long, slow breath. Dev felt nearly lightheaded with relief. *She's not turning it down. At least not yet.* She smiled and carefully plucked the ring from the box Lauren still had clutched in her hand. "Sweetheart, if you had known," she took Lauren's left hand in hers and slipped the ring on her finger, "it wouldn't have been much of a surprise, now would it?" Then she held her breath and waited.

Lauren gasped when she got a good look at the ring. The heavy platinum band was so wide it nearly touched her second knuckle. In its center was nestled a large, flat, rectangular emerald with four small diamonds clustered at its corners. The twinkling glow of the Christmas lights reflected off the dark, green stone. "Oh, Devlyn." Lauren made a fist and held it up a little, allowing the diamonds to pick up the light and sparkle gently. "It's so beautiful," she said reverently, running the tip of her index finger over it.

"I'm glad you like it. I wanted something as beautiful and as special as you are." Dev grinned, reading the look of undiluted joy on Lauren's face and knowing that right now, she was sporting the exact same expression. "And, just like you, it's one of a kind." She paused, "Uh...is it okay? I wasn't sure you'd want to wear one." Lauren looked at her with a gaze so filled with adoration Dev felt a heat creeping to her cheeks.

"Yes, I'll wear it." Lauren tucked a strand of wavy, fair hair behind her ear as she examined the beautiful piece of jewelry. "I've never worn one before." She chanced a glance up at Dev. "I told Judd it was because I really didn't like rings. But that was a lie." Lauren shrugged one shoulder and turned her attention to the tree laden with decorations and ribbon. "I guess I didn't feel like what we had was forever. And I wasn't ready."

"And now?" Dev questioned softly.

Lauren smiled wistfully. "I can't predict the future any better than I could back then." She pressed Dev's hand to her chest, directly over her heart. "But I can't imagine loving you," she smiled warmly, "or your kids more. If anyone's got a shot at forever, Devlyn, it's us."

Blue eyes twinkled, and a slender, dark eyebrow arched. "Yeah. That's exactly what I was going to say. You just beat me to it."

Lauren burst out laughing.

The President gave Lauren's ring a little tug. "Does it fit all right? I had to guess at your ring size. We can have it resized if we need to."

Lauren was about to wipe away the renewed tears that shimmered in her eyes, threatening to fall, but they were happy tears, and such a rare and wonderful occurrence she let them fall. She wiggled the ring with her thumb. It was a bit loose, but wouldn't come off. "It's a little big." Gray eyes found Dev's. "But that's good, right? I've always heard your fingers get bigger as you get older." A sniff. "So this should be fine, and since I don't intend on taking it off, I'll live with it 'as is'."

"Okay, but–"

Lauren's eyes suddenly widened. "Shit!" she exclaimed loudly, causing Devlyn to jump back.

"What?"

"I was supposed to get you a ring, wasn't I?" Lauren threw her hands up in disgust. "I didn't even... Oh, God, I didn't think or plan–"

Dev chuckled, gathering her into her arms. "Sweetheart, the ring isn't the important part of the proposal. The words are, and you had the courage to say the words. That's all that matters. And what matters to me is that, when I march up to that altar, you'll be there."

Lauren grabbed Devlyn's shirt and pulled her forward into a searing kiss. When the kiss ended and they separated, a happy laugh bubbled up from inside Lauren. She cupped Dev's cheeks and looked directly into beautiful, blue eyes, seeing the spirit that had captured her so completely. "That's one thing you don't need to worry about, darlin'. I'll be there."

Monday, December 27th

David watched from the wings as Sharon continued her morning briefing of the press. He was expecting the room to go up in flames in about thirty seconds. David glanced at his watch, wondering how Dev managed to live without one. *Then again, I don't have Liza following around after me, briefing me on my agenda every five minutes.*

"And, finally, the White House is happy to announce the engagement of President Marlowe to Ms. Lauren Strayer of Nashville, Tennessee. The President and Ms. Strayer became engaged just before Christmas and will be wed in the President's home state of Ohio sometime next year. No official date has been set for the wedding."

David smiled at the collective gasp that went through the group. He watched carefully as it took everyone a moment to grasp what Sharon had just said. Then the room erupted in a flurry of questions.

"Who proposed?" the newest CNN correspondent managed to get out first.

"One of the two parties involved," Sharon offered with an absolutely straight face.

Half the room groaned while the other half chuckled. When Sharon responded with this kind of answer...they weren't going to get a damned thing out of her, and they knew it.

Another question. "Where did the proposal take place?"

Sharon sighed inwardly, wishing that Dev had been a little more forthcoming with the details. "The President and Ms. Strayer were at home in the residence over the Christmas season." She held up her hands to forestall what she knew was coming next. "I know, I know. If possible, I will provide more details at a future press conference."

The *Washington Post* reporter politely raised his hand and

Sharon pointed to him. "When *exactly* did this happen?" he asked.

Sharon looked over at the reporter and resisted the urge to be a smartass. "A few days before Christmas. If possible, I will provide more details at a future press conference," Sharon said again. *Ah...my new mantra.*

"What were the circumstances of the President's proposal?" The man from the *Times* held his voice recorder high in the air.

"The exact circumstances surrounding the proposal are a private matter for the happy couple."

Another groan from the more seasoned reporters. That was Sharon speak for "You're never gonna get that particular bit of information".

David's smile shifted into a shit-eatin' grin. He just loved the way Sharon handled the press. *That's it, Sharon; give them your world famous "bite me" answers.*

A new reporter from the *Boston Globe* caught Sharon's eye from the back of the room. "Is this a push by the President for all states to legalize same sex marriages?"

Ahh...an intelligent, if inappropriate, question.

"Absolutely not. This is simply an announcement by the White House to keep the public informed." Sharon sighed and looked down at the podium, even though she had absolutely no notes on the subject.

David had told her only moments before, explaining that Dev was so damned excited she was practically shouting from the roof tops, so Sharon had better make the announcement before it leaked out. Sharon nodded to a tall, black man in the front row.

"Will Ms. Strayer be taking over the traditional duties of First Lady? And will she continue work on the President's biography?"

Sharon pushed her hands into her blazer pocket and stepped away from the podium. "Ms. Strayer will continue to write the President's biography. As far as taking over the duties of the First Lady, that will be for Ms. Strayer to decide for herself."

"Will the press be invited to the wedding?"

"I know this is all very exciting and it's been a hundred years or so since the last Presidential wedding, but this is simply an announcement of the engagement. No wedding plans have been made yet, so the guest list is obviously undecided."

"Will Ms. Strayer continue to live at the White House? Has she moved into President Marlowe's room?"

"Ms. Strayer will continue to maintain her own room within the residence until after the wedding. Just as she has done since her arrival here at the beginning of the year."

David smirked as he watched Sharon finish up the briefing with the announcement that she would take one more question. "Has a spot for a presidential honeymoon been selected?"

"Nothing has been decided as of yet. As soon as the President and Ms. Strayer decide to release more information regarding their nuptials and plans for after, I will let you know. Let's take things one step at a time." Sharon moved back to the podium and picked up her notes. "Have a good day, ladies and gentleman; I'll see you at the five o'clock briefing."

With that, Sharon strode off the small stage and joined David. She nudged him as they began the walk back to the West Wing. "Couldn't she have just declared war on someone? I would have been much better prepared to answer questions about that."

David chuckled. "Ah, Sharon, don't you get it? Knowing Dev's, but most especially Lauren's, penchant for privacy..."

The Press Secretary groaned, imagining the endless questions that Dev and Lauren would never provide the answers to just for spite. "David?"

"Yeah?"

"I want a raise."

Lauren tightened her grip on Dev's hand. *God, I'm more nervous than when I was interviewed by that bitch from* Wake Up, America.

"Relax, Lauren." Dev squeezed her hand reassuringly.

"Everything is going to be fine. And I'm not letting you talk me into any more time. Sharon is announcing it to the press at this very moment." Dev's gaze softened. "Besides, the kids love you."

Lauren nodded. "And I love them. But that doesn't mean they're going to want you to marry me."

The women stopped outside the Game Room. "I *am* marrying you, and they'll be okay. Trust me." Dev cocked her head to the side and listened through the door. Ashley was ruthlessly ordering her brothers around, while the boys fought with each other, her, and generally made the game miserable. She sighed. "Oh, yeah. All three monsters are in there." A glance sideways. "Ready?"

"No."

"Will you ever be ready?"

"No."

"Perfect. I knew this was exactly the right time." The President chuckled. But she truly did sympathize with Lauren, who was now getting a taste of the anxiety Dev herself had suffered with while waiting to propose.

Lauren gathered her courage and said a small prayer. She had been a lousy wife the first time around and she was pretty sure that as far as most children were concerned, she wasn't anything special. Frankly, except for Dev, Lauren considered her "relationship" track record to be abysmal. "God, what makes me think I can be someone's parent?" she muttered quietly, frozen outside the door and completely unaware that she'd spoken the words aloud.

Dev turned and regarded her lover seriously. She reached out and cupped Lauren's chin, tilting her head upward and pinning her with an intense blue gaze. "Do you love them?"

Lauren's brows knitted. "The kids? Of course."

"And you want what's best for them?"

The blonde's hands moved to her hips. "No, Devlyn. I regularly advise them to play in traffic and run with sharp objects in their hands."

Dev bit her lip to keep from laughing. "And you're patient, supportive, and willing to help teach them right from wrong?"

Lauren grinned and scratched her jaw. "I didn't kill them when they gave me the chickenpox. I'm Ashley's English study partner." Gray eyes narrowed. "Though we're still getting a B minus. That toad teacher of hers wouldn't know a simile if it reached up and bit her in the a—"

"Lauren." Dev's voice interrupted Lauren's rant. "You were saying."

"Oh. Right. When the kids in Christopher's class were making fun of his glasses, I told Chris it was wrong to pound them for it."

A dark eyebrow arched. "So you're the one who told him to say that he'd have the Secret Service assassinate anyone who was mean to him!" Dev accused. "He scared those kids senseless!"

Lauren's eyes went round and innocent. "I have no idea where he got such a horrible, vicious idea," she lied unconvincingly.

Dev shook her head but couldn't stop the laughter from tumbling out.

Lauren's face suddenly sobered and her voice dropped to an anguished whisper. "But this is serious, Devlyn. I'm not sure I know how to be a real mom. Not like you are. The kids are smart. They probably know this and won't even want me to."

"Sweetheart," Dev wrapped her arms around Lauren's slim waist, "I've got news for you. You've been a 'real mom' to my kids for months. Getting married is only going to make that official. You've already been doing the hard parts."

"But—"

"No." Dev shook her head with finality. "No buts, Ms. Strayer. It's time to face *our* family." Devlyn rubbed Lauren's lower back with a soothing motion. "Are you ready?"

"No."

Dev rolled her eyes as she pulled open the Game Room door. "You are such a chicken." She tugged the reluctant writer in the room by her shirtsleeve.

"I am not," Lauren mumbled petulantly, smiling when she saw the kids. She decided not to ask why Christopher and Aaron were only wearing their underwear, and their clothes were in a pile in front of Ashley. *Strip "Candy Land"?* Lauren could see the humiliation factor involved in making the losers strip. Unfortunately for Ashley, the little girl hadn't learned yet that humiliation really only works if the people care that they've been reduced to their underpants. Aaron and Christopher were happy as larks. *Naked larks,* she mentally amended.

"Hi, kids," Dev said brightly. Out of the corner of her eye she spied Gremlin and Princess happily snuggled up together on the carpet. *Ooo, she took you back? How can something so hideous be so lucky?*

"Hi!" the children exclaimed in unison, jumping to their feet.

"Wanna play?" Aaron gestured towards the board, his chubby belly bouncing a little as he jumped up and down with excitement.

"Not right this second, pal." Dev ruffled corn-yellow hair. "Lauren and I have an announcement to make."

All three kids quieted and stared right at Lauren, who suddenly felt like a bug who'd been stuck to a cork board with straight pins and was currently being examined by a big magnifying glass. She gulped audibly.

"Don't we, Lauren?" Dev prodded gently, hoping that Lauren wouldn't pass out or throw up. The writer's current pallor wasn't exactly encouraging.

"Uhhh...yes." Lauren looked down at the children. "We do."

"What is it?" Ashley asked.

Lauren looked to Dev helplessly and the President wordlessly asked her if she was ready one more time. This time, Lauren squared her shoulders and nodded.

Dev tried not to look as relieved as she felt. "Okay. The announcement is we–"

"And we really hope you'll be happy," Lauren jumped in, sticking her hands in her pockets to keep from wringing them.

Dev closed her mouth, which was still hanging open from being interrupted mid-word. She swallowed and looked at her children fondly. "Lauren and I have decided to get married."

Silence.

Lauren's eyes flickered sideways to Dev, and the President could see the building panic in the younger woman. Devlyn quickly prodded, "So, kids, what do you think?"

"Will Mom wear a poofy, white dress and carry flowers?" Aaron asked curiously.

"Yes," Lauren blurted out. "If you want her to."

Aaron nodded furiously, his chubby face creasing into a smile.

"Lauren!" Dev complained loudly, giving her a look of pure frustration. "I don't want–"

"Hush. And be grateful the boy didn't say a clown outfit."

Dev let out a grumpy breath. "Fine. Fine. If it'll truly make you happy." She looked at her youngest with pleading eyes, waiting for him to let her off the hook. Which, of course he didn't. "Poofy?" she silently mouthed.

Next Ashley spoke up. "So then Lauren would be our mom, too?" Her chin quivered a little.

Lauren's heart dropped into her stomach, but before she could say a word, the little girl flung herself at Lauren, wrapping slim arms around the woman's hips and pressing her cheek to Lauren's sternum. She squeezed as tightly as she could. "That's great!"

Lauren exhaled shakily, hearing Devlyn do the exact same thing. She returned the embrace. "I think so, too, sweetie."

"You'll be a great mom."

Dev beamed. *Way to go, Moppet! That's my girl.*

Aaron joined Ashley's hug, already thinking about the tall wedding cake he'd seen on cartoons. *Would there be milk?*

Christopher, however, stood silently, his arms crossed over his small chest and his face stony.

"Don't you have anything to say?" Dev asked carefully.

Christopher just shook his head "no" as he fought off tears.

Lauren disentangled herself from Aaron and Ashley and knelt down in front of the boy. "What's wrong, Chris?"

His blue eyes darted to his mom and then back to the woman who knelt in front of him. Lauren turned her head towards Dev and gestured with her chin.

Devlyn nodded and grabbed Aaron and Ashley's hands. "Let's go sit on the couch and discuss the actual meaning of the word 'poofy', shall we?" She tugged them along, giving Christopher and Lauren a moment of semi-privacy.

"Now, do you want to tell me what's wrong?" Lauren asked worriedly.

Christopher sniffed and shook his head, his lower lip beginning to protrude.

"Please?" Lauren asked gently. "It's just the two of us."

When Christopher still failed to say a word, Lauren hazarded a guess. "You don't want me and your mama to get married?"

"No," he said firmly.

Lauren nodded and smoothed back a tuft of pale hair from Christopher's forehead. Of all the children, she never suspected it would be Christopher who would have a problem. Unlike Ashley, he couldn't even remember Samantha, so there was no issue of "replacing" his real mother. "Okay. Can you tell me why? Because I really love her and you guys, too. And want us to be a family."

"But I was going to marry you," he complained quietly, his gaze sliding sideways again to see if anyone was watching. Lauren bit her lip to keep from laughing, but she couldn't stop the smile. "You were?"

"I was just waiting."

Lauren smile turned indulgent. "Oh, Christopher, darlin', that is so sweet."

His eyes brightened. "So you will?"

"No, honey. I can't. I'm gonna marry your mom."

His expression turned sour again.

"Do you know how old I am?" Lauren asked, sitting back on her heels.

"No." He thought for a moment, then guessed, "Sixty-two?"

Lauren's jaw dropped, and she heard the faint sounds of Dev's muffled sniggers from across the room. "Errr...not quite. I'm thirty-one years old."

The boy's eyes widened. "Wow!"

"I know. By the time you could marry me, I'd be older than your mom is now."

His eyes went even wider. "Really? No way!"

Lauren lifted three fingers. "Scouts' honor." The writer grinned smugly when Dev's sniggers abruptly stopped. "And I'm afraid that would be far too old for you."

"I'd still love you," Christopher insisted, causing Lauren's heart to melt.

"Aw, honey," Lauren hugged the boy fiercely, a little at a loss as to what else she could say that wouldn't hurt his feelings.

"Why would you want to marry me?"

"Because I love you and then you'll live in our apartment instead of your room. You'll be able to play with us even more. And we'll be together forever." Christopher tugged on his glasses, subtly reminding Lauren of their special bond.

Lauren laughed softly, wishing she and Judd had had such good reasons. "You do know that I'll be able to live with you guys and see you more often if I marry your mom, right?"

Christopher looked at her blankly for a second, as though the thought had never crossed his mind. "And you'll get to tuck us in and read more stories?"

"I'm sure of it."

Christopher was warming to this idea fast, and it showed by his dimpled grin. "And stay with us forever?"

Tears leapt into Lauren's eyes. This was an easy one. "Forever."

Printed in the United States
114307LV00004B/164/A